TEYSHA W.L.

Magic in the Unmatched

K Corp Novel Book 2

First edition

ISBN: 979-8-9987336-0-4

This book was professionally typeset on Reedsy.
Find out more at reedsy.com

Foreword

I've always believed that stories can be healing, that fiction allows us to say things we sometimes can't say out loud. I write books inspired by my own struggles, and this one was perhaps the hardest to write. It touches on something deeply personal: my identity.

I was diagnosed with autoimmune diseases at a very young age, and they changed the way I looked long before I understood what that meant. I quickly learned how to grow a thick skin, to brace myself for the stares, the questions, and the comments. Like my lead character, I've felt invisible in a crowd and far too visible in the wrong kind of way.

Over the years, I've had many reconstructive surgeries, and while they've helped, I know I will always look different. Dating was never easy. It felt like an exhausting audition for acceptance. But then I met my husband, a man who didn't see my diseases, but saw *me*. His love helped rewrite so many painful narratives I had once believed about myself.

This book is for anyone who has ever felt like they don't fit the mold. For anyone who has questioned their worth because of how the world sees them. It's for those fighting silent battles, physical, emotional, or both, and still showing up every day.

Being different is not a weakness. It's a kind of quiet power, waiting to be embraced.

I hope this story helps you feel seen, helps you find your courage, and

reminds you that love and acceptance are not reserved for the "normal"-
they are for *everyone*.

    With all my heart,

    Teysha W.L.

Acknowledgments

To my dearest family,

Thank you for being the light that guides me and the roots that ground me. Your unwavering support means more than words can hold.

To my children, my brightest stars. Your joy, your laughter, and your willingness to listen to the wild stories I spin have filled my heart with courage. Thank you for reminding me that imagination is a kind of magic, and that love is always the best muse.

To Marie Faulkner, my amazing beta reader, thank you for lending your eyes, your insight, and your quiet brilliance to this story. Your care helped shape its edges and gave it polish. I am deeply grateful.

And to every soul who dares to be different, to dream loudly, and to live boldly-

"If you are always trying to be normal, you will never know how amazing you can be."

- *Maya Angelou*

Chapter 1

Born an outcast, Niamh had known only rejection and disdain, shadows that had haunted her from the very beginning. While society loved to preach that "inner beauty is what truly counts," Niamh knew firsthand that this was nothing more than a comforting lie. The startled gasps, the glances that turned into looks of horror, all these reactions spoke louder than any platitudes. Society had made its judgment, and she was not welcome.

Her first memory, still vivid in her mind, was of her fifth birthday. She invited her kindergarten class to join her at a local kids' play center. Six large pizzas were left untouched because her classmates didn't show up. She cried uncontrollably for an hour until a little girl with blonde hair braided into pigtails came up to her. "Do you want to play?" She asked Niamh. She didn't ask what was wrong, the little girl could see the full pizzas and empty seats and put the clues together. She didn't have to ask. She noticed the girl's strange eyes, but she liked that the girl looked different, unlike the girl who looked like everyone else in her family, blonde hair and blue eyes. There is absolutely nothing unique about them. She longed to stand out, to have something to herself that made her special. She loved that the strange girl had that. She wasn't jealous, though; she admired it.

As Niamh grew older, she longed to be invisible, to melt into the crowd and escape the staring eyes. Yes, she was shy, an introvert who kept to herself, but it wasn't a choice; it was a necessity. Her adoptive parents were given only a single piece of information when they took her in: a name, Niamh. That was the one condition. They agreed, embracing this mysterious child as their own, yet they had no idea just how different their new daughter would be. Years passed in a blur of doctor visits, sterile hospital rooms, and endless tests. But each visit ended the same way: no answers, only puzzled looks and quiet apologies. Niamh was unique, they told her parents, but in ways, they couldn't explain. She knew she was loved by her parents, but she felt so utterly alone in the world.

Yet, there was still one person who made her feel almost normal. With her first and only friend Lidia by her side, she could let down her guard, forgetting for a moment that the rest of the town saw her as an outsider. Together, they created a world where Niamh wasn't "damaged" or "different" but simply herself.

Mirrors were something she tried to avoid, their glassy surface too honest, too revealing. But her mother insisted she keep a large, full-body mirror in her room, convinced it would help her "accept herself." Niamh didn't understand it; how could staring at her reflection, day after day, do anything but deepen the hurt? To her, that mirror was a reminder of her body's betrayal, of the way it had set her apart from everyone else. And it whispered, too, of her birth parents, the ones who'd abandoned her without answers to the questions that haunted her.

Today, she forced herself to stand in front of the tall mirror, hoping somehow to see a different face looking back at her. She held her breath, but there it was again: her reflection, unchanging and unforgiving. Her skin still held that strange, pale tone with its silver-blue hue, a color that seemed almost otherworldly under any light. The sun did nothing to warm it, to lend her the glow that other girls seemed to wear so effortlessly. Her eyes, far too large to be even close to normal, one a deep, inky black, the other an ethereal silver, stared back at her, unblinking, revealing the secrets she wished she could hide. She kept her bangs cut long, hoping they might veil the parts of her that drew the most attention, but they did little to disguise the uniqueness of her face.

With a quiet sigh of resignation, she adjusted the wrap dress her friend had picked out for her, a black floral print that hugged her frame just enough to highlight her shape. Niamh never felt quite at ease in dresses, but that one was…different. It fit her well, almost comfortably, as though the fabric itself was trying to be kind. Maybe, she thought, if her body looked "normal" enough, people would focus on that instead of her face. The thought was fleeting, a thin hope, but she held onto it anyway.

It was her friend Lidia's birthday, and they had planned to meet at her house for a party. Niamh rarely enjoyed parties or any gathering where large groups of people clustered together. In her experience, people grew bolder in groups, and when alcohol loosened their inhibitions, they often found new ways to make her the target of their discomfort or mockery. Parties didn't usually end well for her. But she had promised Lidia she'd go, though she didn't mention that she'd only planned to stay for a little while, hoping to leave before the night unraveled into drunken stares and whispered jokes.

Before leaving to meet her friend, she gave her mom a quick kiss on the cheek and wrapped her dad in a warm hug. As they parted, he pressed a small, familiar object into her hand, a fresh can of pepper spray. "Just in case," he murmured, his eyes heavy with the same concern she'd grown used to seeing in them.

Niamh nodded and slipped it into her purse, a sad smile playing at her lips. She knew her parents worried each time she left the safety of their home. Out there, she wasn't simply Niamh; she was a stranger in the eyes of others, someone to be judged, feared, or mocked simply for how she looked.

Stepping out into the night, she inhaled the cool, crisp air that seemed to settle her nerves just a little. It was colder than usual for this time of year, and its sharpness cut through her apprehension, giving her a small boost of courage. She could do this, she had to. Tonight was for Lidia, her one friend who'd never treated her as anything other than ordinary.

With each block toward the house, her pulse quickened, but she forced herself to stay calm. She steeled herself for the gazes that might follow her, for the comments she'd learned to ignore, but secretly they cut her, leaving a deep wound in her heart. People could be so cruel. Looking the way she did wasn't her choice. She'd give anything to be like them, to be normal. Under the night sky, she allowed herself to feel, even for a moment, like she was no different from anyone else. And maybe, just maybe, this night would be different. A feeble attempt at confidence.

Dozens of cars lined the street in front of Lidia's house, headlights and laughter spilling out onto the road. Niamh felt a pang of relief for her tiny car; it allowed her to squeeze into a spot just down the block, just barely. She was also grateful she'd ignored Lidia's playful insistence on wearing high heels; her flats would make the walk easier, and she didn't need the extra discomfort tonight. The night would bring its own form of torture.

As she stepped out of the car, a group of party-goers strolled past, laughing and chatting loudly amongst themselves. For a moment, Niamh's stomach tightened, an instinctual reaction to laughter she couldn't help but assume was at her expense. Years of being the punchline in others' jokes had left their mark, and she'd grown to believe that every snicker and whispered word was aimed her way. She shook it off, took a steadying breath, and mustered the courage to walk up the street toward Lidia's house, clutching a small can of pepper spray while her other hand cradled her purse next to her body, protecting the carefully wrapped gift safely tucked inside.

The music drifted toward her long before she reached the house, pulsing from open doors and windows like an invitation. The bass vibrated underfoot as she approached, mingling with the laughter and the faint smell of perfume and drinks wafting out into the night air. She followed the rhythm of the crowd, edging her way to the front door, feeling the swell of people surrounding her.

She knew she was never truly safe, not when she looked how she did, but she knew she was as safe as she could be getting close to Lidia. So, she tucked away the pepper spray with a sigh; that tiny can gave her more confidence than she'd known most of her life. But it wouldn't be appropriate to have it out at a party, especially Lidia's party. She'd hate to ruin her friend's day. Her hand felt empty and her heart full of dread, but she pushed on.

Once inside, Niamh began the slow wound through the packed rooms, her eyes scanning over unfamiliar faces, but always holding her head low, in an attempt to hide her face. She headed instinctively toward the kitchen, guessing Lidia would be there, likely setting up drinks and food in her usual spot; she loved making people happy. And she was right; Lidia stood by the counter, a bottle of clear liquid in one hand, pouring it into a punch bowl with a playful flourish. Her face lit up when she spotted Niamh from across the room, her cheeks flush with the familiar rosy tint that always appeared after her first drink or two.

"Niamh!" Lidia's wide smile and open heart lifted her spirits, even if it was just for a moment. In that instant, surrounded by the noise and the stares, she was grateful for this one person who made her feel like she belonged.

Niamh dug through her purse, her fingers brushing past the pepper spray and car keys until she found the small, carefully wrapped box. Lidia's face lit up with excitement as she took it, pulling Niamh into a strong hug before eagerly tearing away the wrapping. Inside, a delicate gold necklace with a tiny snowflake pendant glinted in the low kitchen light. The snowflake dangled in the center, its fine edges catching the light just so. Lidia's breath caught as she gazed at it, her eyes misting over.

"Oh, Niamh… It's perfect! I love it! You're the absolute best!" She slipped the necklace from its box, holding it up as though it were the most precious thing she'd ever seen. Niamh knew how much Lidia missed the snow ever since she'd moved from Michigan to Georgia, she talked about it constantly. And by the look in her friend's eyes, she knew she'd chosen well.

Lidia gave her another tight hug as if to convey how much the gift, and their friendship, meant to her. Niamh, in her shy, reserved way, simply nodded, cheeks pink with quiet pride.

"Glad you like it," she murmured. Finding the perfect gifts had always been her way of showing love. She didn't have much, just a few employees who truly cared for her and her business, her parents, and Lidia. But to Niamh, they were everything. She wasn't the life of the party; she didn't have Lidia's social sway, and she knew she couldn't offer the effortless charm others could. But she could show her gratitude through the time and thoughtfulness she poured into small moments like these.

Lidia had noticed, too. She'd long admired Niamh for even attempting to join the party tonight, knowing how hard crowds could be for her. But Lidia had made it clear to her guests that they'd better treat Niamh with respect. She'd built a reputation over the years as a kind of "queen bee" of their social scene, and her rules were law. If you crossed her, you'd find no invitation from anyone else, and that was a risk few dared to take.

Yet, it wasn't power that drove Lidia's loyalty; it was love. Niamh meant more to her than anyone else, and she knew that beneath the thick skin, Niamh had been forced to develop a deep kindness and quiet strength that the world hadn't yet worn away. Lidia wanted to protect that part of her friend, to nurture it however she could. She understood that Niamh's gift wasn't just a necklace; it was a piece of herself, a symbol of the gratitude she felt for someone who'd stood by her through every high and low, through every cruel remark and whispered judgment.

Niamh glanced down, the warmth in Lidia's smile making her feel seen in a rare way. At that moment, it didn't matter that she was different or that the world hadn't always treated her kindly. Here, with Lidia, she was safe, cherished, and loved.

A loud crash echoed from another room, drawing Lidia's attention. She rolled her eyes, muttering something under her breath before excusing herself to go assess the damage. Left standing alone in the kitchen, Niamh felt her nerves tighten, surrounded by a group of strangers who kept glancing her way with curiosity, or perhaps something worse. She felt her anxiety rising, each glance like a weight pressing down on her. Deciding she needed air, she slipped toward the backyard, hoping for the refuge of quieter spaces and fewer eyes.

As she wove through the crowded room, someone slammed into her shoulder, hard enough to throw her off balance. A small gasp escaped her lips as she stumbled, her heart pounding in that split second when she braced for impact with the floor. But before she could fall, a strong hand caught her by the arm, steadying her with surprising gentleness. She blinked in shock, her pulse quickening; people usually made a point to avoid touching her, as if her uniqueness might somehow rub off. But this man's grip was firm and unhesitating.

"You okay?" a low, rumbling voice murmured close to her ear, cutting through the music's din. His breath was warm against her cheek, and she could feel the heat from his hand seeping into her skin, grounding her as she tried to steady herself. When he pulled back to look at her, she met his gaze, her heart pounding harder now for an entirely different reason.

He was looking directly into her eyes, not with the usual shock or hesitation, but with genuine concern. Her first instinct was to look away, to shield herself from whatever judgment she expected to find in his face. But his expression wasn't one of disgust, nor was it the cold, clinical curiosity she was used to. Instead, he seemed… calm, as if he hadn't even noticed the things about her that made everyone else pull back.

Niamh swallowed, her mouth dry, fighting the uncomfortable vulnerability that always came when someone looked her in the eyes. She waited for him to flinch, to search her face for whatever it was that set her apart. But he didn't. For a brief, unsettling moment, she felt seen, not as an oddity or a spectacle, but as herself.

"Th-thank you," she managed, her voice a whisper over the pounding music. She felt the need to pull back, to shield herself from this unfamiliar attention, but his hand remained steady on her arm as if to anchor her.

He smiled, a slight, genuine curve of his lips that softened his features. "No problem," he replied, releasing her arm slowly, his gaze lingering for just a beat longer than she was used to. "I didn't mean to startle you."

He stared into her mismatched eyes, one dark and brooding like a stormy sky, the other light and ethereal like dawn. Together, they felt like yin and yang, a perfect balance of chaos and calm. Looking into them wasn't just comforting; it was like finding a home he never knew he'd lost. Her gaze wrapped around him like a warm summer breeze, a quiet warmth that seeped into the cold, shadowed corners of his soul. Her presence felt electric, like a rush of Fireball whiskey, but instead of burning, it spread through his veins, igniting something dormant and aching to awaken. He already knew, deep down, that *she* could become addictive.

She tried to speak, but her words dissolved before they could take form. Her pulse raced under his steady gaze, his intensity making her self-conscious in a way she hadn't felt in years. Men like him didn't talk to her, ever. When they did, it was either a cruel joke or a drunken dare. Yet here he stood, so breathtakingly beautiful it felt like the universe was playing a trick on her. Her tongue stumbled over an attempt to introduce herself, the syllables evaporating as soon as they touched the air.

Her hesitation didn't go unnoticed. He saw the way her shoulders tensed and decided to save her from the weight of the moment. Leaning in close, he brought his lips near her ear, his warm breath brushing against her neck, making something inside her loosen its grip. She wanted to give in, to let her hope flow out, but she couldn't trust him. He'd end up like everyone else, proving that she was going to be perpetually alone.

"Do you want to go outside?" he asked, his deep voice a blend of confidence and kindness. "I was heading there anyway. I can lead the way if you'd like."

All she could do was nod, her cheeks burning. His smile in response was so genuine it sent her heart spiraling into chaos. She had to remind herself not to get carried away, or she'd end up hurt again. He loosened his grip on her upper arm, his hand trailing lightly down until his fingers intertwined with hers. Her hand felt small and fragile in his own, yet her touch was grounding in a way he didn't expect. He had to get her alone; the people and sounds were too distracting. He wanted to, no, he needed to have her all to himself.

He pulled her along, bending his arm behind his back, keeping her as tight to his body as possible. He navigated the crowded room; his broad shoulders made him a natural barrier, and people moved aside instinctively, parting like a river around a stone. Niamh followed in his shadow, grateful for the shield he provided. She tucked herself behind him, her heart thudding with a mix of relief and anticipation. Her face rested against the back of his jacket as she walked, inhaling the faint scent of jasmine that clung to him.

It was one of her favorite smells, and it wrapped around her like a soothing memory she couldn't quite place.

Bain felt her touch through the layers of fabric, her warmth breaking through the cool detachment he usually carried. Every soft press of her hand against his back, every step she took behind him, sent his heart pounding. He silently begged the sound wouldn't betray him. Surely, she could hear it, how fast it was racing.

When they stepped outside, the crisp night air hit them like a splash of water, clearing the suffocating heat of the house. Small groups of people dotted the backyard, their conversations hushed under the open sky. Niamh let out a breath of relief, thankful for the anonymity the darkness offered. No one turned to stare as she emerged from Bain's shadow, but when he let go of her hand and spun to face her, her stomach twisted in nervous anticipation.

Out of habit, she reached up, her fingers nervously pulling strands of hair from her bangs as if it could hide her mismatched eyes from his view. But, Bain's gaze never wavered.

"I'm Bain," he said, his voice steady but soft, a small, confident smile tugging at his lips. He noticed her nervous fidgeting, and the urge to pull her hand away from her face tugged at him. She shouldn't hide; *she shouldn't have to hide.* He fisted his hands. Anger rose in him, he wanted to punish all the people who had hurt her, who made her feel so insecure. She was a goddess. He fought the urge to take her somewhere safe, somewhere he could show her how special she was. He made himself release his fists. He didn't want her to notice and thought he had an anger issue. He did, but she didn't need to know that.

"I'm Niamh," she managed to squeak out, her voice barely above a whisper. She glanced down, avoiding his gaze, her heart pounding so loudly she feared he could hear it. She wondered why would someone like him talk to someone like her. Was she part of some cruel game? But as she darted her eyes around, searching for a hint of mockery, a group of his friends laughing behind his back, there was nothing. Just him. She could feel him watching her; his gaze burned through her as he scanned her body but always ended at her face and holding it.

Bain wished she would look at him again, just once more. Those captivating eyes were like magnets, pulling him into her orbit, and he didn't want to leave. He had to keep her talking, he knew she'd probably try and bolt soon. He had to make her remember him, to keep her tethered to him just a little longer. "Are you having fun?" he asked, his voice gentle. He cursed himself for not being able to think of anything better to say. He wasn't used to that; he always had something smart to say, it usually ended up getting him into trouble, but there was always something. Now, it was like his brain was mush; he could only think about her.

"Parties aren't really my thing," Niamh said softly, her gaze fixed on the ground as her fingers twisted through her hair. Her voice was steady, but her heart betrayed her, hammering against her ribs. She wanted to believe this was real, but her mind whispered warnings. Men like him didn't talk to women like her, at least, not sincerely. Still, for a fleeting moment, she allowed herself to feel normal like any other woman being noticed by a man.

Bain leaned closer, the subtle motion carrying warmth and intent. "Me neither," he admitted, his deep voice tinged with understanding. "I only came because Tim guilt-tripped me into it." As he spoke, her soft vanilla and lavender scent wove around him, intoxicating and soothing all at once. She smelled like home and something sweeter, something indulgent, like the most irresistible dessert.

She nodded at his answer, but her silence stretched between them like a fragile thread. Bain could see the way her shoulders stiffened, how her fingers betrayed her nervousness as they danced along the strands of her hair.

"You… you know Tim?" she finally managed to ask, her voice tentative.

"Yeah," he replied with a smile. "We work together."

"Oh, that's nice," she said, the awkwardness of her response making her cheeks burn. *Really, Niamh? That's the best you could come up with?* She cursed her brain for failing her, for shutting down in the presence of this impossibly handsome man. Flirting wasn't a skill she had the chance to practice often.

Bain noticed her discomfort but didn't retreat. Instead, he decided to try a different approach, one he hoped might cut through the tension. "You have such unique, beautiful eyes, Niamh," he said, his tone soft but deliberate. He fought the urge to push her hair out of her face so he could see her more.

Her breath hitched, and she froze, the words hitting her like a wave she wasn't prepared to handle. A compliment, an *honest* one, was something she didn't know how to accept. The memory of all the cruel jokes and mocking smiles she'd endured flickered through her mind. Compliments about her eyes had always been bait, traps set by people who found her differences amusing rather than beautiful.

"You don't have to do that," she said finally, her voice edged with pain. "I'm going to leave now. Thanks for helping me escape that house."

She turned on her heel, ready to flee, but Bain reached out instinctively, his fingers wrapping gently around her arm again. The warmth of her skin surged through him like a current, making his chest tighten. The sensation was almost overwhelming, but he didn't let go. He couldn't.

"Wait," he said, his voice firm but pleading. "Did I say something wrong? I didn't mean to offend you. I do think your eyes are stunning. They're… unique." His words faltered slightly, and he hated the uncertainty creeping into his tone. He wasn't used to feeling this way, off-balance, vulnerable. He craved her gaze, longed for her to meet his eyes and let him in. Since the moment he'd caught her earlier, he'd been lost in her, drawn to her in a way he couldn't explain. She had a power over him he'd never experienced before, and he didn't want to let it slip away.

"I know you didn't mean to," she said, her voice cracking slightly as she tried to keep her emotions in check. "It's just… I've been through this before. People stare and comment, and it's never kind. No one ever compliments me, not seriously. So, I know you're messing with me. Please don't. It's been a long day, and I can't handle this right now."

Her words hit Bain like a punch to the chest, and he felt a surge of anger, not at her, but at the people who had made her feel this way. He wanted to find every single one of them and make them understand what they'd stolen from her. The way she stood before him now, hurt, defensive, and tired, made his heart ache.

"Well," he said, his voice low but steady, "I hope one day you'll believe me because I'm not messing with you, Niamh. I don't think I *could* mess with you. Your eyes, they're unlike anything I've ever seen. And I don't just mean their color. I mean… they're alive. They're you."

She blinked, unsure how to respond, but his words planted a seed of doubt in her certainty that this was just another cruel joke.

Bain reluctantly let go of her arm, his fingers lingering for a fraction of a second longer than necessary, savoring the warmth of her skin one last time. As his hand fell away, he dragged his fingertips lightly along her forearm, desperate to hold onto the connection even as it slipped through his grasp.

"If you leave now," he said quietly, his tone tinged with regret, "I hope you'll remember what I said. Because I meant every word."

Niamh snickered, though it was more bitter than amused, and turned away from Bain. She couldn't afford to let herself believe him, not even for a second. She'd played the fool too many times when she was younger, letting people toy with her feelings like it was a sport. Not anymore. She wouldn't let herself fall for it.

Her mismatched eyes scanned the crowd as she stepped back into the chaos of the house, searching for Lidia. Behind her, Bain's voice cut through the noise, strong and clear despite the chatter around them.

"It was a pleasure to meet you, Niamh," he called after her. "I hope our paths cross again."

She hesitated for a heartbeat, her feet slowing as the words reached her ears, but she didn't turn around. *He can't be serious,* she thought, her chest tightening. *Why would he be?* The idea felt cruel, cruel to even entertain. It was better to walk away than to let herself believe this was anything more than another joke at her expense.

Behind her, Bain stood motionless, watching her disappear into the house. He'd hoped, *prayed*, that she might look back, even for a moment, just to give him one last glimpse of those hauntingly beautiful eyes. But she didn't. The weight of her absence hit him like a blow to the chest.

Her warmth lingered on his skin, faint but maddening, like a phantom touch he couldn't forget. The memory of her was all he had now, her scent, her heat, the way her mismatched eyes had pulled him into a world he didn't fully understand but couldn't resist. It felt like the beginning of a hangover, that aching longing for something he knew he'd never feel again.

Niamh pushed through the crowd, her focus fixed on finding Lidia. The pulse of the music, the chatter of voices, it all blended into one chaotic hum that she wanted to escape as quickly as possible. When she finally spotted her friend in the kitchen, she exhaled a small sigh of relief.

"I'm heading out," she said quietly, giving Lidia a quick, tight hug before stepping away.

"You okay?" Lidia asked, concern flickering in her expression. She sensed something was off with her friend. She'd been there for all the ups and downs, but unfortunately, there were far more downs than ups for Niamh.

"Yeah, just tired," Niamh replied, forcing a small smile. It wasn't a total lie; she *was* tired. Tired of the noise, the eyes, the whispers. Tired of being a punchline.

Without waiting for Lidia's response, she turned and made her way through the sea of bodies, each step bringing her closer to freedom. As the front door closed behind her, the cool night air wrapped around her like a soothing balm. The noise from the party faded into the distance, replaced by a welcome silence.

By the time she reached her car, the quiet had settled fully around her. She leaned against the door for a moment, taking in deep, steadying breaths. It was like she could finally *breathe* again, the weight of the house and the people inside no longer pressing down on her.

Sliding into the driver's seat, she closed her eyes and let her head rest against the steering wheel. Her heart was still racing, but not from the noise of the party. She thought about him, about Bain.

His voice echoed in her mind, the way he'd said her name like it meant something. The way he'd looked at her like she was worth seeing. She hated herself for replaying it, for wanting it to be real.

Her fingers brushed against her too-large eyes in the reflection of the rear view mirror, and she sighed. *Why would he mean it?* she thought, shaking her head. It had to be a joke. That was all she'd ever been to people, a curiosity, a novelty. They never really cared for her.

But deep down, in the quiet space she kept locked away from the world, a small, fragile part of her wished it could be different. That someone might look at her one day and see her, not her flaws, not her scars, but *her*.

She started the car and drove away, leaving the party, the noise, and Bain behind. But as the miles passed, she couldn't shake the feeling that something had shifted tonight. For better or worse, she couldn't forget the stranger who'd looked at her like she was worth more than she dared to believe.

Chapter 2

Back in the sanctuary of her bedroom, Niamh slipped out of the black-and-white dress she hadn't realized matched her eyes until just now. The thought made her pause for a moment, staring at the garment as it lay draped over the chair. She shook her head, brushing away the hint of sentimentality, and changed into her favorite satin pajamas. The soft fabric was a comfort she desperately needed.

At the sink, she splashed cool water on her face, hoping to wash away the lingering thoughts of *him*, the tall, magnetic stranger whose gaze had left an imprint she couldn't seem to erase. Her reflection in the mirror stared back at her, tired and wary, but she avoided looking too closely. Dwelling wouldn't change anything.

Crawling into bed, she pulled the blankets tight around her and drifted into a restless sleep.

Her dream took her back to the party, and there he was again. Bain. The man she wished she could forget, but whose presence lingered stubbornly in her mind.

In the soft haze of her dream, she allowed herself to feel what she'd denied at the party. In this innocent, imagined world, there was no judgment, no cruel jokes. Here, she could be someone else, someone worthy of his attention.

She relived their first meeting, only this time, it wasn't filled with awkwardness or doubt. His warm, strong hand on her arm grounded her, his gaze steady and unflinching as it met hers. The moment burned deeper into her memory, vivid and impossible to ignore.

In her dream, she smiled back at him, confident and unguarded. They laughed and talked, and when the music swelled, he swept her off her feet. They danced together under the glow of a thousand fairy lights, his touch light but grounding, his smile breaking through her defenses like sunlight cutting through clouds.

When the night ended, they kissed under the moonlight, deep and passionate. His scent, warm and inviting, tinged with something heady and irresistible, enveloped her, making her heart race. Her dream self didn't hesitate, didn't pull away. Instead, she pressed closer, letting the world fade away until it was just them.

Her body ached for the dream to stretch on forever, for the warmth of his arms to be real, for the possibility of someone like him wanting someone like her. To be touched the way her body craved. To be loved for who she was.

Waking up felt like a loss.

The sharp contrast between the dream and her reality left her chest tight and her heart heavy. She sat on the edge of her bed for a moment, clutching the blanket as if it could pull her back into the world she didn't want to leave. But the morning light reminded her there was no room for fantasies. Not in her life.

With a sigh, she pushed herself to get ready for the day. Work was her solace, a space where she could exist without anyone's judgment.

The flower shop was quiet, as it often was. It suited her. She'd designed her business to keep her interaction with others to a minimum, relying on online orders to drive most of her sales. Having the post office pick up her packages to go to the post office was far preferable to enduring the stares of customers coming in and out all day. She often didn't even see a single person, she could work in peace.

She arranged a bouquet in one of the display vases, her hands moving methodically as she worked. The cooler hummed softly behind her, and she stepped inside to place the arrangement on a shelf. The chill enveloped her, and a sense of calm settled over her chest.

There was something about the cold that made her feel at peace. Maybe it was the quiet stillness of it, or maybe it was the way it numbed everything else. She felt more at home there than she ever did in the sweltering heat of Georgia.

Someday, she thought, she'd move someplace with snow. A place where the world matched the cool stillness she craved. For now, the flower cooler would have to do.

As she worked, her thoughts drifted back to her dream, to Bain's warm hand and soft smile. She shook her head, forcing herself to focus on the bouquet in front of her.

It was just a dream, she reminded herself. But the ache in her chest didn't subside.

The bell above the shop door jingled, breaking the serene quiet of the flower shop. Niamh froze, her heart leaping inexplicably as she worked up the courage to investigate. She stepped from behind the cooler, her breath catching when she saw the tall, blonde man standing with his back to her.

It couldn't be.

Her pulse quickened. But as he turned, her suspicion was confirmed, it was him. The mystery man from the party. Bain. He was trailing his fingertips over the delicate hydrangeas in the corner, his posture relaxed yet purposeful.

Her pulse quickened. Surely, this was a coincidence. He couldn't have followed her here. Could he?

"Welcome to Royal Flowers," she said, her voice steadier than she felt. She ducked behind the tall foliage lining the counter, using it as a shield. "How can I help you?"

His gaze lifted, and there it was again, that look from last night. Warm, searching, unyielding. It wasn't the look of someone mocking her, nor was it filled with pity or disdain. It was something entirely foreign to her.

"Hi, Niamh," he said, her name soft and deliberate on his lips. "I hope you don't mind... I asked Lidia how I could find you." He rubbed the back of his neck, clearly hoping she wouldn't take offense. He'd pleaded with Lidia for her location, leaning on charm and persistence. To his relief, Lidia had reluctantly given in.

Niamh's jaw tightened. She made a mental note to have a word with Lidia about sharing her private information. "Did she now?"

"I hope you're not mad. I just… I wanted to see you again." He paused, as if gauging her reaction, then quickly added, "And I actually need flowers, too."

She arched an eyebrow, skepticism flickering across her face. "Flowers. Really."

"Yes," he said with a sheepish grin. "For my…" he panicked, trying to think of someone he could buy flowers for, "boss. She's tough to impress, and I figured flowers might soften her up." He mentally kicked himself for saying boss, knowing it would sound weird to buy your boss flowers unless you were romantically involved with them. But he had said it, so he had to keep going with it.

She looked at him quickly.

"Nothing romantic like roses; it's definitely not that kind of situation." he winked, trying to reassure her it wasn't weird to buy your boss flowers. His boss was very cold, maybe the flowers would put her in a better mood when he saw her next and asked for his promotion. She'd been promising him. Maybe his panic choice wasn't so bad after all. Two birds, one stone, rather two happy women, one bouquet of flowers. Or so he hoped.

Her shoulders relaxed slightly. *It's just a business transaction,* she reminded herself. "What's she like? Modern and chic, or more traditional?" Because it didn't matter if it was a romantic situation, she wasn't interested. He could send flowers to whomever he wanted.

"Definitely traditional," Bain replied. "She's a stickler for the old ways."

Niamh's lips quirked into a small smile despite herself. "In that case, I'd recommend Cowslips. We just got them in, and they're one of my favorites. They're considered very special in Ireland."

"Oh?" His curiosity piqued, he tilted his head. "Are you from Ireland? Your name, it's Gaelic, isn't it?"

"No," she replied, shifting uncomfortably. "I'm from here. I was adopted, so I don't know much about my heritage." She kept fiddling with plants around her to keep her hands busy and her eyes off of him.

His face softened. "I didn't mean to bring up anything painful. I should really learn when to stop talking." He kicked himself for opening up his big mouth again. Flirting with her was like learning a new language. He had to learn fast if he didn't want to scare her away.

She waved off his apology. "It's fine. I have great adoptive parents." She knew it was weird to announce that she was adopted to someone she had just met, but she felt more confident when he was around. She felt braver than normal. She made a mental note to not trauma dump on him anymore in the future, though.

For a moment, the air between them felt heavier, more intimate. She noticed how his usual confidence faltered, a rare crack in his armor.

"The Cowslips," he said, clearing his throat. "They sound perfect. Let's go with those."

Niamh ducked behind the counter, relieved to have a task to focus on. "Good choice. I'll have them ready in a few minutes. I'm sure your boss will love them. Sucking up for a promotion?" she teased lightly.

Bain chuckled, the sound deep and warm. "Kind of. And I don't like being on her bad side. She's... intimidating, to say the least."

As she worked on arranging the delicate yellow blossoms in a vase, Niamh found herself sneaking glances at him. He wandered around the shop, his tall frame seeming out of place yet oddly fitting among the rows of delicate flowers.

She took mental notes for later: his strong jawline, the soft curl of his blonde hair, and that infuriating grin that tugged slightly higher on one side. His hands, large and capable, lingered on the petals of a rose, and she couldn't help but imagine how they'd feel brushing against her delicate parts.

She shook herself from the thought, focusing instead on the task at hand. When the arrangement was finished, she stepped out from behind the counter and held the vase out to him. Their fingers grazed as he took it, and an electric jolt shot through her.

Her eyes flicked to his, and she froze. His grin had turned devious, his gaze simmering with something unreadable. Trouble. That's what he was: trouble wrapped in a handsome package.

"I was wondering," he said, his voice low, "if you'd like to grab dinner sometime?"

Her stomach dropped. "I, uh, I'm busy."

"I didn't say what day yet."

"I'm… busy every day."

His grin widened, and he chuckled softly. "If you change your mind, here's my card." He slipped the small piece of paper into her hand, his fingers curling around hers. He soaked up the heat that spread into his body, warming his dark soul.

Her body betrayed her, responding to his touch with a warmth that spread through her chest. She forced herself to meet his gaze, her voice steady. "I won't, but thanks for the offer." It made her heart sink to say those words out loud. She so badly wanted to give in and take the chance with him, but she knew he'd end up being like all the rest.

He placed cash on the counter, winked, and turned to leave. His steps were smooth, confident, and maddeningly graceful.

Niamh watched him go, her heart hammering. She clutched his card in her hand, the edges pressing into her palm.

It had to be a joke, she told herself. *There's no way a man like him could actually be interested in me.*

And yet, the memory of his touch lingered, leaving her mind in a swirl of doubts and possibilities.

As soon as the bell jingled behind Bain's retreating figure, Niamh pulled out her phone and dialed Lidia's number, her fingers trembling with a mix of frustration and nerves.

Lidia answered on the second ring. "Hey, girl! How's the…"

"You told the rando where I worked?" Niamh cut her off, her voice sharp.

Lidia paused, caught off guard. "First off, he's not a rando. He works with my roommate at the ad agency. Second, he's a nice guy. And hot! I didn't think you'd mind."

"Lidia!" Niamh all but yelled. "You can't just tell people where I work! What if he was a serial killer or something?"

"Okay, calm down. He's not a serial killer," Lidia said, exasperation lacing her tone. "We've had dinner with him a few times, and he's totally normal. Did he do something?"

"No… but the fact that he wanted to find me is the red flag! That should've been the first sign to *not* tell him where I was!"

"Honestly, I didn't think you'd react like this," Lidia said, sounding defensive. "You haven't been on a date in forever, and he's gorgeous. You deserved to know he was interested!"

"That's exactly why you shouldn't have told him," Niamh snapped, pacing the shop. "People like that don't go around asking about people like me."

There was a beat of silence on the line before Lidia said, softer this time, "Niamh, stop. You've gotta let this whole 'guys don't like me' thing go. Maybe he really *does* like you. It's possible, you know." She hoped she was right. She so badly wanted Niamh to find love. She just hoped Bain wouldn't let her down like all the rest. She was the risk-taker of the two, she leaped well before Niamh. Sometimes, Niamh needed to be pushed out so she could spread her wings.

Niamh scoffed. "We both know that's not how the world works. A man that looks like him? He's probably dated supermodels and actresses. I'm not in the same league."

Lidia let out a small laugh, though it wasn't mocking. "Girl, you seriously need to find some self-esteem. You are gorgeous and unique with a killer body! He asked about you because he likes you, not out of pity or some weird game. And if you're worried, fine, meet him in public, keep your pepper spray handy. You carry it everywhere anyway, thanks to your dad."

Niamh winced at the mention of her father. "Yeah, you're not wrong about that," she muttered. Her dad had been overprotective since she was a child, hovering so much she could barely breathe. It had its benefits; she was hyper-aware of her surroundings, but it also left her feeling like she was being watched 24/7.

"And honestly," Lidia pressed, "don't you think you deserve a shot at being happy? He seemed genuine to me, and yeah, he's hot, but maybe, just maybe, he sees something in you that you can't see in yourself yet."

Niamh bit her lip, staring out the shop window. She wanted to believe Lidia, but the mirror never lied. Her oddly colored skin, her unnatural features weren't the kind of thing men like Bain fell for. At least, not seriously.

"I'll think about it," she mumbled, knowing full well she wouldn't.

"Good. And if you don't, I swear, I'll set you up with someone else," Lidia threatened lightly. "No more excuses," she laughed gently. Before Niamh was able to hang up, Lidia rushed out, "Hey, are you all packed and ready to go? I'm so excited! I haven't been home for so long! I can't wait to show you around!" Lidia's voice bubbled through the phone, her excitement practically infectious.

Niamh smiled at her friend's enthusiasm. Lidia had talked her into visiting her family in Michigan for the weekend, a trip Niamh had been hesitant about but now couldn't help but look forward to. She'd never been to Michigan, let alone seen snow in person. The thought of a winter wonderland felt almost magical.

"Almost," Niamh replied. "I've still got a few things to pack. Mostly sweaters. I didn't realize how few cold-weather clothes I own. I don't usually get cold." She laughed lightly, knowing her closet was filled with light jackets and cardigans ill-suited for Michigan winters, though she wasn't sure if she'd need the extra layer of warmth.

"I'll never understand how you're always so warm. I freeze if the temperature drops below sixty!" Lidia teased. "But don't worry, I'll pack an extra jacket for you, just in case. Winters are no joke up there, but I promise it'll be worth it. Michigan winters are beautiful."

"I can't wait to see the snow. I've never been to Michigan," Niamh admitted, her excitement growing. "Thanks again for letting me tag along." She'd never been anywhere outside of Georgia. The thought of traveling and having to see even more people frightened her beyond belief, but doing it with Lidia, she knew she'd be safe.

"Are you kidding? I'm thrilled you're coming! I've been trying to get you to visit for years!" Lidia exclaimed. "Plus, it's right around your birthday, so we *have* to celebrate!"

Niamh had almost forgotten about her upcoming birthday. Turning 25 didn't feel like a milestone to celebrate. She still lived at home, though by choice, and hadn't had a serious relationship in years. Still, she didn't mind staying with her parents; her dad worried too much to feel comfortable with her living alone.

Before she could respond, Lidia continued, "Oh, and one more thing… will you call Bain? You know, about dinner?"

Niamh sighed, her fingers brushing the business card sitting on her desk. She hadn't been able to throw it away, though she told herself it didn't mean anything. "I'll think about it," she said vaguely. "Maybe once we're back. One stress at a time."

"Fair enough. But seriously, don't be mad at me, okay? I was just trying to help. And he's cute!" Lidia giggled before hanging up, leaving Niamh shaking her head, tossing her phone onto the counter. She glanced at the business card Bain had slipped into her hand, the edges now slightly crumpled from her grip. She kept asking herself why a man like him would want anything to do with her.

Her heart whispered a dangerous answer she wasn't ready to hear: *Maybe he really does.*

She stared at Bain's card for a long moment. His name felt like it carried too much weight, too much possibility. *Bain O'Clery, Advertising Brand Manager Executive. We build brands that stand the test of time.* His polished title only added to the feeling that he was too good to be true.

What could someone like him possibly see in someone like her? The thought curled up in her chest like a cold knot. She tucked the card into her pocket, locking her feelings away in the same neat mental box where she stored every other impossible dream.

For now, her focus was on finishing orders, grabbing warmer clothes, and packing for the trip. Michigan and the snow awaited her, and for once, she wanted to let herself feel excited about the unknown.

Chapter 3

A long, busy day at the shop left Niamh utterly drained. She slipped into her pajamas, eyeing her neatly packed suitcase on the far side of the bed. Tomorrow was the big trip, but exhaustion tugged her down onto the mattress like an anchor. Sleep came quickly, and with it, her dreams took her back to him.

Bain.

He stood before her, tall and commanding, his presence radiating warmth. His fingertips brushed her cheek, feather-light but electric, sending a shiver down her spine. The touch lingered as his hand traced a path down her neck, a tender exploration that made her pulse quicken. Slowly, his hand slid along her side, resting possessively at the small of her back. With one smooth motion, he pulled her against him, their bodies melting together.

Despite the difference in their height, they fit as if made for each other. His deep gaze locked onto hers, those odd-colored eyes she had always hated about herself now reflected in his as something precious, beautiful. In his arms, her insecurities dissolved. Here, in this dream, she was free.

The faintest mix of their scents swirled between them, intoxicating and inexplicably familiar, like a magic cocoon wrapping them in safety. His muscled arm flexed around her, holding her steady as her body responded, lighting up with sensations she hadn't dared imagine before.

Without thinking, she reached up, fingers threading through his blonde curls. They were softer than she had imagined, yielding to her touch in a way that sent another ripple of desire through her. A quiet, unrestrained moan escaped her, his body tightening against hers in response. Eager to make her repeat that sound.

That crooked, devious smile returned, but this time, there was something knowing in it. Something primal. He wanted her to feel the pull between them—to know his attraction wasn't just her dream's invention.

Her hands roamed up his arms, marveling at the strength beneath his crisp button-up shirt. She hesitated only a moment before undoing the first few buttons, exposing a glimpse of his toned chest and the soft patch of golden hair beneath. She slid her hand inside, reveling in the warmth of his skin and the solidness of his form.

She wouldn't go any further. Even here, in a dream, she wanted to be careful, to keep herself safe. But she could explore the connection between their bodies a little more.

Nestled against him, her face resting on his bare chest, she felt peace so profound it almost didn't seem real. The world seemed to fall away, leaving just the two of them. Weightless, she felt like she was floating.

She glanced down.

They weren't on the ground anymore. Flowers and bushes waved far below them, the earth itself receding as they hovered in midair. Panic started to rise in her chest. She gripped Bain tighter for security, but her gaze caught something in his other hand.

The glint of polished metal.

A blade.

Her breath hitched as she froze, the sharp edge gleaming in the ethereal light of the dreamscape.

Before she could move, Bain raised the knife high above his head. His arm tensed, and his grip on her tightened. His fingers dug into her side, making her gasp in pain.

"No!" she screamed, struggling against his hold.

Just as the blade arced downward, she wrenched herself free. The force of her escape sent her tumbling backward, spinning uncontrollably as she fell toward the earth below. Her arms flailed, her lungs burned with a desperate cry, and then—

She jolted awake, gasping for breath.

Sweat coated her forehead and chest as she sat upright in bed, her heart racing like she'd run a marathon. Her eyes darted around the dim room, her chest rising and falling as she reassured herself, *it was just a dream. Just a dream.*

But the vividness lingered, the way his hands had felt on her skin, the warmth of his body, followed by the icy chill of betrayal.

She wondered what it meant. Was her subconscious trying to warn her? She shivered at the memory of his arm around her, making her feel safe and secure then the knife in his hand, breaking her sense of trust she thought she had. Maybe Lidia was wrong. Maybe Bain was too good to be true, maybe her mind was trying to tell her not to follow her body's desires.

Sleep was out of the question now. Niamh threw off the covers and turned to the safety of busy work, triple-checking her packing for the road trip.

Morning couldn't come fast enough. Michigan, at least, seemed far safer than her dreams.

The back of the car was packed to bursting with luggage and bags, while snacks spilled across the front seat. Niamh and Lidia were finally on the road, heading toward Michigan. Niamh gazed out the window as they drove, the southern landscape blurring past. She'd never seen real snow, though she'd always felt it calling to her, tugging at something deep in her soul. The heat of Georgia had never felt like home. It clung to her skin like an unwanted weight, amplifying the discomfort she already felt in her own body.

"I can't wait to see the snow," Niamh said, breaking the silence.

"I can't wait to show it to you!" Lidia chirped. "It's magical. You're going to fall in love with Michigan." The mention of the word love made Niamh cringe inside. For a second, she was able to forget about the sliver of hope she had when Bain showed up in her shop. The word sent flashes of the terrifying dream back to her. Knowing she wouldn't get many chances to travel to the snow, she was determined to enjoy the trip with her friend. She pushed all thoughts of his handsome face out of her mind.

They split the driving. Niamh took the wheel through the warmer states, but as soon as frost kissed the roads and the threat of ice loomed, Lidia insisted on taking over. "You might be able to handle a lot of things, girl, but black ice is not one of them," she teased.

Relieved, Niamh let herself relax in the passenger seat. The hum of the car and the soft, rhythmic crunch of tires on the road lulled her into a nap. She welcomed the escape, at least, she thought she did.

But he was waiting for her.

In her dream, Bain stood in the corner of a grand, crowded room. Dozens of people mingled around them, yet somehow, he was the only one she could focus on. A strange, almost supernatural clarity surrounded him, like a spotlight cutting through the chaos and highlighting him alone.

He leaned casually against the wall, arms folded across his broad chest, his expression unreadable but intense. Despite the distance, her body moved toward him, compelled by a pull she couldn't resist. The space between them cleared as though the crowd parted just for her.

"Stop," she whispered to herself. But her feet ignored her, carrying her forward until she stood inches from him.

He was otherworldly, his presence nearly glowing, so striking it made her breath catch. His eyes bore into her, studying her with unnerving intensity. She wanted to turn, to flee, but her limbs betrayed her. She couldn't move away, only closer to him.

Her hand trembled as it rose of its own accord, fingertips brushing against his full lips. They were warm and inviting, soft against her skin. His lips parted, and without warning, he captured her finger in his mouth.

A gasp escaped her as his tongue swirled in slow, teasing circles. The warmth of it sent ripples through her, confusion mingling with a visceral reaction she couldn't suppress. But then…

His tongue extended farther than it should have, impossibly long, its forked tip curling around her wrist like a serpent.

Her heart slammed against her ribs as she yanked her hand back, but it was too late. His lips peeled back in a grotesque grin, revealing rows of sharp, predatory teeth.

The room spun. She couldn't breathe.

"Niamh!" Lidia's voice jolted her awake, the world snapping back into focus.

The car was pulled over on the shoulder, and Lidia leaned across the seat, her face a mask of worry. Tears streamed down Niamh's cheeks as she struggled to steady her breathing.

"What happened?" Lidia asked, gripping her friend's shoulder.

Niamh hesitated, then spilled the truth: the dreams, the pull, the terror.

Lidia frowned, confused. "I don't get it. Why would he scare you? Bain seems so normal, sweet, even! You've met him in real life. You didn't feel scared then, right?"

"No… I didn't. But these dreams…" Niamh's voice wavered. "It's like he's in my head, playing tricks on me, trying to scare me. I don't know what's real anymore."

Lidia squeezed her shoulder reassuringly. "Maybe you're just stressed. The trip, the party coming up, everything. Dreams can mess with your head when you're overwhelmed. Let's just focus on this weekend, okay? You need this. We'll have fun, eat too much, and maybe go sledding."

Niamh nodded, forcing a smile for her best friend's sake. "You're probably right."

But deep down, she couldn't shake the feeling that Bain wasn't done with her. Whatever he was, whatever these dreams meant, this wasn't over.

The car glided through the snow-draped countryside, Niamh's eyes glued to the world outside. She didn't sleep again, preferring instead to soak in the wonder of the winter scenery. The trees, coated in thick layers of snow, stood like statues in a frozen cathedral, their branches bowing under the weight. Flurries drifted lazily from the sky, catching the light like tiny crystals. Frozen lakes stretched out like glassy plains, dotted with tiny shacks and bundled-up figures fishing in the cold. It was like stepping into a winter postcard, more breathtaking than she'd ever imagined.

By the time they reached Lidia's parent's house, the sun hung low, casting a golden glow over the over-sized brick home. The circular driveway was coated with salted patches where ice had been carefully warded off, and two enormous flower planters stood like sentinels, their blooms replaced with cascades of snow and ice. Niamh took it all in with a quiet smile.

Lidia wasted no time shrugging on her puffy winter jacket before stepping out into the chill. Niamh, as always, didn't bother. The cold didn't touch her like it did others, something she still couldn't fully explain.

The front door swung open, revealing Lidia's parents. They rushed out with smiles to greet their daughter, wrapping her in tight hugs. Niamh followed behind, standing quietly with her suitcase in hand.

"Mom, Dad, this is my best friend, Niamh," Lidia announced brightly, her voice brimming with warmth. While Lidia had known Niamh most of her life, her parents were not as involved then. They had jobs that took them all over, so Lidia was raised by nannies and staff. Lidia kept her friend's appearance a secret from her parents, knowing they wouldn't be as accepting as she was. They strived for perfection, to not stand out in any way. Niamh was the exact opposite of that. To protect her friend from the cruel world her parents lived in, she kept Niamh a hidden treasure, only for her to admire.

The Prices turned toward her, their polite smiles faltering ever so slightly as they registered her unusual appearance. Niamh saw it happen in real-time, the double take, the flicker of surprise in their eyes, and the subtle stiffness in their posture. It was what she expected. She knew it would happen, it always did. She just hoped they could hide their thoughts about her this weekend so she could enjoy time with her friend.

Niamh extended her hand, keeping her expression calm and pleasant. She knew they wouldn't embrace her, accept her for who she was and not what she looked like. "It's a pleasure to meet you, Mr. and Mrs. Price. Thank you so much for inviting me this weekend. Your home is absolutely beautiful." She knew the drill and how to escalate the situation after a lifetime of encounters like this one.

After a brief hesitation, Mrs. Price stepped forward to shake Niamh's hand, followed by her husband. Their smiles were cautious now, careful.

Niamh knew that look; it wasn't hostility, just discomfort with the unknown. She'd long since stopped taking it personally.

"Thank you, dear," Mrs. Price said, her voice kind but guarded.

"Welcome to Michigan," Mr. Price added, his handshake firm but brief.

They quickly turned back to Lidia, gathering her bags. Niamh hoisted her own suitcase and followed them into the house, slipping off her shoes at the door. Warmth from a crackling fire greeted them, softening the chill from outside. The entryway was grand, with white-and-gray-veined granite floors that gleamed under the light. Twin staircases curved elegantly along the walls, leading to the second floor.

Lidia led Niamh to a spare bedroom down the hall upstairs. The room was cozy, with soft gray walls and an over-sized bed covered in a fluffy white duvet. Niamh dropped her suitcase onto the bed and set her shoes neatly by the door before heading to Lidia's room.

Lidia's room was as vibrant as she was, with colorful throw pillows and an avalanche of blankets piled onto her king-sized bed. The two friends flopped backward onto it in unison, their arms stretched wide like they were making snow angels.

Laughter erupted from them both, light and carefree. For the first time in days, Niamh felt the tension in her chest begin to ease.

"This is what we needed," Lidia said, turning her head to grin at Niamh.

"Definitely," Niamh agreed, letting the warmth and comfort of the moment wash over her. Even if Lidia's parents seemed uneasy around her, she wouldn't let it ruin the trip. She'd learned long ago how to make herself blend in as much as someone with her striking, mismatched eyes ever could.

For now, she was determined to enjoy this rare moment of peace.

Lidia flipped onto her stomach, propping her chin on her hands, her eyes alight with excitement. "So, wanna go out tonight?" Her voice was casual, but the suggestion wasn't optional. She was determined to get Niamh out of her head and out of her house. Lidia's concern for her friend had grown with every mention of Bain and those unsettling dreams. Maybe a night out could shake Niamh out of whatever fog she was stuck in.

Niamh sighed, already resigned. "If you want to." She knew this was coming. Lidia couldn't go more than a weekend without plunging into some social scene.

"That's not an answer, Niamh," Lidia teased, rolling her eyes. "I don't want to pressure you, but honestly, I think you need this. No one here knows you, which means…you can be whoever you want! Let your alter ego out for a spin."

Her lips twitched into a reluctant smile. "Fine. Let's go out."

"Yes!" Lidia clapped her hands together, practically bouncing on the bed. "I know the *perfect* place. It's an underground club that features up-and-coming artists. Like, everyone who's famous now started there. It's super intimate and crazy fun!"

"That actually does sound cool." Niamh tilted her head, imagining herself slipping into a dark corner and enjoying live music. It didn't sound as overwhelming as the typical noisy, neon-lit bars Lidia dragged her to. "Okay, but… what do I wear?"

"I'm so glad you asked!" Lidia jumped off the bed and dove into her closet like a woman on a mission. Moments later, she emerged holding a slinky black dress that sparkled faintly under the light. It had delicate spaghetti straps and a plunging neckline. "This. You. Will. Kill. In. This."

Niamh eyed the dress, doubtful. "Lidia, I don't know… It's not really my thing."

"It's *exactly* your thing. You just don't know it yet," Lidia countered, pushing the dress toward her. "You've got the perfect body for it! Plus, you never get cold, so it's like this dress was made for you. Just try it. If you hate it, we'll find something else."

With a resigned sigh, Niamh slipped into the dress. She avoided the mirror at first, expecting to feel awkward and exposed. But when she finally looked, she barely recognized herself. The dress hugged her curves perfectly, highlighting her natural shape without being too over the top. She felt… powerful.

"I told you!" Lidia crowed triumphantly, watching as Niamh turned this way and that, examining herself from every angle. Before Niamh could say anything, Lidia plucked a pair of black strappy heels from her closet and thrust them into her hands. "These. You *have* to wear these."

Niamh hesitated but slipped on the heels. They added a few inches to her height, making her posture straighten and her confidence rise even further. Maybe this dress wasn't just a dress, it was armor. Something to draw attention away from her eyes, a distraction dress. Something to make her feel like she belonged, even for a night.

Lidia wasn't done yet. She sat Niamh down and worked on her makeup, keeping it light and neutral as requested. She focused on enhancing Niamh's pouty lips, using a soft peach gloss to make them pop while keeping her eyes understated.

"You look amazing," Lidia said, stepping back to admire her work.

Niamh grabbed a curling iron, attempting to add waves to her hair and stretch her bangs as low as possible to cover her eyes. The effort felt futile, though; her eyes, so unnaturally large and expressive, were impossible to miss. She debated adding over-sized sunglasses to her outfit, the kind that screamed *post-eye-surgery patients* would be the only thing to cover hers though.

But something about the way she looked in the mirror stopped her. The dress, the makeup, the shoes, it all added up to something stronger than her insecurities. Maybe, just maybe, tonight could be different.

Chapter 4

Y ou ready?" Lidia asked, pulling on her sequined jacket and giving her hair a final fluff.

Niamh took one last look in the mirror, squaring her shoulders. "Ready as I'll ever be."

"Girl, they are *not* ready for you," Lidia said, grinning as they headed for the door.

The music pulsed through the warehouse, growing louder with every step as Niamh and Lidia approached the club. It was an unassuming building, the kind of place you'd pass by without a second glance. No neon signs or bouncers in sight, just a heavy steel door at the entrance. Despite its plain exterior, the rhythmic bass pouring out onto the street promised a completely different world inside.

Niamh glanced nervously at Lidia, who flashed her a reassuring grin. "Trust me, this place is fun," she said, looping her arm through Niamh's and pulling her forward.

Inside, the atmosphere shifted instantly. The air was thick with energy, heat from bodies packed tightly on the dance floor, and music so loud it thrummed through Niamh's chest. She winced at the intensity, but as the beat enveloped her, she found it strangely liberating.

Lidia wasted no time leading them to the bar. "First things first: drinks!" she declared.

Niamh followed, fumbling with the drink covers her dad had insisted they bring. It felt a bit over the top, but the added layer of safety helped ease her nerves. After a couple of drinks, she felt the alcohol's warmth spread through her, melting away some of her tension.

"Come on, let's dance!" Lidia shouted over the music, tugging Niamh toward the floor.

The dance floor was a sea of movement, every person swaying and spinning to the pounding beat. As expected, Lidia quickly became the center of attention, surrounded by admirers eager to catch her eye. Niamh hovered on the outskirts, letting herself blend into the crowd. The anonymity was comforting, and she began to relax, letting the rhythm guide her body.

Her movements grew freer, more confident. She raised her arms and closed her eyes, swaying to the music without a care. The world around her melted away, and for the first time in ages, she felt weightless, free from judgment, free from her doubts.

Warm hands brushed against her sides, gliding so softly that she barely noticed at first. They moved slowly, tracing the curve of her body, leaving a trail of heat in their wake. By the time they reached her thighs, lifting the hem of her dress ever so slightly, her eyes flew open in alarm.

She spun around, heart racing, ready to confront whoever had dared touch her. But there was no one there.

The wall behind her was bare. No one stood close enough to have touched her.

Niamh convinced herself it was a warm gust of air from the heater that moved her dress, it just felt like fingers, but she barely felt anything, so it was plausible to her. Determined to enjoy the night she pushed her fear to the back of her mind and tried to dance again.

Closing her eyes to sink deeper into the rhythm of the music, her body began to sway to the rhythm. She raised her arms and caressed them in the air, enjoying the freedom music brought her. She had no thoughts in her mind except the music's beat vibrating through her.

"Niamh," a deep whisper called.

Her stomach sank. Wide-eyed in a panic she looked around. But again, no one was close. The music was so loud they'd have to be right next to her to whisper her name. She tried to talk herself out of it thinking someone else may have the same name as her and she just thought it was a whisper.

She knew she had a tendency to be overly cautious because of her past trauma from people making fun of her. Once again, she brushed the feeling aside, gaslighting herself into thinking she wasn't feeling or hearing what she thought she was.

One more look around the room to make sure she was alone in her corner, and she again closed her eyes, letting the beat take over her body.

She spun around with her arms in the air, twirling and jumping, letting herself get lost in the music. A new song started to play, and the crowd went wild, cheering and jumping to the beat in unison. She smiled at the sight of people being so free yet so connected at the same time. She yearned for a feeling like that.

As she joined in and began jumping, she felt a hand on her side, strong and warm. She thought someone just brushed into her by accident, so she ignored it and continued jumping with the crowd. The hand quickly moved up her torso, to sit just below her breast. The strong fingers dug in slightly into her ribs. Before she could move her arms down to brush the fingers away from her body, another hand quickly grabbed her wrists in the air, binding them together above her head. She couldn't turn her head to see who was assaulting her with her arms stretched above her.

A warm body pressed into the back of her. She could tell he was tall, lean, and muscular. His long fingers wrapped around both her wrists with no problem. His eagerness brushed against her. A gasp escaped her lips. She felt ashamed she was slightly aroused by the sensations, but fear quickly overflowed when "Niamh" was whispered into her ear once again. Soft lips grazed her ear as the warm breath traveled down her neck, sending shivers up her spine.

She closed her eyes tightly, hoping to open them to find out it was all a dream. When she opened them, she was alone again, her wrists unbound and no one pushing into the back of her. Only her pounding heart and a slight ache from the fingers digging into the skin under her breast. She rubbed the spot, hoping to brush the feeling away with it.

She couldn't handle it anymore. Her breathing quickened, panic bubbled up in her chest. She didn't like the idea of someone touching her without her permission, but the thought that she may be going crazy scared her more. She searched the room, her eyes darting frantically through the crowd. No one paid attention to her, their attention was on other people. Except for one person. The dark room made it hard to make out exact features, but his curly blonde hair looked a lot like his.

Bain.

The thought lingered in her mind that it may not be him; there were bound to be other men who were gorgeous, lean, and tall like him. But his smile, that was all Bain. His devious grin was unmistakable, even across the dimly lit room. But it couldn't be. Bain was in Georgia, he had no reason to be in Michigan, she thought.

Her pulse thundered in her ears. She tore her gaze away and bolted toward the restroom, pushing through the throng of bodies as quickly as she could. Once inside, she leaned over the sink, splashing cold water on her face in an attempt to ground herself.

"Calm down," she muttered, her voice trembling. "It wasn't real. He's not here. It's all in your head."

But the thought offered little comfort. Her legs gave out beneath her despite her efforts to not touch the disgusting floor. She sank to the tiled floor, pressing her back against the wall, she let the chill soak into her easing her anxiety a little. The panic still clawed at her, but slowly, she forced herself to take deep, measured breaths.

Minutes passed before she found the strength to stand again. She straightened her dress, avoiding her reflection in the mirror, and made her way back into the chaos of the club; she couldn't stay in the bathroom all night. She steeled her nerves, pushing the door open with authority. She wouldn't let a daydream or nightmare ruin her weekend.

Lidia was at the bar, laughing as she ordered another round of drinks. Niamh considered not telling her friend what had just happened. She thought she dreamt it anyway so why bother her with it? She looked like she was having so much fun, ruining her night was not what she wanted to do.

She stood at a distance, contemplating what her next move would be when she felt warm air brush against her neck sending goosebumps up her arms. The sweet smell of jasmine drifted to her, she breathed in the heavenly scent until her brain registered what it meant. She spun around again, but she was still alone. She didn't see Bain or anyone else anywhere near close enough to breathe on her neck.

Niamh couldn't take it any longer. She rushed to Lidia's side, gripping her arm tightly as if to ground herself from the chaos brewing in her mind.

"You okay?" Lidia asked, concern flickering across her face as she looked at her friend.

Niamh nodded, though her hands still trembled. "Yeah," she lied, forcing a smile. "Just needed a breather."

But deep down, she knew something was wrong. Bain wasn't done with her. And she wasn't sure she'd ever be able to escape him, he found her in her sleep and now when she's awake. He had some mysterious hold over her.

Niamh hesitated, unsure how to explain without sounding crazy. But the fear bubbling inside her outweighed her embarrassment. "I… I swear, Lidia, I saw him. Bain. Or someone who looks exactly like him."

Lidia raised an eyebrow, crossing her arms for warmth. "You sure? I mean, I don't want to doubt you, but there's no way he followed us all the way here. That's… it's just not possible."

"I *know* how it sounds," Niamh said, her voice breaking slightly. "But it wasn't just seeing him. I heard someone whisper my name twice. I felt… I don't know, like someone was breathing on me, touching me. And then he was *there*. Smiling at me like he was toying with me. It's the same look he gave me in my dreams."

"Wait, what?" Lidia froze. "Are you saying this is the same Bain you've been dreaming about? With the creepy tongue and teeth and whatever?"

Niamh nodded, her lips trembling. "Yes, but I don't know how that's possible. Maybe I'm losing it. Maybe I'm just imagining things." She buried her face in her hands.

Lidia placed a hand on her arm, her voice softening. "Hey, you're not losing it. You're just stressed, and this trip's been a lot. Maybe some fresh air and a good night's sleep will help. Let's go back to my place, watch a dumb movie, and chill, okay?"

Niamh nodded wordlessly.

"I just need to get out of here. I'm sorry," Niamh pleaded, her voice trembling with desperation.

"Yeah, let's go," Lidia said without hesitation. She leaned in close to the woman she'd been dancing with, murmuring something in her ear. The woman's face fell into a disappointed frown, but she nodded, typing something into her phone before waving goodbye. Lidia turned back to Niamh, gently taking her hand and leading her through the packed crowd. Her grip was firm but calm, trying to steady Niamh's shaking fingers.

As they pushed through the thrumming mass of bodies, the bass reverberated in Niamh's chest, matching the erratic rhythm of her heart. Each step closer to the exit felt like a gasp of air after being underwater. When they finally spilled into the cold night, the biting air wrapped around her, sharp and grounding. It was a relief compared to the suffocating heat of the club. Niamh took in a deep breath, trying to steady herself.

Niamh bent over, bracing herself with her hands on her knees, gulping in breaths of frosty air. Her body trembled as her mind tried to make sense of what had just happened. Lidia stood beside her, rubbing soft, soothing circles on her back.

"Did you drink too much?" Lidia asked, concern lacing her voice. "I knew we shouldn't have had that last shot."

Niamh shook her head, still catching her breath. "No, I didn't even drink as much as you. I had water in between, too." She straightened slightly, her eyes darting around as if expecting Bain to materialize in the shadows. "I just felt... weird in there. It was fine at first, but I swear, I felt like someone was watching me. And then—" She hesitated, her voice dropping. "I swear I heard someone call my name."

Lidia's brows knit together in alarm. "Are you sure you didn't get drugged or something? Should I take you to the hospital?"

"No, no," Niamh said quickly, waving the idea away, though her hands still trembled. "I think I'm okay. I just… I had to get out of there."

Lidia studied her for a moment, unconvinced. "Okay, if you're sure," she finally relented. "I'll call the Uber. They're usually quick around here. You just sit down and take a minute, okay?"

Niamh nodded, collapsing onto the rough, cold curb. She rested her head in her hands, focusing on steadying her breathing. *He wasn't there. He couldn't be there.* She repeated it to herself like a mantra, forcing logic to override her spiraling thoughts. *I'm either exhausted, paranoid, or losing my mind.*

The Uber arrived within minutes, its headlights slicing through the dark street. The ride back to Lidia's parents' house was eerily quiet, the only sound the occasional hum of the car engine. Niamh kept her head in her hands, her elbows braced on her knees as Lidia rubbed her back, a silent gesture of reassurance. Lidia was worried that if she pushed Niamh more, she might break. She'd never seen her friend in that state before. She was always leery and cautious of people, but this was a whole new thing. She didn't know how to help her friend.

When they finally reached the house, the familiar safety of its walls felt like a balm to Niamh's frayed nerves. The faint creaks of the structure and the occasional plop of ice from the freezer filled the silence, grounding her.

They did their normal after-party routine: change into comfortable pajamas, remove makeup, and eat ice cream.

Minutes later, they reconvened in the massive kitchen. Lidia, in her fleece pants and long-sleeved pajamas, grabbed two spoons and a tub of chocolate caramel swirl, while Niamh slid onto the island, her satin pajamas letting the coolness of the cold granite countertop drain some of the heat that always seemed to radiate from her body.

They sat in silence for a while, the occasional clink of spoons the only sound as they scooped small bites of the frozen treat. The weight of the evening lingered, unspoken but heavy.

Finally, Lidia broke the silence. "So, are we gonna talk about tonight?"

she wouldn't be satisfied until she knew her friend was going to be okay.

Niamh sighed, staring down at her spoon. "I'm sorry I made you leave early." Going to redirect the conversation away from where she knew it was going.

"That's not what I'm talking about, and you know it," Lidia said gently but firmly. Her gaze pinned Niamh, urging her to open up.

"I don't know what happened," Niamh admitted, her voice low. "I was fine, dancing in the corner. I could've stayed there a lot longer. But…" She hesitated, gripping the edge of the counter as if bracing herself. "I swear I saw him. Bain. How could he be here? He couldn't be here, right?" Her voice was tinged with desperation, as though begging Lidia to confirm what she already knew wasn't possible.

"Niamh," Lidia said softly, reaching across the counter to place a hand over Niamh's. Her voice was steady, her touch warm. "He isn't here."

Niamh shook her head, her eyes shimmering with a mix of frustration and fear. "I know that. I do. But he's everywhere in my dreams, in my head, and now… now he's in my waking life, too. Why is my brain doing this?" Her voice cracked on the last word, the vulnerability she tried so hard to hide finally breaking through.

Lidia squeezed her hand, her voice firm but kind. "You're not crazy, Niamh. Something's going on, and we'll figure it out. Together."

For the first time that night, Niamh let herself believe her friend.

But Lidia wasn't ready to let the conversation settle into a somber lull. With a mischievous glint in her eye, she suggested, "Maaaaybe you two are soulmates, and your heart is calling to his." She punctuated the idea with a dramatic hand over her chest, leaning into her hopeless romantic tendencies. Humor was her shield, and it was the only way she could think to steer the conversation away from Niamh spiraling into thoughts of insanity or worse, Bain lurking in the shadows.

That earned a snort from Niamh. "Yeah, okay, Lidia. *That's* why he tried to kill me last time." She rolled her eyes, but a faint smile tugged at the corners of her lips. "Maybe I'm just stressed because my birthday is coming up." Her tone shifted, quieter, almost as though admitting it was a burden in itself. She never liked celebrating her birthday. It was always a sharp reminder that her parents had given her away, choosing a life without her. While others saw their birthdays as milestones or celebrations, Niamh saw hers as a hollow marker of rejection.

Lidia's expression softened. "I know, honey," she said, scooping another bite of ice cream and setting it down. "But this year is going to be different. This year, you're taking back the shine they tried to steal from you."

Niamh gave her a skeptical look as Lidia leaned closer, brushing her long hair out of her face to meet her gaze. "You're a strong, beautiful, independent woman," Lidia said emphatically, as though each word was a spell to counter Niamh's insecurities.

Niamh blushed, her instinctive reaction to compliments kicking in. "You're such a dork," she muttered, but her voice was soft with gratitude. She wasn't good at accepting compliments, but she could tell Lidia meant it. After a moment, she let out a small sigh, giving her friend a reluctant smile. "You're right. I can't let their decisions dictate my life."

Lidia beamed, victorious. But Niamh wasn't done. She glanced down at her hands, turning them over slowly. "Still," she said, her voice dipping into something more wistful, "it would be nice to know why they gave me up. Was it because of how I looked? I would understand how having a deformed child would be hard. Did they just not want a kid? Not knowing where I came from…" She paused, searching for the right words. "It makes me feel so alone sometimes."

No matter how many genealogy DNA sites Niamh tried, the answer was always the same: inconclusive. Her parents had no answers either. They swore it had been a closed adoption, a baby left behind with no name, no story, just a phone call that changed their lives. But Niamh couldn't let it go. In secret, she combed through family papers, hoping for a trail, a hint, anything to piece together the past. She wasn't trying to prove her parents wrong. She just wanted to know where she came from. Even a fragment of truth would have been enough.

"You are not alone, you hear me?" Lidia reached across the counter, grabbing Niamh's hand and squeezing it tightly. "You've got me. Always."

The sincerity in her words hit Niamh hard. She set down her spoon and leaned over the ice cream tub, pulling Lidia into a hug. "You're the best," she whispered, her voice tight with emotion. Lidia had been her anchor since elementary school, her safe place in a world that often felt indifferent. Without her, Niamh didn't know where she'd be.

Chapter 5

Though she adored her adoptive parents, their relationship lacked this kind of openness. Especially with her dad; he wasn't exactly a confidant when it came to dating or personal fears. He'd be thrilled if she ended up like King George III's daughters, never marrying and staying at home forever.

But as much as she loved Lidia, Niamh knew the longer they stayed up talking, the more Lidia would try to convince her she wasn't losing her grip on reality. And Niamh wasn't ready for a full-on psych session.

"Let's go see what's streaming." She called to Lidia as she slid off the counter, tossing her spoon in the sink. She paused. "Nothing scary, though."

They both started laughing. They had an unspoken language that most didn't understand. A unique bond they shared.

Lidia found a movie, not scary and not romantic, she didn't want to trigger any more daydreams for Niamh. Maybe a comedy would ease the mood, at least she hoped.

Both of them didn't make it very long into the movie before sleep drug them under. Lidia slept like a dream as usual, but Niamh, her dream went to another place again.

The sky above was a black abyss, void of stars, while the earth below glistened blindingly white, a frozen expanse stretching endlessly. Towering mountains loomed around the valley, their sheer size surreal, their icy peaks clawing at the heavens. Niamh trudged through the deep snow, each step muffled and soundless. It should have been freezing, the kind of cold that bites through skin and bone, but she felt nothing. Only a strange pull, an invisible force compelling her to move forward, though she didn't know where she was going or why.

The pale moon cast long shadows from the skeletal trees, their outlines twisting across the snow like dark, clawed hands. The wind whispered and howled, giving the shadows life, their talons stretching toward her, reaching, grasping. Niamh quickened her pace, but the eerie darkness seemed alive, pushing her closer to the unknown. A sudden, thunderous rumble cracked through the valley, a sound so deep and resonant that it shook the earth itself. Snow erupted in a white plume, falling like ash as the ground beneath her gave way.

A crevasse opened, wide and endless. She scrambled to reach the side, but the ground fell out beneath her too fast, she dug through only air, hoping to catch something to stop her descent into the darkness. She fell, swallowed by the abyss as if she was a flake of snow, small and insignificant. Down, down, into the blackness she plunged, weightless and helpless. Her heart raced as she braced for impact from the inevitable floor at the bottom.

Something snagged her wrist, she reached up with her other hand instinctively trying to grip whatever she was caught up on.

She looked up in a panic, hoping whatever it was that she was clinging to would hold. It was a hand. Warm, firm, and steady, gripping her wrist with an unyielding strength that stopped her descent. With a powerful pull, she was hoisted up from the void. Gasping, she clung involuntarily to her savior, pressing herself against their solid form in an attempt to feel safe after the terrifying ordeal. Relief washed over her in a wave until she finally pulled back to see who had saved her.

Her heart sank, and bile rose in her throat.

Crystal blue eyes stared back at her, their piercing gaze as familiar as they were terrifying. His strong, angular features and short, curly blonde hair were unmistakable. Bain.

The man who haunted her dreams and her waking life had appeared again.

Niamh's relief turned to panic, a far deeper dread than the abyss below had stirred. She tried to step back, to put distance between them, but his fingers slid across her face, brushing her hair away with a careful pinky. The gentleness of the gesture shocked her, but her body recoiled instinctively. She flinched, unused to such an intimate touch, almost expecting something horrible to happen to her as it almost always did in her dreams that involved him. Her wide eyes met his, searching for malice but finding only regret.

He noticed her fear and released his hold on her. His shoulders sagged with defeat. For a moment, the two of them stood in silence, tension crackling like static in the frozen air.

His expression was something that she'd never seen from him. Fear maybe or regret. She felt a draw to him, it was undeniable, but this was something more. He needed her to touch him, to accept his unspoken apology. She needed to touch him, to let him know that she was as confused as he was. That she also felt something for him.

Her breath hitched as she cautiously raised a hand, pressing it flat against his chest. Beneath her trembling fingers, he was warm, too warm. The heat radiated from him, igniting something deep inside her. It wasn't just warmth; it was a fire, burning and consuming, spreading like a wildfire through her veins.

It overwhelmed her.

She tried to pull her hand back, afraid of hurting him or herself, but Bain gripped her arm tightly to hold her in place. His fingers dug into her flesh as if to tether her to him. Her panic flared, her body thrashing as she tried to break free. His face was now plastered with the look of panic.

"Let me go!" she screamed, her voice raw with fear.

But he didn't release her. His hold only grew stronger, and she could feel his fingertips pressing deeper, bruising her skin. The pain and fear churned inside her, a storm she couldn't control. The heat grew unbearable, an inferno consuming her from within.

"Stop!" she cried, her voice breaking.

The emotions, fear, anger, hatred reached a boiling point. She could no longer contain the surge inside her. With a visceral scream, she threw her arms outward, the fire inside her erupted.

It exploded like a bomb.

The force sent Bain hurtling backward, his body twisting and flailing as he scrambled to grasp anything to stop his momentum. Snow and ash swirled violently around her, but she didn't feel relief.

A voice broke through the chaos, piercing the fog of her terror like a beacon of light.

"Niamh! I'm here. You're okay. You're okay. Wake up!"

Lidia.

Niamh gasped for breath, her eyes snapping open as she clawed her way back to reality. Her hands flew to her arms, expecting to find bruises, evidence of his grasp, but there was nothing. No marks, no wounds, just the lingering heat that radiated from her skin.

Her chest heaved as she struggled to calm herself. It was only a dream. A horrible, vivid dream.

Lidia sat beside her, her face etched with concern. She reached out to rub Niamh's arm but pulled back with a sharp hiss. "You're burning up! Are you running a fever?"

Niamh shook her head weakly. "I don't feel sick. It was a dream... it was like I was on fire."

"A dream can't make you *this* hot, Niamh. I can't even touch you without burning myself." Lidia's worry deepened as she stared at her friend. "This isn't normal."

"None of this is normal!" Niamh cried, curling into herself. She pulled her knees to her chest, trembling as tears streamed down her face.

Lidia sat frozen for a moment, unsure how to comfort her friend when everything about this was beyond reason. But she stayed close, her presence a steady anchor in the storm of Niamh's emotions.

Lidia hurried to the bathroom, her concern etched deep into her features. When she returned, she held a washcloth soaked in cold water. Sitting on the couch next to Niamh, she pressed the damp cloth to her forehead, her worry intensifying as the cloth quickly warmed from Niamh's radiating heat.

"This isn't normal," Lidia murmured, her voice betraying her fear. The possibility of a dangerously high fever crossed her mind, and with it, the threat of brain damage. She debated taking Niamh to the hospital right then and there but allowed herself to be convinced otherwise. "If you're still like this in the morning, I *will* take you in," she warned firmly.

Lidia stayed with her to keep a close eye on her friend. She hoped her presence might ward off whatever nightmares haunted Niamh. Her heart ached with worry, but eventually, exhaustion overtook her.

When Niamh stirred, the spot beside her was cold and empty. She reached for Lidia's arm instinctively, but her hand met nothing but fabric. Groggily, she sat up, her damp clothes clinging to her, the remnants of her fever. The suffocating heat from the night before had subsided.

The mirror in the bathroom reflected red-rimmed, puffy eyes, proof that her tears hadn't been confined to the dream. With a sigh, she splashed cold water on her face, letting its sharp chill ground her. It wasn't much, but it was enough to start piecing herself together. She slipped on a T-shirt and jeans, craving normalcy after a night that felt anything but.

The smell of bacon and coffee lured her downstairs, a comforting aroma that wrapped around her like a warm blanket. In the kitchen, Lidia and her parents sat at the table, piles of bacon and golden pancakes stacked high between them. A steaming pot of coffee sat on a trivet, its rich, dark aroma promising a jolt of life.

Lidia rushed over to Niamh and hugged her deeply. Relieved that her temperature went down even more after she last checked on her. She felt like her normal self, minus the puffy eyes from crying.

Niamh gave her a weak smile, knowing that her friend was worried for her.

"Happy birthday!" Lidia said quietly as she waved towards the table.

"Thanks," Niamh replied shyly, scooting into the seat next to Lidia.

"Good morning, dear," Mrs. Price said warmly, glancing up from her magazine. "How did you sleep?"

"Good morning," Niamh replied, forcing a bright tone. "The bed was super comfortable." It wasn't a lie, but it wasn't the truth either. She had no intention of diving into the horrors of her nightmares.

"She had a rough night, Mom," Lidia interjected, her concern apparent. "Bad dreams."

Mrs. Price's expression softened. "Oh, I'm so sorry to hear that. I'll make you some chamomile tea before bed tonight; that always helps me."

Niamh's lips curved into a faint smile, though she doubted tea could do much against the kind of turmoil she faced. It felt like offering a bandage for a broken bone, but the sentiment was kind. "That would be great. Thanks, Mrs. Price."

She gave a curt nod, her expression neutral. The Prices weren't exactly warm toward Niamh, but their tolerance of her was better than outright hostility. She counted even the smallest gestures as victories.

Lidia beamed at her friend, a sparkle of determination in her eyes. "Today is going to be a *good* day, okay? No more bad dreams, no more stress. Just us, pancakes, and… surprises!"

Niamh arched her brow. "Surprises?"

"You'll see," Lidia replied with a mischievous grin, sliding a plate of pancakes toward her.

As Niamh sat down, the warmth of the food and the hum of friendly chatter began to ease the weight of the night before. *Maybe today could be okay. Maybe.* She hoped.

Chapter 6

Lidia spun around to face Niamh, her long blonde hair swinging with her dramatic turn. Mid-eyelash curl, she pinned Niamh with a pointed look. "So, are we gonna talk about what happened last night? I know you like to avoid these conversations, but we *need* to talk about it."

Niamh groaned, burying her face in her hands. "Nope. I was hoping we didn't."

Lidia raised an eyebrow, undeterred. "Girl, you know I'm going to ask. Spill it. What is going on with you?"

Niamh sighed heavily, dragging her fingers down her cheeks. "Ugh, I don't know, Lidia. These dreams are… different. They're too vivid, too real. I can *feel* pain in them, I can *smell* things. It's not like a normal dream."

Lidia set down the eyelash curler and leaned closer, concern flashing in her eyes. "I felt you last night. You actually had a fever. Was that part of the dream?"

"Not a fever exactly," Niamh whispered, "but I was trapped by…" She hesitated, glancing around as if someone might overhear. "Bain."

Lidia's jaw dropped, but before she could say anything, Niamh hurried on. "He grabbed me in my dream, and I…I don't know how to explain it; I kind of exploded. Like, I got so hot I felt like a volcano erupting."

"What?" Lidia practically screeched, sitting bolt upright. "You *exploded*?

What does that even mean?"

"I don't think it was metaphorical," Niamh said, shivering at the memory. "I felt this heat bubbling up inside me like it had nowhere to go. And then... boom." She threw her hands out for emphasis.

Lidia shook her head, trying to process. "Okay, but... why Bain? You've seen the guy, what, *twice* in real life? Why is he invading all your dreams?"

"I don't know!" Niamh threw her hands in the air. "He must've made an impression or something. He did save me in this dream, though. It was a nice change from him trying to kill me."

"He's cute," winking at Niamh, "but not 'let him kill me in my dreams' cute."

"No one's that cute," Niamh agreed with a snort. "But back to the whole 'exploding' thing. It's been happening more and more, Lidia. Last night was the worst."

Lidia rubbed her temples, clearly torn between disbelief and worry. "Alright, here's what we're gonna do. I don't know what to do about your... *hotness,* but we *can* do something about Bain. You're going to call him and set up a meeting when we get back tomorrow."

Niamh's stomach lurched. "What? Why?"

"Because this needs to end," Lidia said firmly. "Either you decide you want to date him, or you figure out a way to get him out of your life for good. Ignoring this clearly isn't helping."

Niamh groaned but knew Lidia was right. She finished her phone out of her pocket, her heart pounding. Bain's name sat in her contacts list, taunting her. She debated even adding him to her phone list before they left for their trip, but a small part of her would always regret it if she didn't. She wanted to enjoy being pursued, just once in her life, even if it ended up being brief. She hesitated before pressing the call button, hoping against hope he wouldn't answer.

The ringing was deafening, her nerves tightening with every second. Then, a familiar deep voice answered, smooth and confident. "Well, hello, beautiful. I was wondering if you'd ever call me."

Niamh rolled her eyes so hard they nearly got stuck. "Yeah, I wasn't sure either," she said coldly, letting her tone carry all the reluctance she felt. "How'd you know it was me?"

Bain chuckled, clearly unfazed. "I knew you'd be calling. I was just hoping it was you. So, when are we going to dinner?"

She wondered if she was the only one he gave his number to. But she brushed off the thought. "Coffee," Niamh corrected sharply. "I'll have coffee with you. Nothing more. Tomorrow at seven."

"Coffee, huh?" His voice was a mix of amusement and satisfaction. "I'll take what I can get. It's a date."

"It's *not* a date. Just coffee," Niamh snapped.

"Whatever you want to call it," Bain said smoothly. "Text me the place. Can't wait."

Before he could say anything else, she hung up and let out a shaky breath. Her heart was racing, but not from excitement, more like dread.

"Okay," she muttered, turning to Lidia. "I see him tomorrow at seven."

"You're not seeing him alone," Lidia declared. "Tim and I will be there. You need backup in case he's as sketchy as you're thinking."

Niamh couldn't argue with that. "Thanks," she murmured. "I appreciate it."

Lidia grinned, the tension breaking slightly. "Alright, now that's done, let's focus on the day! How about ice skating?"

"I've never been, but it sounds fun," Niamh said, grateful for the change of topic. Skating might not fix her dream problem, but at least it was something normal. She could use a little normal right now.

"Grab your jacket and some warm socks, and let's go!" Lidia called to Niamh as she disappeared down the hallway to her temporary bedroom.

Niamh lingered for a moment, leaning against the doorframe as she took slow, deliberate breaths. The tension in her muscles from that awkward phone call with Bain hadn't fully eased yet. She gave herself a small pep talk, then grabbed her things and joined Lidia.

They bundled up well, Lidia did; Niamh knew she wouldn't need as many layers as her friend, jackets in tow, and headed out to the car. Lidia shrugged into her puffy coat immediately, while Niamh, still warm, carried hers under her arm. She felt strangely insulated against the cold, like the chill couldn't quite reach her.

When they arrived, the ice rink took Niamh's breath away. Set in downtown Detroit, it shattered every preconceived notion she had about what an inner-city rink would look like. Her mind had conjured images of grime and litter, but the reality was dazzling. Trees wrapped in white lights bordered the rink, casting a warm, festive glow that reflected off the smooth, ice-like stars in the sky. A massive pine tree dominated one end of the rink. It sparkled with colorful ornaments. It felt like stepping into a dream.

Lidia grinned as she got out of the car, noticing Niamh's stunned expression. "It's pretty, isn't it?"

Niamh nodded, still awestruck. "It's amazing. Almost too pretty to be real."

"Come on, let's go get some skates," Lidia said, leading the way. Niamh followed, her gaze still lingering on the magical scene.

As they approached the rink, Lidia glanced at her friend. "Aren't you cold?"

"Nope, still comfortable," Niamh replied, patting the jacket she carried. "But I have this just in case."

Lidia shook her head in disbelief. "Girl, you're crazy. It's *twenty-five degrees* out here."

Niamh chuckled. "My dad always said I was warm-blooded."

"He wasn't kidding. I wish I had that talent. I would've saved a fortune on sweaters."

They laced up their rental skates, Niamh left her jacket on the bench. She wobbled uncertainly on the thin blades, clutching the wall as she shuffled onto the ice. The sensation was equal parts thrilling and terrifying. She gripped the railing like it was a lifeline, creeping along the edge while Lidia glided effortlessly in the center of the rink. Lidia twirled and spun, looking as natural on the ice as if she'd been born on it.

Niamh envied her grace but stayed firmly glued to the wall. Every time she tried to move away, someone would rush past, the blur of motion unsettling her balance. The cold didn't bother her, but the slippery ice felt like it was mocking her efforts.

As she edged along, a sudden, strong grip closed around her arm. The fingers dug into her skin, just like Bain's had in her dream. Pain shot up her arm, and she gasped, her anxiety rising. She whipped around, expecting to see someone struggling for balance. But no one was there.

Her stomach flipped as she lost her footing, the surprise making her fall hard onto the ice. The impact knocked the air from her lungs, she laid there for a moment, gasping for breath and trying to make sense of what had just happened. Her eyes darted around, searching for whoever had grabbed her. But everyone around her was minding their own business, laughing, skating, or huddling by the wall. No one seemed to notice her.

Lidia, however, spotted her immediately and skated over, worry etched on her face. "You okay?" she asked, crouching beside her.

"Yeah, I'm... I'm fine." Niamh forced a weak smile as she brushed herself off, still rattled. "I think I'm gonna take a break. I'll be on the bench over there."

Lidia hesitated, clearly not convinced. "Are you sure?"

"Yeah," Niamh said quickly. "Go back to skating. I'll just sit for a bit."

"Alright," Lidia said reluctantly, glancing back as she returned to the center of the rink. She resumed skating but kept an eye on Niamh from a distance.

Niamh teetered her way off the ice, clinging to the wall until she reached the bench. She collapsed onto it, grateful for its sturdy reassurance. Her heart was still racing, her mind replaying the moment on the ice. It felt so *real.* The grip, the pain, it wasn't her imagination. But how could it be? No one had been near her.

As Niamh watched the skaters gliding across the ice, a sense of peace settled over her. She admired how carefree they all seemed, spinning, laughing, and moving as if the world outside didn't exist. She zoned out, letting her thoughts drift with the rhythm of their motion, her gaze soft and unfocused. It was a rare moment of quiet in her otherwise restless mind.

"Niamh," a voice called softly.

Her focus snapped back, and she glanced around, startled. Lidia was still on the far side of the rink, twirling with a group of skaters. There was no way it had been her. Niamh frowned, scanning the area, but no one seemed to be looking in her direction.

It's probably nothing, she told herself, forcing a small laugh. Maybe someone else nearby had the same name, though that felt unlikely. She shook off the eerie feeling and turned back to watching Lidia, who seemed to glide effortlessly through the ice's sparkling haze.

"Niamh."

This time, it was unmistakably closer, deeper, and undeniably male. Her stomach twisted, and she whipped her head around. Her breath came faster as her eyes darted over the people milling about the rink, but everyone seemed absorbed in their own worlds. No one was looking at her.

Her skin prickled with unease, and a single thought cut through her: *Am I losing it?*

It wouldn't surprise her. She had no real idea what ran in her family; her past was a puzzle missing nearly all its pieces. Maybe insanity wasn't far behind vivid dreams and unexplained fevers.

A few minutes passed, and the tension began to ease. She settled back into her seat, convincing herself it had been nothing, her imagination getting the best of her. *It's fine. I'm fine.*

"Niamh."

This time, the voice wasn't distant; it was right behind her, so close she felt the warmth of the breath on her neck. The contrast of the cold air around her and the hot puff against her skin made her jerk her body up with a yelp. She spun around, her skates unsteady beneath her, eyes wide and frantic.

There was no one there.

Only cold, empty air.

Her heart hammered in her chest as she scanned the area again. Her logical mind tried to rationalize it, but her gut told her something wasn't right. She was too rattled to sit still, so she pushed herself back onto the ice, desperate to distract herself.

Lidia met her at the entrance, her brow furrowed with concern. "You're not having fun, are you?" she asked, her tone soft but disappointed.

Niamh forced a smile, not wanting to ruin Lidia's mood. "No, it's fun. I'm just… not very good at it."

Lidia tilted her head, unconvinced. "It's your birthday. What do you want to do?"

"Honestly?"

"Always."

"I'd rather go back to your parents' house, order pizza, and binge on junk food while watching movies." She chuckled nervously. "Maybe skating just isn't my thing."

Lidia brightened at the idea. "We can absolutely do that! I just didn't want you to feel like we didn't do anything special while you were here."

"Are you kidding me? A chill night with my bestie is perfect," Niamh said with sincerity. "And you've been talking up this Detroit-style pizza. I'm sold."

Back at the house, they wasted no time swapping their layers of winter gear for cozy pajamas. Lidia raided the kitchen, returning with a feast of snacks, which she spread across the coffee table like a proud hunter presenting her catch. Thick, cheesy slices of Detroit-style pizza joined the mix, their crispy edges and rich, saucy centers stealing the show.

They curled up on the over-sized couch, legs tangled under heaps of soft blankets, munching and laughing at the ridiculousness of the movies they picked. Niamh felt lighter than she had in weeks, soaking in the normalcy of the moment. The unease from earlier began to fade, replaced by the comforting warmth of friendship.

But as the hours ticked on, her eyelids grew heavier. She fought the pull of sleep, knowing Bain's presence awaited her on the other side of consciousness. Yet, exhaustion won out. With her head resting against Lidia's shoulder, she drifted off, the sounds of the movie fading into the background.

The black starless sky above, and the blindingly white blanketed earth was below. With mountains that seemed too tall to be real, towered above the valley she was in. White glistening snow puffed up around her legs as she waded through it. Without the bite of cold she was expecting from the snow, she walked around, feeling the urge to move, like a gravitational pull, but not knowing where to.

The bright moon made the trees cast dark shadows across the white snow, the wind gave the shadows movement like clawed hands were reaching out for Niamh. They swayed and stretched toward her as she walked, reaching out their pointy talons closer and closer to her. A deep rumble and cracking sound shook the valley and the mountains, making snow puff up from the vibration. Beneath her, a large crevasse opened up in a violent wave. She was swallowed up by the white powder falling with her into the blackness below. As her mind was expecting to fall deeper and deeper into the nothingness, strong hands wrapped around her waist, lifting her up almost effortlessly.

Once her feet were safely on the ground, she instinctively embraced the mystery savior, grateful for not disappearing. She pulled away to examine the rescuer, only to find a certain strong-featured, blonde, short, curly-haired man staring back at her with crystal blue eyes. Niamh felt a rush of panic far greater than when she felt like she was falling into oblivion. This man has haunted her dreams and her wake since they met. He loosened his grip on her waist and swooped her hair out of her face with his pinky. She flinched at the gesture. She wasn't used to people touching her, especially not wanting to see her eyes more. This was uncharted territory for her.

He sensed her fear and pulled his hand away as if she burnt him. He hung his head in defeat. She stood there a moment, deciding what to do. She slowly raised a hand to touch his chest, it was firm and warm. She rested her flat hand on his body. The heat rose in her; she was used to feeling warm, but this was something else. It burned from the inside, eating away at her resolve until her entire body felt like it was in flames. She attempted to pull away from him, not wanting to hurt him too. But he grabbed her around the waist tightly with determination. She fought to escape his grip, but he squeezed tighter. His fingertips dug into her flesh at her hips as she struggled to break free. A painful scream escaped her throat.

She felt the pain, fear, and hatred deep inside her starting to boil up. Like a pot of water on the stove with the burner up too high. There was no containing the amount of heat in her. A vicious scream escaped her as she threw her arms to the sides and let the heat burst out, detonating like a bomb. It threw Bain, twisting and flailing across the ground, trying to grab anything to stop.

A sharp pain ripped across her ankle as he flung his arm to the sides, hoping to grab onto anything or anyone to stop him. She screamed in agony; the searing pain tore through her. She reached down to hold her hand on the wound to instinctively stop the bleeding, but the effort was futile. It quickly leaked through her fingers and pooled on the white snow beneath her foot.

Lidia's voice broke through her terror, pulling her back to reality like a beacon. She followed her friends' voice with every ounce of energy she had, knowing her life might depend on it. The dreams started to feel too real to her.

Lidia held Niamh tightly, her own heart aching at the pain and confusion written across her friend's face. She stroked Niamh's hair gently, her voice soft and steady. "You're here. You're safe. No one can hurt you while I'm here, okay?"

Niamh nodded weakly, clinging to Lidia's words like a lifeline. She wiped at her face, trying to push back the storm of emotions swirling inside her. "It felt so real, Lidia. I could feel the snow, the wind, even the pain… That's not supposed to happen in a dream, is it?"

Lidia hesitated before answering, choosing her words carefully. "Dreams can feel real sometimes, especially when they're tied to things we're going through or feeling in real life. But Niamh, this sounds like something more. It's not just your imagination running wild."

"It was more than a dream. I felt the pain of a scratch on my ankle," bringing her ankle up to touch it where she felt the ache. Sticky liquid clung to her fingers when she pulled it away. Blood was still dripping down her ankle.

Both the girls let out a gasp.

"M… maybe you scratched yourself in the dream?" Lidia asked unconvincingly.

With her hand wrapped around the deep cuts in a futile attempt to stop the bleeding, she said, "I don't have sharp nails, Lidia."

Lidia didn't say a word as she left the room, returning with a first aid kit. She wrapped Niamh's ankle, inspecting it as she covered it with gauze. "Maybe we should get you to a doctor. This looks pretty deep. It doesn't look like ligaments or arteries were hit, but I'm also not a doctor."

"No, no doctors. They'd never believe how this happened." Lidia knew she was right. Doctors would probably lock her in a loony bin if she told them about her dreams. No, there had to be another explanation, and she was determined to find it.

"I just don't get it, though. Why would he try to hurt you?"

Niamh sighed, "they don't start off as him attacking me. He usually starts off mysterious and gentle; the scenery is usually very beautiful. Then something changes, it gets dark, and something always happens, and I think he tries to save me, but ends up hurting me." She rubbed her face with her free hand, knowing what she just said aloud sounded crazy even to her.

"I wish I knew what to say to make this all make sense, Niamh. This all sounds so out of this world." She rests a hand on her friend's shoulder, knowing her words would just fall flat in this situation.

"I just want to get back home, I need to talk to Bain. I have a weird feeling he's somehow the cause of everything happening to me. I don't know how, and I know it sounds crazy, but this stuff only started when I met him."

"Okay, if you're sure. I just don't want anything else to happen to you." Lidia said, sounding like a mother hen protecting her chick.

"I'm sure. I just want to get home and deal with this."

"I'll start packing our stuff. You just sit and rest."

"I'm sorry to cut our last day short."

"No, you are more important than anything Niamh. I just want you to be safe. I can only take so much of my parents anyway." She said laughing.

With that, Lidia headed up the large set of stairs to pack both of their bags. Niamh sat on the couch, contemplating the recent events. She felt helpless; she couldn't help her friend pack, and she couldn't help herself out of this crazy dream situation.

They said their goodbyes to Lidia's parents, a look of concern was plastered on their faces as they hugged Lidia. She reassured them everything was fine, and something suddenly came up, so they had to leave early. It wasn't a complete lie. Niamh felt guilty making her leave early, she felt like a big inconvenience, affecting everyone around her.

Chapter 7

L idia drove the entire trip back to Georgia, gripping the wheel tightly as if the force alone could ward off the creeping sense of dread. Niamh sat rigid in the passenger seat, her eyes red-rimmed but wide open. She didn't dare risk falling asleep. Every time her eyelids grew heavy, the memory of her dream jerked her back to alertness.

The two made small talk during the journey, their voices strained as they avoided the looming shadow of what had just happened. Lidia recounted funny stories from school, trying to distract them both, but Niamh's responses were clipped, her mind too preoccupied to truly engage.

As they pulled into the driveway, Niamh barely had time to gather her thoughts before her parents rushed out, their faces full of concern.

"Lidia texted that you'd been hurt. Are you okay?" her father asked, wrapping her in a protective hug before she could respond.

Niamh shot a sharp glance at Lidia, irritation flashing in her eyes. *Couldn't she have warned me?* she thought bitterly, already mentally drafting a conversation about boundaries. Lidia only shrugged, guiltless, as she handed Niamh's bags to her mom.

"Here, let me help you," her dad insisted, holding her arm as she hobbled toward the house. She gritted her teeth against the discomfort, unwilling to show just how much the pain in her ankle still throbbed.

"I'll call Dr. Brown. He still makes house calls," her dad said as they reached the door.

"No, Dad," Niamh said quickly. "I'm fine. I just want to rest in my room."

Her dad's skeptical frown deepened, but he relented with a sigh, watching her closely as she shuffled toward the stairs to her room. Once the door to her bedroom clicked shut behind her, she leaned back against it, exhaling deeply. She wasn't ready to explain this, not to anyone. What could she even say?

She eventually made it over to her bed, she reached for the stack of DVDs on her desk and grabbed her favorite horror movie. If she wasn't going to sleep, she needed something to keep her mind busy. She popped a few chocolate-covered coffee beans into her mouth, savoring their bitter sweetness as the opening credits rolled. She was determined to not sleep… to not see Bain in her nightmares again.

Three movies later, her body was exhausted, but her mind raced. She stared at the now-blank screen, wondering if she'd ever feel safe closing her eyes again. Just as she began to question her sanity, a golden burst of light filled her room. The air shimmered like sunlight on water, glittery and bright.

The wind whipped her hair across her face, and she instinctively yanked her blanket over her head, her heart pounding in terror. *This can't be happening again.* Slowly, she peeked out from under the blanket, bracing for Bain's familiar, unsettling presence.

But Bain wasn't there.

Instead, two strangers stood in her room: a woman with fiery copper curls and an air of fierce determination and a tall, broad-shouldered man whose gray-streaked hair and calm demeanor exuded authority. Niamh froze, her breath catching in her throat. She couldn't scream. She couldn't move.

"Hi," the red-haired woman said gently, her tone almost soothing. "We're sorry to startle you. We're here to help."

"Help?" Niamh managed to stammer, her voice shaking. "Who are you?

How did you get in here?"

"I'm Aoife (EE-fa)," the woman said, offering a small smile. "This is Nick. We help people affected by magic. We got a hit that you were in trouble."

"Magic?" Niamh repeated, her disbelief breaking through her fear. "Magic isn't real. You're crazy. And you need to leave before I call the cops." She grabbed her phone, her finger hovering over the emergency call button.

Nick stepped forward, his hands raised in a calming gesture. "We're not here to hurt you. And trust me, magic is very real. You wouldn't be experiencing all of this if it weren't."

"All of what?" Niamh snapped, clutching her phone tighter. "You don't know anything about me."

Aoife's expression softened. "You don't know, do you? About yourself?" She hesitated, glancing at Nick before continuing. "You're not... entirely human."

Niamh's stomach dropped. "Excuse me?" Her voice cracked, her panic rising. "I don't know what you're talking about. I'm normal. I'm..." She stopped, the words catching in her throat.

Nick spoke up, his voice steady and kind. "You're the child of two magical beings. It's in your blood. Your eyes," he gestured gently, "are a giveaway."

She blinked, self-conscious. People had commented on her eyes her whole life, how unnaturally big they were. "They're just... different," she said defensively. "A birth defect."

Aoife shook her head. "No. They're a mark of your heritage. Neither of your biological parents were human. You didn't know?"

"I was adopted," Niamh said, her voice trembling. "My parents don't know anything about my birth parents."

Nick stepped closer, his expression both apologetic and earnest. "You're not alone in this. We can help you. But you are in danger."

Niamh stared at them, her mind a whirlwind of confusion and fear. The ground beneath her felt like it was crumbling. Everything she thought she knew about herself, about the world, was slipping away. But one thing was clear: nothing would ever be the same again.

"Um... okay," Niamh managed to squeak out, her voice trembling as her mind struggled to keep pace with what was unfolding before her.

Aoife stepped in gently, her tone warm and reassuring. "I know this is a lot to take in. Trust me, I was in your shoes not too long ago. It's overwhelming, I get it. But I'll be with you every step of the way if you'll let us help."

"You're magic?" Niamh asked, her voice edged with disbelief.

"Yup," Aoife replied with a small laugh. "My family was cursed generations ago. The curse gave certain members of my family magical abilities, but no one really understood it. My parents didn't have magic, so I was alone. But I learned how to control it. With Nick's help," she said, leaning into the large man and lightly touching his chest, "I tracked down the coven responsible for the curse. I had a choice: keep my magic and use it for good, or give it up entirely. I chose to keep it and dedicate my life to helping people in need. Now I work to make the world safer for those like you, who are caught in the crossfire of dangerous magic."

"That's… a lot," Niamh said, trying to process it all. "Okay. Are you a witch?"

"No," Aoife said, shaking her head with a smile. "I don't practice witchcraft. I just have abilities. They call it manifestation. For example, I can create portals that allow me to travel instantly between places."

"Well, that's pretty cool. Can I do that too?" She was amazed at how quickly she adjusted to thinking of magic. She'd always felt like she was an outcast from society, but maybe it just wasn't her society. A flicker of hope ignited in her, she just wanted to find where she fit in.

Aoife chuckled softly. "Probably not. Everyone's abilities are different. But we don't know what yours are yet. That's where Njeri comes in, she's amazing at helping people discover their gifts. If you're interested, she'll help you figure it all out."

Niamh nodded slowly, her anxiety ebbing just enough for curiosity to creep in. "So, what happens after I figure that out? I mean… what's next?"

"Figuring out who's targeting you and why," Aoife said seriously. "That's usually the hard part. But once we know, we can work on a solution. You don't have to face this alone."

Niamh hesitated, looking between Aoife and Nick. "It's not like I could do this on my own, right?"

Aoife gave her a knowing look and shook her head. "Probably not."

Niamh exhaled deeply, feeling both daunted and relieved. "Okay, I'm in. I've been an outcast long enough. If there's a chance I can find out where I come from, maybe even meet people like me, I want to take it."

Aoife's face lit up with a warm smile. "Great! Do you want to leave a note for your parents? Just so they won't worry. You don't have to mention the magic. Most humans struggle to handle anything outside their normal reality."

"Yeah, I'll leave a note," Niamh said, rising to grab a pen and paper. "It'll be easier than answering a million questions I don't have the energy to lie about."

Aoife gave her a sympathetic nod while Nick moved toward the doorway, giving Niamh space to write. When she finished, Aoife held out her hand. "Whenever you're ready."

Niamh hesitated for a moment before reaching out to take Aoife's small, soft hand. Nick, noticing her struggle to balance on her injured leg, stepped forward without a word and scooped her up into his strong arms. Niamh let out a startled gasp, but Aoife just gave him a warm, approving smile.

"Hold on tight," Aoife said, holding her hand in front of her. A golden whirlwind erupted in the center of the room, glittering and swirling with a force that sent Niamh's hair flying. She squeezed her eyes shut, instinctively retreating into herself. *If I don't see it, it can't hurt me,* she thought.

When she finally opened her eyes, her bedroom was gone. They were standing in what looked like a small, clinical office. A padded examination table sat in one corner, two plastic chairs lined one wall, and a sleek computer hummed quietly on a desk near a rolling chair.

"Where are we?" Niamh asked, her voice unsteady as she took in the unfamiliar surroundings.

"Oh, you're in my building, K Corp, in Canada. This is home base," Nick replied matter-of-factly. "We have locations all over the world."

"You… portaled us to Canada?" Niamh's eyebrows shot up. "Is 'portaled' even a word?"

Aoife chuckled warmly. "It is here, and yes, I did. Pretty cool, right?"

"It's… something," Niamh muttered, unsure what else to say.

Aoife took a step closer, her tone gentle. "We thought you could use a visit with our doctor first, to patch you up. She's the best in her field, I promise. Then we'll figure out the rest."

Before Niamh could reply, the door opened, and a woman stepped in. She was stunning, with skin so deeply smooth and radiant it seemed unreal. Her thick, coiled hair framed her face in a way that made Niamh think she belonged on a runway rather than in a sterile office. For a moment, Niamh was so captivated by her beauty that she didn't notice the subtle flickers of something unusual, camouflaged within the woman's hair.

"Aoife. Nick." The woman greeted them with a curt nod, her voice calm and professional. She turned her attention to Niamh, her dark eyes softening. "I'm Doc B., I'll get you fixed up and on your way. I see your ankle is injured. Any other pain or injuries I should know about?"

"I… I don't think so," Niamh replied, her words faltering as the doctor gently lifted her leg and extended a panel from the examination table to rest it on.

"Well, these are deep gashes," the doctor said, inspecting the wound with a critical eye. "I'll need to stitch them, and I'll give you a salve to speed up the healing."

Niamh nodded, still in shock from everything that had happened in the last few minutes. She barely registered the sound of Aoife and Nick settling into the spare chairs as the doctor began cleaning and stitching her wound.

As the doctor worked, Niamh's gaze wandered to her thick, curly hair. She thought she saw something, a pair of slender shapes nestled within the coils. Were they… moving? They twitched slightly as the doctor leaned in closer to focus on her work. Niamh squinted, trying to make sense of it, completely forgetting the pain in her ankle.

"Done," Doc B announced, startling Niamh from her thoughts. The wound was expertly bandaged, and the doctor handed her a small container of green gel. "Apply this twice a day. It'll reduce inflammation and speed up the healing process."

Niamh blinked, realizing she didn't have her purse to carry the gel. Aoife seemed to read her mind, smiling as she handed over the bag.

"Thanks," Niamh murmured, touched by the gesture. *Women are so intuitive,* she thought. Having Aoife there felt grounding, like having a close friend who just *got* it. Nick was kind, but he didn't carry the same calming presence.

Niamh slipped the container into her purse, which she draped over her shoulder. Almost immediately, she noticed her ankle felt better, not just numbed, but like the wound was already beginning to heal. She marveled at the effect but didn't dare question it. Whatever the gel was, it worked, and she wasn't going to complain.

The doctor gave her shoulder a light pat before leaving the room. As she turned, Niamh caught a glimpse of something... unusual. Beneath the doctor's jacket, something seemed to shift, tips of delicate wings, glimmering with shades of purple and blue, like butterfly wings caught in the sunlight. Niamh blinked hard, confused.

No, that can't be right, she thought, shaking her head. *Stress. I'm imagining things.* Still, the image lingered in her mind long after the doctor was gone.

The slight ache in Niamh's foot was barely noticeable as she followed Aoife and Nick down the quiet, sterile hallway to an elevator. She glanced at the floor indicators as the elevator moved, but there were no windows to tell her whether they were ascending or descending. Everything felt enclosed, as though she'd stepped into a secret world where direction and time lost their meaning.

Aoife broke the silence. "We'll go see Dr. Aba Fahr next. She'll help you figure out your lineage."

Niamh only nodded. The idea of answers was both thrilling and terrifying.

The elevator dinged softly, the doors gliding open with precision. Another hallway stretched before them, identical to the last, and Niamh found herself trailing behind them again. Her mind raced. *They healed my ankle... they don't seem dangerous... right?* she thought, repeating the question like a mantra. Trust wasn't easy to come by, but for now, it was all she had. These doctors weren't like any she'd ever known. Bodies don't heal that fast, she repeated in her mind. Something was off here, but she didn't know what. She didn't feel unsafe, though. Just off…

They stopped at a door marked "MBS. Magical Being Services". Nick pushed it open, revealing a tall, elegant woman waiting inside. She had almost ethereal skin, so pale it shimmered faintly in the fluorescent light, and shoulder-length teal waves framed her angular face. Large, retro-framed glasses perched delicately on her button nose, giving her an air of quirky brilliance.

"I'm Dr. Aba Fahr. Most leave off the Fahr though, Dr. Fahr was my mother," she said with a small laugh. "It's a pleasure to meet you," the woman said warmly, extending a slim hand.

Niamh shook it tentatively. "I'm Niamh."

The doctor's office was striking in its simplicity. The room was nearly empty save for a sleek glass desk, a transparent molded chair, and another chair mounted on the wall like modern art. Dr. Aba slipped into her seat with practiced ease, motioning for Niamh to take the wall chair. Niamh hesitated; it didn't look particularly comfortable, but she obliged, perching stiffly on the edge. Aoife and Nick remained standing near the door, their watchful presence reassuring but unnerving at the same time.

"Let's see if we can get you some answers," Dr. Aba began, her voice calm but charged with purpose. "Tell me everything you know about your family, and we'll go from there."

Niamh wrung her hands in her lap. "I don't know anything about my birth parents. My adoptive parents are Margaret and James Johnson. That's all I've ever known."

She nodded and turned to her computer, her long fingers gliding over the keyboard with effortless precision. The soft tapping filled the room, each keystroke tightening the knot in Niamh's chest. After a few minutes, the doctor paused, her eyes scanning the screen with interest.

"Ah, I see," she said cryptically, continuing to type.

Niamh's stomach churned as the silence stretched on. She glanced nervously at Aoife, who offered a reassuring smile. Finally, with one last decisive click, Dr. Aba stood and gestured toward the ceiling.

Lights streamed down like beams from a stage, swirling in intricate patterns until they coalesced into a holographic family tree suspended in midair above the desk. At the top was Niamh's name, branching downward into a network of names she didn't recognize.

Dr. Aba smiled softly, pride flickering in her eyes. "Thanks to our network's extensive record-keeping, I was able to track your lineage."

Niamh's breath hitched as the doctor continued. "Your birth mother is Cailleach, and your birth father is Aamon."

The names hung heavy in the air, unfamiliar yet impossibly significant. Niamh's fingers curled around the edge of the chair. "Who...what are they?"

Dr. Aba's expression softened as though she understood the weight of her revelation. "Your mother, Cailleach, is a goddess. She's often called the Queen of Winter because of her dominion over cold weather and storms. She can influence the very elements."

Niamh's heart pounded in her chest. *A goddess?* She felt like the air had been sucked out of the room.

"And your father," Dr. Aba continued, "is Aamon, a shadow creature. Some call his kind wraiths, beings of darkness and mystery."

Niamh sat frozen, her thoughts spinning out of control. Her mouth went dry as she managed to croak, "So... they're not human?"

Smiling kindly, "No, they're not. It simply makes you... unique. And perhaps, very powerful."

"Are they evil?" She was almost scared to ask, but she had to know.

"Evil is a strange word, isn't it?" Dr Aba said, "What makes people perceived as evil is often consequences of dire situations they were put in or put themselves in. We try to think of everyone as good around here until they prove to us otherwise. But your mother has had her fair share of run-ins as she's tried to accumulate powers. We haven't heard anything about your father for quite some time now, though he was known for dream hopping and causing mischief."

She wondered if he was the one causing the distress in her dreams. Could her own father want to hurt her, she wondered.

Niamh sat in stunned silence, the revelation about her parents washing over her like a tidal wave she hadn't been prepared for. *Goddess. Wraith. Monsters,* she thought bitterly, the word clinging to her like a thorn. She stared at the glowing tree still floating above the desk, her name intertwined with the unfamiliar names of her parents, like a puzzle piece she didn't belong to.

As if sensing her turmoil, Aoife stepped closer and placed a comforting hand on her shoulder. "You are not a monster, Niamh," she said gently, her voice filled with conviction. "You were born unique and beautiful. Don't assess your value based on who your parents are."

The words pierced through the fog in Niamh's mind, loosening the knot in her throat just enough for her to swallow hard and nod. "So… what does that mean for me?" she whispered, her voice shaky but determined.

Dr. Aba leaned forward, clasping her hands on the desk. "It means we need to figure out what abilities you inherited. With parents as powerful as yours, it's very likely you have some latent abilities of your own. Once we know that, we can help you understand who's targeting you and why. For now, as long as you're here at K Corp, you're safe. Our shields are impenetrable."

Niamh nodded again, though her thoughts felt like a chaotic storm she couldn't calm. The sheer magnitude of what she'd learned left her hollow and numb, like a marionette going through the motions. "Okay," she managed, her voice distant, "so what's next?"

Aoife knelt slightly to meet her eye level, her expression soft with understanding. "I know this is overwhelming. I've been where you are, believe me, but it's crucial that you stay here. Whatever is after you can't reach you while you're inside K Corp. We need to keep moving, though. I mentioned Njeri earlier, she's our next stop. She'll help you uncover your abilities."

Niamh blinked at Aoife, trying to ground herself in the sincerity of her words. "No, I'm fine," she said quickly, the words spilling out before she could think too much. "I'd rather keep going. If I stop now, I'll probably have a breakdown, and I… I just need to stay busy."

Aoife exchanged a glance with Nick and Dr. Aba, and the three began speaking in a low, fluid language Niamh didn't recognize. The unfamiliar words danced in her ears, but she didn't have the energy to care what they were saying. She'd been the subject of hushed conversations her entire life, this was nothing new. *Probably just figuring out what to do with me,* she thought bleakly, her mind too numbed to spiral.

Dr. Aba finally nodded, squeezing Niamh's shoulder lightly as she passed her. "You're stronger than you think," she said before stepping out of the room.

"Come on," Aoife said softly, gesturing for Niamh to follow. "Njeri will know what to do."

Without a word, Niamh rose and trailed behind Aoife and Nick, her legs carrying her down another endless hallway to yet another elevator. The doors closed with a quiet swish, and the familiar sensation of motion reminded her how far she'd come from her ordinary life. She didn't even bother trying to guess what would happen next. After tonight, the concept of normal felt irretrievably lost.

Chapter 8

Niamh gasped as she entered the room, overwhelmed by the sheer size and vibrancy of the space. It was cavernous, with high ceilings and open expanses interrupted only by inflatable obstacle courses scattered haphazardly across the floor. Along the walls were sleek, glass-walled cubicles that looked like futuristic offices or private observation rooms. Her awe was momentarily interrupted by a booming laugh as Nick was fake-punched in the stomach by a tall, striking woman with rich dark skin and long, intricately braided hair. She then smacked Aoife on the shoulder, sending her a step forward.

The woman turned her sharp, discerning gaze on Niamh, and her face broke into a welcoming grin. "I'm Njeri. Step into my office," she said with a wave, gesturing toward one of the glass rooms in the corner.

Niamh followed the group inside and sat in the lone chair at the center of the minimalist space. She clasped her hands together, trying to process how much her life had changed in such a short time. The surreal events of the night washed over her. She'd longed to understand herself, to feel like she belonged, but never, in even her wildest imaginings, had she envisioned *this*.

Njeri's voice cut through her spiraling thoughts. "So, your ma is the Queen of Winter, and your pops is a shadow, huh? Quite the mix! I bet you've got some unique secrets behind those eyes. Let's find out what you can do!" Njeri grinned and placed a glass of water in front of her. "Alright. Let's start with something simple."

Niamh blinked, frowning at the glass. "You want me to drink it or something?"

"Girl, *what?* No! I want you to *do something* with it. Ever felt something unexplainable before? A weird sensation? Focus on that, it could be your powers trying to come out."

The instructions made no sense to Niamh. She wasn't special. Sure, her eyes were unusual, but beyond that, she was just... her. She focused on the glass anyway, staring hard at the water, willing something, *anything*, to happen. Nothing. Not even a ripple. She tentatively touched the glass, hoping it might trigger something. Still nothing.

Njeri picked up the glass, inspecting it. "Not even cold. Hmm... interesting."

Undeterred, Njeri set the glass aside and brought out foam balls. Aoife and Nick chuckled behind Niamh, and she felt a spark of curiosity as she guessed there was a story behind the laughter.

"Alright," Njeri said, her tone upbeat. "Let's try something else. Turn into a shadow and dodge these."

The first ball hit Niamh square in the chest, taking her by surprise. She winced but tried again, closing her eyes and imagining herself fading into the darkness; she was a professional wallflower anyway. It would make social gatherings much easier on her if she could literally disappear, she thought. Ball after ball pelted her, each one chipping away at her hope. She clenched her fists, focusing harder, but nothing happened. The shadow she longed to become remained unattainable.

Finally, she threw up her hands, her voice breaking as she said, "I can't do any of this! I'm a freak with no powers!" Tears welled in her mismatched eyes, and despite her efforts to hold them back, they spilled over, running down her cheeks in hot, angry streams.

Njeri crouched in front of her, gently lifting her chin to meet her gaze. Her expression was tender but fierce. "First off, you are absolutely not a freak. Look at those eyes, like Yin and Yang. You are *stunning*. You're perfect just the way you are. Second, we've barely scratched the surface. These things take time."

Niamh sniffled, barely mollified. "I just… I don't know. What if there's nothing? What if I really *am* just… broken?"

"It took Aoife here a while to figure out her powers and even longer to master them. Only when she was forced to use them to protect someone did she truly begin to understand the extent of them." Njeri pointed at Aoife and smiled.

Aoife stepped forward, her expression warm and encouraging. "It's true, it took me *forever* to figure out my abilities. I was so frustrated that I almost gave up. Poor Nick had foam balls raining on him all day because I couldn't control my portals."

Nick chuckled, and Aoife rolled her eyes at him before turning back to Niamh. "The point is this is hard for everyone at first. But you *will* find it, and when you do, you'll master it. You're not alone in this. We're here for you every step of the way."

Niamh nodded slowly, the words sinking in. Though the tears still blurred her vision, a small ember of hope began to glow in her chest. Maybe, just maybe, there was something more to her after all.

"Why don't you two go get something to eat while Niamh and I play around with more stuff," Njeri said, her voice slipping back into that unfamiliar, melodic language. She was addressing Aoife and Nick, and once again, Niamh felt the tug of curiosity. That language was nothing like anything she'd heard before. She mentally bookmarked it as something to ask about later, whenever things stopped spiraling into chaos.

Aoife offered her a reassuring nod before she and Nick excused themselves, leaving Niamh alone with Njeri. The silence that followed seemed heavier than it should have been. Njeri motioned for her to follow, leading her into a larger, more imposing room.

"Okay," Njeri began, flipping a dial on the wall, her eyes bright with purpose. "We need to think outside the box. Your mom can control weather, any kind, really, but she's always preferred the cold. Maybe there's more to you. Let's see if you can tap into something else."

Her words hung in the air for a moment as Niamh hesitated. A fleeting thought crossed her mind: why did she always feel so at home in the cold? The cooler room was her favorite spot, and no matter how low the temperature dropped, she'd never felt the bone-deep chill that others did. Could it mean something? She was about to voice this thought, but before she could, a roar of fire shot out from a tube in front of her.

The flames erupted without warning, a feral blaze of heat and color, forcing Niamh to dive instinctively to the side. Her shriek tore through the room as terror clawed its way up her chest. She scrambled, wide-eyed, looking to Njeri for help. But Njeri didn't turn off the fire, she cranked the dial higher.

The flames leapt higher, wilder, licking closer to Niamh. Panic set in as sweat beaded on her forehead, her body trembling. She tried, desperately, to push the fire away, to keep as much distance between it and her, but nothing happened. Her mind screamed for escape, but she was trapped. The flames closed in, and for one heart-stopping moment, she was certain she would burn alive.

Just as she raised her hands to surrender, to beg Njeri to stop, her fingers grazed the fire. Instinctively, she yanked her hand back, bracing for pain, for blistering heat, for anything. She inspected her hand, but there was nothing. Her skin was untouched, unmarked. The fire hadn't burned her.

It *had touched her*, she felt its warmth, but instead of consuming her, it danced over her skin, harmless. She stared at her hand, flipping it over in disbelief. Her breath caught in her throat. She had no idea what to think, or how to tell Njeri.

Njeri, oblivious, finally turned off the fire. "Well," she said casually, "that's a no to fire. Let's try wind."

Niamh stayed silent. She didn't know why she kept it to herself, but for a moment, the knowledge of what had happened felt like a tiny victory, a secret bit of power that was hers alone. It wasn't much, but it was hers.

Another dial spun, and this time, a powerful gust of wind surged through the room. The force of it hit Niamh like a wall, sending her sliding across the floor. She dug her feet in, barely managing to stay upright. The wind roared louder, battering her relentlessly until she was forced to the ground, her arms thrown over her head for cover.

From across the room, Njeri's voice was calm, too calm. "Hm. I have another idea." She gestured for Niamh to follow her again, her movements brisk and purposeful.

Reluctantly, Niamh obeyed, her steps slower now, her trust in Njeri rapidly eroding. It wasn't that she didn't want to find her powers, if she even had any, but she wasn't sure she'd survive Njeri's methods. *There might be someone out to get me,* she thought, *but Njeri might finish me off first.*

They entered another room, smaller, enclosed. Njeri closed the door behind them, sealing them in. Without a word, she turned another dial on the wall. Instantly, the temperature dropped. The air cooled so rapidly that Niamh's breath puffed out in visible clouds. The chill seeped into the walls, the floor, the very air they breathed.

Niamh looked to Njeri for direction, unsure of what to do. But Njeri was in the corner, hugging herself tightly, her teeth chattering as she shivered uncontrollably. Niamh blinked, confused. She felt fine, normal, even. The cold was there; she could see it in the frost forming on the walls, but she didn't feel it. She never had.

It hit her then: this wasn't new. She'd always known she didn't feel the cold like others did. Another thing that made her different. Another thing that marked her as a freak. She wrapped her arms around herself, trying to hide the truth.

"Looks like we found it," Njeri said, laughing weakly between shivers. Her excitement was contagious, but Niamh didn't share it. "You don't get it, do you?" Njeri said, still trembling but grinning now. "This is big. Like, *real big!*"

Niamh frowned, confused. How could being immune to cold be a power? She couldn't *do* anything with it. It wasn't like her mother's ability to summon storms or shift the weather. This felt small, useless.

But Njeri's eyes were bright, and her grin only widened. "You've got no idea what you're capable of, do you?"

Still uncertain, Niamh just shrugged, her confusion evident. She didn't understand why Njeri was so excited. A moment later, Njeri practically bounced over to her, wrapping her in a bear hug so tight that Niamh thought she might crack a rib.

"Okay, okay, I get it, you're excited," Niamh wheezed, patting Njeri's back awkwardly.

Njeri finally let go, stepping back to look her over like she was appraising a rare gem. Her eyes widened in realization. "Wait a second. You're not cold at all. Like, *at all*. And, holy crap, you're warm! You're actually warming me up!" She laughed, her grin stretching from ear to ear. "You might be able to share this power. Think about it: keeping people warm in freezing conditions? This could be *huge!*" Njeri pushed herself up, laughing through her shivers as she crossed the room to turn off the dial. "It's *huge*, Niamh. This isn't just some party trick to keep warm in a blizzard." She paused, rubbing her hands together to warm them. "It's deeper than that. Your mother's powers aren't just about creating weather, they're about commanding it. And you've inherited at least a part of that. You're attuned to cold, immune to it even. That's step one. Step two is figuring out how you can manipulate it."

Niamh blinked, still unsure of how to respond. She'd always seen her odd immunity to cold as just another thing that set her apart, another thing that made her feel like a freak. But the way Njeri talked about it, this wasn't just some weird quirk. It was something that could matter. Something that could help.

Before she could process it, Njeri's tone shifted back to its usual playful self. "Okay, but seriously, can we get out of this room now? You're warming me up, and I have a girlfriend, you know. She'd *definitely* kill me if she thought I was warming up to someone else!" She laughed at her own joke, and Niamh couldn't help but blush, ducking her head.

"Right. Sorry," Niamh mumbled, stepping aside to let Njeri pass.

Njeri shot her a grin. "So, we know you're hot, I mean, you have the power of being warm," she corrected herself quickly, waving a hand as if to brush away the slip. "What we don't know is what your dad gave you.

If anything, Other than that gorgeous onyx eye of yours." She paused, her expression turning more serious. "Are you up for more? Or do you need a break?"

Niamh hesitated for a moment. The truth was, she felt like curling up in a corner and crying. Everything about this situation, her powers, her past, the uncertainty of it all, was exhausting. Deep down, she longed for her bed, a safe space where she could hide from all of it. But she didn't have that option anymore. Not until they figured this mess out.

"We can keep going," she said, her voice steady despite the knot in her chest. "I need answers."

Njeri nodded, her grin returning. "That's the spirit! Let's see what else you're hiding, Niamh."

Niamh furrowed her brow, skepticism taking over. "But I can't create frost or ice or anything like that. I tried with the water earlier, and nothing happened."

"Not yet," Njeri corrected, her tone sharp but encouraging. "You've spent your whole life suppressing this part of you, whether you realized it or not. It's going to take time to wake it up. But trust me, if you can withstand freezing temperatures like they're nothing, then cold isn't just a comfort zone for you; it's your *element*. You've already got the foundation. Now we build on it."

Niamh exhaled deeply, processing Njeri's words. It still felt strange to think of herself as someone with powers, let alone the child of gods and shadow creatures. But the idea that cold had always been her refuge, her safe space, resonated. She thought about all the times she'd found comfort in winter, how she'd loved the crisp air when everyone else was complaining, how her favorite places were always the ones that made others shiver.

"Okay," she said quietly, as she fiddled with a string on her shirt nervously. "So… what now?"

Njeri grinned, her confidence infectious. "Now? We practice. I don't know what your full potential looks like yet, but I promise we're going to find out."

As they stepped out of the cold room and back into the larger training space, Niamh felt a flicker of something she hadn't felt in a long time: hope. For the first time, it didn't feel like her differences were burdens. They were *gifts*, pieces of a puzzle she was only beginning to understand. She still didn't know what the future held, but for now, she was willing to see it through.

Njeri's voice snapped Niamh out of her spiraling thoughts. "I have another idea," she said, leaning forward with a look of determination. "They told me you've been having trouble in your dreams. Like someone's in there with you?"

Niamh nodded hesitantly, her stomach twisting at the memory of her last nightmare.

"Well," Njeri continued, her tone gentle but firm, "that might be where you're weak. If you have a power in the dream world but don't know how to use it, it could be leaving a door open, letting someone, or *something*, in." She paused for emphasis, then asked, "Have you ever meditated before?"

"No, not really," Niamh admitted, her skepticism evident. The idea of sitting and chanting "om" didn't seem like it would help her battle shadowy intruders in her mind.

Njeri grinned, catching the doubt in Niamh's tone. "Okay, listen. It's easier than you think. Meditation is just…chilling. It's about finding the space between consciousness and the unconscious. That's where your power might be hiding. We're going to sit here, relax, and see what we find. Clear your mind and let your muscles relax. I'll be right here with you."

Still unsure but willing to try, Niamh lowered herself onto the padded floor. Her body felt stiff, weighed down by fear. The memory of her last dream was too vivid: the towering shadows, the suffocating terror. Sensing her hesitation, Njeri reached out and touched her hand.

"I'm here with you," Njeri said softly, her voice steady and warm. "You're safe. We have protections in this building, so nothing can hurt you here. And if anything tries, I'll protect you. That's a promise."

Niamh looked at her, startled by the sincerity in her words. Despite her lingering doubts, she allowed herself to relax, trusting Njeri more than she realized. If anyone could fight off the darkness, it was her. Njeri was a warrior through and through. She'd trained with the best Fae warriors and high knights in the realms. She was a highly sought-after soldier for royalty in the dimensions.

As Niamh closed her eyes and let her body soften, a strange sensation seeped into her mind. Darkness crept in, quiet at first, like ink spilling into water. Shadows swirled and danced, moving in strange, fluid shapes, black and grey, sifting and churning like a storm. The swirling smoke began to form something solid, something *large*. It towered over her, a shapeless mass of shadow that loomed closer, bending down as if to swallow her whole.

Her heart pounded, the air growing thick and oppressive. She tried to move, to scream, but her body felt frozen, trapped in the haze. The shadow folded over her like a tidal wave crashing down on a helpless surfer.

Just as it was about to consume her, a hand gripped her shoulder and shook her hard. "Niamh! Wake up!"

Gasping for breath, Niamh's eyes flew open. She found herself staring into Njeri's dark, concerned gaze. "You're okay. I'm here," Njeri said, her voice soft but steady. "You're safe. That was intense."

Niamh clutched her chest, her heart still racing. For the first time, someone had witnessed what she'd been experiencing. She wasn't crazy, her dreams weren't just nightmares. They were alive, and they were dangerous.

"What's changed since you started having these… dream attacks?" Njeri asked gently, crouching beside her.

Niamh hesitated, her thoughts swirling. What had changed? She ran through the possibilities in her mind, and one stood out: a person. "I met someone," she said finally, her voice uncertain. "He was nice. Handsome, even. But he gave me weird vibes. I don't know why. He didn't *do* anything strange, but…" She trailed off, searching for the right words. "He wasn't weirded out by my eyes. Everyone is, at least at first. But he wasn't."

Njeri's brow furrowed. "Was it a chance meeting, or did it feel… planned?"

Niamh frowned, considering the question. "Now that you mention it, it didn't feel random. But I could be wrong. He does work with my best friend's roommate, so maybe it was just a coincidence."

"No," Njeri said firmly, her tone sharpening. "Trust your gut. Don't brush that feeling off. People with magic are powerful, but those who are new or who don't fully understand their abilities are the most vulnerable. He might have been after you for a reason." She leaned back, her expression pensive. "Being part shadow makes you especially vulnerable in your dreams. It's a sub-shadow state, your powers might be bleeding into your dreams and making them unstable. You can learn to control it, to block others out, but it'll take practice."

Njeri paused, her eyes narrowing slightly as she studied Niamh. She seemed to sense the tension building in her. "I think that's enough for one day," she said at last. "We've got a good starting point for your powers. Let's pick this up again tomorrow."

Niamh's heart sank at the mention of tomorrow. "I can't stay here overnight. My parents will be worried."

"Oh, we've already taken care of that," Njeri said with a reassuring smile. "Your parents think you're staying with your friend for a few days. Your friend's been briefed, just the basics. We wanted to cover all possibilities. You're in good hands."

Niamh's shoulders slumped. "I can't rest easily. My dreams, those things, they're trying to kill me."

Njeri winked and gave her a playful finger gun. "We've got that covered too. Our witches cast a protection circle around your room. Nothing's getting through tonight. I promise."

"Oh," Niamh mumbled, overwhelmed. "That's... a lot to take in."

"I know it's a lot," Njeri said gently. "But this is what we do. You're not the first person we've helped, and you won't be the last. You're safe here, Niamh. We've got you."

"Oh my god, I completely forgot, I had a coffee date set with a guy." I didn't tell him I wouldn't be there with all this going on, it slipped my mind."

"I'm sure he'll forgive you."

"The thing is, I thought it was the cause of my bad dreams, but that's crazy. Right?"

Njeri shrugged. "I've seen some pretty odd things happen around here.

That wouldn't even make the top 100."

Before Niamh could respond, the elevator chimed. Aoife strode out with an easy confidence, her presence lighting up the room. Niamh couldn't help but admire her. Aoife exuded a strength and self-assurance that Niamh wished she possessed.

"You're all set for the night," Aoife said, flashing Niamh a reassuring smile.

As Niamh stood, Njeri pressed a small card into her hand. "Here's my number. Call me if you need anything. No question is too small."

Niamh nodded, clutching the card tightly. She wasn't sure what tomorrow would bring, but for now, she allowed herself to be led by Aoife, grateful for the momentary reprieve.

"We heard it went well!" Aoife said brightly as Niamh approached. "That's so exciting! Great job! I know today has been a lot, though. Let's get you to your room for the night."

Niamh nodded and followed silently, exhaustion weighing her steps.

When Aoife opened the door, Niamh froze. The room looked like it belonged in a completely different world than the sterile corridors they'd walked through. A stunning, intricately carved four-poster bed dominated the space, draped in soft fabrics that seemed to invite her to sink into them. A wood-burning fireplace flickered warmly, casting a golden glow over the plush rugs scattered across polished wooden floors.

Aoife turned and smiled, clearly catching the awe on Niamh's face. "I know, it still takes my breath away. This was my room when I first got here, too. It holds a special place in my heart. I hope it can bring you some peace during this hard time."

Niamh stepped inside, running her hand along the edge of the bedpost, the smooth wood cool beneath her fingertips. "How did you deal with it?" she asked softly. "All of this new stuff, I mean?"

Aoife leaned against the doorframe, her expression thoughtful. "Oh, I won't lie to you. The first few days? I felt like a zombie, just going through the motions until something clicked. For me, it took almost losing someone close to me to realize how much I could do to help others with my powers. That wake-up call changed everything." Her voice softened, and a faint smile played on her lips. "Since then, I've never looked back. Adjusting wasn't easy, but it's been the best journey of my life. And you have that chance too. But you have to learn about your magic and take control of it. Being magical makes the people around you vulnerable. If you want to protect those you love, you've got to embrace what makes you different. You've got a fire in you that most people can't even comprehend. Own that power, Niamh."

Niamh blinked, surprised by how much Aoife's words resonated. "That… was actually helpful," she admitted. "I'm sorry about your friend, though. That must've been horrible. I hope they're okay now. But… I'm glad you're here. It's comforting to know someone's been through all this."

Aoife nodded, her smile growing warmer. "Thank you, and I'm glad I'm here too. But I won't keep you up. You've had a long day." She gestured to a tray on a small table. "I had the restaurant send up some tea and special cookies. They'll help you sleep tonight, without dreams."

"Special?" Niamh asked, a playful edge creeping into her voice.

"Not *that* kind of special," Aoife laughed as she made her way to the door. "Tomorrow is a fresh start, and you've got a strong support system. Lean on us. We won't let you fall." She paused, her hand on the doorknob. "Oh, and if you need anything, my room's 600. Just knock."

And with that, Aoife was gone, leaving Niamh alone with her thoughts, a situation she dreaded.

The silence felt heavy, almost suffocating after the whirlwind of the day. Desperate to stave off the creeping anxiety, she picked up the tea and sipped it cautiously. The warmth spread through her, soothing the edges of her frazzled nerves. She nibbled on a cookie, it was sweet, buttery, and spiced with something she couldn't quite place.

Needing a distraction, she began to explore the room. Every detail was elegant, like something plucked from a wealthy estate in Europe. There were no personal touches, no photographs on the walls, just a striking carved wooden "K" above the fireplace, framed by an intricately detailed wreath.

A fully decorated Christmas tree stood in the corner, its soft lights casting a cozy glow. It was simple but beautiful, and she found herself oddly comforted by it. Next to the tree was a small table, set with a single chair. On the side table by the bed, where she half-expected a Bible to be, sat a Christmas book instead.

"Odd," she murmured, picking it up. She turned it over in her hands, curious but too tired to read. "Maybe they just really like Christmas here," she mused aloud, setting it back down.

For now, she decided, she wouldn't think too hard about the book, the carved "K," or any of the oddities in the room. There had been enough mysteries for one day. All she wanted was to curl up under the soft blankets and let the magic of the tea and cookies lull her into a dreamless sleep.

Niamh changed into the soft, flannel pajamas left for her in the bathroom, appreciating their warmth and comfort. She brushed her teeth using the hygiene kit neatly arranged on the counter, its thoughtful presentation a reminder of how prepared these people were for her arrival.

Sliding into the bed, she couldn't help but marvel at how luxurious it felt; the thick, flannel sheets hugged her like a cocoon. Aoife had promised her a dreamless sleep, but Niamh wasn't convinced. It had been days since she'd truly rested, and her dreams had become a battleground.

Pulling out her phone, she saw missed calls from her dad and one from Bain. Guilt bubbled up in her chest, but she couldn't summon the energy to return them tonight. "Tomorrow," she thought, making a mental note to at least call her dad in the morning. She was still unsure what to do about Bain; he was the least of her worries. For now, she needed to shut out the world.

Chapter 9

To her surprise, sleep came swiftly. It was deep, heavy, and free from the usual torment of her dreams. When she woke, she felt oddly refreshed, a sensation she hadn't experienced in what felt like forever.

She changed into the clean clothes left out for her. Shock took over as everything the K Corp employees left for her fit perfectly, which was both impressive and unsettling to her. As she looked in the mirror, she noticed something different about herself. The word "freak" didn't scream back at her from her reflection like it usually did. Instead, she saw someone stronger, someone who had survived so much already. Maybe discovering the truth about herself was bringing a sense of empowerment and strength.

She ran her fingers around her eyes, they felt less of a defect now. A sudden knock at the door startled her, pulling her from her thoughts. Heart racing, she cautiously peered through the peephole. On the other side stood a tall, blonde woman in a crisp white dress shirt, pushing a rolling cart.

With hesitation, Niamh opened the door.

"Hi! I'm Cami," the woman said cheerfully, her smile bright and disarming. "Aoife thought you could use some breakfast."

"Um, sure," Niamh replied, stepping aside to let her in.

"Aoife picked her favorite for you, but if it's not your thing, I can bring something else. I also brought coffee, orange juice, and tea, I wasn't sure what you'd prefer."

"Coffee sounds great, and I'm sure whatever Aoife chose is fine. I'm not picky. Thanks, though."

Cami lifted the silver dome covering the plate to reveal an eggs benedict with salmon. The savory aroma wafted through the room, making Niamh's stomach growl loudly enough to embarrass her.

Cami chuckled. "Looks like Aoife made the right call. Let me know if you need anything else. And welcome to K Corp. This place is something special, you're in good hands."

With that, she gave a warm smile, turned the cart, and rolled it back out the door.

Niamh sat down at the small table, savoring the first bite of her meal. The rich flavors melted on her tongue, grounding her in a way she desperately needed.

As she ate, her thoughts swirled, trying to process the whirlwind of revelations. She had magic, a gift inherited from her birth parents, one a shadow creature and the other the Queen of Winter. That alone would have been enough to upend her world, but there was more. Someone was after her. Someone dangerous. And, by extension, her family could be at risk.

Her chest tightened as she thought of her parents and how much she wanted to see them, to tell them everything. But she knew she couldn't. Not yet. Until she understood her powers and could protect them from the threats that followed her, distance was the safest option.

With a sigh, Niamh sipped her coffee and steeled herself. This was only the beginning. She had a long way to go, but for the first time, she felt a flicker of hope that she could face whatever came next.

Speaking of family, Niamh knew she couldn't put it off any longer. She had to call her dad. The guilt gnawed at her, and with a deep breath, she summoned the courage to press the call button. She'd never ignored his calls before, and she could already feel the weight of the lecture coming her way.

The phone rang barely twice before he answered.

"Niamh, where have you been? I know you're not at Lidia's. I called her! Where are you? Are you okay?" His voice was thick with worry, a mixture of panic and frustration that made her stomach churn.

"Dad, I'm fine," she said, trying to sound steady. "I'm 25. You don't have to check on me, you know."

"That's not the point," he countered, his tone softening only slightly. "You aren't usually out all night, and you were acting strange earlier. Then you left that vague note. I've been worried sick. Are you…" He paused, his voice dropping to a conspiratorial whisper. "Are you taking drugs?"

That startled a laugh out of her. "No, Dad, I'm not on drugs," she assured him, shaking her head at the absurdity. "I'm fine. I just… I'm away for a work trip."

"A work trip?" he repeated, clearly not buying it.

"Yeah, it's a… flower meeting. In Canada," she added, wincing at the ridiculousness of her excuse. It wasn't entirely untrue. She was in Canada, apparently.

"A flower meeting in Canada?" His tone was skeptical, bordering on incredulous.

"Yes," she said, leaning into the lie. "It's been great! I'm learning a lot."

There was a long pause on his end, and she could almost feel him debating whether to push further. Instead, he surprised her.

"Hey," he said, his voice softening. "I just worry because I love you, you know."

Niamh's chest tightened, guilt clawing at her. "I know, Dad. I love you, too. I do."

"Are you *sure* you're okay?" he asked again, his concern unwavering.

"I'm okay," she lied, her voice barely above a whisper. "I really do have to go, though. I'll call you soon, alright?"

"Alright, honey," he said reluctantly. "But remember, I'm here. Day or night. Anytime you need me."

"I know," she said, her throat tightening. "Thanks, Dad."

Before he could ask another question she couldn't answer, she ended the call.

Niamh stared at the phone in her hands, the guilt weighing heavier now that she'd hung up. She hated lying to him. Her dad had always been her rock, her safe place, and she knew he deserved the truth. But how could she tell him? That she was in danger? That someone was hunting her? That she was trying to track down her birth parents—not because they mattered to her in the way her adoptive parents did, but because her family's safety might depend on it?

Her real parents would always be the ones who raised her, who stayed up with her when she was sick, who loved her unconditionally. The people who gave her life, just a shadow and a queen, were only pieces of a puzzle she needed to solve. For now, the truth would only put her dad in danger, and that was something she could never allow.

Setting the phone down, Niamh exhaled shakily. She'd called him. That was something. But the heaviness in her chest lingered, a reminder of how much she had to lose.

Feeling replenished and highly caffeinated, Niamh called Aoife's room number, itching to get the day started. The confines of her room, while comfortable, were beginning to feel stifling.

"Hey, Niamh, good morning! How'd you sleep?" Aoife answered, her voice bright and warm.

"I slept better than I have in days, thanks to you guys! So, what's the plan for today?"

"Well, I thought we could work with Njeri again if you're up for it. Practice makes… better. No such thing as perfect, right? I hate that saying."

Niamh chuckled. "Sounds good. Should I meet you there? I think I remember the way."

"It's a plan. I just need to say goodbye to Nick, and then I'll be on my way."

In the background, Niamh could hear Nick giggling as Aoife said something playful to him. They sounded so happy, so in sync. A pang of longing stirred in her chest. She hoped that someday she could find a connection like that, someone who made her feel safe and whole. A "power couple" didn't matter, but just being part of any couple for once sure would be nice.

When she arrived at Njeri's training arena, she immediately noticed how the room had transformed. Large industrial fans were set up around the space, along with a snow-making machine she recognized from ski resorts. The hum of the equipment filled the air, and Niamh's stomach sank as she tried to guess what was in store.

Aoife entered right after her, taking in the scene with a smirk. "Yeah, Njeri doesn't do anything subtly," she said, laughing.

"Guess not. This seems… excessive," Niamh said, eyeing the snow machine warily.

"Maybe," Aoife admitted, shrugging. "But she's amazing at helping people find what makes their powers tick. This is definitely a 'trust the process' situation."

"Uh-huh," Niamh replied, not quite convinced.

Across the room, Njeri's voice rang out. "Who's ready to spread their magical wings, so to speak?" She strode over, dragging an extension cord slung over her shoulder like a makeshift cross-body bag. Her energy was contagious, even if Niamh still felt unsure.

Niamh managed a small, hesitant smile. She didn't have much of a choice in the matter, not if she wanted to protect everyone she loved. She couldn't risk losing control again—or worse, never gaining control in the first place.

"So," Njeri began, dropping the cord onto the floor as she clapped her hands together. "We know you're most vulnerable when you're asleep; that's your Achilles' heel. But we also know that cold doesn't affect you, which means that's where we'll focus today. Strengthening your powers might give you better control over other parts, too. At least… that's the hope," she added, her grin tight.

The unspoken *no guarantees* hung in the air, but Niamh swallowed her doubt. If this was her chance to grow stronger, to learn how to protect herself and the people she cared about, she'd take it. She paused, closing her eyes, gathering what was left of her frayed nerves. She blew out a breath, her eyes open, shining with determination, even if her confidence wavered.

"Alright," Niamh said, exhaling a shaky breath. "Let's do this."

Niamh stood at the center of the room, her heart pounding as Njeri pointed to her position.

"Stand here," Njeri instructed, tossing a pair of large safety glasses her way. "To protect those beautiful eyes of yours." Then, with a playful grin, she stepped behind a protective barrier where Aoife was already waiting.

As soon as Njeri flipped the first switch, the fans roared to life, sending powerful gusts of wind swirling around Niamh. Her hair lifted wildly, whipping above her head in all directions. The instinct to tame it was almost overwhelming, but she fought against it. It reminded her of that day in school—the day she realized just how different she was. Her classmates had laughed and pointed at her, a moment seared into her memory that left her wary of standing out.

Not today, she told herself, shaking off the memory. She steeled her resolve and focused on the storm building around her.

The second switch triggered the snow machine, adding flurries of icy white to the chaos. The snow stung her skin like tiny needles, and without thinking, she crouched to the ground, wrapping her arms around herself for protection.

"Stand up and fight it like a woman!" Njeri's voice cut through the howling wind. "Use your heat!"

Niamh hesitated but found the strength to rise. Slowly, she pushed herself to her feet, bracing against the force of the storm. The glasses were nearly useless as snow accumulated on them, and she squinted to make out anything through the blinding white.

Out of the corner of her eye, she saw Njeri and Aoife huddled behind a paintball obstacle, their hair dusted with snowflakes despite their attempts to shield themselves. They looked cold, miserable, even, and something deep inside Niamh stirred. She wanted to help her new friends. She owed them so much; the urge to keep them safe overwhelmed her.

Her chest filled with warmth, a familiar heat that seemed to grow stronger with her determination. It was like a reservoir of molten energy, and now it was overflowing. With every ounce of strength she had, Niamh clenched her fists and allowed the scream building within her to rise.

The visceral cry tore from her throat as an explosion of heat erupted from her body. It burst out in a wave like an atomic shockwave, radiating power and light. The heat quickly concentrated, transforming into fiery tendrils that snaked outward, seeking the sources of cold.

Flames wrapped around the fans, causing them to groan to a halt, their mechanisms melted into unrecognizable blobs of plastic and metal. The snow machine sputtered and hissed as it succumbed to the heat, its remnants dripping onto the scorched floor. The flames retreated back into Niamh's fingertips with a whooshing sound.

Niamh stood at the epicenter, her eyes squeezed shut, her body trembling with exhaustion. She struggled to catch her breath, her mind racing to process what had just happened.

"Well," Njeri said, breaking the silence with a laugh, "I don't think we'll be getting our security deposit back."

"That… was… amazing!" Aoife exclaimed, rushing over to Niamh's side. She inspected her with wide eyes, marveling at how not a single strand of her hair or thread of her clothes had been touched by the flames.

As Niamh's breathing slowed, a smile began to spread across her face. It wasn't just relief, it was pride. For the first time, she felt like she had some control, like she'd taken a step toward mastering the magic that had turned her life upside down.

"I did it," she whispered to herself, her voice trembling with disbelief and satisfaction.

Aoife clapped a hand on her shoulder. "You sure did. And you're only just getting started."

Niamh's smile grew wider, but the thought lingered in her mind: *Can I do it again?*

One step at a time, she reminded herself. For now, it was enough to savor the victory.

Niamh stood straighter, emboldened by her success. Her fingertips still tingled with residual warmth, and the memory of controlling the flame filled her with cautious excitement. She inspected her hands, they looked no different than before. She just felt more like herself with every task she completed.

"Let's try something more refined now that we know you can create fire. Light these candles. One by one, not melting the candle past the wick."

She nodded, exhaling deeply, and focused on the first candle. Deep Inside her she felt the warm flicker form the flame, begging to be let out again. She pictured it leaping into an invisible hand inside her, as she held onto it, pulling it closer to the surface. She focused on the candle.

Flames shot out of her fingers, wild and uncontrolled. Niamh struggled to contain it. Without any guidance from Niamh, the fire wrapped around the first candle, causing it to melt into a puddle within seconds from the extreme heat. Her head dropped in defeat.

Njeri called out, "It's okay girl, that's why we're practicing. Try the next one." She nodded her chin towards the thick pillar candle next in line.

Reaching down, embracing the heat inside her once again. She extended her hand, palm outward, and felt the familiar heat build within her again. Flames snaked out from her fingers, wobbling like an unsure dancer. The stream of fire was difficult to control, its energy chaotic and eager to lash out in every direction.

"Steady, Niamh," Aoife encouraged, her voice calm but firm.

Niamh narrowed her eyes, willing the fire to obey her command. She focused solely on the candle wick in front of her, visualizing the small spark she needed. Slowly, the flame steadied, stretching toward the wick. The wax glistened as the heat melted its surface, and soon the wick smoldered before bursting into a soft, flickering flame.

"Yes!" Niamh exclaimed, recalling the fire once again. This time it felt smoother, more natural, as though the energy truly belonged to her. She drew the flame back to her but not letting it go out.

"Now you're getting it!" Njeri said, her grin returning. "Keep going. Don't stop until all of them are lit."

Niamh moved to the next candle, her confidence growing with each success. By the third candle, her movements were getting more fluid, and the fire seemed to respond faster to her will. The stream of flames danced through the air with surprising grace, lighting the remaining candles one by one until the room glowed with warm, golden light.

As she extinguished the last tendril of fire, she turned back to Aoife and Njeri, her heart pounding with exhilaration. "I did it. I really did it!"

"You're a natural," Aoife said, her eyes shining with pride.

"Not bad for a beginner," Njeri added with a smirk, though her tone betrayed her genuine approval. "Now, imagine what you can do once we refine that control."

Njeri gave a loud laugh, clapping her hands. "This is just the beginning. You've got more power than you realize. And when you finally tap into all of it? Watch out, world."

For the first time since this whirlwind began, Niamh felt more than fear. She felt the possibility. And for the first time, she allowed herself to hope she might not just survive this strange new life but thrive in it.

Niamh's laughter echoed through the room, her joy mingling with the golden light of the flames. The heat from the candles surged in response, almost as if they were celebrating with her. She took a steadying breath, realizing her emotions were more deeply connected to her magic than she had imagined. Slowly, she extended her hands again and, with deliberate focus, reined in the energy, calming the flames until they settled into steady flickers.

Aoife stepped forward, her smile wide and full of admiration. "You didn't just do it, you *owned* it. That was incredible, Niamh. You're getting stronger and more in tune with your power already."

Njeri crossed her arms, nodding with approval. "You've got raw talent, no doubt about it. But what's even better? You're *feeling* it now. Magic isn't just in your head; it's in your heart, your emotions, your instincts. The more you connect with it, the more control you'll have."

Niamh let their words sink in, the validation bolstering her resolve. "I still have so much to learn, though," she said, her voice quieter. "What if I mess up when it matters most? What if I hurt someone?"

Aoife stepped closer, placing a reassuring hand on Niamh's shoulder. "Mistakes will happen, and that's okay. What matters is that you're learning and growing. You're not alone in this, we're here to guide you."

Njeri's grin turned playful as she chimed in, "And for the record, if you ever do mess up, we'll make sure to keep a fire extinguisher handy."

That earned a laugh from Niamh, easing the weight of her worries.

"So, what's next?" she asked, her tone more determined now.

"Next," Aoife said with a twinkle in her eye, "we test how well you can maintain control under pressure. Njeri's got a few tricks up her sleeve, I'm sure."

"Oh, you better believe I do," Njeri said, her grin widening. "And trust me, Niamh—by the time we're done, you'll be ready for anything."

Niamh nodded, determination blazing within her. For the first time, she didn't just see her powers as a burden; she saw them as a part of herself, a part worth embracing and mastering.

Chapter 10

The phone in Niamh's pocket buzzed against her hip, pulling her out of her thoughts. She fished it out and answered, her tone brisk, "Hey Dad, can I call you later? I'm kind of in the middle of something."

"No, honey," her father's voice was unusually heavy, laced with urgency. "I'm sorry to pull you away from your flower workshop, but we need to talk. Something has happened."

Those three words froze Niamh in place. Her breath caught as her mind scrambled through worst-case scenarios. Was it her mom? The shop? The possibilities crowded her head, each one more unbearable than the last.

"It's Lidia."

Her knees buckled as the words registered, and she collapsed onto the cold cement floor. Her chest felt hollow as if her heart had been torn out and left behind. The phone trembled in her grip, and her voice emerged in a thin, shaky whisper. "What... what happened?"

Njeri and Aoife exchanged alarmed glances, rushing to her side. They stayed silent, their presence a quiet anchor as they crouched near her, their eyes full of unspoken concern.

Her father sighed on the other end of the line, the weight of the situation evident in his tone. "She's missing. Her phone and purse are still in her apartment, but she's gone. Her roommate says she hasn't heard from her in almost a day."

"That doesn't make sense," Niamh said, her voice barely audible. Her mind raced, scrambling for explanations. "Lidia always tells Tim where she's going. She wouldn't just disappear. Everyone loves her. This... this can't be real."

"I know, sweetheart. I know." Her father's voice cracked slightly before regaining composure. "Was there anyone who might have been jealous of her? Anyone who would've had a reason to hurt her?"

Niamh shook her head, even though her father couldn't see her. "No one. She's the kindest, most genuine person I've ever met. She didn't have enemies, she didn't even argue with people. I... I'm coming home, Dad. I have to be there."

"Oh, honey," her dad said softly, "there's nothing you can do here. The police are involved. You'd just be sitting around and waiting, like the rest of us."

"I *can't* just sit here," she snapped, tears stinging her eyes. Her voice softened as it cracked, raw with emotion. "I need to do something. Lidia's my best friend, Dad. She's... she's my only friend."

Her father let out a long, heavy breath, his own pain evident. "It's up to you, Hun. But promise me one thing: be careful. Don't go anywhere alone, you hear me?"

"I will, Dad," she said, choking on the lump in her throat. She paused, her voice trembling. "Hey... Dad? I love you."

"I love you too, honey," he said gently, his voice a balm to her fraying nerves. "Always."

The line went dead, and the weight of her father's words slammed into Niamh with the force of a tidal wave. The composure she'd fought to maintain crumbled entirely. Her shoulders heaved as sobs overtook her, the pain and fear spilling out in waves that felt impossible to contain.

Aoife dropped to the floor beside her, gently pulling her into a tight embrace, steady and grounding. Niamh clung to her as if she were a lifeline, her cries eventually softening into hiccuping breaths, though the ache in her chest refused to subside.

"What can we do to help?" Aoife asked softly, brushing the tear-dampened strands of hair from Niamh's face. Her green eyes were warm and earnest, silently promising she wouldn't let Niamh face this alone.

Niamh shook her head weakly. "Unless you can find my friend…" Her voice cracked, and she took a shuddering breath. "Nothing. But, thank you. I have to get home now."

Aoife and Njeri exchanged a glance, their silent communication swift and resolute. Njeri gave a sharp nod, and Aoife's grip on Niamh tightened slightly. "I think we may be able to help," Aoife said, her tone firm.

Before Niamh could question what they meant, Aoife stepped away, pulling her phone from her pocket. She moved a few paces away, her voice low and purposeful as she made a call. Njeri helped Niamh to her feet, her grip firm but reassuring.

"Let's go to the conference room," Njeri said. "Aoife's got a plan."

Niamh allowed herself to be led, sandwiched protectively between the two women. Their presence was steadying, but her thoughts felt far away, tangled in worry and fear for Lidia. Each step down the quiet hallways felt heavy, her body moving almost on autopilot.

They reached the elevator, and Niamh leaned into the silence that surrounded them. The only sound was the faint hum of the elevator and her occasional gasping breaths as she struggled to push back the tears still threatening to spill over again. She didn't trust herself to speak; her emotions felt too raw, too close to the surface. If anyone asked her for anything- words, answers, even the smallest shred of energy- she feared she might shatter entirely.

The elevator doors opened, and they walked down more twisting hallways, Niamh barely registering the path. She hoped she wouldn't need to find her way back; everything felt blurred, like she was walking through a fog. She was glad neither Aoife nor Njeri pushed her to speak; they seemed to understand she couldn't yet. All she could do now was move forward, step by step, and pray they truly could help her.

Niamh followed Aoife and Njeri into the expansive room, her nerves frayed to the breaking point. A massive table dominated the space, its surface scattered with papers, maps, and strange glowing objects she couldn't immediately place. Chairs lined its edges, most of them occupied. Niamh blinked, certain her stress and exhaustion were playing tricks on her. Did she just see *cat-like ears* twitching on one person? And scales gleaming on the neck of another? She quickly shook the thought away, this was neither the time nor the place for her imagination to run wild.

At the head of the room stood a towering man, built like a tank and exuding authority. His military-cut hair and rigid posture made him seem carved from stone. He surveyed the room with a heavy gaze, his voice thick with a Russian accent as he spoke.

"I am Viktor," he began, his tone clipped and efficient. "I'll be heading up this op. We're investigating a possible civilian abduction." His eyes moved briefly to Niamh, sharp but not unkind. "We've been tracking suspicious activity in Georgia. It's unusual because there are no registered citizens in our database in that area. This activity coincides with your residence, Niamh, so we believe there may be a connection. We're deploying a small team to investigate."

Niamh's chest tightened as the room went still. This wasn't just some discussion. These people were about to act, and for a moment, it felt surreal. Then determination sparked inside her. She shot to her feet.

"I want to go with them," she said, her voice trembling but steady enough to turn heads.

Viktor's hard eyes locked onto hers, and he shook his head immediately. "No. Absolutely not. You are a civilian, untrained, and by my reports, unable to reliably control your magic reliably. It is not happening."

"If this involves Lidia," Niamh said, standing her ground, "I'm going."

He sighed, exasperated, and made to dismiss her, but Aoife's voice cut through the tension like a blade. "I'll look after her, Viktor," she said, stepping forward with quiet authority. "If Lidia is connected to this, Niamh might be able to help. We can't afford to overlook that."

Viktor let out a low growl, clearly weighing his options. His eyes narrowed as he assessed Niamh again, then he finally threw up his hands.

"Fine," he barked. "But you're Aoife's responsibility. Let the record show I am against this."

Niamh let out a shaky breath, relief mingling with nerves. Aoife gave her a reassuring squeeze on the shoulder, her touch warm and grounding. "You've got this," Aoife whispered. For the first time in hours, Niamh felt a small spark of confidence.

Viktor turned back to the group, his voice booming. "Here's the plan. Aoife will open a portal for our team. We'll track the magical residue and pursue both the civilian target and the perpetrator. Civvies' safety is our top priority; capturing the perp or perps and registering them comes second. Niamh, you stay by Aoife at all times. She'll watch your six."

The team broke into motion with military precision, gathering supplies and preparing for the portal jump. Niamh sat frozen in her chair, still absorbing the whirlwind of activity. This was real. These strangers, these professionals, were preparing to risk their lives to find Lidia, someone they didn't even know. That spark of hope she'd felt earlier began to burn brighter, chasing away the shadows of despair.

As the room buzzed with readiness, Niamh clung to that flicker of hope. Soon, they'd be on their way to finding Lidia. And she dared to believe, for the first time since her father's call, that her friend would return safe and sound.

The group followed Viktor through yet another hallway, the sterile scent of disinfectant growing stronger as they entered an area that looked like something out of a sci-fi movie. Machines of every shape and size beeped, blinked, and whirled, their functions a mystery to Niamh. Walls were lined with shelves holding glass containers of various sizes, filled with substances that ranged from glowing liquids to shifting sands. Scientists in crisp white coats huddled in clusters, gesturing at screens or examining samples with intense focus. The entire room buzzed with purpose and energy, making Niamh feel like an intruder in a world far beyond her understanding.

Her gaze was drawn to a massive circular device dominating one wall. Its surface shimmered faintly, almost alive, and its sheer size made her stomach tighten with unease. As she stared at it, a scientist leaned toward her, his voice a low murmur.

"We used to rely on that portal for field operations," he said, nodding toward the machine. "But now that Aoife has mastered her abilities, she's our living portal. Trust me, you're better off with Aoife. That old thing had... let's just say some *unpredictable* side effects."

Niamh glanced back at the circle with a mixture of curiosity and dread, imagining what those side effects might have been. She managed a weak smile and nodded at the man, though she was too overwhelmed to respond.

Before she could process further, Viktor's booming voice cut through the hum of the room. "Fall in, everyone! It's go time!"

The shout startled Niamh, making her heart leap into her throat. Her nerves were already strung tight, and she could feel the weight of the moment pressing down on her. What if she wasn't strong enough? What if she lets Aoife or worse, Lidia, down?

The group formed a single-file line behind Aoife, who stepped to the center of the room. Niamh watched in awe as Aoife raised her hands, a calm focus radiating from her. Swirls of golden dust materialized around her, spiraling upward like a living cyclone. With a graceful motion, Aoife pushed the golden vortex onto its side, the swirling dust collapsing inward to form a glowing oval. She pulled her hands apart, widening the portal, and with a final push, it stabilized into a window-like frame.

Through its shimmering eye, Niamh could see Lidia's living room, just as she remembered it, cozy, with mismatched cushions on the couch and a stack of half-read books on the coffee table. The sight hit her like a wave of nostalgia, and for a moment, she could almost pretend everything was normal.

Aoife turned and gave her a reassuring nod. "You're going to be fine," she said softly, her voice cutting through Niamh's spiraling thoughts.

Niamh took a shaky breath as Nick gently took her arm and nudged her forward. Her steps felt wooden, her body moving almost against her will. As she approached the portal, she braced herself for something, she didn't know what, fearful of what it might feel like.

The moment she stepped through, there was a rush of wind that tugged at her hair and clothes as if she'd been swept into a sudden gale. And then, just as quickly, it was over. The golden light faded, the hum of the portal disappeared, and Niamh found herself standing in the familiar warmth of Lidia's living room.

Her chest tightened as she glanced around, taking in the space. It looked untouched, the usual coziness unchanged, but knowing that Lidia was missing made the room feel eerie, almost hollow. She swallowed hard, forcing herself to focus. Whatever happened next, she was here now. She had to hold onto that spark of hope burning inside her.

For Lidia.

As the last of the team stepped through the swirling portal, Aoife followed, sealing it with a graceful motion of her hands. The golden cyclone dissipated into stillness, leaving only the faint hum of anticipation in the room. She approached Niamh, standing shoulder to shoulder with her, a silent pillar of support. Around them, the team immediately set to work, producing sleek, handheld devices that blinked and beeped intermittently. They fanned out across the house, scanning every corner with methodical precision.

The faint chirps of their equipment suddenly escalated to a frantic pace. A voice called from another room, sharp and alert: "We got a hit."

The team gathered in Lidia's bedroom, where the air felt heavy, charged with the tension of their search. Niamh hesitated at the threshold, feeling like an intruder in a space so personal, yet knowing it was necessary. She lingered near the door as the man from earlier gestured to his screen.

"It's pulling up an unregistered signature," he explained, his voice clipped and professional. "We can track it."

The room buzzed with activity as buttons were pressed and technical jargon flew. Niamh tried to follow their conversation but quickly gave up. The words were a blur, and she felt like a ghost haunting the edges of their world. Her attention wandered to Lidia's dresser.

Her fingers hovered over the framed photos perched there, the memories captured in each image feeling like an anchor. She smiled faintly at a picture of them from high school, arms slung over each other's shoulders, carefree and wild. Another showed the ribbon-cutting ceremony at her flower shop,

Lidia beaming as if it were her own accomplishment. Then, one of Lidia on a family trip with Niamh's parents, her refusal to move away with her own family before graduating solidifying her bond with Niamh's.

They weren't just friends, they were sisters. Every memory was a thread tying them together, and now, someone was threatening to sever that connection forever. The thought sent a searing heat coursing through her, anger blooming in her chest, raw and unstoppable. Her hands clenched into fists, the beginnings of her power sparking just beneath her skin.

Then, her phone buzzed.

The sharp vibration jolted her, derailing her spiraling emotions. She fumbled it from her pocket, her stomach dropping as she read the text message.

"Come alone to the Pooler warehouse, I've sent you a pin. If I see anyone with you, you'll never see Lidia again."

Her blood ran cold. Bain. The name burned in her mind like a brand. She had known something about him didn't sit right, but she hadn't wanted to believe it. Now, there was no denying the truth: he was involved in Lidia's disappearance. And he was playing her. Fury flared anew, but it was tempered by the icy grip of fear.

She had no choice. If Bain wanted her alone, she would go alone. Lidia's life was worth any risk. She would deal with Bain herself, no matter the cost. She knew she should probably coordinate with the combat team from K Corp, but she couldn't risk Lidia's safety if she went against Bain's wishes; she didn't know how unpredictable he was. She knew if she was watching this on a movie, she'd be so mad at the girl for sneaking around and not telling the people that could help, but the saying was true: "you never know how you'll react until you're in that situation".

Niamh tapped Aoife on the shoulder, keeping her voice casual despite the storm inside her. "Hey Aoife, I'm going to swing by and see my parents real quick while you guys are on the trail, okay?"

Aoife turned, her brow furrowed with concern. "Are you sure? I can come with you."

Niamh shook her head firmly. "No, no. I'm fine. I just miss them, and since we're so close, I figured it'd be a good time to stop by. Don't worry about me."

Aoife studied her for a moment, clearly unconvinced. "Okay, if you're sure. I can portal you to your house."

Niamh forced a tight smile, waving off the offer. "No, I'll just call an Uber. You've got enough to handle here. Thanks, though."

Aoife's gaze lingered, skeptical, but she eventually nodded and returned to the team. Niamh stepped outside, her heart pounding as she pulled out her phone. She summoned a ride, sharing the address Bain had sent her.

The car pulled up minutes later, and she climbed in, the driver oblivious to the storm of emotions roiling beneath her composed exterior. She gave the address, her voice steady despite the tremble in her hands.

As the car pulled away, she exhaled shakily. This was it. She was heading straight into danger, but for Lidia, there was no other choice.

The warehouse loomed ahead like a dark monolith, its sparse, flickering lights doing little to dispel the suffocating gloom. Niamh's stomach churned, her instincts screaming at her that this was a colossal mistake. The oppressive air felt wrong, heavy with the weight of something sinister. But the thought of Lidia, her best friend, her sister in all but blood, kept her rooted. She couldn't abandon her, not when this might all be her fault.

A deep voice cut through the silence. "Well, well. Hello, pretty lady."

Niamh whirled around, her heart leaping into her throat. Bain stepped out of the shadows, his sharp features catching the faint glow of the overhead light. His light hair glowed, the illusion of a halo mocking her as he smiled. But there was nothing angelic about him.

"Where's Lidia?" Niamh demanded, her voice tight with anger, every syllable forced past the lump in her throat.

Bain smirked, his hands casually slipping into his pockets. "Oh, she's safe. Don't you worry about her right now."

Her hands balled into fists. "Why did you do this, Bain? What did I ever do to you?"

The smirk widened into something colder, darker. "Oh, it wasn't you, darlin'. You're beautiful—that's the problem. I can't stop thinking about you. You stood me up, and now you won't return my phone calls."

Niamh blinked, stunned. "This is about a *date?*"

Bain chuckled, the sound low and unnerving. "Well, I'd like to do more than date, but yes."

Desperation gripped her, and she scrambled for a way to de-escalate. "Okay. Let Lidia go, and I'll go out with you. Anywhere you want. Just let her go."

His smile faltered, his eyes narrowing. "If only you'd agreed to that before. Now, it feels... insincere. Like you're only doing this for her."

Her voice pitched higher, urgency creeping in. "No! That's not it! I thought you were cute when we met at Lidia's party. I just... I didn't think you'd want someone like me. You could have anyone."

It wasn't entirely a lie, and she hoped her trembling voice sold the illusion. Bain tilted his head, considering her words, a flicker of pride flashing in his eyes.

"Right. And I want you."

Niamh swallowed hard. "Why me?" Her hands instinctively moved to her hair, tugging it forward to shield her face. It was a habit she couldn't break, a way to hide the part of her she despised the most.

Bain's expression darkened as he stepped closer, his leather shoes crunching the gravel-strewn pavement with each deliberate stride. Niamh's pulse quickened, and she flinched when his hand rose toward her. His lips twitched into a mock pout, but he didn't stop. Instead, he brushed her hair aside, tucking it gently behind her ear.

Her stomach twisted as her face was laid bare under his gaze.

"There. That's better." His voice was quieter now, almost reverent. "I like your face. It's unique. And no one's unique these days. Everyone wants to look like those over-processed celebrities, with their Botox and silicone. But you... you're special."

The intensity of his gaze made her skin crawl. She had no idea how many hours he'd spent obsessing over her, watching her from the shadows, cataloging her every move. She didn't know he'd followed her for weeks before they'd "met" at Lidia's party. Bain's fixation had only deepened as he observed her obliviousness to the world around her. It had sparked something possessive, a need to protect her innocence or, more accurately, to control it.

Niamh dropped her eyes, her voice trembling. "I'm not special. I'm deformed. I'd change how I look if I could."

She hated the spotlight her distinct features brought. Her eyes were her curse, and over the years, plastic surgeons had unanimously declared there was nothing to be done. She was trapped in a body she resented.

Bain's face darkened, his voice suddenly sharp. "Don't ever say that!"

Niamh recoiled, her breath hitching, certain for a moment that he might lash out. He noticed her reaction and softened, though his fervor didn't wane. "Don't you see? You're perfect the way you are. No one's ever going to hurt you, not while I'm around."

She lifted her hands, palms out, her voice a shaky whisper. "Okay, okay."

But Bain wasn't done. He stared at her as though she were a puzzle he had to solve, a treasure only he could claim. Niamh's mind raced. She couldn't let him dictate the pace; she needed to regain control, somehow. But every move felt like a step deeper into his trap.

"If you come on a date with me, my choice of place, I'll let Lidia go." His voice was smooth, almost playful, but there was a glint of something darker in his eyes. He knew Niamh would do just about anything to save her friend. That was the game, and he was already winning.

What Niamh didn't know was that he had no intention of harming Lidia. Hurting her would mean hurting Niamh, and that wasn't part of the plan. But he wasn't about to let her know that.

"I'll go," she blurted, the words tumbling out before she could stop them. "I'll go." Her chest tightened as she spoke, her mind too consumed with fear to think of the consequences. All that mattered was Lidia.

"Great!" he said with a grin, clapping his hands together like an excited child about to dig into dessert. The casualness of his reaction made her stomach churn.

"Let's go," she said quickly, trying to seize control of the situation. "You need to let Lidia go first, though."

He shook his head, his smile sharpening into something cold. "Nope, princess. That's not how this is gonna work. Date first, Lidia later."

Her heart sank. She should've known it wouldn't be that easy. "You promise she's safe?" she asked, her voice trembling despite her attempt to sound firm. She didn't trust him; how could she? But what choice did she have? This was the only path forward, the only way to keep Lidia out of harm's way.

"She's safe," he said smoothly, his tone almost mocking, as if her fear amused him. "As long as your little K Corp friends stay out of this. Just you and me, princess. That's the deal."

Niamh clenched her fists, her mind racing. She hated the way he smiled, the way he held all the power in this moment. But for Lidia's sake, she swallowed her pride and nodded.

"Fine," she said, her voice barely above a whisper. Inside, every nerve screamed at her to run, to fight, to do *anything* but agree. But she knew she couldn't risk it. Not with Lidia's life hanging in the balance.

Chapter 11

Niamh hoped, against all reason, that the K Corp group wasn't as skilled as their reputation claimed. But deep down, she knew better. They were good at what they did, and that terrified her. Lidia's fate was uncertain, and it was her fault. She had to go through with this, there was no other choice. She had to save her friend.

"I have this great little place in mind," he said with a grin, his tone casual, like this was any ordinary date. "Hardly anyone knows about it. Come, my Niamh." He held out his bent elbow, waiting for her to take it.

She stiffened at the words *my Niamh*. The bile rose in her throat as though the phrase itself was something poisonous. The way he said it, as if she belonged to him, like she was his property to do with as he pleased, it made her skin crawl. Every fiber of her being screamed to fight, to run, but she knew she couldn't. Not if she wanted to save Lidia. She forced herself to play along, plastering a strained smile on her face as she slipped her hand through his arm.

Her muscles didn't relax for a second. Instead, they coiled tighter with each step. The warmth of his arm under his suit jacket was undeniable, and for a fleeting moment, her traitorous mind noted the strength beneath his polished exterior. She cursed herself for even *thinking* about it.

He led her down a narrow alley behind the warehouse, the air heavy with silence. Each step felt like walking toward her doom. Her thoughts swirled as she wondered if she'd even survive this so-called date. Would she make it out alive? Did it even matter, as long as Lidia did?

The sudden shatter of glass snapped her out of her thoughts. He smashed a small bottle against the ground, and the sound echoed in the empty alley. Startled, Niamh jumped and tried to pull away on instinct, but his arm tightened around hers like a vice, locking her in place. Panic surged through her, and she twisted in his grip, her heart hammering wildly.

"Relax," he murmured, his voice too smooth, too controlled. "We're just getting started."

Before she could react, the broken glass gave way to something impossible. A glowing white circle appeared in the air in front of them, shimmering with otherworldly energy. Her eyes widened in disbelief. It wasn't just light; it felt *alive*, buzzing and humming like it had its own pulse.

"No!" she gasped, trying to dig her heels into the cobblestones, to stop him from pulling her closer. But he was too strong, and with a firm tug, he dragged her forward.

The white light swallowed her whole, blinding and consuming. She shut her eyes against its intensity, but the brightness still burned through her lids. The ground shifted beneath her feet, and for a moment, she felt weightless, untethered.

Then, as suddenly as it came, the light faded.

Niamh opened her eyes to a crisp, blue sky. The air was sharp with cold, and before her stretched a snow-covered cobblestone street. Rows of old houses with thatched roofs lined the path, their windows frosted over with ice. Snowflakes swirled lazily in the breeze, occasionally lifting from the ground in small gusts of wind.

But the street was eerily silent. No sounds of laughter, no footsteps crunching through the snow—nothing. The stillness pressed down on her, and a chill settled deep in her chest, one that had nothing to do with the icy air.

"What is this place?" she whispered, her voice barely audible. The cold seemed to swallow her words, leaving them to hang in the air unanswered.

He didn't respond. He simply stood beside her, a satisfied smirk curling at the edges of his lips as if he owned not just the space but her as well.

And for the first time, Niamh realized that saving Lidia might come at a far greater cost than she'd ever imagined.

Niamh's breath hitched as she took in the scene around her. The quaint snow-covered cobblestone streets might have been picturesque under different circumstances, but now they felt suffocating in their stillness. The eerie silence pressed down on her, amplifying the sound of her own shallow breathing and the crunch of snow beneath their feet. The thatched-roof houses lining the street seemed to stare at her like silent witnesses, indifferent to her plight.

Bain tugged her forward, his grip on her arm firm but not painful. His smug smile was fixed in place, as if this isolated winter wonderland was the crown jewel in his collection.

"Beautiful, isn't it?" he asked, his voice full of pride.

Niamh didn't respond. Her mind raced with plans, most of them flawed. Every instinct screamed at her to fight, to flee, but the thought of Lidia kept her tethered to the moment. She forced herself to stay calm, to bide her time.

Bain noticed her silence and leaned in closer, his breath warm against her ear in contrast to the icy air. "I picked this place just for you, you know. I thought you'd appreciate the charm, the… uniqueness."

Niamh flinched, leaning away as subtly as she could. "Where are we?" she asked, her voice steady despite her growing dread.

Bain straightened, a satisfied smirk pulling at his lips. "A little pocket I like to call home. Off the beaten path, just like me. No one knows we're here. No one can find us."

The finality of his words hit her like a blow. No one can find us. She clenched her teeth, trying to keep her fear from showing. If the K Corp group couldn't track her here, then it was truly up to her to handle Bain and save Lidia. She glanced around, hoping for some clue, some sign of escape.

"Come," Bain said, guiding her down the deserted street. "The restaurant is just this way. I think you'll love it."

She had no choice but to follow, her boots crunching against the snow as she moved. As Bain led her, he began talking about the architecture, the history of the area, even pointing out a few of the buildings as though giving her a personal tour. But Niamh wasn't listening. Her focus was on memorizing the path, noting every alleyway, every possible hiding spot or escape route.

Finally, they arrived at a small, warmly lit building at the end of the street. Bain opened the door, and the scent of spiced wine and roasting meat wafted out. The interior was cozy, with wooden beams and a roaring fire in the hearth. A single table was set in the middle of the room, adorned with a white cloth and flickering candles. It was clear the place had been prepared just for them.

"After you, princess," Bain said, gesturing for her to enter.

Niamh hesitated but stepped inside, her eyes darting around for anything she could use as a weapon. The room was vacant except for one table, already set with cloches covering plates, the small stone fireplace crackling, and a small bar along one wall with a few bottles of wine resting on top of the old countertop. Bain followed her in, closing the door with a resounding *click* that echoed in her chest.

"Please, sit." Bain pulled out a chair for her, his smile never wavering.

Niamh sat stiffly in the creaky old wooden chair, afraid it would collapse under her weight, her heart pounding as she tried to keep her face neutral at her unnerving company. Bain took the seat opposite her, folding his hands on the table as he stared at her with intensity.

"Now," he said, his tone soft but laced with something dark. "Let's enjoy this meal, and then we can talk about the future. Our future."

Niamh swallowed hard, her mind racing. She needed to keep him talking, to buy time, to think of a way out. But most of all, she needed to keep Lidia alive, and that meant playing along, for now.

Niamh clenched her fists under the table, the rough wood of the chair biting into her palms as she forced herself to maintain a neutral expression. Every fiber of her being screamed to run, to fight, to do *something*. But she couldn't, not with Lidia's life in Bain's hands. Instead, she forced her breathing to steady and plastered a hesitant, fragile smile across her lips.

"Thank you," she murmured, her voice as brittle as cracked glass. He lifted the cloches off the plates with flare. Niamh was unimpressed but tried to look at least pleasant for Lidia's sake. "The food looks… lovely," she gritted out.

Bain's face brightened, his grin spreading with a smug satisfaction that made her stomach churn. Bain poured them each a glass of red wine, swirling and smelling his as if he were a sommelier. He raised his glass in an exaggerated toast. "To a night of new beginnings, my Niamh."

My Niamh. The words clung to her like oil, suffocating and unshakable. Her throat tightened, but she mimicked his motion, lifting her own glass. She sipped carefully, the cool water doing little to ease the storm in her chest. Her eyes darted around the cafe as her mind raced for a plan. The eerie silence of the place gnawed at her. No bustling staff, no clinking of dishes or cheerful conversations. Just empty tables and oppressive stillness. It felt like a trap; no, it *was* a trap.

Bain's voice pulled her back. "Eat. You'll need your strength for what's to come."

His words sent an icy shiver down her spine. "What's to come?" she asked, her voice trembling despite her best efforts to keep it steady.

Bain leaned forward, his hands clasped, and smiled as if sharing an exciting secret. "A future, Niamh. Our future. Together. You're special, something more than you realize. And I've been searching for someone like you for a very, very long time."

Her stomach dropped. His obsession wasn't just about her appearance or the idea of control. He wanted her magic, her very essence. Panic clawed at her chest, but she forced herself to appear calm. She couldn't afford to let him see her fear. If she played her cards right, she might learn enough to save both Lidia and herself.

"You keep saying I'm special," she said, leaning into the uncertainty. "But I don't understand what you mean."

Bain's gaze softened, his eyes practically glowing with self-satisfaction as though she had finally asked the right question. "Your eyes, your presence, your *magic*… Niamh, you're extraordinary. The world is full of the mundane, the ordinary, but you…" He stopped, his piercing gaze locking onto hers. "You're like a diamond among rocks."

Her pulse thundered in her ears as the weight of his words sank in. He wasn't just infatuated, he was obsessed with what he believed she could become. She had to tread carefully. He was unstable, and pushing him too far could endanger Lidia.

"I don't even know what I'm capable of," she whispered, her voice trembling with what she hoped sounded like vulnerability. "I don't understand any of this… magic stuff."

His hand shot across the table, covering hers in what he likely thought was a reassuring gesture. Niamh's skin crawled at the contact, but she didn't flinch. "That's why you need me," Bain said, his voice thick with conviction. "I can guide you, teach you. Protect you. Together, we'll unlock your full potential."

Her jaw tightened, and bile rose in her throat, but she forced herself to nod slowly. "Maybe… maybe you're right. I don't have anyone else to help me."

The lie tasted bitter, but it worked. Bain's chest puffed with pride, and his grip on her hand tightened slightly. He didn't notice how she forced herself not to recoil at his touch. He didn't know just how much "her little friends" had helped her out already. She held those cards close to her chest, though, not ready to reveal her hand.

"Exactly," he said with a smile that made her blood run cold. "You can trust me, Niamh. I'll take care of everything. All you have to do is follow my lead."

Niamh mirrored his smile as best she could, her thoughts a whirlwind of desperation. She needed more time, more information, *anything* that could give her the upper hand. For now, she would play the role he wanted, a frightened, naive girl willing to be molded. But deep inside, she knew this wasn't over. If Bain thought she was going to sit quietly and let him pull the strings, he was dead wrong.

Niamh toyed with her fork, her fingers pressing into the cool metal as she shifted the food around her plate. Each bite felt like a test, a precarious balance between keeping Bain pacified and safeguarding herself from whatever might be lurking in the meal. Her head tilted slightly, the corners of her lips curling into a half-hearted smile. "It's very thoughtful. I don't usually do fancy, so you made the right choice."

Bain's chest swelled at her words, his grin widening like he'd won some unspoken contest. He leaned back in his chair, his demeanor effortlessly smug. "I thought so. You're not like the others I've known. Simplicity suits you, it's refreshing."

Not like the others. The phrase coiled around her spine, chilling her. She didn't dare ask who or what *the others* were, fearing the answer. She focused instead on lifting her glass of wine and mimicking the swirling motion he'd shown her earlier. The deep crimson liquid moved in lazy circles, catching the light from the sconces above. Her hesitation lingered as she brought the glass to her lips.

Bain noticed. "It's not poisoned, you know," he said with a laugh that lacked humor. "I wouldn't waste a wine like this on a trap."

Her throat tightened, but she took a small sip, the sharp tang of currants and earthiness of truffle flooding her senses. She swallowed, forcing herself to meet his gaze. "It's... rich. Definitely not something I've had before."

He chuckled again, his fingers tracing the stem of his glass. "Few have. It's a rare vintage, much like you."

The compliment hung between them, heavy and unwelcome. Niamh didn't flinch outwardly, but inside, a war raged between the desire to lash out and the need to stay composed. She forced a polite nod and set the glass down carefully. "It must've taken a long time to find something like this."

Bain smirked, swirling his wine as if the motion contained the answer. "I have time. And when something, or someone, is worth it, I make the effort."

The way his eyes lingered on her as he spoke made her skin crawl, but she managed to hold his gaze. She couldn't let him see her fear, though every instinct screamed at her to flee. Instead, she pressed on, her voice soft but steady. "It must've been hard to leave such a... bustling place behind."

Bain's expression shifted, his smile faltering for a fraction of a second before he recovered. "Change is inevitable. Places like this come and go.

People… they come and go too. But some things remain constant, Niamh." His voice dropped, growing softer but no less intense. "Some things are worth holding onto."

The double meaning wasn't lost on her. She gripped her fork tightly under the table, her knuckles whitening as she fought to keep her breathing steady. "You must have a lot of stories from those days," she said, feigning curiosity to keep the conversation moving away from herself.

He laughed, a sound that was equal parts amusement and something darker. "Stories, yes. Too many to count. But not all of them are meant for polite company." He leaned forward, his elbows resting on the table as his eyes searched hers. "Perhaps someday, when you're ready, I'll share them with you." He wouldn't bare his soul to her, she was far too bright and beautiful to be tainted by his dark soul and what he'd done through the centuries to survive.

Her stomach turned, but she nodded, forcing a small smile. "I'd like that." The lie tasted bitter on her tongue, but she hoped it was convincing enough to satisfy him.

Bain sat back again, his expression softening as if imagining a future where they shared his twisted past over countless dinners like this one. "Good," he said simply.

Her breath hitched, but she quickly masked it with another sip of wine. The room suddenly felt colder, the weight of his words pressing down on her like iron chains. *Stay calm,* she told herself. *Keep him talking, keep him happy. For Lidia.*

But deep inside, a spark of defiance burned brighter. She didn't know how or when, but she would find a way to break free, and she would take Lidia with her.

Chapter 12

❧

Niamh's mind raced as Bain helped her to her feet, his touch soft yet suffocating. Her hand trembled slightly in his grasp, but she forced herself to smile, a weak, reluctant smile that she hoped would keep him pacified. The kiss he placed on her knuckles lingered like an unwelcome brand, and her skin burned under his gaze.

"You're quiet tonight," he said as he led her toward the door, his voice smooth but carrying an edge that made her pulse quicken. "I thought you'd be more excited to spend time with me."

Her throat tightened, but she pushed out a response. "I'm just… nervous, I guess." The words felt true enough. "This isn't exactly a normal date for me."

He chuckled, the sound dark and low, sending a shiver down her spine. "Ah, but normal is boring, isn't it? You deserve something extraordinary. Something… unforgettable."

She bit the inside of her cheek, willing herself to stay composed. Each step toward the exit felt like walking a plank, the unknown stretching out before her like a dark abyss. Her heart ached with the thought of Lidia, trapped somewhere, depending on her to endure this nightmare. *Just keep him happy,* she repeated silently. *Don't provoke him.*

Outside, the cobblestone street was still eerily silent, the snow crunching softly beneath their feet as Bain guided her down the narrow path. He seemed content, humming a tune she didn't recognize, his grip on her arm both possessive and oddly tender. She glanced around, searching for any sign of life, any hint of escape, but the town was a ghostly shell.

Niamh's stomach twisted with a mix of fear and uncertainty, flipping relentlessly like a bird trapped in a cage. She couldn't stop wondering what else Bain had planned for her. The unknowns loomed like a shadow, and the possibilities terrified her.

"Shall we?" he asked, his voice dripping with charm as he extended a hand toward her. The gesture, so polite and poised, felt at odds with the weight of her situation.

Reluctantly, she lifted her trembling hand to his, her movements hesitant and slow. He took it with practiced ease, giving her knuckles a feather-light kiss before tucking her hand into the crook of his arm once again. The touch sent an unwelcome warmth spreading through her, a tingling sensation she couldn't ignore, no matter how hard she tried. Her body betrayed her, reacting against her better judgment.

She used to dream about moments like this, someone treating her like a delicate treasure, a gentleman sweeping her off her feet. But now? Now, she would give anything to go back to being invisible, unnoticed, and free.

Bain reached into his coat and pulled out another small glass bottle. With a flick of his wrist, he smashed it against the cobblestone road. The sound of shattering glass echoed around them, and once again, a glowing white circle appeared. Snowflakes drifted out from its edges, swirling briefly in the air before dissolving like they'd never existed.

"Off on another adventure!" Bain declared cheerfully, his excitement so incongruous with the tension clawing at Niamh's chest. Without waiting for her response, he pulled her through the circle.

The world shifted again. Blinding white gave way to a sharp, piercing blue sky. The air hit her lungs like a blade, thin and icy, as the scene around them came into focus. They were standing atop the tallest peak of a snow-covered mountain. The endless expanse of white stretched out in every direction, broken only by jagged cliffs that plunged into oblivion below.

Her stomach lurched as vertigo took hold, her knees threatening to buckle beneath her. She stumbled, swaying dangerously close to the edge, but before she could fall, Bain's arms wrapped firmly around her waist. His grip was strong, unyielding, and steady, like the trunk of a tree rooted in the earth.

"Careful now," he said, his tone light, almost teasing, as if her near-plunge into the abyss was nothing to worry about.

Her heart pounded, not just from the height but from the sudden closeness. He was holding her so securely, as if he might actually save her if she fell. The thought sent conflicting waves of relief and resentment coursing through her. Bain hadn't hurt her yet. But that didn't mean she trusted him. Trust was a luxury she couldn't afford. Not now. Not with him.

She straightened herself, stepping out of his grasp as quickly as she could without drawing attention to it. He let her go, his hands lingering just long enough to remind her that he could catch her again if he wanted to.

"What do you think?" he asked, gesturing to the breathtaking expanse of snow and sky. His smile was wide, confident, and far too pleased with himself.

Niamh swallowed hard, her voice caught in her throat. She wasn't sure what terrified her more, the dizzying heights around her or the man standing next to her.

The biting wind swept across the mountaintop. Her heart was pounding from the abrupt transition, the vertigo, and she hated to admit it, the way Bain's arms had steadied her so effortlessly. His presence was as unnerving as it was grounding.

She glanced at him warily, still reeling from his earlier touch. His expression was calm, yet his eyes sparkled with something she couldn't quite place. Admiration? Desire? Either way, it left her uneasy. And yet, there was something about his gaze, like she was the most precious thing he'd ever seen, that made her pulse quicken, a reaction she immediately scolded herself for.

Turning her attention back to the breathtaking scenery, Niamh let herself be momentarily distracted by the sheer beauty of the world around her. The silvery glow of a massive moon bathed the snow in soft, shimmering hues, casting an ethereal light over the landscape. Below, pine trees stretched toward the sky, their dark green needles a striking contrast against the endless expanse of white.

Her breath hitched in her throat. It was beautiful, *achingly* beautiful. For a fleeting moment, she forgot about Bain, her fear, and the danger lurking behind this surreal adventure.

Then, her gaze shifted, catching something she hadn't noticed before. Behind the enormous moon was a second one, smaller, tinged with a faint, otherworldly pink. It peeked out cautiously, as though unsure if it should reveal itself. The sight jolted her.

The eerie realization hit her like a punch to the chest: she had no idea where she was. This wasn't her world. The familiarity of snow and pine trees suddenly felt foreign, as though the beauty she'd admired seconds ago now cloaked something ominous.

Bain's voice broke her reverie. "I'm glad you like it. I tried to think of somewhere new to surprise you."

His tone was gentle, almost… tender. It wasn't what she had expected, and for some reason, that unnerved her even more. Against her better judgment, she stole a glance at him and immediately wished she hadn't.

In the moonlight, his face was softer than usual, the sharp edges of his confidence blunted by an almost boyish joy. There was a genuine delight in his expression as if her awe had been a gift to him. But beneath that innocent veneer, something darker lurked, a hunger that gleamed in his eyes. It wasn't obvious, not entirely obvious, but it was there, and it made her cheeks flush hot despite the biting cold.

"It's beautiful, thank you," she murmured, her voice quieter than she intended. Her breath formed small clouds in the frigid air, but even those felt fragile, ephemeral. She pulled on her hair, attempting to keep it from blowing in the breeze. The wind had other plans, though, freeing the strand almost instantly.

Bain reached out before she could react.

She flinched. It was instinctive, her body recoiling before her mind could process the movement. The moment his hand paused mid-air, the weight of what she'd done hit her. His smile faltered, the corners dipping just enough to reveal something unexpected. Was that…that emotion he was showing? Hurt?

He hesitated, his gaze searching hers, but after a breath, he moved again, slower this time, deliberate. With the utmost care, he tucked the strand of hair behind her ear. His fingers brushed her cheek, barely a touch, but it was enough. The warmth of his skin lingered, burning like a brand, and for a horrifying second, she had to fight the urge to lean into it.

Her stomach churned at the thought of wanting Bain's touch and knowing she had no idea where she was and not knowing how to get back to her world. This wasn't normal. None of this was normal. The moons hanging in the sky, *two moons*, and the stillness of this strange place whispered an undeniable truth: she wasn't in her world anymore. She didn't belong here.

Her heart began to pound, her chest tightening as fear wrapped its icy fingers around her. Every fiber of her being screamed that she shouldn't trust him, that she shouldn't let him close. And yet, here she was, his touch still warming her skin, his dark eyes holding her gaze as though daring her to look away.

"I'm glad you think it's beautiful," he said softly, his voice low and careful as if he were trying not to scare her off. But Niamh wasn't sure if it was the gentleness in his tone or the *unspoken threat* in his presence that terrified her more.

His hand lingered near her face before he lowered it. "There's a cabin just down this trail," he said, gesturing toward the slope. "We can go there for a bit."

The way he said it left no room for argument, though his tone was softer than before. Niamh wrapped her arms around herself, not because of the cold but to shield herself from the tumultuous feelings Bain stirred in her. Her body was a traitor, responding to his touch and his gaze in ways that made her stomach churn with self-loathing. She couldn't allow herself to forget who he was, what he'd done.

To her surprise, he didn't take her hand this time, though he walked close enough that she could feel the heat radiating from his body. She was grateful for the space, even if it was just an illusion of freedom. As they began their descent toward the cabin, the crunch of snow underfoot was the only sound between them. Each step felt heavier than the last, as though the weight of what might happen in that cabin pressed down on her shoulders.

Her mind raced, trying to piece together a plan, an escape, anything. But for now, all she could do was follow Bain down the snowy trail, praying that Lidia was still safe and that she wouldn't lose herself entirely before this was over.

The cabin was a masterpiece of rustic craftsmanship, exuding warmth and intimacy despite the circumstances that had brought her there. The golden-hued logs were lit by the two moons. They lay stacked on top of one another, flowing through each other like a river of wood. The naturally curved ends jutting out gave the structure an earthy charm. The arched front door, with its hand-carved detailing, set the tone for the cabin, a place built with care and an artist's touch. Everything seemed organic, natural, as if the cabin had grown from the mountain itself.

Inside, the live-edge wood stairs leading to the second floor caught her eye, their raw edges polished to perfection, while the stick-and-branch railing wove into an intricate, spiderweb-like pattern that felt both delicate and unbreakable. The massive stone fireplace crackled softly, filling the room with warmth and the faint, comforting scent of burning wood. She tried not to let the beauty of the cabin ease her guard, but it was hard to deny its appeal. If she weren't Bain's hostage, she might have genuinely enjoyed this place.

On the kitchen table sat another bottle of wine, resting in an ice bucket, accompanied by two glasses. Bain, ever the showman, gestured toward it with a flourish. "You didn't seem to enjoy the red much, so I thought white might suit your taste better. Château d'Yquem, 1811."

His tone was filled with pride, and she could tell he was watching for her reaction. She didn't have a clue what the brand or year meant, but the number alone told her this wine was as rare and expensive as the least. She forced a neutral expression as he opened the bottle; the pop startled her as it echoed in the silence. He poured the golden liquid into the glasses and offered one to her, holding it delicately by the stem. Reluctantly, she took it. At least she'd seen him open it. If there was poison or drugs in this one, it would've had to come from the bottle itself.

She casually looked around, stalling the first sip. She'd hoped Bain would taste his first so she knew it would be safe for her to drink. He moved to the large couch and lounged back in it, sinking into the leather, lifting one leg so his ankle rested on his knee. He tried his hardest to hide his nerves. But Niamh made him nervous. He was putting on his best moves, but she didn't seem the least bit impressed. She was truly an enigma.

He lifted his glass in the air as a cheers then took a sip, closing his eyes, savoring the flavors. She found herself focusing on his lips, the way he licked them after he took a sip, his tongue so delicate and precise with its motions. She cursed herself as she almost let out a small moan.

He gave her a look of anticipation or frustration, she wasn't sure which, but she knew she had to sip it eventually. So, she did. She took a very small sip, expecting bitterness, but was instead surprised by its sweetness. The wine tasted like honey and pineapple, light and luxurious. Against her better judgment, she liked it. She tried to mask her reaction, but Bain caught the subtle shift in her expression.

"I'm glad you like it," he said, his voice tinged with satisfaction. His grin was soft but victorious, and she hated the way it made her feel like he'd won something. She quickly looked away, trying to keep her tone cold.

"It's good. Thanks."

Her detachment didn't faze him. Bain was too focused on her to notice. He'd begun cataloging every tiny detail about her, the way she scrunched her nose ever so slightly when she disliked something, the curious way she paused before taking a second bite of anything she liked, as though savoring the mystery of it. He was determined to learn everything that made her happy, to know her in ways no one else did, because somehow, she had become the center of his world.

"Please sit." He motioned to the space next to him.

Niamh moved reluctantly to the far end of the couch, hoping to keep as much space between them as possible. But Bain slid ever so gracefully across the smooth leather to sit down beside her. Heat from their bodies touching immediately seeped into her as his knee pushed against hers, not in an invading way, but in an inviting manner. She froze for a moment, her mind battling her body. Part of her wanted to pull away, to maintain some semblance of distance, but the other part, traitorous and weak, craved the warmth.

His scent hit her next, a faint, heady mix of jasmine and something earthy, like rain-soaked pine. The familiarity of jasmine tugged at her, reminding her of home, of safety. She clenched her hands around the thin wine stem, trying to ground herself. *It's just my mind playing tricks,* she thought. *This isn't comfort, it's a trap.*

Bain draped an arm over the back of the couch, his fingers dangerously close to her shoulder. She shifted slightly, angling her body away, trying to create a buffer without being obvious. Her nerves were a live wire; every inch of proximity made her hyper aware of her surroundings, her breathing, and the pounding of her heart.

"Are you comfortable?" he asked, his voice soft but tinged with expectation.

She didn't answer right away, instead focusing on the flickering flames in the fireplace. "It's warm," she said at last, keeping her tone neutral.

If Bain noticed her unease, he didn't let on. But the way his eyes lingered on her, the faint smirk playing on his lips, made her feel as though he was perfectly aware of the effect he had on her—and it both terrified and infuriated her. She was done feeling like the mouse in this game. She knew she needed to start making some strategic moves to get ahead in this game of chess he was playing. She didn't know where she was or how to get back, so all she could do was to get as much information out of him as she could. Hoping he'd share the wrong piece and she'd finally gain the upper hand.

Niamh tried to keep her tone light, masking her nervousness. "So, do you come here often?" It was a cliché, but she just needed to get him started talking. She knew men like him liked to gloat about themselves, so she was aiming for his ego while trying to make him still feel in control.

Bain's deep chuckle resonated through the cozy cabin. "No, not really.

It's my boss's place. She lets me use it once in a while."

"Your boss sounds pretty cool if she lets you borrow her cabin." Niamh's voice was casual, but her mind was racing. She still didn't know who his real boss was, he clearly wasn't just an advert exec.

"She has her moments," Bain said with a shrug. "Usually when she's trying to get something from us. She doesn't do anything out of the joy of helping others. She'll only do something if it'll better herself somehow." Not unlike himself, he thought, though he wouldn't tell Niamh that.

"Then why work for her? Why choose that company specifically?" Niamh prodded, feigning interest while hoping he'd let something slip. She shifted slightly, angling her body toward him, trying to seem engaged.

Bain smirked, leaning back against the couch. "She's the best in the business. Very powerful. Why not aim for the top?"

Niamh couldn't hide the way her brows furrowed in subtle disapproval. "Me personally, I prefer integrity and substance over power. But to each their own." She shrugged, hoping to trigger him just enough to share more on the subject of his boss.

Her comment was an intentional dig, and Bain caught it, but he didn't flinch. His ego was too well-practiced in brushing off criticism. Instead, he countered smoothly. "But you started your own business, didn't you? Surely, you must enjoy a little power yourself."

She sighed, shaking her head slightly. "That's not why I started it." Her voice was firm, but her eyes flickered with something softer, a hesitation, a vulnerability Bain hadn't seen before.

Curious, Bain leaned forward slightly, resting his elbows on his knees. "Why, then?"

Niamh looked down at her lap, at the wine glass she clutched in her hands. She didn't want to share, but something in his quiet attention made her feel cornered. She relented with a sigh. "I started it so people wouldn't look at me. Every job I've had before, I worked directly with the public. They weren't exactly accepting of my… appearance."

Her voice dropped at the end, and she focused intently on the wine glass, refusing to meet Bain's gaze.

He frowned slightly, his brow furrowing as he considered her words. Gently, he reached out and tilted her chin upward with the side of his finger, forcing her to look at him. His touch was surprisingly tender, his eyes soft but intense. "You are beautiful, Niamh. You took my breath away when I first saw you."

She let out a bitter laugh. "Yeah, in horror, I'm sure." Her self-deprecation cut through the room, sharp and raw.

Bain's expression grew serious, his hand steady as he kept her gaze locked with his. "No, Niamh," he said, his voice low and earnest. "You are unlike anyone I've ever met. You're beautiful, inside and out. And those eyes of yours…" He exhaled deeply, almost as if the thought overwhelmed him. "They feel like they stare directly into my soul. And I'll be honest, it's uncomfortable because my soul is not something your innocent heart should ever experience."

His words struck her harder than she wanted to admit. She felt her chest tighten, a flicker of sympathy sparking against her will. For a moment, she wondered if she'd misjudged him. Maybe he wasn't as heartless as she'd thought.

But then, the image of Lidia, her best friend, locked away somewhere, frightened and alone, flashed through her mind. Niamh steeled herself against the softness creeping into her opinion of him. Bain was her captor, no matter how gentle his words or how much sincerity shimmered in his eyes.

She straightened her shoulders, forcing herself to break away from his gaze. "Thank you," she said, her voice cool and detached. "But words don't change what you've done."

The flicker of emotion in Bain's eyes dimmed, replaced by a shadow of disappointment. He leaned back against the couch, giving her space but not looking away. "Maybe not," he said quietly, swirling the wine in his glass. "But I meant what I said."

"So why don't you change and become a better person?"

"Easier said than done. I only know people on the dark side, I would have to start from nothing if I wanted to do things the honest way. Failure isn't really something I've ever accepted either, so I like to take the guaranteed route."

"Nothing is guaranteed. It's never too late to make a change and to be better, Bain." She wanted to connect to his good side; maybe that side would want to let her and her friend go.

He laughed a little. "I'm far too old to start over."

"You couldn't be a day over thirty. There's plenty of time."

"I'm older than I look." He said coldly, changing his mood quickly.

"Well, then you have that going for you! You look young so I'm sure you can get hired in someplace else easily."

"We'll see, princess."

"Why do you call me princess?"

"Oh, uh, a funny story I'll share with you sometime. Not now." She wasn't ready for it now. She'd surely want to leave, and she wouldn't even give him a chance.

"Um, okay."

"More wine?" he asked.

Niamh hadn't realized she had drunk all her wine during their conversation.

"Sure, why not? I guess I did like it."

"I'm glad. Plenty more where that came from," he said as he poured more warm amber liquid into the narrow opening glass.

He sat back down next to Niamh, handing her the delicate, thin-stemmed glass. She hesitated for a moment before taking it, then turned to face him fully, crossing her legs in front of her. Her gaze locked on his, searching for answers she wasn't sure she wanted.

"So," she began, her tone measured, "why did you do all this, Bain? You don't strike me as the type of guy who has trouble getting what he wants. Why resort to measures like… this?"

He leaned back, his posture relaxed, but there was tension in his jaw. "I was under a time crunch," he admitted, swirling the wine in his glass. "I didn't have the luxury of letting you fall for me naturally. And," he added, his eyes meeting hers pointedly, "you wouldn't even give me the time to talk to you in person."

Niamh blinked, taken aback. "I was out of town. If you'd just waited, we could've grabbed a coffee or something when I got back."

"Like I said," he replied, his voice steady but firm, "I didn't have the time."

Her frustration bubbled over, and her tone sharpened. "But you *had* time to kidnap my friend and then drag me on a series of dates?" Her voice rose, punctuated with disbelief. "Dates, Bain? Really?"

His composure cracked, and he ran a hand through his hair, exhaling heavily. "I just… I wanted to get to know you better before…" He stopped abruptly, the words hanging in the air between them.

"Before *what*?" Niamh pressed, leaning forward, her eyes narrowing.

His lips parted as if to answer, but he hesitated, the silence stretching too long. Finally, he muttered, "Nothing. I'll tell you later."

"It doesn't sound like nothing," she shot back. "It sounds like something I *should* know. Bain…" Her voice wavered slightly, betraying the fear tightening her chest. "Are you…are you going to kill me?"

"What?" he yelled, his shock reverberating through the room. His eyes widened in disbelief. "No! I'm not going to kill you. After everything I've done, you think I went through all this just to kill you?"

His indignation was so genuine that it threw her off. Still, she raised her glass defensively, trying to create some distance between them. "Well, you have to admit," she said, waving her free hand around the room, "this is all… a little weird." Her gesture sent the wine sloshing over the rim of her glass, a golden splash landing squarely on his shirt.

She gasped, her heart dropping into her stomach. "Oh no! I'm so sorry. I didn't mean to…" The words tumbled out of her mouth in a rush, panic gripping her. She held her breath, waiting to see if the spill would push him over the edge.

Bain looked down at his shirt, then back at her, his expression softening. "I know," he said evenly. "No harm done."

Relief flooded through her, and she sagged against the couch as he stood. "I'm just going to clean up," he added, his tone calm. He disappeared into another room off the living room, leaving Niamh to sit in uneasy silence.

Niamh sat frozen for a moment, listening as the door clicked softly shut. She hated the silence that followed, it pressed down on her, thick and suffocating. She couldn't just sit there, waiting for him to come back. Not when this might be her only chance to find some answers.

Her heart raced as she slid open the nearest end-table drawer, careful to move slowly, keeping the wood from creaking. Empty. Her fingers hovered for a moment before she closed it and checked the one beneath it. Nothing. Frustration prickled at her nerves. Either he didn't use this place often, or he'd cleared it out ahead of time.

Refusing to give up, she stood and padded to the kitchen, her bare feet silent against the cold floor. The drawers there had to hold *something*. She started opening them one by one, her movements quick but quiet, her eyes darting over utensils and neatly arranged kitchenware. All mundane. All useless.

A sound made her pause, a faint rustle coming from the other room. She crept back toward the doorway, leaning just far enough to peek inside. Her breath caught at the sight before her.

Bain stood in the dim glow of the moonlight filtering through the window, his back to her. The room was dark except for the silver-blue light that washed over him, giving his silhouette an otherworldly glow.

He reached up, pulling his shirt over his head in one fluid motion, revealing a broad, muscular back. Niamh swallowed hard. His shoulders and spine were perfectly defined, each muscle shifting with the motion, like something carved from stone. But her gaze caught on something else, a scar.

The raised, jagged line ran a few inches down his shoulder blade, interrupting the smooth expanse of his skin. Though it had healed, it was obvious the wound had once been deep, raw. A wound that didn't heal cleanly. The scar seemed out of place on him, like it didn't belong on someone who carried himself with such confidence, such control.

Her mind wrestled with the image. *Who had hurt him? How did it happen?* And why, for some inexplicable reason, did it make her feel something other than fear? She clenched her fists, forcing her thoughts to refocus. Bain was dangerous. Whatever scars he carried weren't her concern, and letting herself soften toward him, even for a second, was a mistake she couldn't afford to make.

She stepped back into the kitchen, shaking her head as if to physically dispel the lingering image of his scarred, muscular back. Refocusing, she opened another drawer, her fingers trembling slightly now.

She couldn't let him get in her head. Not like this.

Niamh glanced quickly over her shoulder, then back at the drawer. She had to make a choice.

Her instinct screamed at her to get back to the couch, to pretend like she had been sitting there the entire time. As she rounded the corner, Bain reappeared from the hallway, now dressed in a fresh shirt. His gaze immediately locked on her, his eyes narrowing ever so slightly.

"What are you doing?" His voice was calm, but there was tension in the way he stood that made Niamh's stomach flip.

"Nothing," she replied too quickly, a forced smile on her lips. She tried to act casual, to make it seem like she hadn't been snooping through his things, but her pulse betrayed her, hammering in her ears. "Just… getting more wine. It really is delicious." She finished off what was left in her glass and reached for the bottle to refill it.

"Are you looking for something?" Bain's voice rang out from the doorway, smooth and steady, cutting through the silence like a blade.

Niamh froze, her pulse thundering in her ears. *Caught.* She spun around quickly, trying to mask the panic bubbling inside her.

He was leaning casually against the doorframe, one arm braced above his head like he'd stepped out of a magazine spread. His sculpted figure and relaxed posture sent an unwelcome jolt through her. She had to steady herself, forcing a deep breath before she could speak.

"I, uh, was just getting more wine," she stammered, clutching the bottle like it was a lifeline. "And maybe a snack. I didn't eat much earlier, and, well, I don't like drinking on an empty stomach." She moved quickly, pouring more wine into her already-full glass, her movements deliberate but shaky.

Bain raised a brow, the faintest smirk tugging at his lips. "Hm," he murmured, studying her like he knew there was more to her story. "What do you feel like? I'll grab it for you."

"Anything, really. Crackers or chips, whatever you have is fine," she replied quickly, hoping to redirect his attention.

"Crackers or chips," he repeated as if turning over the simplicity of her request. "Alright. I'll grab something. But don't you go anywhere."

The playful lilt in his voice made her skin prickle, and before she could respond, he reached into his coat and pulled out yet another glass bottle. He shattered it effortlessly against the ground, the now-familiar white circle blooming to life at his feet.

She watched as he stepped through the glowing portal, disappearing in an instant. Niamh exhaled sharply, finally allowing herself to breathe. Her mind raced, not just with the fear of being caught but with questions that continued to pile up. *Where does the glass go when it shatters? How many bottles does he even have? And why?* She shook her head, cutting off the thought. She had bigger things to worry about than Bain's endless supply of mystery bottles.

The white circle reappeared moments later, and Bain stepped through, his long, muscular legs striding confidently back into the room. In his arms, he carried a wicker basket, his lips curved in a warm, almost disarming smile.

"I grabbed a few things," he said, his tone light as he placed the basket on the coffee table in front of her. He knelt and began unpacking it, laying out an array of carefully arranged breads, rolls, crackers, and cheeses.

Niamh's brow furrowed slightly as she looked over the spread. It was more than she'd expected, more than anyone would typically prepare for a casual snack. The presentation was almost elegant, thoughtful.

She didn't know if she should be impressed or unsettled. *Where does someone even get all this on a whim?*

Bain glanced up at her, his expression softening as if he'd caught the flicker of confusion in her eyes. "You may not be well-traveled," he said casually, almost as if reading her mind, "but I'm determined to bring the world to you."

His words, sincere and strangely tender, sent an uncomfortable knot tightening in her chest. She forced a small smile, not trusting herself to speak. She didn't know what unnerved her more, the kindness in his gesture or the ever-present reminder that none of this was by her choice.

She snacked on cheese, crackers, and wine to keep busy. Bain added logs to the fire, if this wasn't the thing of nightmares it might actually be romantic. He did look good standing by the fireplace she thought then regretted it. Her mind was a traitor and kept drifting where it shouldn't.

He turned to catch her eye as she walked from the kitchen. He took a few steps closer, the warmth of his body invading her space once again. There was a softness in his eyes now, the hardness from before gone, replaced by something she couldn't quite decipher.

"Why did you ask if I was going to kill you?" he said suddenly, his voice low. It wasn't an accusation, just a question.

Niamh's eyes flickered to his, then back down to the wine glass she was still holding. She shifted uncomfortably. "I don't know. I guess… after everything, I thought maybe you were keeping me here for something else. Something darker."

"Like what?" Bain's expression darkened, his jaw tightening again.

Niamh met his gaze, her heart racing. She couldn't quite bring herself to say the words, to voice the fear she'd been holding on to. But she had to ask, had to understand what was going on in his head, no matter how twisted it seemed.

"I don't know," she admitted quietly. "You've kidnapped my friend; you've kidnapped me. I didn't know what to think."

Bain's eyes softened, a hint of regret flashing across his features. He opened his mouth but paused as if reconsidering what he wanted to say. After a moment, he spoke, his voice barely above a whisper.

"I'm not going to kill you, Niamh. I value you too much. There are things you do not yet know. Things that involve you. But I would never put you in harm's way. Of that, I speak the truth." He looked away, running a hand through his hair, clearly frustrated.

Niamh held her breath, trying to process his words. She had no idea what he meant by *things that involve you*, but she didn't want any part of his plans if this was how he solved his issues. She couldn't trust him. Not after everything.

Still, a strange ache stirred in her chest, and she found herself wondering, for just a moment, if maybe, just maybe, there was more to Bain than the monster he'd tried so hard to appear to be. She was ever the tender heart, always trying to find the good in people even after they'd repeatedly hurt her. She searched for love and acceptance her whole life; the draw of that potential feeling overpowered even her instincts sometimes.

She carefully nibbled on crackers, trying to appear calm despite the unease swirling inside her. Bain was unpredictable, and every word he spoke seemed to shift the ground beneath her. Feeling the warmth spread through her chest. She knew it was easy to get lost in the moment, to let the tension slip away with each glass, but she couldn't afford to let her guard down completely. Not yet.

"So, your boss is the one who makes those portals?" she asked, trying to keep her voice casual as she set her glass down.

Bain's smile faltered for a brief moment, his gaze darkening as he looked her directly in her eyes. "Yeah. She's the one with all the power. I just... use what she gives me."

"Why don't you use it to, I don't know, free yourself?" Niamh pressed, her curiosity getting the better of her. "You don't seem like the type to let someone control you."

Bain's eyes flickered to hers, and for a moment, she saw something like hesitation pass across his features before it was masked again with that smug, almost carefree expression. "I told you. Failure isn't something I've ever accepted. And starting over? It's not as easy as it looks." His tone was darker now, and she could hear the edge of frustration in his voice.

"You don't have to start over," she countered, hoping he would hear her. "You just have to start *now*."

He laughed, but it was hollow, a sound that didn't quite reach his eyes. "You really think it's that simple?"

She shrugged, her frustration mounting. "Maybe not simple, but possible. You've done things, Bain. But it doesn't mean you have to keep doing them."

For a moment, he got lost in thought, considering her words. Could he turn good after centuries of only knowing darkness? He did things, things he wasn't proud of, but they were things he needed to do to survive. It didn't make them any less horrible. No, he thought he'd been bad for too long; there was no going back for him. "Enough of this. You're here now, and you might as well just enjoy the wine. The rest of the talk can wait." His words felt like an easy escape, a way to change the subject without facing any hard truths.

As she sipped, she found herself watching him closely. There was more to Bain than he let on, more than he was willing to admit. Maybe his boss was the source of his power, but it was clear Bain wasn't just a pawn in some game. There was ambition behind those eyes, a desire for control that he wasn't quite ready to let go of.

Niamh leaned back in her chair, breaking the silence with a question that had been nagging at her for a while. "What exactly does she want from you? This boss of yours. You've never really said."

Bain's eyes narrowed slightly, his jaw tightening as if the question hit a little too close to home. He didn't answer right away, instead reaching for the wine bottle to refill her glass, as if it would help deflect the pressure of her question.

After a long pause, he finally spoke, his voice low and guarded. "She wants power. Control. And she's using me to get it." He looked at her, his gaze sharp. "But we're not all that different, are we? You want something too."

Niamh's brow furrowed. "I'm not here to take control, Bain. I'm here because I want to help people."

He chuckled softly, shaking his head. "Maybe, but everyone has their price, Niamh. And everyone has something they're willing to trade for what they want."

She met his gaze steadily. "Not everyone. Not me."

Bain's expression softened for a moment, almost imperceptibly, before he looked away, his fingers tapping the side of his wine glass. "We'll see about that."

There was something in his tone that sent a shiver down her spine. It was like he knew something about her that she hadn't realized yet. Or maybe, just maybe, he was starting to see her as more than just a captive.

The thought made her uneasy. She couldn't let herself get caught up in the strange mix of emotions swirling between them. She had a mission. Lidia needed to be freed. And Bain, complicated as he was, was still the key to understanding what was going on.

But as the night stretched on and the wine continued to flow, Niamh couldn't help but wonder: *What if Lidia wasn't the only one in need of saving?*

"Are you a witch?" Niamh asked, narrowing her eyes slightly as she studied him.

Bain threw his head back and laughed, a deep, genuine sound that echoed through the quiet room. "No," he said with a smirk. "Not a witch. Or anything close to it."

"Care to elaborate?" she pressed, tilting her head. "I thought we were supposed to be getting to know each other."

Her tone was light, but there was an edge of determination beneath it. She knew he wouldn't open up easily; he was like a vault, locked tight and full of secrets. But she was equally determined to crack it open, even just a little, to get a glimpse of the truth hidden inside.

He sighed, the sound heavy with reluctance, and leaned back slightly. "Alright," he said finally, as if conceding a battle he hadn't meant to fight. "I can't make portals. My boss can. She makes me these."

Reaching into his pocket, he pulled out one of the small vials she'd seen him use before. He held it up in front of her, letting the faint white glow illuminate the space between them. Shimmering flecks swirled lazily inside the glass as if suspended in some kind of ethereal liquid.

"I told you," he continued, his tone shifting into something smoother, more self-assured. "I like powerful people. They're... useful. Very handy."

Niamh's brows knit together as she eyed the vial. "So, you don't have any powers?"

"Not really," he admitted after a pause, his voice quieter this time. The words came out reluctantly, and for a moment, his confidence seemed to waver. He hated saying it out loud; it felt like peeling back a layer of armor, exposing something vulnerable.

Because that was the truth of it: Bain was a trickster, someone who manipulated and schemed to get what he wanted. He used the power of others to prop himself up, pretending to be someone he wasn't. And deep down, he hated how much that truth stung.

But Niamh wasn't convinced. She recognized the slight shift in his tone, the way his eyes darted briefly to the side before meeting hers again. He was slipping back into his sly, slippery ways. Always dodging. Always deflecting. Still, she decided to let it go for now.

Without a word, she picked up a piece of bread from the basket and broke off small pieces, nibbling to keep her mouth and her restless thoughts occupied. The bread was dry, and she took small sips of wine to wash it down.

Bain, however, seemed far more invested in her wineglass than she was. Every time it dipped even slightly, he was ready, refilling it with a smile that teetered between charming and insistent.

She glanced at him briefly, trying to gauge his intentions, but his expression remained as unreadable as ever. The more time she spent with him, the more she realized he was a puzzle, pieces scattered everywhere, with no clear way to put them together.

<h1 style="text-align:center">Chapter 13</h1>

Niamh hadn't realized how much wine she'd drunk until Bain set the empty bottle into the trash can with a soft clink. Her head felt light, as though the edges of her thoughts were beginning to blur. She slid down onto the couch, letting her body sink into the cushions as a wave of fatigue washed over her.

Bain noticed. Without a word, he reached for the woven blanket draped over the back of the couch and spread it over her with surprising care. His touch was gentle, almost tender, and it sent a confusing ripple through her. But before she could think too much about it, the weight of the blanket and the warmth of the wine lulled her into darkness.

When she opened her eyes, the room was dim, illuminated only by the flickering glow of the fire. Bain sat nearby, crouched in front of the hearth, prodding the embers with a long metal hook. Sparks flared up with each movement, dancing briefly before fading into the shadows.

Her mouth felt dry, and a dull ache had settled behind her eyes. She groaned softly, sitting up and rubbing her temples. On the coffee table in front of her, a large glass of water and a small packet of pills waited.

"Good morning," Bain said without turning around, his voice low and smooth, almost teasing. "Thought you could use some aspirin after all that wine."

His words sent a jolt of self-consciousness through her. She hadn't meant to drink so much, certainly not enough to let her guard down around him. She reached for the glass, her fingers brushing its cool surface, but hesitated, stealing a glance at him.

Bain finally turned, resting the hook against the hearth. His expression was unreadable, a flicker of amusement in his eyes but no hint of malice. Still, she couldn't shake the unease coiling in her chest.

"Um, thanks," Niamh said, her voice hoarse as she gestured to the water and aspirin. She avoided his gaze, focusing on the rippling firelight instead. "And sorry. I don't usually drink that much, but… well, it was an unusual night."

"You're fine," Bain replied, leaning back in his chair with a small shrug. "I probably should have stopped you, but I was just glad you were relaxing and enjoying the wine."

Niamh stiffened slightly, her stomach twisting. She hesitated, then blurted, "We uh… didn't…"

Bain's eyes widened, and his face flushed a deep shade of pink. "Oh god, no!" he exclaimed, sitting upright so quickly he nearly knocked over the fire hook beside him. "Not, not that I didn't want to! But I'm not a total creep. I'd *never* take advantage of a woman like that." His words rushed out in a flustered tumble, and for a moment, the self-assured Bain she'd come to know seemed completely disarmed.

It caught her off guard. He looked… cute when he was flustered, she realized, and the thought hit her like a slap. She regretted it immediately, shaking it off with a subtle, annoyed exhale.

"Okay, good," she said, pulling the blanket tighter around herself. Not because she was cold, she wasn't, but because the flush of her embarrassment made her feel exposed.

Bain's sheepish expression softened into a familiar smirk, and the glint of his usual confidence returned. "But," he drawled, the teasing lilt back in his voice, "if you ever *doooo* want to, just say the word." He punctuated the remark with an exaggerated wink.

Niamh's jaw clenched. *So much for being a better guy,* she thought, rolling her eyes internally. "I'm good, thanks," she said curtly, brushing off the comment like it was nothing.

But it wasn't nothing. As much as she hated to admit it, the thought *had* crossed her mind, briefly. She'd never tell him, of course. Bain didn't need any more ammunition for his relentless charm.

Instead, she focused on the fire, willing her thoughts to stay firmly rooted in her annoyance rather than the flickers of curiosity she didn't dare entertain.

His lips curved into a small smile, but he didn't respond, leaving the air between them thick with unspoken words.

She downed the aspirin and the water quickly, hoping the combination would clear her head, but deep down, she knew she was more affected by Bain's presence than she wanted to admit. He was charming in his way, and that wink he gave her… she'd be lying if she said it didn't make her heart flutter, even if she didn't want it to. She had to stay focused. *This is about Lidia. This is about getting out of here.*

"So, I have some stuff to do today," Bain said casually, standing and brushing off his pants. "I hope you don't mind. I have to leave you for a bit."

"What?" Niamh sat up straighter, the blanket sliding off her shoulders. "Leave me? Here? I don't even know where I *am!*"

"I know," he said, his tone almost apologetic, though it didn't quite reach his eyes. "Sorry about that, but I promise I'll be back later."

She stared at him in disbelief. "That's not the point, Bain! You can't just leave me here. I have no idea where I am, no way to get back, and no one I can even ask for help!"

He sighed, rubbing the back of his neck as if her protests were a minor inconvenience rather than a valid argument. "Do you need me to bring you anything while I'm out?" he offered, deflecting her concerns with an infuriating calmness.

Niamh's glare could have burned a hole through him. "How about bringing me *home?*" she snapped, her voice taut with frustration.

He winced slightly but didn't relent. "Can't do that. Not yet, anyway." His lips curved into a playful grin that only made her angrier. "But I'll bring you a surprise, though. Be back soon!"

Before she could argue further, Bain blew her a kiss, his charm cutting through the tension like a blade. Then, with his usual flourish, he smashed another glass bottle at his feet.

The glowing white circle appeared, and within seconds, he was gone.

Niamh sat frozen for a moment, staring at the space where he'd stood. The sound of the portal's hum lingered in her ears, fading slowly until she was left in complete silence.

The reality of her situation settled heavily on her chest. She was alone—in an unfamiliar, alien world with two moons and no clear way back. Her gaze drifted to the windows, where the silver and pink moons loomed like watchful eyes, offering no comfort.

Her mind raced with worry. *What if he doesn't come back?* The thought crept in unbidden, its weight sinking deep into her stomach. Bain was unpredictable at best, and his promises meant nothing. He'd left her here with no plan, no answers, and no way to even begin solving this mess on her own.

She wrapped the blanket tightly around herself, trying to ward off the creeping chill of isolation. For now, all she could do was wait—and hope she wasn't as abandoned as she felt.

After some time went by and Bain didn't return, Niamh got antsy.

She got up, still feeling a little off-balance, and began to pace around the small living area. It was sparsely decorated, with just a few pieces of furniture and nothing that could give her a clue about where they were or why Bain seemed to be taking his time to deal with her.

She was all alone in an unknown place. Her cell phone didn't work. She'd been checking as often as she could to see if bars popped up, but no service since they left the warehouse. She snooped through the rest of the cabin, looking for clues. The cabin was void of any personal belongings. She was upstairs when she heard voices. She peeked down through the wooden web railing to see who it was. She saw Aoife's gold tornado and her copper hair flying in the wind. Nick stepped through, then Njeri.

Chapter 14

Niamh rushed down the stairs, her socks sliding against the gleaming wood. She barely caught herself from falling, her momentum nearly sending her crashing into Aoife. Instead, she collided with her friend, wrapping her arms around her in a desperate hug.

Aoife hugged her back tightly, then held her at arm's length, inspecting her with wide, worried eyes.

"You're okay?" Aoife asked, her gaze darting over Niamh's face and body as though searching for any sign of harm.

"I'm fine." Niamh's voice trembled, the relief overwhelming her. "How did you find me? Did you find Lidia?" She clung to Aoife's arms, unwilling to let go. Her touch felt like a lifeline in an ocean threatening to pull her under.

"We did," Aoife said gently, giving her a reassuring squeeze. "She's okay. Bain sent us a message with her location. She's safe. She's fine. Don't worry." She paused for emphasis, her voice steady. "She's with one of our teams for now. Let's get you home."

Niamh nodded, her heart pounding as she reached to grab Aoife's hand. But before their fingers could touch, something yanked her backward with a force so sudden and strong it stole her breath.

A gasp escaped her lips as an unseen grip tightened around her arms, pulling her away from Aoife. The sensation was unmistakable, Bain's strong fingers, unyielding and inescapable.

"Niamh!" Aoife lunged forward, her hand outstretched, but she was slammed to the ground by a burst of white energy. The force pinned her in place, a shimmering shield pressing her down like a weight.

"Stay down!" Niamh cried, panic flooding her chest as Aoife struggled beneath the glowing barrier.

Nick rushed to Aoife's side, his face twisted in determination. He tried to shield her body with his own, but the white energy resisted his touch. He hissed in pain, recoiling as it burned his skin.

Across the room, Njeri leaped toward Bain with feral intensity, her movements quick and precise. But Bain was faster.

Before she could even come close, he wrenched Niamh through a glowing white portal. The world blurred into blinding light, and in an instant, they were gone.

She was tired. Tired of hitting him, tired of crying, tired of being the helpless mouse in his twisted little game. Her body felt heavy, drained of every ounce of fight she had left, but something inside her refused to give up completely.

With a shaky breath, Niamh pushed herself to her feet. She wiped her tear-streaked face with trembling hands, then looked Bain dead in the eye, her voice sharp and furious.

"What is *wrong* with you?" she yelled, her words echoing off the empty silence around them.

Bain didn't flinch, though something in his expression shifted, subtle, almost imperceptible. "I'm sorry," he said, his voice low, almost pleading. "I just have one more thing I need to do. I couldn't let you go yet. I let your friends know where Lidia was, though, just so you know. She's safe. I won't go after her again."

Niamh let out a bitter laugh, the sound raw and hollow. "How am I supposed to believe anything you say? You're a liar and a cheat!"

He didn't deny it. "I may be those things," he admitted, his tone steady but tinged with regret, "but I also gave my word to someone, and I have to keep it."

Her hands curled into fists at her sides. "So, you'll keep your word for *someone else* but not me?"

Bain's head dipped, shame clouding his features. "I'm sorry," he said again, softer this time. "It's just not that simple."

She wanted to scream at him, to shake him until he understood what his choices were doing to her. She wanted him to feel the same helpless fury that was boiling inside her. And maybe, just maybe, he already did. But his guilt didn't make her feel any better.

"I'm just a pawn in your game," she said, her voice cold and sharp. Her chest ached, but she forced herself to ignore it. Any small, fleeting feelings she might have had for Bain were shoved down, buried deep where they could never resurface. She wouldn't allow herself to feel anything for someone who had done this to her.

"You're so much more than that, and you know it," Bain said, his gaze fixed on her with an intensity that made her want to look away. "But I have to follow through with this." He sighed, running a hand through his hair. "Come on. Let's get it over with, and we can both get on with our lives."

With a sharp breath, she pushed past him, her shoulder slamming into his chest as she shoved him out of her way.

He let her go, saying nothing, but she didn't care. She refused to let him think he had the upper hand.

Niamh's mind spun, tangled in the rush of emotions tearing through her. Fury, heartbreak, and an overwhelming sense of defeat churned inside her like a storm. Her hands still trembled from the surge of anger that had fueled her strikes against Bain, but now, standing before him, her chest heaving, the anger began to slip away. It was as though she would have been drained, leaving behind nothing but exhaustion.

Safe. The word echoed hollowly in her head, a fragile promise that didn't bring the comfort she so desperately wanted. Lidia was safe, for now. But at what cost? Bain had once again pulled her strings, dragging her back through that accursed white portal, leaving her friends, her real allies, helpless on the other side.

Her body ached, though it wasn't the physical strain that weighed on her the most. It was the bitter weight of defeat pressing on her chest, curling like a stone in the pit of her stomach. She had been so close to freedom. So close to escaping him.

"You…" Her voice wavered as she tried to muster her fury again. "You let me go, Bain!" she spat, the words shaking as they left her lips.

Bain sighed heavily, his expression softening, though the guarded look in his eyes didn't falter. "I didn't want to do this, Niamh," he said, his voice quieter than before. "I didn't want to pull you back here, but I couldn't let you leave. Not yet."

His tone lacked the usual bite, but that only made his words more unsettling.

"Then *why?*" Niamh demanded, her voice rising in pitch as frustration overtook her. "Why are you doing this to me? Why kidnap me, why play these twisted games, if you weren't planning on…"

Her voice broke, and she stopped herself before finishing the sentence. A lump rose in her throat, thick and suffocating, threatening to unleash a torrent of emotion she couldn't afford to let loose. She clenched her fists at her sides, grounding herself in the tension before the tears could fall again.

Bain's gaze flickered, his eyes catching hers with a faint flicker of regret, so faint she wasn't sure if she imagined it. "I never meant for this to go on this long," he said, his voice barely above a murmur. The vulnerability in his tone was jarring, but it didn't make his actions any less infuriating.

He reached a hand toward her, hesitating mid-gesture, as if he wanted to touch her arm but thought better of it. His expression shifted, his eyes darting between frustration and something that almost resembled guilt. "I didn't want it to get so complicated. I didn't want you to hate me," he said, his voice tinged with something unfamiliar. "But I needed you to understand. You will understand in time why I did this."

"I just want to go home," she continued, her voice rising with conviction. "I want to be with my friends, to make sure Lidia stays safe, and to leave this whole mess behind. I want my life back."

Her words hung heavy in the air, cutting through the tension between them. She saw Bain flinch, just slightly, but he didn't respond. Instead, his eyes searched hers, as if looking for some crack in her resolve, some opening he could exploit.

But Niamh stood firm, the weight of her exhaustion giving her strength. She wouldn't let him break her, not now, not ever.

He took a slow step closer to her, though he didn't touch her. There was something in his eyes, something she didn't quite understand, an invitation, a plea. She could feel the weight of it pressing on her chest. "I *can't* let you go yet, Niamh." His voice was nearly a whisper. "There's still something you need to see. Something I need to show you."

"Why?" Her voice trembled with frustration. "What could you possibly need to show me after everything? I don't trust you. You've made sure of that."

He looked at her for a long moment, the silence hanging thick between them. The air in the room felt charged, crackling with a tension neither of them wanted to acknowledge. Finally, Bain's eyes softened, and his posture relaxed. He didn't seem like the same man who had dragged her here in the first place.

"I never wanted to hurt you, Niamh. I don't want to be your enemy. But you're too important to just let go." His voice was low, almost hoarse. "Please, just let me explain. One last time. If you hear me out, I swear I'll let you go. I'll even help you get back to your life. No more games, no more tricks."

Niamh swallowed, her heartbeat pounding in her ears. "What do you need from me?"

Bain looked at her for a long, drawn-out moment, as though debating whether to continue. Finally, his gaze locked with hers, and in his eyes, she saw a deep, unspoken truth—one she wasn't sure she was ready to hear.

"I need you to trust me," he said quietly. "Just for a little while longer. Once you understand, you'll see that I'm not the bad guy in this story. I'm just trying to protect you from something worse."

Niamh felt her stomach twist. *Protect me?* But she couldn't shake the feeling that there was more to his words than he was letting on. She wanted to say no, to push him away, to demand answers. But something inside her, something that felt raw and terrifying, told her to listen. To understand.

But could she trust him?

He gestured for her to walk in front of him, but she didn't move immediately. It was only then that she realized she hadn't even taken in her new surroundings. She had been so consumed by her emotions that she hadn't noticed anything beyond Bain and the weight of her anger.

She stared at him, her chest tight, before stepping forward. She couldn't look at him any longer. She pushed past him, her shoulder colliding with his chest, shoving him aside in a silent act of defiance.

They walked down a winding path, the earth beneath their feet gleaming as if kissed by starlight. The pavers, smooth yet irregular in size, shimmered like crystal, each stone a different unearthly shade catching the faint light from the glowing plants that lined the edges of the path. As Niamh moved, the colors rippled under her feet as though the stones were alive, shifting with each step she took. The path wound through an ethereal landscape, and the air felt charged with a magic she couldn't quite understand, humming with energy that seemed to vibrate against her skin.

The trail eventually led to a cave, its entrance framed by massive doors made of what looked like stained glass but unlike any she'd ever seen. The glass shimmered in hues of gold, blue, and violet as if it were alive with color. Niamh glanced back at Bain, catching him looking down, his expression unreadable.

He noticed her gaze and motioned for her to go ahead.

There was no escaping. She had no choice.

With a sharp exhale, she shoved open the doors, the glass rattling as they slammed against the stone walls behind them. The sound echoed down the empty hall, a resounding thud that made her skin prickle with tension.

She marched down the hallway, her steps deliberate and loud, the smooth, shiny stone floor beneath her feet reflecting her mood. She wanted to make it clear to him, make it clear to herself that she was not happy with this. The walls felt too close, the air too heavy.

This was not the end she had imagined. But now, it was her reality.

Tall white crystals, their jagged edges like the teeth of some ancient beast, grew from the ground in clusters, jutting out in every direction. Some rose high above her head, while others bent in wild angles, their surfaces glistening with frost-like markings that seemed to shift and move as though the stone itself was breathing. It was beautiful, yes, but also unnerving, the kind of beauty that promised both wonder and danger in equal measure. The crystals flickered with an inner light, like stars trapped within their clear prisms, casting eerie shadows that twisted around her legs as though something were watching.

Niamh glanced back at Bain. He was looking down, avoiding her gaze, his expression unreadable. She caught him watching her out of the corner of his eye, and his gaze flickered with something she couldn't place.

The hallway before her stretched onward, the walls gleaming with smooth, polished stone, more reflective than any surface she'd seen before, light and bright, almost blindingly bright. Niamh could feel the weight of the place around her, the magic pressing down from every corner, thick like a heavy fog, almost suffocating.

But there was only one way forward. And for now, she was stuck in his world, the one he'd brought her to.

The hallway led to only one door, a towering structure of frosted glass that gleamed faintly in the glow of the room beyond. Its ornate silver handle twisted in an intricate, swirling pattern that looked like it belonged to another time, delicate yet strong. She didn't wait for him to tell her what to do this time, she knew she had only one choice. She wouldn't give him the satisfaction of ordering her around again. Niamh reached out, pushed the door open with force.

As she stepped inside, the room before her was unlike anything she had ever imagined. It was surreal, like stepping into a dream that she couldn't quite place. Large, jagged crystals erupted from the floor, rising in sharp angles like a forest of translucent, otherworldly spires. They were similar to the ones outside, but here, their scale was almost overwhelming, crisscrossing overhead like support beams, holding up the very air around her. Each crystal emitted a faint, ethereal glow, a soft light that bathed the room in a cool, almost ghostly ambiance.

The walls were pristine, gleaming white, with no color to distract from the intensity of the light. It was so bright it almost hurt her eyes, the sharp contrast of it all making her feel small and out of place. Everything in the room seemed to be some variation of white, from the polished marble floor beneath her feet to the clear surfaces of the furniture. It felt as though she had stepped into an abstract painting, monochromatic, minimalist, and cold. The space was both beautiful and unsettling, as if it was designed to leave no room for anything personal, no trace of emotion.

A thick, crystal-clear desk sat in the center of the room, sleek and uninviting. Behind it, a massive wall of bookshelves stretched across the far side, laden with books that appeared almost weightless in their simplicity. The spines were blank, with no titles or authors visible, just shades of pale white and muted grey, like the room itself; they seemed to belong to a different world. The floor, made of smooth crystal, reflected the light in soft veins of silver and grey, creating the illusion of movement beneath her feet.

Despite the pristine beauty of the room, it felt sterile, like a place designed to remove all traces of life, of warmth. The air felt too still, too perfect, as if no one had ever dared to leave a fingerprint or leave anything personal behind. The only touch of color in the room came from a small vase on the desk. It was a delicate arrangement of bright yellow cowslips, their tiny petals bright and alive against the otherwise sterile setting. She recognized them instantly, her suggestion had been right and wrong all at once. Cowslips were simple, humble flowers, but here, in this stark place, they felt misplaced, like a single flash of color in an otherwise dull world.

She wondered why Bain's boss was so difficult to impress. And for a brief, almost absurd moment, she regretted suggesting the cowslips, wishing she'd chosen something more fitting for this cold, sterile place, maybe calla lilies or wisteria. She mentally scolded herself for focusing on such trivial thoughts at a time like this.

"Have a seat," Bain's voice cut through her thoughts, and she turned to see him motioning to a white molded chair beside the desk. The chair was pristine, its sharp angles and glossy surface making it look more like a modern sculpture than a place to sit. As Niamh slid into it, her knees buckled slightly, the weight of the room's coldness making her feel small and unsteady. She quickly adjusted herself, forcing her posture straight, but the discomfort lingered.

Bain took a seat beside her, his body tense but his presence unmistakable. He wanted to reach out, to reassure her with a simple touch on her shoulder, to let her know that everything would be okay, that she'd soon be going home. But he knew she wasn't open to that. Not yet. He let his hands rest on his lap instead, his gaze flickering toward the door. "She should be here soon," he said, his voice low, almost hesitant. The words were heavy in the air, as if the very space around them had paused, waiting for the arrival of someone important.

"Who?" Niamh asked, her voice thick with confusion.

"Your mother," Bain replied, his tone flat but serious.

"My mom is here? Did you take her too?" Panic rose in her chest, making her breath catch.

"No, your other mother. Your birth mother."

Her stomach sank. Her breath stuttered, and her mind froze. He brought her to meet her birth mother. Niamh couldn't process the words, couldn't form a coherent thought. Everything seemed to whirl around her in a storm of fear and disbelief.

"The queen of hell or whatever you all call her?" Niamh snapped, the edge of sarcasm in her voice, the words coming out thick with anger and a tinge of dread.

"The Queen of Winter, but yes." Bain's voice was calm, like he was used to the confusion, maybe even the anger. "That's why I called you princess, by the way. You are a princess. The daughter of a goddess."

"She is not my mother," Niamh spat, shaking her head as her words picked up speed. "My mom is the woman who raised me. The woman who kissed boo-boos and checked for monsters in my closet. Turns out she should've been looking for my birth mother in there. She's the real monster we should've been fearing." Her voice cracked slightly on the last word.

"Fair," Bain said quietly, his gaze steady on her, though she could hear the hint of regret beneath his words. "But you should know the whole story before you judge her too much."

"You work for my birth mother?" Niamh's voice grew louder, the shock still cracking through her words. "This whole time, you've been talking about her? The flowers," she said, gesturing sharply, "were for her? Those were my favorite! Now, I have to find a new favorite. Thanks for that." Her hands trembled, frustration burning through her.

"Yes," Bain responded, his voice soft but firm, almost too calm. "But I was intrigued by you the second I met you. I would have pursued you even if your mother hadn't hired me."

"Whatever." She waved him off, her lips curling in disdain, though the flicker of something darker, something like anger and pain, shifted across her gaze. Her dark eyes gleamed with tiny flecks of red, the color glowing faintly as her emotions twisted inside her.

"It's true," Bain added, as though trying to reach through the walls she was putting up. "I know you probably don't believe me, and you have no reason to, but it's true."

Her gaze shot back to him, raw and unguarded. "What does she want from me?" The question came out sharp, biting at the air between them.

"I, I'm not sure, actually. She just said she needed to find you."

Niamh clenched her fists at her sides, her chest tightening with the weight of unanswered questions. "What do you get out of this?" she asked, voice low, almost dangerous.

"She promised me a role by her side," Bain answered, his eyes flicking to the side, as though unsure how much to reveal.

"So, you did all this in blind trust that she'd help you out?" Niamh scoffed, shaking her head in disbelief. "It's a good thing you're pretty because you are not very bright."

"We'll see," he murmured, sinking lower into his chair, discomfort radiating from him as he tried to make himself small. But it was clear to her that his words didn't sit well with him either.

After a few minutes of Niamh stewing over how angry she was, the large frosted door opened with an almost imperceptible whisper. A woman entered, her presence so striking that the air seemed to still in her wake. She was breathtakingly beautiful, with long, flowing white hair that shimmered like snow under a winter moon. Her eyes, the color of a frozen lake, held a chilling depth as though the very cold of winter resided within them. The gown she wore was an intricate masterpiece, the fabric hugging her form like a second skin. Beads, sparkling like icicles, trailed across the fabric, ringing softly as she moved. Niamh couldn't help but wonder why she was so extravagantly dressed, her intuition prickling with the sense that this was all a performance, a show of power, perhaps, or control.

"My Niamh!" The woman's voice was high-pitched, almost shrill, as she glided toward Niamh with a grace that seemed almost otherworldly. She wrapped her arms around Niamh in a sudden, forceful hug, and Niamh stood stiffly, arms slack at her sides, her heart thundering in her chest.

Pulling back, the woman held Niamh at arm's length, inspecting her with an intensity that made Niamh feel like she was being weighed and measured. "You have your father's eye," she said, her tone carrying a sharp edge. "That lovely silver one, that's from me!" She said the last part with a note of pride, her eyes gleaming as if the silver in Niamh's eye were some sort of trophy. "You can call me *Mother*."

Niamh's heart twisted at the word, bitterness flooding her throat. "I'd rather not," she shot back, her voice cold. "I already have a mom."

The woman's smile faltered for a moment, and her eyes flickered with fury. Her lips curled into a sneer, and her once-charming features took on a more menacing edge. "That woman isn't your mother," she hissed, her voice thick with contempt. As she spoke, her eyes glowed brighter, a frost settling in the air around her as her anger rose. "You were taken from me before I even got to see you. Your father stole both mine and your chance at a happy future and gave you to those… humans." She spat the last word, as though it tasted foul on her tongue, her face twisted in disgust.

The words struck Niamh like a slap, but they only solidified her resolve. "You don't get to decide what I call anyone," Niamh said, her voice steady despite the storm raging inside her. She couldn't shake the cold dread creeping down her spine, the realization that this woman had been waiting for this moment, for her, long before Niamh ever understood what was happening. "Speaking of, "her voice tinged with defiance, "where is my dear old 'dad'?"

The woman's expression darkened instantly, and her lips curled into a snarl. "Last I heard, someone was trying to vanquish him. Good riddance. He was the one who banished me to this hellhole of a dimension." Her words were sharp, filled with venom, and she spat on the floor as though the mere mention of her former lover was a bitter taste she couldn't expel fast enough.

Niamh's curiosity couldn't be contained. "Did you two ever love each other? Or was I born in some weird magical way?"

The woman seemed to savor the question, sitting slowly, her movements deliberate and dramatic. She swept her long, ice-blue gown to the side as she settled into a clear, crystalline chair that shimmered like glass, and she fluffed her silken white hair as if she were preparing to relive a cherished memory. "Once upon a time, we did love each other," she mused, her voice softening momentarily with nostalgia before turning bitter. "He stabbed me in the back and had me banished to this vile plane of my existence. I've been stuck here ever since while he roamed free, unscathed." She inhaled sharply, eyes flashing with resentment. "Let's say we parted ways and be done with that conversation."

Niamh stood silent, the weight of those words sinking in. Her mother, her *real* mother, wasn't just some estranged figure. She was filled with bitterness, rage, and a resentment so deep it could freeze a river.

"So, tell me about you," the woman continued, her voice brightening, as if the personal history had been closed for now. "What amazing powers do you have?"

Niamh frowned, suspicion creeping into her gut. "Why do you want to know?"

"Well," the woman said with a sly smile, leaning forward, her eyes sparkling with ambition, "you are the princess, my heir to the throne. I'd like to know how you can protect our kingdom."

"I want nothing to do with your throne, or your legacy, or anything else that has to do with *you*," Niamh shot back, her words firm and resolute.

The woman's eyes flashed with anger, her lips curving into a smile that didn't reach her eyes. "You may not have a choice in the matter, my dear. Not if you want to survive what's coming."

Bain stepped forward, his voice tense but respectful. "My Queen, she's very new to magic. She's still learning. Please, forgive her."

The queen scoffed, her icy gaze flickering from Bain to Niamh with disdain. "You'd take her side?" she sneered. "How did you feel knowing Bain was the one who permeated your dreams?" Her tone was dripping with malice, as if relishing in her small victory, proud to have outed him.

Bain fell silent, his shoulders tense, his expression unreadable.

Niamh turned sharply to him, her voice rising with disbelief. "You've been in my dreams on purpose? It was you all along?"

Bain hesitated, his gaze dropping. "Yes," he answered quietly. "But I only meant to open your mind to thinking of me. You didn't seem into me."

"I wasn't not into you!" Niamh shot back, her voice laced with frustration. "That's not a good way to get someone to think about you! Did you try and kill me in my dreams?"

"No!" Bain rushed to clarify, his voice cracking with sincerity. "I promise I'd never hurt you. I tried to stop it, actually. The potion she made me give you to trigger the dreams had some unforeseen side effects."

Looking at Bain, bewildered, "Wait, you gave me a potion?"

He rubbed his neck sheepishly, forgetting that he had meant to tell her that earlier. "Yeah, uh, well, I only used a little. It was a transdermal potion, so when you grabbed my hand..." he trailed off, uncomfortable with how the conversation was going. He knew it looked bad, and it was.

Niamh was fuming, she turned her body away from Bain's, refusing to look at him as he attempted to pat her leg to apologize. Her discomfort became more apparent as he went on. Luckily they were interrupted "That's your dad's doing dear. He was a weak man who could only attack people in their dreams. Apparently you inherited his weakness." The queen spoke with disgust at her father's legacy.

"I am *not* weak!" Niamh's eyes flared with an intensity that matched her words.

"That's not what I meant," Bain stammered after her mother's confession. "All we meant is that part of you is from your father, and he wasn't exactly known for being… a ray of sunshine."

"I meant what I said child" she inspected her long, pointy nails as she spoke as if they weren't interested in any of the conversation.

"I can't believe you, Bain, after all those conversations about trusting you." She thought she could feel her heart shattering as they spoke.

"Enough of this bickering, children!" The queen's voice was like a sharp blade, cutting through their conversation. She glared at them both before turning her attention fully to Niamh. "We have business to discuss. You will join me as the princess, and you will help me rule."

"I will not," Niamh declared forcefully, standing her ground despite the weight of the queen's presence.

Bain quickly interjected, trying to soften the moment. "My queen, she doesn't know what she says. Give her time to adjust."

"There is no time!" the queen snapped, her voice crackling with urgency. "I need my heir to help me rule, *We* need to use our magic together to escape this dimension."

"She's not ready for this yet, my queen," Bain protested, his tone earnest but measured. He felt a deep need to protect Niamh, he felt the queen's rage close to boiling over.

The queen's eyes flickered with disdain. "Why are you helping her? You work for *me*! I thought you were an opportunist, Bain. You disappoint me." Her voice dripped with condescension, each word laced with power.

"I'm not taking sides," Bain replied, his voice steadier now. "I did my job and brought her to you. I just want you to see how amazing she's turned out to be. She has something special about her."

The queen's eyes narrowed, her gaze sharp and calculating. "You think she's special, huh?" She cocked her head, considering him with a predatory intensity.

His voice now tinged with desperation. "Just give her a chance."

"Oh, I don't give chances." The queen's lips twisted into a cruel smile. "I expect people to bow to me as their queen."

Niamh's fists clenched at her sides, her voice low but dripping with defiance. "You are not my queen."

The queen's eyes flared with frozen fury, her icy exterior cracking, revealing a core of rage. The air around her seemed to grow colder, her power swelling like a storm about to break.

Bain stepped forward, his gaze steady despite the tension in the room. "She didn't mean that," he said, his tone soft but firm. "Let me take her back, and you two can slowly get to know each other over time. There's no need for this to go any further."

For a moment, the queen stood still, her fury palpable. Then, with a deep breath, she turned her eyes back to Niamh, her expression unreadable.

"I don't want time," the queen shot back, her voice firm and unwavering. "All I have is time. What I want is for my family to respect me." The queen's lips twisted into a sneer.

"Respect is earned. You've done nothing to earn my respect." The words felt liberating as they left her mouth. For once, she was saying exactly what was on her mind, unfiltered. All the years of silence, of accepting the cruelty and manipulation, were gone. She was done being used.

The queen's icy fingers shot out to grab Niamh's arm, but before she could make contact, Bain surged forward, pushing the queen aside with an unexpected burst of strength. The queen's eyes blazed with fury, her voice like a whip. "You dare to go against me?" she hissed. "Bain, I thought you knew who was more powerful here."

Niamh barely noticed the sting of the queen's talon-like nails as they grazed her arm. She looked down, seeing a small scratch weeping blood. She wrapped her other hand around the wound, trying to stanch the flow, but the pain was secondary to the chaos unfolding around her.

"You are most powerful, My Queen," Bain said, his voice a mixture of respect and defiance. "But I respect Niamh. She's loyal, honest, trustworthy… and worth saving from your evil hands."

The queen's lips curled into a cruel smile, her eyes glowing with an eerie coldness. "Why, you little," she hissed, her voice thick with venom. Without another word, she lifted her hands, her fingers snapping in the air like a storm gathering force. A blast of cold wind ripped through the room, slamming Bain against the stone wall with an almost unnatural force. The explosion knocked the wind out of Niamh. As she gasped, trying to sort out her surroundings, she noticed Bain slumped against the wall.

The queen exhaled, a bitter gust of frost rushing from her lips. Bain's skin started transforming, turned an unnatural shade of icy blue, the crystals forming around his eyes and mouth like delicate frostbite. He gasped, struggling to breathe as the cold continued to suffocate him.

"No!" Niamh cried, her heart pounding. Panic surged through her, and her hands scrambled over Bain's body, searching for the vial he always carried. She had seen him use it before, small glass bottles filled with a magical substance that allowed him to transport them out of danger. Her fingers closed around one in his pocket, and with a sharp twist, she tore it free.

Without a moment's hesitation, she hurled the vial into the air, shattering it against the stone floor. A blinding white circle of light appeared in front of her, the portal swirling with energy. Niamh didn't hesitate, she threw herself against Bain, her muscles straining as she used her full weight to drag him toward the circle. His body felt impossibly heavy, frozen in place by the queen's magic.

With a cry of exertion, she pulled him through, her strength fueled by sheer desperation. She didn't care where they landed, only that they were far away from the queen, from her cruelty, from the suffocating cold that threatened to consume them both.

Instinctively, Niamh kept pulling his limp body, dragging him across the rough, uneven cement ground, no longer on the smooth marble floor that had been their prison just moments ago. The sudden shift in terrain jolted her, but she didn't stop. She couldn't stop. It was only when she paused, gasping for breath, that she realized they were no longer in the queen's cruel realm. They were somewhere else, somewhere far from the hell they had just escaped.

Chapter 15

Niamh dropped to the ground beside Bain, her hands shaking as they reached for him. His lips, once full of warmth and color, were now an unnatural shade of blue. His eyes, the brilliant cerulean she had come to trust, were fading, shifting into a lifeless, sickly gray.

Panic gripped her heart like an icy vise. *No, no, this can't be happening.* He had defended her. He had protected her from that horrible woman. Bain had stood between her and certain death. He had saved her life. And now, he was slipping away.

Tears began to pour down her face, hot and fast, dripping onto his cold, motionless form. The shock of everything that had transpired, everything that had happened so quickly, left her mind reeling. She didn't know what to do, where to go, or how to save him. All she could do was bury her face in his chest, the steady rhythm of his heart barely audible under the cold. She sobbed for a moment, letting herself fall apart, feeling his frozen body beneath her fingertips. It wasn't enough to make the pain go away, but it was all she could do.

When the sobs subsided, she pulled away, her eyes red and swollen. She looked at him, her breath hitching in her throat as she saw where her tears had fallen on his skin. The ice crystals on his face began to melt, but instead of returning to normal, the areas where her tears had touched him were turning an unnatural, sickly pink, further highlighting the bluish tint of his skin around them. Her heart sank.

He's not going to make it, is he?

Her gut twisted, a gut-deep certainty that he was fading fast, and there was nothing she could do to save him. She couldn't lose him, not like this. Not after everything. Her mind raced, desperately grasping for some answer, some way to stop this, some way to undo the damage the queen had done, the damage Bain had taken for her. She had to save him. She had to.

With trembling hands, she pulled him closer, not knowing what else to do but unwilling to let go of him, even if the world itself was crumbling around them.

A gust of wind behind her cut through the stillness, drawing Niamh's attention. She turned, seeing Aoife and Nick stepping through the portal. Nick moved quickly, kneeling beside Bain, his hands hovering over him, inspecting the damage. Aoife closed the portal circle behind them, her eyes darting around the unfamiliar surroundings.

"We've been looking for you! Are you okay?" Aoife's voice was soft but urgent as she slid onto the cold pavement next to Niamh.

"I'm... I'm okay," Niamh replied, her voice shaky. Her breath caught in her throat as she glanced at Bain. She couldn't bring herself to speak anymore, the lump in her throat growing with every breath.

Nick's gaze softened as he gently placed his hand on her shoulder. "What happened?" he asked quietly, his voice careful, not wanting to startle her.

"The Queen... my... my mother tried to kill me, I think." Niamh's voice broke as she spoke the words she never thought she'd have to say. "But Bain jumped in front of it."

Aoife and Nick exchanged a look, one filled with silent understanding, but Niamh couldn't shake the feeling that they were speaking a language she didn't understand. She hated that. She hated being kept in the dark, especially when it came to her own life.

"Let's get him back to K Corp. The witches can help; I'm sure of it," Aoife said, her voice steady and hopeful.

"He wouldn't survive the move," Nick replied solemnly, his voice tinged with sorrow.

Niamh's chest tightened. "I can't just let him die. I would be dead if it wasn't for him." Her voice wavered, the weight of her words pressing down on her. Bain had sacrificed everything for her, and she couldn't just let him slip away. She wouldn't. Not like this.

"Your heat, Niamh," Aoife said urgently. "Use your heat to warm him."

"I don't know how to control it," Niamh said, her voice trembling with fear. "I'm afraid I'd burn him, kill him by accident."

"He's fading away anyway," Aoife said, her words hitting Niamh like a sharp jab to the chest. "It's worth a try. If we move him in the state he's in, he'll most likely die."

The word *die* hung in the air like a heavy cloud, and Niamh felt her heart falter. She knew the truth in Aoife's words but hearing them spoken aloud made it feel all the more real.

For a long moment, Niamh was paralyzed with fear, but then, something in her shifted. Aoife was right. She couldn't just sit there and watch him fade away. She had to try.

Without another word, Niamh leaned over Bain, her body trembling as she touched her chest to his. The cold radiating off him was like ice seeping into her very bones. She imagined the cold entering her, spreading through her own body, and in return, she would give him her warmth. She could feel her own energy pulsing within her, the heat flowing from her core. She focused, willing herself to control the heat, to direct it into him without letting it flare into flames.

With every breath, she exhaled warmth, the heat rolling off her in gentle waves. Her hands moved over Bain's cold arms, rubbing them softly, trying to bring him back. She focused on warmth, on light, on the feeling of the sun against her skin. She thought of safety, of home, of the things that made her feel alive and whole.

She lost herself in the rhythm of it, her mind focused solely on Bain. But then, a hand touched her back. The touch was gentle but firm, and it sent a jolt of surprise through her. She snapped her head around, her heart skipping a beat.

Aoife and Nick were standing at Bain's feet. Aoife was wrapped in Nick's arms, her tears streaking down her face, but neither of them had touched her. The hand that had rested on her back was cold. So cold.

It was Bain's hand.

Niamh's breath caught in her throat. She looked down, her eyes wide with disbelief. Bain's fingers twitched slightly, the movement slow but undeniable. His once lifeless body was now responding to her heat. His skin, still pale, was no longer as frigid.

He wasn't gone. Not yet. He was still with her.

The wave of relief that washed over Niamh was overwhelming. She collapsed beside him, her hands shaking as she continued to radiate heat, her heart pounding in her chest. He was alive. And he was fighting. They both were.

Bain's breath was slow, still coming in ragged gasps, but there was something almost magical about how his body was responding. Slowly, as if testing the waters, the color in his lips deepened, returning to a light pink, still not quite as vibrant as his usual color, but closer. His eyes, once a dull gray, flickered with the faintest hint of cerulean, but with specks of white scattered throughout, resembling stars on a pale blue sky. It was a sign. He was coming back.

Then, as though his body had gathered strength, his hand moved. The chilled fingers gently traced Niamh's cheek, skimming along her smile line before they brushed over her lips. The sensation made her shiver, but not from the cold. Her breath caught in her throat. The moment felt suspended in time, his touch a silent promise, a gentle apology, a reminder of how close they had come to losing each other.

Niamh closed her eyes, savoring the tender touch. The knot of guilt in her chest, the fear of losing him, started to melt away, replaced by something warmer. Something lighter. Optimism. Euphoria. She wasn't sure which emotion she was feeling more intensely, but for the first time since everything had spiraled out of control, she felt a glimmer of peace.

Bain's fingers slid to the back of her neck, pulling her closer until their lips met. The kiss was frantic, born from fear and longing, the raw emotion of almost losing one another pressing against their lips. His hand roamed across her shoulder and back, grasping at her like he was trying to pull her even closer, to solidify the reality of her being there, of her safety.

But Niamh pulled away, her breath shallow as she leaned back, forcing herself to collect her thoughts. Bain lay there, panting, his eyes wide with need, silently pleading for her to come back to him, to keep kissing him. She couldn't, not yet. There were things left unsaid, things she needed to hear from him.

He spoke first, his voice hoarse, almost breaking under the weight of his regret. "I am so sorry, Niamh. I didn't know she'd try and hurt you. I thought she just wanted to meet you. That's how she explained it to me. I… I didn't know." His words were sincere, but there was an ache in them, the kind that came from realizing how much damage had already been done.

Niamh's voice came soft but steady. "I believe you." It was all she could say, and it felt like enough for now.

"If I could go back and do it all differently, I would," Bain continued, his words raw and regretful. He sounded as though he would have given up anything to turn back time, to change what had happened.

Niamh didn't respond right away. Her silence hung between them like a fragile thread, the air thick with the weight of what they had both just survived.

Finally, Bain spoke again, his voice softer, almost reverent. "Everything I said in there is true. I think the world of you. You are kind and compassionate and have the biggest heart I've ever witnessed. And… I think you're the most beautiful creature I've ever laid eyes on."

The sincerity in his words struck deep, too deep, and it was as though her heart cracked wide open. Tears welled in her eyes, brimming with emotion she couldn't control.

And then it hit her, the anger, the frustration, the heartbreak. The realization that Bain's actions, no matter how well-intentioned, had robbed her of the chance to have her own happy beginning with him.

"Damn you, Bain!" she screamed, her fists pounding against his chest with all the frustration and grief she couldn't keep inside anymore. "Damn you for doing all this! Why couldn't you have let our romance flourish in its own time? You stole our… my chance at happiness! Damn you!"

She hit him again, her tears now mingling with the rage that burned inside her. She needed to scream, needed to get it out. Bain didn't fight back. He didn't pull away. Instead, he calmly reached out, gently taking her wrists, holding them still against his chest. The action, so tender, made her collapse into him, her body trembling with the weight of everything she had been holding in. He would have sat there all day and let her work out her frustration, but he knew there was more to it. He knew he'd hurt her; she'd trusted him, and he broke that. He broke her heart.

She cried. She cried for the loss of the dream they had almost shared, for the reality that their love had been thrust into something neither of them had been ready for. She cried for the future she had wanted, the one she'd dreamed of, and the pain of having it torn away before it could even begin.

Bain let her cry. He didn't speak, didn't try to make it better or erase her pain. He just let her feel everything she needed to feel, and at that moment, Niamh realized that he wasn't trying to fix her, he was just there. And that, in itself, was something she needed more than she realized.

Lost in her grief, she didn't realize when Bain's grip went slack on her wrists. Not until his fingers slid from hers, hitting the ground loosely. His eyes still showed empathy, but his pink skin tone was being taken over by a blue hue. She then noticed the ice growing around them as if it were alive.

Niamh's heart raced as she watched the ice creep closer to Bain, its cold tendrils wrapped around his boot, slowly freezing it to the ground. His scream of pain sent a sharp pang through her chest. She was in too much shock to know what to do, but she knew she had to do something. There was no time to think, just act.

With trembling hands, she tried to pry his leg free from the ice. She could feel Bain's pain, his struggle. Though weak as he was, he still fought. He was fighting to survive, but also fighting for her; he knew she wouldn't be the same if she saw him die like that. He couldn't let that happen to her.

Bain's breath came in sharp gasps, his body stiff with the cold. The sight of him so vulnerable, struggling under the weight of the magic she knew was coming from her mother, made her feel helpless. But she couldn't give in to that feeling. Not now.

"Hold on," she whispered, more to herself than to him, as her hands found the edges of his boot, trying to loosen the ice, to break the bond between him and the frozen ground. But it was no use. The ice was too strong, and her strength alone wouldn't be enough.

Aoife's voice rang out through the storm. "Niamh, we need to stop this before it gets worse! If we can't get him free from the ice, the cold will kill him!"

Her stomach dropped at Aoife's words, the severity of the situation hitting her like a freight train. She could feel the ground beneath them tremble with the weight of her mother's wrath.

Niamh's mind raced. She needed to think. She had magic. She *was* magic. The magic called to her, begging her to let it out. She'd worked so hard on ignoring it all her life, she hadn't realized how strong she felt it.

Her chest tightened, and she focused on her breath, imagining the fire within her being channeled outward towards the man who'd taken everything from her but also given her every reason to live too. She pushed the heat out of her body, picturing it wrapping around people like a warm blanket. Keeping the frigid cold at bay. Hoping it was enough.

The air around them shimmered, the temperature rising for the first time in what felt like an eternity. Bain's body relaxed. He wasn't in visible pain anymore. She held her breath as she waited for a more definite sign that she did the right thing. But there was nothing, just the roaring wind and pelting ice from the storm still brewing behind them.

A tear slipped down her cheek, unbidden. Niamh tried to hold them back, to cling to the last shred of strength she thought she had, but it was futile. The fear clawing at her chest was too much, too heavy. She wasn't strong enough, not now, not anymore.

More tears followed, tracing hot, stinging paths down her face. She closed her eyes tightly, as though shutting out the world could somehow erase the pain. She wanted to unsee him, his beautiful, infuriating face burned into her memory. But it was no use. He was everywhere, lingering in the corners of her mind, the spark he'd forced into her heart refusing to fade.

When a hand brushed her cheek, wiping the tears away with a touch so gentle it made her breath hitch, her body froze. She gasped, her chest tightening, too afraid to open her eyes.

"Look at me," he demanded, his voice raw and trembling.

She shook her head, her lips pressing into a thin line as more tears slipped through her lashes. She couldn't. She *wouldn't.*

She was scared. Scared that it really was him, standing there so steady, so alive, with that insufferable mixture of confidence and vulnerability. If it was him, she'd have to admit the truth she'd been shoving down, deeper and deeper with every interaction: she was starting to fall for him. That thought terrified her more than anything.

But she was equally terrified that it wasn't him. That it was some cruel trick, another of her mother's games. That when she opened her eyes, she'd find nothing but a hollow illusion designed to break her completely. To shatter her heart and leave her soul irreparably scarred.

Every possibility was terrifying, and she felt trapped in the moment, unable to move forward, unable to pull back.

"Please." His voice softened, breaking through her spiraling fear, carrying a weight that felt almost unbearable.

Releasing her breath, she hadn't realized she'd been holding, she slowly opened her eyes. Her heart threatened to beat out of her chest. Silver blue eyes looked back at her, his full lips now a sickly shade of grey moved into a weak smile. He wiped more tears away from her cheek with the back of his hand, his skin was so cold against hers. She knew he wasn't out of the woods yet. She knew he wanted to send her a sign that he was still fighting, though.

It was all he could muster, but he wanted her to know he was okay. She brought his hand up to her mouth, laying gentle kisses ferociously across it. As if each kiss would warm his body, she wanted to give him every ounce of love she had, with it, every bit of heat she had.

The storm still brewed behind them, the wind whipping Bain's hair around his face. It brought Niamh back to reality. He wasn't out of the woods yet.

She gave his hand one last kiss, then steadied herself on her feet. Rage burned deep inside her. How could her mother hate her own daughter so much? How could she have tried to kill her and almost kill the man she loves? She already knew that woman was not the mother she'd hoped for, but now she'd shown her repeatedly that Niamh was just a tool to get what she wanted. She never cared for Niamh, never loved her, not really. She loved power; Niamh was just something to be used to gain more power.

She turned to Aoife, who was still struggling to maintain the portal, the gold light flickering with every icy blast that hit it. "We can't keep this up for much longer. We need to stop her!"

Aoife nodded, her face set with determination. "I know, but I can't hold the portal forever with this much pressure. We need to get Bain out of here, and we need to do it now."

The air thickened with the storm's suffocating weight, crackling with unspent energy. The ground trembled beneath them, a warning of the chaos building above. Around them, the ice was beginning to refreeze, creeping closer with each passing second, sharp and unrelenting.

But Niamh wasn't done. Not yet.

She'd had enough of running, of cowering, of being powerless. Her magic surged inside her, roaring like a firestorm, no longer willing to be contained. She felt the heat rising, the flames licking at her anger as if begging for release. This time, she wouldn't hold back.

Fixing her gaze on the storm's icy heart, she called to the red flame deep within her, fanning it with all the rage and defiance burning in her chest. It leapt eagerly, feeding on the kindling of her emotions. With a scream that tore from her very core, she unleashed it.

The blazing red ball shot into the sky, cutting through the freezing air with molten fury. Snowflakes sizzled and evaporated as they met the heat, droplets of water falling in their wake.

The explosion hit its target with a deafening roar. The ground beneath her feet bucked wildly, sending small pebbles skittering into the air. A burst of fiery red streaked across the stormy sky, spreading in violent, swirling waves of crimson. The fire twisted and churned, colliding with the cold white fury of the storm. It was as if the elements themselves were locked in battle, fire and ice waging war in the atmosphere.

Niamh stood mesmerized, her breath stolen by the chaos she had created. Her little flame, *her* flame, had turned the tide. The beauty of it, the power of it, held her captive.

"Go!" Aoife's sharp, commanding voice jolted her out of her daze. "We need to move, *now!*"

The snowflakes and hail pounding the earth were replaced by heavy droplets of water, the sky an angry clash of red and white, neither element giving way.

As they ran, a fierce pride ignited in Niamh's chest. Part of her reveled in the damage she had caused, in the chaos she had unleashed on her birth mother's storm. For the first time, she felt like she was reclaiming a piece of herself, one that had been stolen long ago.

Her steps quickened, and though fear still clung to the edges of her mind, something else burned brighter now. *Hope.*

Aoife pulled her hands further apart, her fingers trembling as she widened the shimmering portal. The golden cyclone swirled violently, throwing off sparks of light that danced against the chaos around them. She groaned with effort, her face tight with concentration as she fought to keep it stable. Gritting her teeth, she nodded sharply toward Niamh, her silent command clear.

Niamh's heart thundered in her chest, the sound deafening in her ears. She didn't hesitate. Rushing to Bain, she slid an arm around his shoulders, pulling him to his feet. His weight bore down on her as he leaned heavily against her, his body still weak from whatever torment he'd endured.

But in his eyes, those tired, stormy eyes, there was something more. A spark. A flicker of hope that hadn't been there before.

"Come on," she whispered, her voice steady despite the whirlwind of fear and adrenaline coursing through her. "We're almost there."

The moment they stepped through the portal, the world of ice and fury vanished behind them, swallowed by the golden light. The raging storm, the relentless cold, it all fell away, replaced by the stillness of a new, safer place. But Niamh's heart refused to calm. She knew it wasn't over. Not by a long shot. Her mother would come for her, for them, and next time, they needed to be ready.

People in lab coats rushed toward them the instant they arrived. The blur of movement was disorienting as they took Bain from her, gently but firmly guiding him onto a waiting gurney. Monitors beeped to life as they hooked him up to IVs and sensors with practiced precision. At the same time, members of the coven surrounded him, laying crystals in a meticulous pattern around his body and beginning to chant.

It all happened so fast, a whirlwind of activity that left Niamh standing frozen, dazed, watching as they worked to stabilize Bain. Her emotions teetered on the edge of chaos, the fire within her still smoldering with anger and confusion.

Through the tangle of bodies surrounding him, Bain's gaze found hers. Despite the weakness in his features, he searched for her with a quiet desperation, as though grounding himself in her presence. Their eyes met for only a moment, but it sent a wave of emotion crashing over her. She couldn't hold it back anymore.

Niamh's chest tightened, her breath shallow and uneven as the enormity of everything pressed down on her. She had saved him, dragged him back from the brink of death, but nothing felt settled. Everything was spiraling out of control. The fire that had fueled her, that had burned so brightly in her anger, now felt like a restless ember, dampened by the icy reality of their situation.

Her hands trembled as she tried to steady herself, searching the room for something, *someone*, to anchor her.

Aoife was there, at her side, her hand slipping into Niamh's with a reassuring squeeze. Niamh turned her gaze to her friend, who was watching her with calm, determined eyes. That simple touch steadied her, grounding her in the midst of the chaos unraveling around them.

"Breathe," Aoife murmured, her voice low and steady. "You're okay. He's okay. Just breathe."

And for a moment, Niamh let herself believe it.

Aoife's calm presence helped, but Niamh's thoughts kept swirling back to her mother. The storm, the ice, Cailleach's wrath- it all seemed so personal, so deeply rooted in the hatred her mother had for her. Niamh wasn't sure what to do anymore. She had known from the beginning that she was caught in the middle of something much larger than herself, but now that she had seen the extent of her mother's fury, it felt suffocating.

"She won't stop, will she?" Niamh asked quietly, her voice shaky despite the resolve in her tone.

Aoife squeezed her hand again, her eyes full of understanding. "No, she won't. But that doesn't mean you have to face her alone."

Niamh nodded, her thoughts a tangled mess of anger and uncertainty. She had been thrust into this battle, and now there was no going back. Her heat had saved Bain, but it was a double-edged sword. What would happen if she couldn't control it? What if Bain resented her for saving him? What if she lost herself in the power, became more like her mother than she ever intended? The guilt from earlier, the confusion about Bain's intentions, everything felt like too much to carry.

But she wasn't alone. She couldn't forget that. Aoife, Nick, and Lidia were with her, and Bain, he had risked his life for her. He had been the one to shield her from the storm, the one to face her mother's wrath head-on. He had shown her a side of himself she hadn't expected. Even though she was torn, she couldn't ignore the way he looked at her. The way he cared. It was different from everything she'd expected from him. Maybe it wasn't too late to see what they could be, but the uncertainty gnawed at her.

As they wheeled Bain into a separate room, Niamh lingered for a moment, her gaze meeting his. He smiled weakly at her, and for a brief second, she saw a flicker of the connection they had shared in the midst of the chaos. His eyes, despite the pain, were still full of warmth, and that gave her a small sense of hope.

As they left the lab, Aoife led her down the hallway into silence, a drastic change from the lab they were just in. She could see the well-oiled machine that is K Corp and their medical team working efficiently to stabilize Bain, the low hum and beeping of machines, the background noise of the medical team talking with each other over him. They were doing everything they could, but the tension in the air was thick. The worst wasn't over. It wouldn't be until her mother was dealt with.

"I'll be here when you wake up," Niamh whispered softly, more to herself than to him.

Aoife gently tugged on her hand, guiding her toward a nearby seat. "He's in good hands, Niamh. He'll pull through."

Niamh sat down, her mind racing. "I don't know what to do, Aoife. I feel like I'm being torn in a million directions. I'm so angry, and I don't even know where to focus that anger. I'm scared that I'm losing control of everything."

Aoife sat beside her, her posture relaxed, but there was an intensity in her eyes that told Niamh she wasn't alone in her struggle. "Anger is a natural response to what you've been through. But you don't have to let it define you. You control your power, not the other way around."

"I don't know if I can control it," Niamh admitted, her voice tinged with fear. "Every time I use it, it feels like I'm about to explode. What if I hurt someone? What if I hurt Bain?"

Aoife's expression softened, and she placed a hand on Niamh's shoulder. "You've already proven you can control it. You saved Bain. You didn't burn him up, you didn't destroy everything around you. You used your magic when it mattered most. And you have people here who'll help you learn to control it, to shape it into what you need it to be. You're not alone in this."

The words were comforting, but Niamh's mind still buzzed with worry. "But how do I fight my mother? She's too powerful."

Aoife took a deep breath. "We don't have to face her directly just yet. We'll figure out how to protect you, how to keep you safe until you're ready. There's a way through this, Niamh. And we'll find it."

Niamh looked at her, feeling the weight of the promise in Aoife's words. For the first time in a long while, she let herself believe that maybe, just maybe, they could win this fight.

With Bain's recovery underway and Aoife by her side, she had a sliver of hope to hold onto. But the storm wasn't over yet. Cailleach would come again. And Niamh would be ready.

"You have had a very, very long day. Why don't you take a rest? Your room is ready for you whenever you are. You should go visit Lidia too, she's been asking about you. We kept her here until we were sure she was out of danger." She paused. "If you're having trouble calming your mind after the day, I highly recommend taking a swim or just sitting in the hot tub. It does wonders for the body and mind. It's one of my favorite things here." She said with a wink and left her with a gentle hug.

"Thanks… for everything, Aoife." She managed a small, half-hearted smile.

"Hey, you did a great job today. You should be proud of yourself. You were very brave."

Niamh scoffed. "I don't feel very brave. I didn't do anything to stop that evil witch."

Aoife put a hand on Niamh's shoulder. "She's very powerful; stopping her would be extremely hard. But you stood up to her and used your powers for good. That alone is something to celebrate. Not many people, especially new to magic, would be able to resist the pull of power."

Niamh just nodded, appreciating the compliment but not knowing how to respond. She wove her way down hallways hoping she chose the right ones, the elevator ahead made her sigh in relief. She was almost back to her room where she could have a breakdown, and no one would know.

The shower washed off the now-dried blood from the cut on her arm, washed off the remaining scent of Bain's Jasmine cologne off her body and out of her mind, and washed away the lingering hopes of meeting her birth mother for the first time. She needed a clear head when she visited Lidia. She was worried her best friend would hate her, she wouldn't blame her if she did. It was her fault she was in danger.

Chapter 16

Dread set in as she stood outside of Lidia's room; her heart was beating so quickly, it felt like hummingbird wings, her stomach was full of butterflies, and her mind went to dark possibilities of what could be to come. She was trying to work up the nerve to knock on the door when it opened in front of her. Lidia stood, straight faced, blocking the door frame. She couldn't read Lidia's emotion; her heart was about to shatter. She felt bad news coming. She braced for impact. But an embrace is what she got instead. Lidia hugged her so tightly that she struggled to breathe.

In dismay, Niamh stood with her arms at her sides while Lidia cried into her neck. It took her a few moments to realize her friend wasn't mad at her, or if she was, at least right at that second, she wasn't. Finally wrapping her arms around Lidia felt like home. Her resolve shattered, the tears streamed down her face as her legs gave way, and she crumbled. They sat in a heap on the floor. Lidia held Niamh tightly until they both gathered enough composure for Niamh to stand on her own again.

As Niamh gently pushed their shoulders away so she could look at her best friend again; Lidia slapped Niamh's arm, "Bitch, I thought you were dead!"

Niamh laughed and cried at the same time, wincing at the pain that shot through her as she slapped her cut, not knowing it was there. "I thought you were, too. Luckily, neither of us are."

"Come in. Why are you just standing there?"

"You were blocking the door."

"Oh… yeah. Sorry"

Lidia sat cross-legged on the plush bed and pulled a pillow to her lap to hug it. Niamh reluctantly sat on the edge of the bed, still not fully feeling confident her friend had forgiven her.

"Are… are you okay?" Niamh reluctantly asked, not fully sure if she was prepared for the answer.

"Oh yeah, I'm fine. How are you, though? They wouldn't tell me anything!" she said, surprisingly upbeat.

"I'm okay. Still digesting everything that happened. He took me to meet my mother." She looked up through her lashes to see Lidia's reaction.

"Like your birth mother? Oh my god, how was it? I mean, what was she like?"

"She was… a lot. She wanted me to take over her kingdom with her. I'm apparently a princess." She sat up straighter and did a princess wave as they always did when they pretended to be famous; it made Lidia laugh.

"Are you okay?"

"I'm fine. Just a little confused, disappointed, angry. there's a lot of emotions right now."

"Understandable."

"I knew you were always special. But you didn't need that title to make you important, you know." She paused. "So, are you going to go with her, wherever she is?" She was afraid to ask that question, for fear that Niamh would want to go and be the princess she was meant to be. She deserved to be in a place where she was appreciated and cherished, not feared and hated.

"No, I don't want anything to do with that woman. I tried telling her no, but she wasn't having it and tried to kill me!"

"What? Apparently, she needed more mommy and me classes, huh?" She tried to make a joke to lighten the mood. Lidia's heart broke for Niamh. The first time meeting her birth mother and she tried to kill her? Niamh used to make up stories and pretend what her birth mother would be like; that was never one of the scenarios, though.

"She's definitely not winning any 'Mother of the Year' awards."

"Well, I'm glad you're okay!"

"I wouldn't have been if it wasn't for Bain."

"Bain? Like the Bain that had you and me?"

"One and the same. He jumped in front of me and took the hit for me."

Lidia's eyes went wide at the revelation. She'd suspected there was more to the story, but hearing it confirmed made her heart twist. She'd never fully believed Bain was as bad as everyone thought. There had to be something more to him.

"As far as kidnappers go, he wasn't too bad. For me, at least. I don't know what he was like with you, but he was a perfect gentleman with me. I imagined being stuck in a trunk or chained up in a basement, but he put me in a hotel room and ordered room service. I wouldn't call it kidnapping, more of a vacation." Lidia sat back dramatically, mimicking a lounge chair pose, complete with an imaginary drink in her hand.

Niamh couldn't respond immediately, her mind processing everything she'd just heard. "You were in a hotel? Like a one-star, roach-infested kind?"

"No, like an expensive, granite-floor, king-bed kind with 1,000-thread-count sheets." Lidia grinned.

"Huh. I wasn't expecting that," Niamh said, stretching out on the bed, face down, arms crossed under her head.

"Girl, me neither! It was like a vacation other than worrying about you."

"You were worried about me?" Niamh asked, glancing over.

"Well, yeah. He said he needed to take you somewhere and that I needed to stay there for our safety. He said that if I was safe, you wouldn't worry about me." Lidia's voice softened. "Do you think he meant to hurt you?"

"No, actually, he treated me well, too. I don't think he ever intended for me to get hurt. I kind of grew to like him, as hard as I tried not to, because who kidnaps someone to get a promotion?"

"Mobsters," Lidia said with a smirk.

"True. But what are the chances of it happening to someone like us?"

"Apparently, not zero!" Lidia burst into laughter.

"Right?" Niamh laughed along, her chest feeling lighter than it had in days. She rolled over onto her back to stare up at the ceiling, letting the sound of their laughter fill the room.

"Girl, you fell for him? The whole kidnapping thing didn't turn you off?" Lidia asked with a teasing smile.

"I mean, I didn't love being forced to go with him, but he went above and beyond to get things he thought I'd like. He never tried anything inappropriate. He never hurt me or did anything weird. He didn't even seem like he was trying to brainwash me or anything. If it wasn't for the kidnapping part, it would have been a great date! We went to a cabin in the woods, had great food and wine… too much wine, and I passed out on the couch. I woke up wrapped in a blanket, and he was sitting there, looking like a god by the fireplace. It wasn't all bad, I guess." Niamh couldn't help but smile at the memory.

"Stockholm syndrome much?" Lidia raised an eyebrow, a mischievous glint in her eye.

Niamh threw her head back in laughter, "No. This isn't that. Don't make it weird."

Lidia shrugged, a smile playing on her lips. "He was a nice guy before all this. He didn't do anything weird or violent. Maybe he had good intentions but just went about it the wrong way." She paused, her expression turning more serious. "What happens now?"

Niamh exhaled slowly, her gaze dropping to her hands. She wasn't sure. Not yet. "I'm not sure, really."

"Hey, you have blood on your sleeve."

She looked down at the dots of dark red on her shirt, surprised that the tiny cut was still bleeding. "Oh, it's nothing. I got a scratch."

"Hm, keep an eye on that."

"Yes, mother."

They both went silent then looked at each other and burst out into laughter, the word 'mother' would never feel the same to them.

There was a brief pause in the conversation. "Hey, Aoife said the pool here is great. I can't sleep yet. Care to go for a swim?"

"Sure. Why not? I saw a few swimsuits in the drawer when I was snooping around." Lidia opened the drawer, tossing a one-piece suit toward Niamh and saving the two-piece for herself. She knew Niamh wouldn't want to wear the two-piece.

Their laughter filled the halls as they walked toward the pool, the weight of their day lightened for a moment. It was hard to believe that just hours ago, they had been wrapped in chaos, kidnapping, meeting her birth mother, and narrowly avoiding death. The usual scent of chlorine wasn't there. Instead, the fresh, salty air of the sea greeted them, and for a fleeting second, the world felt normal again.

They placed their towels on lounge chairs near the pool, and Lidia broke the silence. "So... have you seen or talked to Bain yet?"

"No! Why would I?"

"Um, because he saved you? You're not the least bit curious about him?"

"I'm trying not to think about it." In truth, it was all she had been thinking about. He'd crept into her mind every few seconds, no matter how much she tried to push him out. She hadn't succeeded.

"And how's that going?" Lidia asked, raising an eyebrow.

"Not well," Niamh admitted, burying her face in her hands. Lidia laughed, and Niamh couldn't help but smile in response.

"Well, whatever you decide, I got your back."

"Thanks, Lidia. Now, can we please stop saying his name? My brain needs a Bain break."

"That's a tongue twister, but you got it." Lidia winked, following it with a cheesy finger gun. Niamh couldn't help but smile more at her antics.

Niamh stepped slowly into the pool, allowing the cool water to soothe her as she submerged past the angry scratch on her arm from earlier. She winced as the salty water stung the wound. Lidia, on the other hand, was more daring, cannonballing into the pool with a splash that sent water flying in every direction. She flipped her wet hair toward Niamh, a playful gesture that always seemed to lift her spirits.

"Thanks." Niamh's voice was soft as she watched Lidia's cheerful energy.

She couldn't shake the guilt, the feeling that everything they had gone through was her fault.

"You know I always have your back," Lidia said firmly, her tone sincere.

"No, I mean it. Thanks for everything. Thanks for not hating me for putting you in danger. Thanks for not freaking out about all this. And especially, thanks for being my friend." Niamh's eyes shimmered with gratitude, the weight of her emotions breaking through.

Lidia blinked, her own eyes softening. "Are you kidding? I should be thanking you! You make my life so much better. I couldn't imagine not having you in my life."

That made Niamh's eyes well up, the overwhelming love and appreciation for her friend settling in her chest like a comforting weight.

"Girl, don't you start crying, or I'm gonna start crying, and we both know I'm an ugly crier. Don't do that to me." Lidia's words pulled a laugh from Niamh, who knew full well that Lidia didn't do anything ugly.

But still, Niamh couldn't fight the tears, her heart swelling with gratitude for the unwavering friendship Lidia had given her. The world seemed a little less heavy with her by her side.

The door to the pool room swung open with a soft squeak, drawing their attention. Nick held the door open as Aoife slipped past him, her fingers brushing his silver-streaked beard as she grinned up at him. Aoife's gaze quickly swept over the women already in the pool. "Hey, do you want some privacy? We can come back later."

"Oh, no. Please join us," Niamh said, waving them over with a smile.

Aoife grabbed Nick's hand, pulling him along as she picked up speed and jumped into the pool, hauling Nick along with her. The splash echoed through the room as they surfaced, both laughing. Niamh watched them, a small pang of envy in her chest. They were so effortlessly happy together. Niamh had only ever had a few relationships, all short-lived and strained by the constant stares and whispered comments about her appearance.

"So, how are you adjusting here, Niamh?" Nick asked, his voice warm and understanding.

"Well, everyone is very nice," Niamh said, floating on her back. "I'm just still trying to wrap my head around all this. This place, all the different things I've seen since I've been here, and the fact that my birth mother tried to kill me. It's been… a lot, to say the least." She sighed, the weight of it all pressing down on her.

Aoife's voice softened. "I get it. This place was completely overwhelming for me at first, too. But then I found my strength, and I knew I belonged here. I knew I could help people. It just felt like home quickly." Nick glanced at her, his eyes bright with pride as a grin spread across his face.

"We don't want you to feel pressured to stay here or do anything," Nick added. "We just want you to be able to protect yourself so you can live the life you choose. We'll always be here for you, no matter what. Even if you choose to go somewhere else, we're a safe haven for people and creatures affected by magic. And that goes for you too, Lidia. If you ever need us, just call." His words were firm and reassuring, offering comfort with every syllable.

"Thanks, Nick, that's nice of you," Lidia replied with a grateful smile. "I half expected you guys to just wipe my memory with one of those light, flashy things from the movies," she laughed, lightening the mood.

"No light, flashy thingies here, but we do have witches for those who can't handle knowing there's more out there," Nick said, his voice steady. He wasn't joking. The witches had wiped memories before to protect their world and would do it again if necessary. They'd sworn to safeguard the magical community, K Corp included.

Lidia's eyes widened. "They can erase memories?" She swallowed hard, processing the weight of his words.

"Sure. But we rarely need to do it. Most humans we deal with have a loved one with magic, so they try to embrace the world to support them. Like you're doing," he said, offering Lidia a warm smile.

"I love every part of Niamh, even before I knew about her magic. She was already magic to me. My soul sister," Lidia said, her voice thick with emotion as she flung an arm around Niamh's shoulder. Their heads leaned together, and Niamh could feel the tears threatening to spill. She fought them back, blinking hard to keep her composure.

Lidia pulled back slightly to look at Niamh. "Hey! Your scratch is gone!"

Niamh looked down at her arm, surprised. The angry scratch that had marred her skin earlier was now just a faint pink mark. "Huh, that's weird," she said, puzzled.

"You got scratched? When?" Nick's voice shifted to urgency.

"Um, at the queen's palace," Niamh said, trying to downplay it. "It was just a tiny scratch. It's no big deal."

"Everything the Cailleach does is a potential threat," Nick replied sharply. "Did she draw blood?"

"Maybe a tiny bit," Niamh said, unsure why he seemed so worked up. To her, it felt insignificant.

Nick exchanged a look with Aoife. "We need to look into this," he said, and Aoife nodded in agreement.

Niamh couldn't understand why they were making such a big deal over a small injury. She'd had worse from rose thorns. It didn't seem worth the stress. Wanting to shift the focus, she asked, "How did you decide to stay, Aoife? If you don't mind me asking."

"I didn't want to at first," Aoife admitted, her voice softer now. "I felt trapped. Like I didn't have a choice but to stay, and that made me want to leave even more." She chuckled lightly, then continued. "Then I realized, I'd spent so much time battling in my everyday life that I was just fighting this instinctively. I started to let my guard down, let people in, and a whole new world opened up for me here. And I'm so glad I did. This is my home. These are my people now." She kissed Nick gently, her affection for him clear.

Niamh listened closely, her mind swirling. "I'm not sure I have much to give here. You seem to have found your powers useful. I'm just warm. That's not much of a useful power."

"Are you kidding?" Aoife replied, raising an eyebrow. "Without you, Bain would be dead right now. And we'd all have a lot more injuries to heal. No one survives Cailleach's ice influence. She's not exactly known for letting people who cross her live. You're lucky you were there. I bet there's more use for your powers than you think, especially here in Canada. It's not exactly warm here." Aoife's words were sincere, reassuring.

Lidia and Niamh both winced at the mention of Bain again. Aoife hadn't been there for their earlier conversation, and they weren't close enough yet to casually discuss it. Niamh just shrugged, unsure how to respond. She still questioned how useful her powers were.

Changing the subject, Nick said, "Sorry the pool is so cool today, we're having trouble with our heating system."

"I don't mind it," Niamh replied with a shrug.

"Of course you don't," Lidia laughed. "But some of us don't have your super space-heating superpowers."

"Why don't you try to warm it up, Niamh?" Aoife suggested with a playful glint in her eyes.

Niamh hesitated, worried that she might accidentally boil everyone like lobsters. She focused, pushing aside the worry, and thought of gentle warmth. It wasn't the same as when she was igniting a fire; it was soft, like rolling waves of heat. Slowly, warmth radiated from her body, spreading through the water. The gentle difference in temperature was visible, with ripples and swirls where the warm and cold waters met, like one ocean meeting another.

"Ooh, that's nice!" Lidia said, her voice slow and content, sinking deeper into the water as she swam in slow circles on her back around Niamh.

"See? You're already helping out," Aoife added, smiling.

"Cool, I can be the official pool heater," Niamh said sarcastically, but a small smile tugged at her lips.

"Don't cut yourself short, Niamh. You are powerful," Aoife said, her tone unwavering and sincere. "If you weren't, I bet money that Queen Cailleach wouldn't want anything to do with you. She's only drawn to things that make her more powerful or things she can control. And you? She wanted you by her side for a reason. She knew you were powerful."

Niamh absorbed Aoife's words, feeling both comforted and burdened by the weight of them.

"Well, we didn't mean to interrupt your conversation earlier," Aoife said with a small laugh. "Nick and I are going to swim some laps, then we're going to check on Bain if you want to join."

"Oh, um. Sure. Why not? Thanks." Lidia let out a little giggle at the mention of Bain's name again, shaking her head.

Aoife winked at Niamh before she and Nick swam off toward the other end of the pool, ready to start their laps. Lidia was still floating lazily around Niamh, her movements slow and peaceful. She splashed Niamh gently to snap her out of her deep thoughts.

"You okay?" Lidia asked.

"I'm... going to be, I think."

"I could say his name one more time if it would help you feel better."

Niamh gritted her teeth at Lidia's bad joke, she sure loved prodding her.

"You know, you could stay here. You don't have to go back to Georgia. I know it's not easy at home with how people treat you. It might be an easier life here," Lidia said, her voice soft but convincing. "By the way, have you seen the tail on the lady behind the front desk? It's pretty cool!"

"What? No!" Niamh's eyes widened in surprise.

"Yeah, it seems most people here are... unique, like you are."

"I hadn't noticed much. I need to start paying better attention."

"Oh, and look out for the tall, skinny people with iridescent glowing skin! It's pretty epic. I wish I had skin like that!"

"Lidia, be happy you are normal."

"Normal?" Lidia laughed. "What's normal anyway? Around here, I'm the odd-looking one. I don't have horns, a tail, or glowing skin. No one even bats an eye at your... well, eyes."

Lidia's offhand comment made them both burst into laughter at her unintended pun.

"It *is* nice to not feel like a freak here," Niamh admitted, her laughter fading into a quieter smile. "I thought they were all just ignoring my eyes, but maybe they don't mind how I look."

Lidia nodded, her tone turning sincere. "I think you should consider staying here. Even though I'd miss you so damn much if you didn't come home. Promise me you'll visit me a lot! And I promise to send you fresh peach cobbler and our favorite fried green tomatoes from Home Grown so you won't get homesick."

Niamh chuckled, the weight of her thoughts easing, if only for a moment. "Deal. If I stay." The thought of staying hadn't crossed her mind until now. She had her parents, her flower shop, and Lidia back home. But that was also where she'd always felt like an outsider. She wondered if it would be possible to stay in K Corp, to fit in somewhere for once. Maybe even do some good, help others. She added those thoughts to the already long list that constantly buzzed in her mind.

"You don't have to decide right now," Lidia continued. "Feel it out. Talk to more people around here to see their perspective of this place. Like they said, you can stay as long as you want. We'll be home waiting for you. You know your employees got the store handled; they don't need you micromanaging. They'll be fine. And I'll make sure to do surprise check-ins to keep them on their toes."

Niamh smiled at Lidia's teasing, grateful for the distraction. She knew her flower shop would survive just fine without her. She'd hired good people she trusted completely. They were fantastic at what they did, creating beautiful arrangements without needing her constant oversight. But still, she liked to keep busy, to stay behind the scenes. The shop had grown so successful with her well-trained team that she didn't need to be there, and that should have made her proud. Yet, the thought of staying, finding a place to truly belong, pulled at her heart. She felt torn between two lives, two worlds.

As Aoife and Nick finished their laps, meeting at the end of the pool in an embrace, small giggles drifted through the air, pulling Niamh's attention. She watched them, happy for their connection, but a tinge of jealousy twisted in her chest. She couldn't help it. The ache of betrayal by Bain still gnawed at her heart.

Aoife's voice broke through her deep thoughts. "Hey, we're done here, and we're gonna head up to check on Bain. If you wanted to see him and didn't want to do it alone, we'd be happy to be mediators."

Niamh hesitated, a flicker of relief flashing through her. "Sure, that would make me feel better. Thank you so much." She knew she couldn't face Bain alone right now. There were too many emotions tangled up. If she went alone, she might make a rash decision—either something irreversible would happen to him, or she'd fall into bed with him. Neither option seemed like a good idea when she couldn't fully trust herself around him.

Aoife smiled, giving her a reassuring nod. "Kay, we'll be ready in about ten minutes. Meet you in the lobby?"

"It's a plan."

After they left, Lidia couldn't hold her curiosity in anymore. "So, what are you going to do about *he who shall not be named?*"

Niamh sighed, pulling her towel tighter around her. "Undecided. I was so busy trying to process the whole mother situation, I haven't really had time to sort out my feelings for Bain… or if there are any feelings left. He may have been playing me the whole time."

"I don't know," Lidia said thoughtfully. "He seemed sincere when he talked about you. Before the incident and after."

"I guess we'll see. I'm trying to keep an open mind. This whole situation has taught me that an open mind is important. I mean, there's freaking magic, other dimensions, and creatures other than humans and animals. So yeah, an open mind here is important." Niamh ran her fingers through her damp hair, her mind still reeling from everything. It was almost too much to absorb all at once.

"Well, I'll let you three do your magical world thing together, and I'll just be in my room, gorging on delicious food that Cami keeps bringing me!" Lidia grinned, her usual playful demeanor returning.

"I know, right? If I keep eating here, I'll have to start a strict workout routine, or I'll be packing on the pounds so fast."

Lidia rolled her eyes dramatically. "It would be worth it. The food is sooo good!"

They shared a laugh, their lighthearted moment offering Niamh a much-needed distraction from the heavy thoughts swirling in her mind. Together, they dried off and made their way back to their rooms, each with their own questions and uncertainties, but at least they had each other.

Niamh sat on the edge of her bed, her mind drifting back to Bain's words.

"I never meant to hurt you." "I like you." "You're special." Each phrase echoed in her thoughts, but the questions lingered just as strongly: Was any of it true? She wanted to believe him—wanted to believe that his feelings were genuine, but deep down, she knew he had motives. He had been sent for a reason, to use her, to manipulate her. She couldn't shake the feeling that there had always been a hidden agenda, even if he claimed that wasn't the case anymore.

The idea of confronting him, of hearing those words again, made her heart ache. Would he still say them with the same sincerity the next time she saw him? Or would it all unravel like a bad dream?

Shaking her head to rid herself of the spiraling thoughts, Niamh took a deep, cleansing breath. She stood up, forcing herself to focus on the task at hand. She grabbed a towel and dried her damp hair as best as she could, her hands working mechanically. When her hair was mostly dry, she pulled her bangs down over her eyes; old habits die hard. The concealment was comforting, even if she had grown used to the people here not reacting to her appearance. It still felt safer, like a shield.

She dressed in her usual, comfortable style: jeans and a flannel top. Nothing flashy, just something that felt like her, something that would blend in but not demand attention. She didn't want to seem like she was trying too hard to impress anyone. But the simple clothes felt like an armor, offering her a small sense of control in a world where so much was beyond her grasp.

One last look in the mirror. She adjusted her bangs one more time, fidgeting with them as if somehow that would make the weight of her thoughts lighter. With a quiet exhale, she decided she was ready, or as ready as she could be.

"Okay," she whispered to herself, standing up straight. "Let's do this."

With a final deep sigh, she headed toward the lobby, where Aoife and Nick would be waiting. She didn't know what to expect from this meeting with Bain, but she knew she couldn't avoid it forever. No matter how much she wanted to stay hidden from the storm that was brewing inside of her.

Chapter 17

Niamh lingered behind Aoife and Nick as they entered the sterile, hospital-like room. The sharp hum of machines and the harsh fluorescent lights immediately set her on edge. She was grateful for Nick's towering frame, using him as a shield for as long as possible, clinging to the illusion of safety he provided.

Before Nick or Aoife had a chance to start the conversation, a deep, gravelly voice broke the rhythm of the beeping machines. "How is Niamh?" Bain asked, his words rolling over her like a physical force, sending an involuntary shiver down her spine. His first thought was Niamh. That small gesture made her trust him slightly more, just slightly, though. Too much had happened to be easily swayed.

Niamh hesitated but finally stepped out from behind Nick, her movements drawing Bain's immediate attention. His eyes locked on her as he scrambled to sit up, the restraints on his wrists clicking loudly against the bed rails.

"Careful," Aoife warned gently, but Bain ignored her, his focus entirely on Niamh.

He attempted to shift into a more dignified posture, but his weakened state betrayed him. His smile stretched wide, forced and a little too eager. Even now, with his body visibly frail, he clung to the image of himself he wanted her to see.

But the Bain before her wasn't the confident, effortlessly alluring man she had come to know. His skin still carried a strange bluish tint in patches, and an unnatural dewiness clung to it. The healthy glow she'd once associated with him had vanished, leaving behind something that looked hollow and worn.

His eyes, normally vibrant, sparkling with mischief, were dulled, rimmed with dark circles that made the grey within seem clouded and tired.

Niamh noticed how hard he was trying to appear composed, to conjure a semblance of his usual charisma. It was a weak attempt, but she could still feel the tug of his effort, a whisper of the man who had once been so maddeningly sure of himself.

And for a moment, her heart twisted. Against her better judgment, she almost pitied him.

"Hi, Niamh! I've been asking about you, but no one would let me talk to you. How are you?" Bain's voice, though still deep and rumbling, carried an undercurrent of nervous energy she wasn't used to hearing from him.

"I'm, um… fine. How are you? You're the one who almost died," she replied, her voice awkward as she tried to ignore the strange cocktail of emotions churning in her chest.

"Well, thanks to you, I didn't. So, I'm doing great!" Bain attempted his signature uneven grin, throwing in a wink for good measure. But the effect was lackluster, his pale complexion and gaunt appearance undercutting the charm he was so accustomed to wielding.

It was clear he wasn't used to being in this position, stripped of his usual magnetic allure. A flicker of something crossed his face, a fleeting frustration at his vulnerability. He glanced away briefly as if struggling to suppress his thoughts. Niamh could almost hear the self-assessment happening behind his now dull grey eyes, could imagine him pitying men who lacked his typical good looks. The vanity was palpable, but he bit back the words he wanted to say, suppressing the shame he felt for himself.

"That's… good," Niamh replied, forcing herself to focus on the moment. She wasn't going to point out how unwell he still looked. She could see his body struggling, and she didn't feel the need to add to his bruised ego. She hated to admit to herself, she didn't ever want to see him hurt, but the last thing she wanted to do was to be the cause of the pain itself.

"You look well," he said, leaning into another smile. It fell flat, his usual confidence absent. "Beautiful as ever."

"Yeah. Aoife and Nick have been great. And Lidia has been keeping me company." She paused, meeting his gaze. "Thanks for keeping her safe, by the way. Even though you kind of kidnapped her, too."

"For the record, she wasn't kidnapped," Bain said quickly, his tone defensive. "She could have left at any time. I just wanted her to be safe so you didn't have to deal with her getting hurt if something went wrong." He hesitated, then added quietly, "I did kind of kidnap you. And I am sorry for that."

"So, you've said."

"And I'll keep saying it," he replied earnestly, leaning forward as much as the restraints allowed. "Until you believe me."

"That might be a while."

"As long as you need, princess." His voice softened at the last word, a term he had used before, but now it felt different, less playful, more genuine.

Aoife, sensing the tension thickening, interjected smoothly. "Bain, we have a few questions about Cailleach if you're up for it."

"Shoot," Bain replied, his casual tone undercut by the heavy atmosphere of the conversation.

Nick stepped forward, his tone sharp and focused. "According to our records, she's banished to a dimension. How did she manage to reach you to do her bidding?"

Bain's expression hardened slightly, the humor fading. "She *is* banished and can't leave. But that doesn't stop her from trying to find a way back. She's gathering powerful allies, looking for people who could help tip the scales in her favor. She has these lower-level ghilan that can travel between dimensions. They're the ones who carry her messages and promises to those of us who might..." He hesitated, a shadow of shame passing over his face. "...be open to a profitable proposition."

"Ghilan?" Nick asked, tilting his head. "Like ghouls?"

"Yeah, just older," Bain replied with a smirk, his humor resurfacing briefly. "And smellier. They don't exactly believe in bathing between dimensions."

Nick ignored the attempt at levity and pressed on. "These ghilan, what kind of messages do they send? What did the queen offer you?"

"Power." Bain's response was simple yet heavy with meaning. "That's usually enough for most of us. Who wouldn't want to be the right-hand man of someone with that kind of dominance? She promised me abilities I could only dream of. Being an Abarta, I don't have any unique skills of my own, so the idea of finally having *something*, well, it was tempting."

Nick's brow furrowed. "Tricksters with more power? That would've been a disaster. Good thing you changed your mind and made the right choice in the end."

Bain leaned back against the bed, the restraints clinking faintly as he let out a wistful sigh. "It wasn't much of a choice, honestly. I couldn't let Niamh get hurt because of me. But…" He let out a small, bitter chuckle. "The powers would've been cool. Just saying."

"You still made the right call," Aoife chimed in, her tone kind yet firm.

Bain's expression softened as he turned his gaze to Niamh. His eyes seemed to pierce through the distance between them, locking onto hers with an intensity that made her heart skip. He looked at her like she was the only person in the room, his voice dropping low and earnest.

"I'd choose you again and again," he said, the weight of the words settling heavily in the air around them. And he would. He would gladly give up any possible powers or status for her. Abartas were tricksters by nature, always looking for more, never satiated with what they had. He had never felt satisfied with his life until he met her. She showed him there was more to life than constantly seeking more.

Niamh's breath caught at his confession. She had always struggled with eye contact, but with Bain, she couldn't look away. For once, it didn't feel like a threat; it felt like safety, like something she wasn't sure she was ready to admit she wanted.

"So, how are you really doing here?" Niamh asked hesitantly, her voice soft but steady.

Bain gave her his signature smirk, though it lacked its usual charm. "Oh, ya know, living the life. Got maid service, a personal chef. Not bad, really, aside from these lovely bracelets." He rattled the handcuffs against the bed frame with a playful jingle.

Her lips quirked in a faint smile. "So… you're going to be okay?"

Before he could answer, the doctor poked her head around the curtain, her expression both stern and amused. "He'll be fine. Honestly, he could stand to be humbled more often. But physically? He'll be back to his cunning self in no time. You, my dear, are the real hero here. Cailleach's powers are extraordinary, but you managed to counter them. That's no small feat. We'll monitor him, but we don't foresee any issues. Just a nice long life for this one," she patted his foot firmly with her hand. "He's lucky you were there."

Niamh's cheeks flushed a deep red. "Th-thank you," she stammered, unsure how to take the compliment.

The doctor gave her an encouraging smile. "No, thank *you*. You made my job easier. Your abilities could be a real asset around here. I can already think of so many ways we could use someone with your talents if you decide to stay, that is."

Nick cleared his throat, breaking the silence. "Bain, we'll need to keep you here for observation. Until we're confident you're not a danger to us or anyone else and that Cailleach is still securely locked away in her dimension. I hope you understand."

"Sure thing, big man." Bain's tone was light, though a hint of irritation crept into his smirk. "As long as you keep feeding me this five-star cuisine, I'll stick around as long as you need."

Nick's jaw tightened, his expression unimpressed. He let out a low grunt of disapproval but didn't dignify Bain's comment with a response.

Bain shifted slightly in his restraints, his sharp gaze searching for Niamh. She had retreated toward the back of the room during the doctor's visit, half-hidden in the shadows. Bain leaned forward as far as his bindings allowed, craning his neck to catch a better glimpse of her. His eyes softened when they finally found hers, though the distance between them felt as vast as an ocean.

Nick, ever the protective wall, stepped slightly to the side, effectively blocking Bain's view. His broad frame acted as a fortress, one he wasn't planning to lower until Niamh signaled she was ready. She appreciated his silent support, but her heart still ached under the weight of Bain's penetrating stare.

"So, Niamh," Bain began, his voice dipping into a teasing yet sincere tone, "you, uh, wanna grab dinner sometime? Maybe come to my place, since I'm kind of stuck here for a while."

Her brows lifted in surprise, caught off guard by his casual attempt at charm. "Um, I'll… think about it."

His lips curled into a hopeful smile. "Please do. I'd like a chance for a redo. If you'd let me, that is. I know this isn't the most romantic setting, but I'll take what I can get. Maybe the good doctor would let us light some candles?"

From behind the curtain, the doctor's sharp voice cut through. "Absolutely not."

Bain chuckled, shrugging with as much flair as his restraints allowed. "Worth a try," he said, still grinning.

Niamh opened her mouth to reply, but her thoughts betrayed her. Every question she'd wanted to ask him dissolved under the weight of his presence. His full lips, those piercing blue eyes, and the sharp angles of his face made her stomach flip in ways she wasn't ready to admit. Even the dark circles under his eyes and his pallor couldn't dull his allure. She desperately tried to refocus her thoughts, grasping for anything to distract her from how maddeningly attractive she found him, but her mind offered no reprieve.

Sensing her struggle, Aoife stepped in, her tone brisk and efficient. "We'll check back in with you later. If you need anything, let the doctor know. And if you think of any other useful information about The Queen, don't hold out on us. The more you tell us, the more reason we'll have to trust you." Her sharp gaze lingered on him, clearly skeptical.

Bain raised his brows, a mock salute thwarted by his handcuffs. "Will do," he said lightly, but the glint in his eyes shifted when they landed on Niamh. He gave her a soft, almost pleading smile as she turned to leave with Aoife and Nick. His eyes spoke of an unspoken hope, a silent request for something she wasn't ready to give. Not yet.

Niamh didn't return his smile. Too much had happened, and her heart wasn't ready to forgive or forget. She let the door close behind her without a second glance, her resolve shaky but holding firm.

But even as she walked down the hall, her mind couldn't escape Bain. His sickly appearance haunted her, stirring an ache she didn't want to feel. He'd looked so vulnerable, so uncharacteristically subdued. Every instinct in her screamed to help him, to stay by his side and make sure he got better.

But then the memories of his betrayal came flooding back, the lies, the manipulation, the danger he'd put her in. She clenched her fists, trying to push down the swirling storm of emotions. Confusion. Anger. Pain. Desire. It was all too much.

She quickened her pace, eager to put more distance between them. Whatever connection she felt to Bain was dangerous, and she knew it. Nothing good could come from being so close to someone who'd already hurt her so deeply.

Staring at the unfamiliar ceiling, Niamh let her mind wander to the countless "what-ifs" swirling in her head. This hidden sanctuary in the middle of nowhere Canada had begun to feel oddly comforting, a world away from the stares and whispers that had defined her old life. The town freak. The weight of that label had been suffocating. Here, though, she didn't have to hide. No long bangs to shield her face, no shrinking into the shadows.

She imagined what life could have been like if she'd grown up in a place like this, a community that accepted her instead of making her feel like a mistake. Maybe she'd have been the kind of woman she admired: confident, assertive, unapologetically herself. But then again, could that ever really be her? Or was she too shaped by years of retreating inward?

With a deep sigh, she shook off the thought. Dwelling on the past wouldn't change it. What's done is done. All she could control was what came next.

The shrill ring of the phone startled her, yanking her out of her thoughts. She reached for it, her hand trembling slightly.

"Niamh, we have a problem," Aoife's urgent voice spilled through the receiver. "Bain just told us he just got a message from one of the Queen's underlings. She's planning an attack tonight. He won't tell us where; it has to be you. Can you meet us down there right away?"

Niamh's pulse quickened, her grip tightening on the phone. An attack? Tonight? Her birth mother's relentless pursuit was no surprise, but it still sent ice through her veins. Why couldn't Cailleach accept her decision and move on?

"Yes, of course," she replied, her voice steady despite the panic bubbling under the surface. "I'll be there right away."

She hung up, her mind racing. This isn't over. It might never be over. She shoved her lingering doubts and fears into the back of her mind. Right now, she didn't have the luxury of second-guessing. Lives could be at stake, and Bain, despite all the confusion he stirred in her, needed her.

Throwing on her jacket, she bolted out the door, ready to face whatever awaited her.

Bain was sitting up, a scorched shred of thick, rough paper clenched in his hand, the faint scent of burnt edges lingering in the air. His normally cocky demeanor had been replaced by an uncharacteristic seriousness. As Niamh stepped into the room, his eyes immediately found hers.

"I'm sorry I didn't tell you all right away," he began, his voice low and slightly hoarse. "But I needed Niamh to hear this first. I want you to know, I had no part in this. The only reason I know what she's planning is because someone owed me a favor, and I called it in."

"Just spit it out, Bain," Nick growled, his patience wearing thin.

Bain held up his hands defensively, his cuffs clinking faintly. "Alright, alright. She's targeting your parents. If you leave now, you might be able to get there before her."

Niamh's heart dropped into her stomach, the words hitting her like a physical blow. Her parents? The people who had loved her, raised her, given her a home when her birth mother had abandoned her? Fury and fear tangled in her chest. How dare Cailleach stoop so low?

She cursed the day she'd ever met her birth mother. Nothing good had come of it, no sense of wholeness, no closure, no family bond. Instead, it had left her feeling more broken than before, like the void inside her had only grown wider. But if anything happened to her parents... no, she couldn't even think about that. It would destroy her.

Without a word, Niamh turned and followed Aoife and Nick out of Bain's room. In the hallway, Aoife stopped and turned to Nick. "You ready?"

He nodded curtly.

Aoife's gaze softened as she turned to Niamh, placing a steadying hand on her arm. "You don't have to come. We can handle this if it's too much."

"No," Niamh said, her voice firm despite the panic bubbling beneath the surface. "It's my parents. I'm coming."

She squared her shoulders and lifted her chin. The hours she'd spent training to control her powers surged to the forefront of her mind. She was ready, she had to be.

Aoife studied her for a moment before nodding, a flicker of pride crossing her face. Niamh wasn't the same uncertain, withdrawn girl who had arrived here weeks ago. She was stronger now, more determined.

With a wave of Aoife's hands, a swirling gold vortex sprang to life in front of them, whipping their hair and clothes in its relentless wind.

Nick stepped through first, his hulking frame vanishing into the glowing portal. Niamh followed close behind, her heart pounding as the vortex pulled her forward. Aoife brought up the rear, sealing the gateway with a deft flick of her wrist.

When they emerged, the world had shifted. They stood on the familiar front porch of Niamh's home in Georgia. The air was brisk, the scent of pine mingling with the faint warmth of the southern winter. Her parents' porch was festively decorated, with a slightly out-of-place plastic snowman family standing cheerily in the corner.

The sight stabbed at her heart. Her parents had no idea of the storm heading their way. But Niamh was here now, and she would do whatever it took to protect them.

Niamh's heart thundered in her chest as she rushed to the front door, the chill of the air forgotten in her desperation. She gripped the doorknob, only to find it locked. Her breath hitched, and she fumbled beneath the snowman for the hidden spare key. Her fingers trembled as she unlocked the door and pushed it open, revealing the warm interior of her childhood home.

Everything looked so normal and yet so wrong. The cozy, inviting aroma of home-cooked meals was replaced by a stench that churned her stomach. It was rancid, sharp, and suffocating. Her eyes darted to the kitchen, where two cups of tea still steamed on the counter. An open book lay beside them, its pages creased mid-read.

Her parents were nowhere in sight.

"Mom? Dad?" Niamh called, her voice shaking as she bolted for the stairs.

She took the steps two at a time, Aoife and Nick close behind her. The familiar photos lining the walls, the smiling faces of her younger self, her parents on vacations, family holidays blurred as she ran past them. Memories flashed in her mind, each one a contrast to the dread threatening to consume her.

Reaching the doorway to her parents' room, Niamh skidded to a halt. A dark, smoky shadow loomed before her, blocking the entrance. It writhed and pulsed, its edges curling like smoke caught in an invisible wind. She squinted, her breath catching as she saw through its semi-translucent form.

Her parents.

They were bound on the floor, gags muffling their cries. Their wide, tear-filled eyes met hers, and a gut-wrenching wave of helplessness crashed over her.

"Mom! Dad!" she cried, stepping forward.

Nick's firm hand on her shoulder stopped her mid-step. "Let me handle this," he said, his voice calm but commanding.

Niamh hesitated, torn between charging through the shadow to reach her parents and trusting Nick. She didn't know what that thing was or how to fight it, but the desperation clawing at her chest made her want to try.

Aoife stepped up beside her, squeezing her arm reassuringly. "We've got this. Trust us," she said, her voice steady.

Niamh swallowed hard and nodded, stepping back just enough to give Nick room. Her fists clenched at her sides as she forced herself to wait, every muscle in her body taut with restrained urgency. She couldn't lose her parents. Not now. Not ever.

"Ghilan! What is it you seek here?" Nick's voice thundered through the room, commanding and unyielding.

The shadowy form swirled violently, pulling itself together until it loomed taller and broader than Nick, its edges crackling with dark energy. The stench of decay grew unbearable, a nauseating assault that made their stomachs twist.

"I seek my queen's favor," it hissed, the words dripping with disdain. "She desires these humans'…" the creature spat the word like venom, "lifeforce to wither into nothingness. I serve her will. This is no concern of yours, *hominid*."

Nick took a deliberate step forward, his broad frame blocking the ghilan's path. His voice dropped, low and dangerous. "Humans are under our protection. You will not harm them."

The ghilan's smoky form expanded, its darkness pressing against Nick like a physical weight. "I don't take orders from your kind," it growled, its voice like grinding stone.

The pressure between them grew, a palpable force radiating from the creature as it puffed itself up further, encroaching on Nick's space. But Nick didn't flinch. His boots stayed firmly planted on the floor, his chest rising with calm, controlled breaths as he resisted the invisible push.

"This is your last warning, ghilan," Nick said, his voice unwavering. "Leave now, or we'll take action."

The ghilan's form quivered, its edges rippling like heat waves as it leaned closer. "I refuse," it snarled, its tone brimming with defiance.

The room fell deathly silent, the tension between them crackling like a storm on the verge of breaking.

Nick nodded at Aoife, their silent communication honed from countless battles together. Without hesitation, Aoife summoned a swirling gold portal and disappeared into it. Moments later, small gold flecks shimmered in the bedroom behind the creature. Aoife emerged like a whisper of light, her sharp eyes locking on the bound figures of Niamh's parents. With practiced efficiency, she pulled a small, sharp knife from her boot and cut through the ropes holding them.

"Move!" she urged in a low, urgent tone. She helped Niamh's mother to her feet and guided her through the still-spinning portal as her father stumbled close behind.

The ghilan stiffened, sensing movement. It turned with unnatural speed, its smoky form twisting and writhing as it lunged toward the portal. Its translucent arms flailed wildly, reaching for anything it could seize. Its claw-like grip found Niamh's father's ankle, yanking him backward with brutal force.

"Dad!" Niamh screamed, her voice breaking as she watched her father dragged back into the room.

He kicked frantically, his foot passing through the creature's form as though it were nothing but mist. His struggles only seemed to amuse the ghilan, its strength relentless as it pulled him farther from safety.

Niamh's instincts ignited with the ferocity of her love and fear. A gut-wrenching scream tore from her chest as flames erupted from her hands, glowing tendrils of fire lashing out like living whips. Her power wrapped around the creature in a burning embrace, the heat consuming everything in its path.

The creature writhed, its form distorting under the fiery assault. The room filled with a cacophony of hisses and crackles as flames licked at the carpet, climbed the drapes, and kissed the ceiling. The ghilan released Niamh's father with a guttural snarl, its smoky form recoiling. Her father scrambled through the shrinking portal just as it sealed behind him, leaving the creature trapped.

The ghilan's mouth stretched open in a grotesque howl, rows of razor-sharp teeth gleaming through the black smoke. It let out an ear-piercing screech that sent waves of pain through the room. Nick and Niamh clutched their ears and shut their eyes tightly, their heads pounding as the sound resonated like a physical attack. A second ghilan appeared as if he'd summoned another one. They briefly looked at each other, then the second one disappeared, leaving a pit in Niamh's stomach.

Even blinded by the pain and frustration, Niamh refused to relent. Her tendrils of fire grew hotter, brighter, forcing the creature into a tightening inferno. She poured every ounce of strength into her flames, her resolve burning as fiercely as the fire she controlled.

The ghilan's shrieks faltered, replaced by the crackling roar of fire as the flames consumed it. When the sound finally stopped, Niamh opened her eyes. Smoke hung heavy in the air, stinging her throat and filling the room with an acrid scent.

The creature was gone. All that remained was a smoldering pile of ash and the red-hot flames devouring the room, their heat pressing against her skin like a warning.

Nick grabbed Niamh's arm, pulling her toward the stairs as smoke thickened around them, stinging their eyes and lungs. She stumbled, her legs refusing to cooperate as panic clouded her focus. Each step felt like an impossible feat as she tripped and stumbled down the stairs.

"Come on, Niamh!" Nick shouted, urgency sharp in his tone. His grip on her arm tightened, steadying her before she could collapse entirely.

Just as they began to gain momentum, the brittle wood of the stairs gave way beneath Nick's weight. His leg plunged through with a sickening crack, pinning him in place.

"Nick!" she cried, dropping to her knees beside him.

He yanked at his leg, gritting his teeth against the pain. The flames were closing in, their oppressive heat licking at the edges of their reality. His shirt ignited, a small blaze spreading across the fabric.

"No!" Niamh slapped at the fire, her hands moving faster than her thoughts, extinguishing the flames before they could do serious damage. But the boards surrounding Nick's leg refused to budge.

"I'm stuck," he growled, his voice tight with pain and frustration. "Go, leave me. I'll be right behind you," he demanded.

She wasn't about to leave him. He'd saved her countless times, if she'd learned anything from him and K Corp it was that they fight to the end for what's right. And leaving Nick behind would never be right.

Fear gripped her as the fire crept closer. Every instinct told her they wouldn't make it, that this was the end. But then she remembered Njeri's training. The flames hadn't hurt her before. Could she control them now?

"Please," she whispered, as if pleading with the flames themselves.

She raised her hands, feeling the power stirring inside her. Summoning the fire felt like tugging on an invisible string. The flames wavered, then angled toward her, flickering as if considering her command. A reverse funnel formed, the fire twisting and coiling toward her like a living thing.

The heat surged, her skin prickling as though it might blister, though she knew it wouldn't. But the strain was unbearable; every muscle in her body screamed as she held her ground. A guttural, primal scream tore from her throat as she drew in more of the flames, pain blazing through her core like molten lava.

Nick stared at her, his eyes wide with astonishment. "What the hell…"

Nick broke free, splintering the wood around his leg. Relief flooded his face.

Her breaths came in ragged gasps, but she managed a weak smile. She glanced at the charred remains of her home. The fire was gone, leaving behind a skeleton of blackened wood. Small puffs of smoke rose from the smoldering structure, but it was over.

Nick smiled through his coughing, his eyes shining with pride despite the chaos. "You did it."

Niamh nodded, her strength slowly returning. She let Nick help her to her feet, leaning on him as they carefully made their way down the ruined staircase.

The fresh night air hit them like a salve, cool and cleansing. Niamh inhaled deeply, her lungs grateful for the reprieve, but Nick staggered, a fit of coughing overtaking him.

"You okay?" she asked, her voice still raspy.

Nick waved her off, his hand bracing on his knee as he bent over, gulping in clean air. "Just… smoke. I'll be fine."

Niamh barely noticed her breathing was steady and easy, the smoke and heat inside her causing no discomfort. Her body hummed with residual warmth, as though the fire she had absorbed still flickered somewhere within her.

As Nick caught his breath, they turned their attention to the scene before them. Aoife stood in the front yard, her stance protective, a small knife in her hand. Behind her, Niamh's parents huddled together, fear etched into their faces.

Niamh's heart ached at the sight. She stepped forward, hands outstretched, her voice soft but steady. "Mom, Dad, it's okay. You're safe now."

Her mother's eyes darted between Niamh and the ruins of their home. "Niamh… what did you…?"

Niamh looked down at her hands, the faintest shimmer of gold light lingering at her fingertips. "It's a long story," she said, her voice heavy with exhaustion. "But you're safe. That's all that matters."

Her father swallowed hard, his lips pressing into a thin line as he nodded. "Thank you, sweetheart."

Nick straightened beside her, giving Aoife a quick nod of acknowledgment. "We should move," he said, his voice still rough. "This isn't over."

Niamh glanced at the house, her childhood, her memories reduced to ash and soot. But her parents were alive. They were here.

And for now, that was enough.

The second creature loomed over Aoife, its shadow darker now, blending seamlessly with the night around it. Its presence seemed to suck the light from the air, leaving a suffocating void. Aoife stood her ground, her shoulders squared as she shielded Niamh's parents behind her. But her defiance faltered as the creature's maw stretched open, revealing jagged, yellowed teeth that glistened like rot.

A sickening gray fog poured out from the ghilan, smothering Aoife's face in an instant, covering it in a thick blanket of blackness. She clawed at the smoke, her movements frantic as she gasped for air. Her body convulsed with effort, but the suffocating fog refused to clear.

"Aoife!" Nick shouted, bolting to her side. He waved his arms wildly, trying to push the fog away, but his hands sliced through nothingness. The tendrils of darkness clung to her like a second skin, unyielding. Terror twisted her features as her strength began to wane.

Niamh's chest tightened. Her thoughts swirled in a chaotic storm of helplessness. *I can't lose her. I can't lose anyone else.* Panic clawed at her throat until her voice broke through in a desperate cry.

"Stop!"

She hadn't expected it to work; it was nothing more than a feeble, desperate cry for help. But the creature froze. Its glowing eyes blinked, slow and deliberate, as if her voice had struck some chord. The smoke stilled, then swirled backward, receding into the creature's gaping maw. Aoife collapsed into Nick's arms, coughing violently, her legs trembling under the strain.

The ghilan's gaze shifted to Niamh, its eyes locking onto hers. It stood silent and unmoving as though awaiting instruction.

"Tell it to go!" Nick called out to her, his voice rough with urgency as he steadied Aoife.

Niamh's pulse thundered in her ears. Her mind raced, but she found her voice. "Go back to where you came from," she commanded, her voice stronger than she felt. Then, almost as a plea, she added, "And never come back here again!"

The creature blinked again, its expression unreadable, then began to dissolve. The thick, oppressive smoke dissipated into the night air, carrying with it the nauseating stench of decay. As the last tendrils vanished, the air felt lighter, cleaner.

Niamh's parents peeked out from behind Aoife and Nick, their bodies trembling but alive. Relief flooded through her, a weight lifted from her chest.

Their eyes, glassy with unshed tears, were a mix of fear and overwhelming gratitude. But as their gaze shifted to the house, their expressions faltered. The broken windows, melted siding, and thick black smoke streaks above the openings told the story of what had happened.

Niamh had stopped the fire, but not in time. The damage was done.

Chapter 18

H er parents seemed frozen, caught between two conflicting emotions: the profound relief of surviving and the devastating new truth about their daughter.

Nick was crouched beside Aoife, his hand rubbing her back as she sat hunched over, her head resting on her knees. Her breaths were ragged, but her color was returning, and her shoulders began to relax.

Niamh knelt between Aoife and her parents, her voice soft. "Aoife, are you okay?" her question aimed at all of them.

Aoife lifted her head slightly, her lips quirking in a weak smile. "You never cease to impress me."

Niamh let out a shaky laugh, but her eyes betrayed the weight of everything she had just endured. Her home burned behind her, her family shaken, and the memory of that creature's soulless eyes still lingered in her mind. But for now, they were safe. For now, they had survived.

"Niamh, what was that thing?" her dad finally worked up the courage to ask.

Niamh didn't know how to answer, she didn't even know what it was. Luckily, Nick spoke up, "It was a ghilan, like a ghoul but worse. They serve whoever offers them the most power."

"W, what?" her mom squeaked out.

"Mom," Niamh took her mom's hand, "My birth mother found me." She said, taking a deep breath. "She... she is something not human. That's why I look the way I do. She's the Queen of Winter, they call her. She's not a good queen though; she's a goddess, but she's very, very bad. I'm so sorry you guys got caught up in all this. I know you haven't had it easy choosing me as your child, and now this?" She cut off fighting tears. "You guys didn't deserve everything I've put you through."

"You didn't know your birth mother would do something like this?" her mom asked with a pleading look in her eyes, hoping for the right answer.

Niamh just shook her head. Unable to find words that would fit the heartbreak she felt for her parents.

Her dad spoke up, "Darling, you were a blessing. We've loved every part of being your parents. We've never regretted choosing you, not even for a second." They looked at each other lovingly and gave a small smile to one another. "As for *her*... we know you wouldn't do anything to hurt us; she is the one responsible. We aren't hurt anyway, the house can be replaced. You are what's important. We do not blame you."

"I just feel so bad you almost got hurt because of me."

Niamh's dad scooted closer, placing a comforting hand on her shoulder. His eyes, filled with unwavering love, met hers. "Listen to me, sweetheart. You are *not* to blame for any of this. None of it. You're our daughter, our *miracle*. The day we picked you up from the adoption agency was the best day of our lives, and nothing, not even this chaos, can change that."

Niamh's lips trembled as her father's words washed over her. She looked to her mom, whose hand still gripped hers tightly. Her mom's tear-filled eyes softened, and she gave Niamh's hand a gentle squeeze.

"Your dad's right," her mom said, her voice wavering but firm. "We didn't choose you because we thought it would be easy, Niamh. We chose you because we loved you. And we always will. No matter what."

His brows knitted together, deep in concentration, trying to figure this odd situation out. Facing Niamh, holding her gaze lovingly. "So... do you mind me asking, you said she wasn't human, does that mean you aren't either?" he paused, noticing her face had changed expressions slightly. "Not that it would matter to us; we love you just the way you are. Forgive us, we don't know how to handle this situation," he rushed out, trying not to offend her.

Niamh glanced at Aoife and Nick, searching their faces for reassurance. They nodded back in unison, giving her the silent okay to spill the truth. She took it upon herself to share the news of her past with him.

She took a deep breath, steadying herself. "So… you know about my birth mother," she began, her voice trembling slightly. "She gave me the white eye. My father was a wraith, a shadow creature, you could say. He gave me the dark one. Maybe that's why I was able to control the ghilan. The shadow part of me… it let me order him to leave. At least, I think so. I don't really know." She paused, her shoulders sagging under the weight of her own admission. "I'm still figuring all of this out."

Her throat tightened as the next words threatened to stick. "I… I do have powers," she confessed, the statement hanging heavy in the air. She hesitated, her voice softer now. "But if this is too much, too soon, I can wait to tell you more. Or… I don't have to tell you at all, if it's too much for you to handle."

Tears welled in her eyes as she searched their faces for any sign of rejection. Her adoptive parents had always been her haven, the only ones who had ever truly made her feel loved and accepted. The thought of losing that, of them turning away now, broke her heart in ways she couldn't put into words.

But she had to respect their decision, no matter how much it hurt.

She braced herself, holding her breath as she waited for their response.

They exchanged a glance, their eyes speaking volumes, before turning back to her. Her mother smiled softly, her voice steady but filled with warmth. "We want to know, honey. We love all of you. Most people change and evolve as they grow older; you just one-upped everyone else." Her father chuckled, nodding in agreement.

Her mother continued, "We've been ready for this moment… well, maybe not *this exact* moment, but we want to know everything about you. All of you. We're ready."

Relief washed over Niamh like a wave, her chest loosening for the first time in what felt like hours. Still, she hesitated, unsure how to begin. Words felt clumsy and inadequate, so she decided to show them instead.

Taking a deep breath, she extended her hand, palm up. A small red flame appeared, flickering to life with a soft *whoosh*. She had chosen this color deliberately—it felt less unnatural, less intimidating than the others.

The crimson flame danced across her palm, its movements smooth and hypnotic. Niamh wiggled her fingers, guiding the fire as it weaved effortlessly between them, moving like a serpent under her control. The glow illuminated her face, casting warm shadows across the room.

"It doesn't burn me," she said quietly, her voice steady but soft. "It doesn't hurt at all. It's... a part of me. My friend."

She let the flame flicker brighter for a moment before letting it shrink to a gentle ember, her gaze fixed on her parents. She wanted them to see not just the fire but the connection she had to it. It wasn't a weapon; it was an extension of herself.

Her heart pounded as she waited for their reaction, but in the warmth of their expressions, she found reassurance.

Once their expressions leveled out, Niamh let them take it in at their own pace before she spoke again. "I have other colors," she said gently. "They all do something different. Do you... want to see what it can do?"

Her father nodded slowly, curiosity flickering in his eyes. Her mother gulped, her hesitation clear, but she didn't say no.

Taking a steadying breath, Niamh flicked her wrist toward the yard. The small red flame leapt from her hand, obedient and controlled. She willed it to stay small, to do as little damage as possible. She didn't want to scare them more than they already were.

With an excited little crackle, the flame launched itself into the air. When it hit the grass, it let out a small, sharp *bang*, like the sputtering backfire of an old lawnmower. Her parents both jumped, their eyes wide, as the flame left a neat, baseball-sized divot in the grass.

Niamh turned back to them, her heart racing as she waited for their reaction.

Her mother was the first to speak, her voice unsteady. "So... you have bombs inside you?"

Niamh bit her lip, unsure whether to laugh or cry at the question. "Well, kind of," she admitted with a small shrug. "But they do what I say. The flames listen to me. They obey me. That's how I stopped the fire, I drew it into myself. The ones inside me aren't all bombs, though." She paused, a faint smile tugging at her lips. "But they all do something amazing."

Aoife stepped in, her voice filled with compassion as she addressed Niamh's parents. "She *is* amazing, Mr. and Mrs. Johnson. You should have seen her. She's saved so many people from harm."

Aoife's words carried a sense of pride that Niamh hadn't expected, and when she glanced over, Aoife gave her a reassuring smile that felt like a lifeline.

"You, you've saved people?" her mother asked.

She nodded, her voice steady but tinged with emotion. "They were in danger. I couldn't just stand around and let them get hurt." She hesitated, her gaze dropping for a moment. "And Bain… he was hurt. I did my best to keep him warm and safe."

The words hung heavy in the air, and Niamh felt her chest tighten.

Her parents exchanged a glance, their expressions shifting. It wasn't just what she'd said, it was how she'd said it. This was the first time Niamh had ever mentioned a boy to them, *ever*. And they caught on to it quickly.

"This *Bain*, he's safe now?" her father asked.

Niamh nodded.

"I'm so proud of you, honey. Does this Bain treat you well?"

"Dad," Niamh said softly, her tone firm but tinged with exhaustion, "you can stop saying *this, Bain*. It's… complicated with him." She hesitated, choosing her words carefully. "I believe he has a good heart. He just goes about things the hard way." She exhaled slowly. "We can talk about him later. Right now, I just want to make sure you guys are safe."

Her parents clung to each other, their bodies trembling slightly as they took in the remains of their home. "We will be," her dad said, his voice thick with emotion. Tears welled in their eyes as they glanced at the charred siding, the shattered windows, and the blackened streaks above the door.

A lump rose in Niamh's throat as guilt crashed over her. She tried to swallow it down, but the tears she'd been holding back spilled over anyway. "I'm so sorry," she whispered, her voice breaking. "I didn't mean for any of this to happen. I didn't even know she'd... she'd come after you like this."

Her mom stepped forward and pulled her into a tight embrace, her arms trembling as they wrapped around her daughter. "You didn't bring this upon us, baby. *She* did. This isn't your fault." Her voice was soothing but firm, cutting through Niamh's self-blame. "We're safe now, and we're together. That's what matters."

Her dad joined the hug, his strong arms wrapping around them both, pulling them closer. "Your mom's right," he said, his voice steady despite the emotion in it. "We'll rebuild, and we'll move forward. Just promise us you'll be careful, okay?"

Niamh nodded against her mom's shoulder, her tears soaking into the fabric. "I promise," she whispered, her voice trembling but resolute.

Nick cleared his throat softly, stepping forward to address the group. "Your parents are tougher than most people I know, Niamh. But it's best if they stay somewhere safe for a while. The Queen won't give up easily, and I have a feeling this isn't over."

Niamh's parents exchanged a nervous glance, their hands tightening around each other, but eventually nodded in agreement.

Her dad was the first to speak, his voice steady but warm. "We always knew you were special, Niamh. That you were born for something more. So, we know it might seem crazy that we're just... accepting all this so quickly, but the truth is, we've always known you wouldn't take the same path as everyone else. We just could never have imagined it would be this...unique".

Niamh's eyes widened, and tears began to well up, glistening in the firelight. "You... you did?" she asked, her voice barely above a whisper, almost not daring to believe him.

Her mother stepped in, her voice soft but filled with love. "Honey, we did. We always knew you were destined to do something big. We just never imagined it would be... this dangerous."

The lump in Niamh's throat swelled again, but this time it wasn't from guilt or fear, it was the overwhelming wave of love and understanding from the two people who had always been there for her.

"We're sorry you got involved. We didn't realize how hard she'd fight to get her daughter back. And we didn't think she'd be able to go after you." Aoife spoke kindly to Niamh's parents.

"She's our daughter," her dad said proudly.

Niamh's heart twisted as she saw the raw emotion flicker in her mom's eyes.

Niamh stepped closer, taking her mom's hands in her own. "I know. I feel the same way. But this world is real. And it's not just my world anymore. It's *our* world. We're all part of it now. We'll figure it out together. We always have." She paused, then added, "And you're not alone in this. Lidia's learning too. She's been through some of the same things, trying to understand what's going on. Maybe you can talk to her, get some clarity."

Her mom shook her head, almost laughing. "Lidia?"

Niamh felt her heart sink, but she nodded. "I know it's a lot to take in. But she's learning how to deal with it too. She's been there for me through the beginning when I thought I was going crazy, even now, helping me sort it all out. Maybe she can help you understand more about it."

Nick spoke up, sensing the tension. "If this is too much, we have ways of making people forget about magical interactions. It's an option," he added.

Her mom looked at Nick, her face still a mixture of disbelief and confusion, but something in his calm, unwavering voice made her pause. "So, you're saying you can make people forget all of this?" she asked, her voice small.

Nick nodded, his expression serious. "Yes. We can do that. It's the safest way to protect both them and our world. Some people aren't ready for this kind of truth. Some can't handle it at all, they don't like their reality to be challenged. We have to keep the magical community safe. Just know that if you choose this, we will not think any less of you. It's a lot to process."

Niamh could feel the weight of her mom's gaze as she looked at her dad, who was trying to keep it together for her. Her heart ached at the thought of them being thrust into a world so foreign to them.

Her dad, though still processing, gave a quiet but steady response. "We get it. It is a lot. But we've always had each other, and we've always protected Niamh. This… this changes things, but it doesn't change that. We'll adjust." Her parents shared a look with unspoken words between them.

"We don't want to erase any part of you," her mom said quietly, her voice cracking slightly, tears welling in her father's eyes once again.

Aoife stepped forward, offering a comforting smile. "It's okay," she said gently. "You don't have to decide right now. We just want you to know that you're not alone in this. You have Niamh's back, and we have yours too."

Her mom looked back at Niamh then, and though she still looked overwhelmed, there was something softer in her eyes. "I know, honey. I just… I need a little time to understand all of this. It's a lot to take in, but we'll figure it out. We always have."

Niamh's chest tightened, her eyes burning with unshed tears. "I love you both so much. I'll make sure you're safe. You won't have to carry this alone." She wiped her eyes quickly, trying to pull herself together. "I just… I just want to protect you."

Her dad smiled warmly, though the concern still lingered. "We know, Niamh. We know."

Nick gave a small, encouraging smile. "And now you've got all of us, too. We'll make sure you're safe, and we'll help you through this. Just say the word."

Niamh felt her chest tighten with emotion, but it wasn't fear or sadness—this time, it was something warmer, something stronger. "We're going to get through this," she said softly, looking at both of her parents. "We always do. And now, we've got the strength of this… this new world behind us."

Her mom nodded slowly, a small but genuine smile forming. "Well, I'm not sure I fully understand all of it yet, but if it means keeping our family safe, I'm willing to try."

"Good," Nick said, clapping her dad on the shoulder. "That's all we can ask for. Now, let's get everyone settled. One step at a time."

Her dad raised an eyebrow. "One step at a time. Yeah, that sounds nice… But for now, I could use a drink."

Niamh's mom smirked. "I'm sure the first step is making sure we're all safe, and then we can get you that drink."

Her dad chuckled, the moment of lightness a welcome relief amidst the heaviness of everything.

As Aoife and Nick spoke quietly among themselves, Niamh looked at her parents, at the people who had raised her, loved her, and always did their best for her. The weight of everything, of the life she'd stepped into, still pressed on her chest, but for the first time in a long while, she felt like maybe, just maybe, they could handle it together.

"We can call the Thornes. They are long-time family friends. I'm sure they'll let us stay there temporarily while we get this fixed. We'll figure something out. No need to worry yourselves." Her mom said.

"Mom, it's no trouble. If you ever change your mind, please let me know. I did this, I owe you." She knew her parents were putting on a strong front for her. The guilt of everything was eating her up. They always had a hard time accepting help, so she was surprised they were letting Nick and Aoife help as much as they were now even.

"If you need any help with anything, we have teams worldwide with a wide range of skills, including architects and builders, if you need any assistance. This is what we do." Nick added.

Niamh knew her parents would never accept help. They hated people thinking they couldn't handle things on their own. It would wound their pride. Aoife seemed to know what she was thinking. She leaned over to her and said, "It's up to them what help they want to accept, but we'll help them get set up with a new wardrobe and essentials. Then they can let us know what they need from there. It's hard, but they have to make their own choices. We can't force someone to accept our help."

The weight of Niamh's thoughts felt heavier than the charred remnants of her home. She stood there, frozen, staring at the destruction, the ash swirling in the wind. She had failed to save it, failed to stop the fire in time to preserve the place she had called home for so long. The smell of burnt wood lingered, biting at her throat, mixing with the exhaustion and guilt that consumed her.

Her parents, standing in the distance, looked like shadows of themselves, defeated, broken by what they had just witnessed. Tears stained her mother's cheeks, and her father stood with his hands on her mother's shoulders in an attempt to comfort her, their eyes red from smoke burning them. The house, their home, was gone. Niamh's heart ached, the overwhelming pain of helplessness sinking deep.

She was so used to trying to fix things, trying to control the uncontrollable. But this… this was beyond her reach. And as she looked at the remains of her childhood, it seemed as though all the power in the world couldn't undo what had been done.

Aoife's voice broke through her spiraling thoughts. "I didn't know you could do that with the fire."

Niamh glanced at her, forcing a weak smile. "I didn't either," she admitted, her voice barely above a whisper. "I just… had a feeling I wouldn't get burned. I had to try."

Nick looked at her then, his face softening as he stepped closer. "I'm glad you did, or I wouldn't be standing here," he said, his words sinking into her chest, easing the weight there. His smile was sincere, and the warmth in his voice gave her something to hold on to. "You saved me."

The words hit her harder than she expected, the tears threatening to spill once more. He was right. If she hadn't acted, they would all have been consumed by the flames. She had done something powerful, something right.

"For that, I will be forever grateful," Aoife added, her voice thick with emotion as she leaned in to hug Nick more deeply. Niamh tried to swallow the lump in her throat, but it wouldn't go away.

And then, there it was again: the overwhelming sense of guilt. She'd saved them, yes, but she couldn't save everything. She couldn't save her parents from the pain of losing their home. It was her home too, but for some reason, she felt more of a loss for her parents than for herself. That was the home they had built and raised a family in. They'd spent a lifetime collecting memories in it. She didn't share the same bond with the house; she was sad, of course, but more heartbroken for her parents.

She couldn't erase the damage, couldn't take back what had been lost. She was supposed to protect them, to make it better, but she wasn't sure she had.

Niamh's eyes shifted back to her parents. Her heart clenched as she saw the tears streaking down her mother's face, the quiet grief in her father's eyes. The guilt was suffocating, threatening to drown her.

She thought about her birth mother, about the power, the darkness, the dimension that called to her. Maybe it would be easier to disappear into that other world, to leave this pain behind, to leave her family safe. Maybe her presence here only brought destruction, only brought them closer to danger.

Maybe it would be better for everyone if she just left.

But the thought of leaving them, of walking away from everything she had ever known, made her stomach turn. She couldn't, she wouldn't, abandon them. Not after all they had done for her. Not after everything they had already been through.

Chapter 19

Niamh stood in the shower, the warm water cascading over her, its soothing touch a sharp contrast to the storm raging inside her. The black soot, the remnants of her childhood, washed away in streams, but no matter how many times she scrubbed, she couldn't erase the feeling of failure. The dirt clung to her, both on her skin and in her heart, a constant reminder of everything she couldn't save.

Her tears mingled with the water, dissolving into nothing, as if they had never existed. As if her pain and her guilt could simply be washed away with a rinse. But she knew better. The house, her home, was in ruins. Most of her memories, too, were now just ashes in the wind. She had waited too long. She should've acted faster. She should've known.

Her parents were settling in with their good friends now. The insurance was in place, new records were requested, and everything was getting back to normal, except it wasn't. Not for Niamh. They were rebuilding their life, but it wasn't the same. It would never be the same. Not without the home that held the pieces of who they once were.

She had been the one to call the shots, the one who had chosen to act, and now it was her responsibility to make things right. The guilt gnawed at her like a fire steadily growing inside her, feeding off her regrets, consuming her. Every moment that passed was another ember adding to the blaze in her chest.

Niamh knew she couldn't keep going like this. She had to change how the story was going. She no longer wanted to always be the damsel in distress. She vowed to make sure nothing like this ever happened again.

She clenched her fists, the water now running cold against her skin and the sound of her own heartbeat pounding in her ears. She had to find a way. She had to become stronger, faster, better. For them. For herself.

There was no other choice.

Sleep wouldn't come to Niamh no matter how hard she tried. There was no way her mind could quiet enough for rest. After pacing the room, hoping to tire herself out to no avail, she finally gave in and decided to go for a swim. It had helped her relax in the past, maybe it would help her now.

The salty water helped soothe the tension in her aching muscles, but it didn't touch the emptiness gnawing at her heart. After swimming a few laps and soaking in the hot tub until she was well and truly pruney, she gave up and dried off. Deciding what to do next because she knew her mind still wouldn't let her sleep. She knew Lidia was already asleep, safe and sound in her room, so Niamh didn't want to disturb her. But Bain? He had no such luxury of peace. He was the reason all of this was happening, the reason her parents had suffered.

With her heart burning with anger and frustration she could no longer contain, Niamh stormed down to the medical wing. Her steps were quick and purposeful, each one fueled by the storm of emotions swirling inside her.

She knew Bain would be there, peacefully sleeping without a care in the world, oblivious to the chaos he'd left in his wake. The thought of his calm, untroubled rest only made her anger boil hotter.

She wanted him to feel it, to feel even a fraction of the rage, the sadness, and the betrayal that churned inside her. She wasn't going to hold back this time. He'd see all of it. She was about to unleash the weight of her heartbreak and fury on him, showing no pity.

The hospital room was dim, illuminated only by the soft light of machines, their constant beeps and whirs filling the otherwise still air. Bain lay in the bed on his side, handcuffed only to one of the side rails now. His face was slack with relaxation, a picture of calm.

And yet, all Niamh felt was rage. The sight of him, looking so comfortable, so relaxed, tore at her. Pain curled in her chest, the weight of it suffocating her. She could barely contain herself as she stormed to his bedside. Without a second thought, she swung her arm and slapped him across the face.

His eyes flew open, wide with fear, and his mouth gaped in surprise. The pink mark on his cheek blossomed as he stared at her, confused and uncomprehending. Her pulse roared in her ears. She tried to ignore the fact that he looked healthier, his eyes clearer, his skin more vibrant. The thought made her sick. He was recovering in a pampered style while her parents were trying to rebuild their lives, while everything she had known was in ruins.

Bain sat up slowly, his movements careful as he tried to regain some composure. His voice was small, almost hesitant. "I take it things didn't go well?"

He kept his tone measured, knowing that one wrong word, one wrong move, could set her off even further. The sting of her earlier hit still lingered, not on his skin but in the weight of her fury. He hadn't expected her to strike him, but strangely, a part of him felt… proud.

She had found her strength, the fire inside her that she'd always been too afraid to let out.

He looked at her, standing tall and brimming with emotion, and decided he would take whatever she needed to throw at him. If it would help her feel even a little better, it was worth it.

After all, he knew deep down that this was all his fault. She was in this situation because of him. Taking her anger was the least he could do.

"Not really!" she screamed, her silver eyes flaring with light, illuminating the room in a harsh glow. She didn't care about the hospital's quiet or the patients who might be sleeping nearby. All that mattered in that moment was making Bain feel even a fraction of the pain she was carrying.

"Are… are your parents okay?" he asked, his tone shifting, now cautious, as though sensing her near breaking point.

"They are, but everything else is destroyed!" Niamh's voice cracked as the weight of it all overwhelmed her. "Their home is gone, my home is gone! Everything they've worked for, everything they had, is gone! They're starting over, and they were so close to retirement…" Her words faltered as tears welled up, burning her swollen eyes. She hadn't realized how much she was holding in until now.

Bain's face softened, his voice quieter. "I'm so sorry. Truly. I never meant for any of this to happen. I didn't think your mother would hurt the people who raised you. I tried to keep Lidia safe…"

"Stop calling her that!" Niamh's voice hissed, a growl escaping from deep within her. "She's not my mother! She's a demon. My parents are my real parents! Not her!" The words felt like acid in her mouth, each one more painful than the last.

"I apologize for the poor choice of words," Bain said, quickly realizing that any further missteps could cost him dearly. He swallowed hard, knowing that the only thing keeping him alive was the delicate thread of their conversation.

Niamh stood next to Bain's hospital bed, tears streaming steadily down her cheeks, each drop falling onto her chest. It was only then that she realized she hadn't changed out of her swimsuit. In the heat of her rage, she must have gone straight to the hospital after the pool, not even stopping to think. She could feel Bain's eyes on her, trying not to look at her exposed form in the cutout swimsuit, but it didn't matter. She felt his gaze, and for a brief moment, the urge to cover up with anything, anything at all, swept over her. But she refused to give in. She was not going to cower. Not now. Not in front of him.

She stood strong, tall, her posture rigid, masking the insecurity threatening to surface.

"Why didn't you do anything to stop that creature?" she asked, her voice shaky but fierce.

Bain shifted slightly in his bed, clearly uncomfortable, his handcuffs jingling with the movement. "Well, honey, I was a little tied up," he said, trying to inject some humor into the situation, but it fell flat.

"You could have done something!" Her words came out sharper than she intended, her frustration spilling over.

"I don't have the kind of power it takes to control an underling," he said, his voice quieter, more resigned. "I… I have no real powers."

Silence filled the room like a heavy weight. Niamh's chest tightened, and she stared at him, not knowing whether to believe him. His words seemed genuine, but Bain had a knack for twisting truths to suit his needs. She wiped her tears away, trying to gather herself, and stood a little taller. The tears had stopped, but the coldness that settled into her heart was only growing. Bain could see it. He saw her wall rising, each brick of hurt and anger stacking higher and higher around her heart. She needed to protect herself any way she could, and right now, it meant closing her heart off from heartache again.

"Niamh, I… I am so sorry," Bain said, his voice softer now, almost pleading. "If I could have stopped him, I would have; I just don't have that kind of power. I didn't want you to get hurt in any way."

"Don't worry, I'm powerful enough," she snapped, her voice cold and unyielding. "I stopped him. I don't need your pity. I don't need your excuses. And I certainly don't need you or your help."

With that, she turned on her heel and walked out of the room, her footsteps echoing in the sterile silence that followed her. Bain watched her go, the weight of guilt heavy on his chest. He knew she didn't trust him; how could she? He had betrayed her in so many ways. All he had left was his hope, a hope that one day, she might see the effort he was putting in. He wasn't a good person. He was bad at being good, but he would keep trying for her, even if it seemed like everything he did only made things worse. He would have given anything to take her pain away, but he was the cause of it.

As he lay there, still handcuffed to the bed, all he could do was hope that one day, Niamh would let him prove he could be better.

Niamh lay still, staring at the smoothness of the ceiling above her bed, her mind adrift in the silence. She tried to will herself to float into white nothingness, to escape her thoughts, but sleep slowly overtook her despite her best efforts. She found herself in a familiar place, the Detroit skating rink Lidia had taken her to just days before. The glow of the lit-up pine tree illuminated the rink, making it look magical, almost otherworldly.

The ice was perfectly smooth, glassy, and pristine, untouched by the sharp blades of skates. Tiny, fluffy snowflakes fluttered down around her, each one seeming to hang in the air before gently landing on the ice as she spun, taking in the peaceful, sparkling scene. Everything felt quiet, the darkness of the night blending with the soft glow of the lights.

Then, the deep, sensual laugh came. It vibrated through the air, sending a shiver down her spine. Niamh froze her senses on high alert. She looked around but saw no one. The rink was empty.

She stepped out onto the ice in her shoes, the coolness of the ground seeping through her soles as she searched the surroundings. She spun in slow circles, eyes darting in every direction. But still, there was no sign of anyone. The laughter came again, closer this time. It was low rumbling, like it came from deep within, and she could feel it in her chest.

Her pulse quickened as the realization hit her. She recognized the laugh.

"Bain!" she called out, her voice commanding, her tone sharp. "Show yourself!"

But there was no answer. The only sound was the whisper of the wind as it passed by. And then, there was warmth on the side of her neck. A soft touch on her cheek. Her brain said to run! Run away fast! But her body betrayed her, responding with a warmth that sent a shiver through her.

Traitor, she cursed herself.

She wanted to shout, to demand he stop, but the words caught in her throat, trapped by something far stronger than her will. The touch continued, soft, tender kisses gliding up her neck to her earlobe. She could feel his warm breath against her skin, sending heat flooding through her. Fingers tracing up her body. They moved with purpose, with a slow, deliberate touch, from her thigh, around her hips, to her waist.

His presence behind her was undeniable. His body pressed close, searching to please, to consume. Niamh felt the pull of him, her body betraying her more with every second.

Then, as if from nowhere, a voice.

"Wake up!"

Lidia's hands shook Niamh's shoulders, pulling her out of the haze of sleep. Her eyes fluttered open, the dream dissipating like smoke.

"Girl, you're moaning and making it real awkward for me right now," Lidia said with a teasing smirk.

Niamh blinked a few times, still trying to gather her thoughts. She felt the heat in her cheeks as she tried to make sense of the lingering sensations from the dream.

"That was… weird," she muttered, her voice shaky. She paused for a moment, the remnants of the dream still clinging to her. "Good… but weird."

Lidia raised an eyebrow, a playful grin tugging at her lips. "Sounded like a 'good' dream."

Niamh just groaned and buried her face in her hands. "Don't ever mention that again."

Niamh threw a pillow at Lidia, and it landed with a soft thud as they both collapsed onto the bed, laughing. That was what Niamh needed, a moment of carefree laughter. It grounded her, even if the echoes of the dream lingered in the back of her mind. Whatever had happened in that dream, she could've done without it… unless it stayed confined to her dreams.

Lidia rolled onto her side, still giggling, and shot Niamh a grin. "What are you doing here anyway?" Niamh asked, wiping away the last of her laughter.

"Oh, I was tired of waiting to hear about your parents, and Aoife told me I could come up. Hope you don't mind. Even if you do, I don't care," Lidia teased, knowing full well that Niamh wouldn't mind her company.

"Did Aoife say anything about my parents?" Niamh asked, her voice quieter now, the weight of her emotions slipping back in.

"She gave me the cliff notes of it. I'm really sorry about your house. But I'm so glad they're okay! That's what matters. Everything else can be replaced. It's crazy that you stopped it. Did you know you could do that?"

Lidia asked, her voice filled with awe.

Niamh let out a stressed laugh, shaking her head. "I had no idea. That was a new trick. I didn't do it in time, though. Most of it was gone by the time I realized what was happening. But they were almost hurt because of me. I can't…" Her voice wavered for a second, and she had to swallow the lump in her throat. "I can't keep the people I love safe. Not with her trying to get to me. I don't know what to do."

Lidia was quiet for a moment, her expression softening. "You saved them. That thing tried to kill them. You *did* stop it."

Niamh shook her head again, her hands curling into fists. "That thing was only there because of me. The wicked witch of the other dimension… she wants me. And now she's going after everyone around me. I'm supposed to protect them, but all I'm doing is putting them in danger. I can't keep doing this."

Lidia shifted, sitting up and pulling Niamh into a hug, the comforting weight of her friend's embrace making her feel a little less alone in her turmoil. "You don't have to do it alone," Lidia said quietly. "You've got us, Niamh. Aoife, Nick, and me… we'll help you. You don't have to carry all this by yourself."

Niamh clung to her for a moment, trying to steady her breathing, but the anxiety and fear were still there, lingering. "I just… I just want this to be over. I want to stop feeling like I'm a walking target."

Lidia pulled back slightly, looking her in the eye. "You'll figure it out. You always do. You're stronger than you think. You don't need to have all the answers right now."

But at that moment, Niamh didn't feel strong. She felt like she was just one wrong move away from losing everything she held dear.

"Will they come here? I'm sure they'd let them."

"They don't want to. They're staying with the Thornes for a bit until they figure out what they're going to do."

"Oh, I love the Thornes. That was very nice of them!"

"Yeah, Nick said he'd send someone over to put a cast on the house to protect them, so that makes me feel a little better too," Niamh murmured, trying to focus on the positive.

Lidia tilted her head, a little confused. "I'm not sure what that means, but if it helps keep them safe, then I support it," she said, her tone light.

"I'm not exactly sure either, but I'll do anything to keep them safe," Niamh said with a small, weary smile.

Lidia paused, sensing the heavier undertone in Niamh's words, but decided to change the subject, trying to bring back some levity. "So… are you going to tell me who you were dreaming about?" she prodded, unable to resist.

Niamh hesitated, feeling the heat rise in her cheeks as she considered the dream. "I honestly don't know. I didn't see anyone, I just felt… a lot," she admitted.

Lidia raised an eyebrow, leaning in. "What exactly did you feel?"

Niamh let out a short laugh. "Not what you're hoping to hear about," she joked. "Just someone being close to me, gentle touches. And no, no place inappropriate to talk about before you ask…. Though it was heading in that direction. If you hadn't have woken me up…" she gave Lidia a devious smile.

Lidia snapped her fingers in mock disappointment. "My bad. I'll work on my timing. We have to get you a date, girl. It's been so long; you're making up invisible people in your dreams now."

Niamh rolled her eyes, but the edges of her lips curved into a smile. "I think it was someone, I just didn't see anyone. I… I was hoping it was someone I knew, maybe."

Lidia tapped her chin thoughtfully. "Would this someone be tall, blonde, and smexy?" she asked with a teasing smirk.

"Possibly. Is that weird?" Niamh asked, her voice betraying the uncertainty she felt about the whole situation. "I don't want to like him. He's hurt me so many times and keeps doing it! Unintentional or not, it doesn't matter. Danger follows this man around like a shadow."

Lidia's grin softened, and she shook her head. "No, not weird. Just a little sad," she said, her tone turning more serious but still light-hearted. "You've never been drawn to the dangerous guys, so I'm just surprised."

Niamh pouted jokingly, knowing deep down that Lidia was right. It *was* a little sad. To want someone who had hurt her so much. To still feel that pull, despite everything. But she couldn't deny it. A strange ache in her chest made her wonder if there was more to Bain than she'd seen or maybe just more to what she wished he could be.

"I mean, he did save you, and he does seem convincing that he likes you," Lidia mused. "Maybe he's not such a bad guy. Maybe we just haven't seen the best side of him yet. And maybe you'd like to see his best side," she added, finishing with a wink.

Niamh blinked, the pull of her emotions fighting against her better judgment. "I don't know…" She let the thought trail off, unsure how to even feel about Bain anymore. She wanted to believe Lidia was right, that there was something redeemable in him. But every time she thought of him, the weight of everything he had done pressed down on her chest. He hadn't earned her trust. He hadn't earned her anything.

But that lingering feeling from the dream, that pull… it made it hard to ignore. She couldn't tell if it was just the aftermath of her desire for connection or if something deeper, more complicated was starting to happen.

"I can't think about this now. I have too much going on. He will have to wait," Niamh muttered, still trying to push away the pull Bain seemed to have over her thoughts. There was no room for him right now.

Lidia's eyes softened, but her smile stayed teasing. "Just don't make him wait forever."

Niamh shrugged. "If he likes me, he'll wait as long as it takes." She said it with more hope than conviction, wishing desperately that Bain might somehow prove different from all the others in her past who had come and gone. But deep down, she knew, if he was anything like the rest of mankind, he'd be onto the next best thing in no time.

"Speaking the truth, girlfriend! Know your worth!" Lidia said as she snapped her fingers in the air flamboyantly, her voice playful but the encouragement was there.

Niamh sighed and leaned back on her bed. "What am I going to do about the queen? It's not like I'd ever have a healthy relationship with her, especially after she tried to kill my parents. How could it get better after that?"

It wasn't the first time Niamh had questioned what it would mean to confront her birth mother. It wasn't even that she wanted to; it was just a deep, gnawing ache she couldn't ignore. For most of her life, the idea of her bio mother had hovered in the back of her mind, not as a person but as a concept, disappointment wrapped in a question mark. She knew she had to sever ties, but the idea of facing that pain still felt insurmountable.

Lidia looked at her with understanding in her eyes, her voice steady. "I can't answer that for you. But I do know she can't be left to hurt more people. You can't be afraid to make friendships or have relationships because you're afraid they'll get hurt by her. She needs to be dealt with."

Niamh nodded slowly, the weight of Lidia's words sinking in. She couldn't keep hiding from her bio mother forever, but the thought of confronting her was terrifying. She had to get stronger, learn to control her powers more, and somehow find a way to protect the people she loved. But for now, she needed to take things one step at a time.

"I don't know how to stop her, but I do know I have to get better at controlling my powers. Wanna meet Njeri today? I think you'd like her. She's pretty badass," Niamh suggested, needing a distraction from the tangled mess of thoughts in her mind.

Lidia grinned, her energy infectious. "Sure! Not like I have a lot to do around here. I think I've gained ten pounds since we've been here. I have to do other things than eat. I'll be your Robin, but I won't actually help in any way. I'll just be the funny sidekick." She paused, "But I am kind of hungry. Can we grab food before your physical activities?"

Niamh laughed. "You're always hungry."

"It's true, but this place has amazing food, and did I mention it's all free? I kept asking who to pay, and no one would take my money. So, I'm taking advantage of this!

Someday, I'll meet some man or woman who loves a little fluff on their future wife." Lidia gestured dramatically as if presenting herself as some kind of future treasure.

Niamh couldn't help but laugh. "You're beautiful inside and out, no matter what size you are. And this food does beat the microwave dinner or leftover meatloaf I'd probably be having if I were home. Food will get my mind off things. What sounds good?"

"I've been talking to the chef. There's not much to do around here, so I made friends," Lidia said with a laugh. "Anyway, he's been having fun surprising me with new food each time. Want to be surprised with me?"

Niamh smirked. "Lidia, you're so much."

"No, I am just the right amount," Lidia said, sitting up straight with exaggerated confidence.

Niamh rolled her eyes with a grin. "Yes, I'll have whatever you're having or whatever they send. Just no brains or weird organs, okay?"

Lidia raised a hand in mock solemnity. "Deal! I already told him nothing Andrew Zimmer would eat."

They shared a laugh before Lidia bounded out of the room, ready to tackle whatever came next. Niamh's mind still lingered on her birth mother, Bain, and her powers, but for the first time in a while, she felt a little lighter. Maybe today, just for a moment, she could forget about everything she couldn't control and enjoy what was in front of her.

Not long after Lidia placed the call, there was a knock at the door. Niamh opened the door, and the beautiful blonde waitress from before was standing there pushing a cart loaded with covered plates.

"Cami! How are you?"

"Oh, I'm great! Thanks! You guys must be hungry. There's a lot of food here!" she joked.

"We are hungry, but the chef was apparently going to surprise us. Lidia has been making friends, I guess."

"Yes, she's a bit of a social butterfly, isn't she? It's been great having new people around here. Things have been… quiet lately."

"She is over here!" Lidia called from the open bathroom door, touching up her makeup. "And yes, I pride myself on being a butterfly, not an actual one, of course… I wish, though," Niamh and Cami quietly giggled.

"Quiet can be good though, right? It means no one is in danger." Niamh spoke softly, unsure if she wanted to hear the answer.

"True." She paused, "When Aoife arrived here, her human friend was attacked while she was learning how to control her powers."

"What happened?" Lidia prodded as Cami sat the food on the small table.

"Aoife's ex was jealous and attacked a woman who helped her escape his grasp. Luckily Aoife could portal there and she and Nick stopped it in time, but if she couldn't have used her magic that well, it would have been a very different outcome. The coven almost prevented us from helping. They warned me to not say anything, but I couldn't just sit around and not help."

"That's terrifying. I'm glad she's okay." Cami didn't explain about the coven anymore, it was still a sore subject around the building. "But everyone knew the coven was corrupt. Nick quickly got them in line, whether they liked it or not. I'm not telling you this, to scare you. I'm telling you this, so you know how fragile human life is and to urge you to protect the people you love. At all costs."

"I am starting to realize this myself. We had an… incident with my parents earlier. They're okay," Niamh saw the concern on Cami's face. "But I have to get stronger to keep them safe. And I'm not letting Lidia leave until I am sure she's safe. Sorry, but you'll be seeing a lot more of her around here." Niamh chuckled.

"Looking forward to it. The chef hasn't been this happy to have someone test out his new recipes in a long time. I'm a vegetarian, so his talents are wasted on me," Cami added.

"I didn't know. That's cool."

"Yeah, being a banshee and knowing what death feels like, I can't bring myself to eat those innocent creatures. But don't worry, I don't judge others who do."

"I didn't know. Wow, that must be really hard. I couldn't imagine sensing death all around you. I was feeling sorry for myself with the powers I had. Now, I feel a little grateful for what I have. It could have been much worse. Not that your powers are worse," she added, trying not to insult Cami.

"No, you're fine. It's not much fun. But it makes me appreciate life even more. It is what it is, ya know. Well, your food is all ready for you!" she said, changing tones. "I'll be leaving you to it. Let me know if you need anything else."

She turned to leave but said, "It's not all bad here ya know. The last time we had a newcomer bring a human friend along, he became my boyfriend," she said with a wink.

Lidia raised her hand, "Where do I sign up for a magical boyfriend?"

They all laughed.

She started to walk out the door, Niamh called to her, "Hey Cami?"

"Yeah?" she spun around.

"Thanks for telling me. I appreciate it."

Cami just nodded, gave a small grin, and left the room.

Niamh sat at the table, the weight of Cami's words still heavy in her mind. To live with the constant awareness of death, to feel it hanging around you like a shadow, that was something she couldn't even imagine. She felt a pang of guilt for having been so consumed with her own struggles, but in a way, it helped her see things from a new perspective. She wasn't alone in having to deal with extraordinary circumstances. Maybe that was why she needed to focus more on the people around her, those who had their battles to fight, just like she did.

Lidia, clearly unfazed by the heavier conversation, dug in with enthusiasm. "Man, this food looks amazing. I might have to find myself a chef around here just for the food alone."

Niamh smiled weakly, picking at her plate. She couldn't quite shake the feeling that Cami had given her something to think about, something more important than the food, or the dream, or even Bain. *Protect the people she loved.* That was her responsibility now. She had to get stronger. But more than that, she had to learn how to lean on others. Cami had a point, even if it was hard to swallow; she couldn't do it alone.

"Cami's right, though," Niamh murmured, staring at her plate. "I have to focus on what I can control. I need to get better at my powers, better at protecting my family." Her voice was quiet but firm.

Lidia nodded, her usual teasing demeanor softening a little. "You're right.

And you will. You're tougher than you think, Niamh. But don't forget, we're all here for you. Even if you don't always need us, we'll still be around. And who knows, maybe you'll need a magical boyfriend too, one day," she added with a wink, trying to lighten the mood again.

Niamh chuckled, the weight on her shoulders feeling just a little lighter. She didn't have answers for everything, but she did know one thing for sure: she wasn't going to face it alone. The road ahead would be difficult, but with people like Lidia and Cami by her side, maybe it wouldn't be as impossible as it seemed.

"Alright, alright, I'm done," Lidia said, leaning back in the chair with a dramatic sigh. "But seriously, you've got *the* guy downstairs, and you're over here talking about magic training like it's a 9-to-5 job. A girl's gotta wonder, you know?" She raised an eyebrow, clearly enjoying teasing Niamh.

Niamh buried her face in her hands, groaning. "I swear, you make everything sound like some soap opera." She couldn't help the small smile tugging at the corners of her lips, though. Lidia had a way of making the serious feel just a little bit lighter.

"I'm just saying, there's magic here, literally and figuratively," Lidia continued, tapping her chin. " I'm talking about the kind where a girl gets to explore all the fun and danger that comes with a guy who looks like he walked off a romance novel cover."

Niamh rolled her eyes but couldn't stop the warmth that spread through her chest. "I'm not thinking about him, okay? I'm focusing on getting stronger. My family… my friends. I need to protect them. I can't afford distractions."

Lidia grinned, her teasing tone softening. "I get it, but just remember that you're allowed to have *some* fun, too. It doesn't make you weak. In fact, it might just make you stronger. And I'm not talking about getting all googly-eyed, but there's nothing wrong with a little spark."

Niamh nodded, appreciating the reminder. "You're right, Lidia. I need to keep my balance. And you… you just need to keep being the awesome, supportive friend that you are."

Lidia beamed, tossing her hair over her shoulder. "It's what I do best, babe., I'm your Robin anytime… but I don't do anything; I'm just here to look good. Now, when do I get to meet this Njeri person you're so fond of? I have to see what kind of trainer you've got."

"She's amazing. Stronger than anyone I know," Niamh said, her face lighting up a little at the thought of Njeri. "But she's different. She's… not like anyone else here."

"I'm down for whatever. I might even pick up a few moves along the way." Lidia stood up, stretching dramatically.

Niamh laughed, feeling the warmth of the moment wrap around her. Life was chaotic, unpredictable, and often overwhelming, but at least she didn't have to face it alone.

"Girl, I can't wear these pants anymore," Lidia complained, tugging at the waistband. "Got anything with an elastic waistband I can change into before we go?"

"Honestly, I have no idea what's in those drawers. Feel free to check."

Lidia tossed a pair of grey sweatpants in Niamh's direction, then quickly slipped into a black pair herself before collapsing onto the bed with an exaggerated sigh. "So, you ready to go kick some butt, or whatever it is you do during your magical practice?"

Niamh rubbed her stomach, still feeling a bit too full from the rich meal. "I shouldn't have eaten that much, but luckily Njeri's training is more mental than physical."

"Ooh, switching teams finally?" Lidia grinned playfully. "What have I told you? Girls have more fun." Lidia knew Niamh was straight, but it never stopped her from lightening the mood with queer humor.

Niamh let out a laugh, shaking her head. "Um, no. No judgment for anyone on that team, but I like men far too much."

Lidia pouted dramatically. "Can't say I didn't try and warn you."

"You'll like Njeri," Niamh added, pulling a fresh shirt over her head. "But just to warn you, she's taken."

Lidia's face fell for a moment before she raised her hands in mock surrender. "Oh, no fun. You're killing my dream girl fantasy over here."

Niamh chuckled, offering a hand to help Lidia up from the bed. "Okay, let's go see if Njeri can help me out. Come on, time to get to work."

Chapter 20

Lidia gasped as she stepped into the training room, her eyes wide with awe. The space was large and open, with padded floors and an inflatable tower looming in the center. Niamh's gaze immediately found Njeri across the room, lying on the floor, her long braids cascading beneath her as she knocked out crunches with practiced precision. Lidia gave Niamh a mischievous look, then without warning, sprinted toward the inflatable tower.

She made a bold leap, but it didn't quite go as planned. Instead of sticking the landing, Lidia bounced off the second layer and tumbled gracelessly to the padded floor. Niamh couldn't help but burst into laughter, and Lidia joined in, her infectious giggle filling the room.

Njeri, having noticed the spectacle, slowly made her way toward them, her expression unreadable. "Impressive… try," she said dryly, offering a slight nod, though it was clear she wasn't going to be handing out any compliments for the failed attempt.

Lidia stood up, dusting herself off with a flourish. "Thanks. I was going for the 'bug on the windshield' effect."

"Well, then you nailed it." Njeri gave her a thumbs-up and chuckled, her lips quirking into a brief smile before turning her attention to Niamh. "Had a feeling you'd be swinging by. Ready to get your magic under control?"

Niamh shrugged with a sheepish grin. "How'd you know we'd... Oh, never mind. Obviously, Aoife talked to you about the situation earlier."

"It's a tight community here," Njeri said, her tone matter-of-fact. "Word travels fast. I knew you were a quick learner, but I didn't think you'd have it mastered after only a few sessions."

Niamh smiled, a little proud of how far she had come. "I'm still not sure I've mastered anything, but I'm definitely getting the hang of it."

She turned to Lidia, who was still recovering from her impromptu tumble. "Oh, Njeri, this is my best friend Lidia. She's staying here for a while too, but I'm sure you already knew that."

Njeri's eyes softened for a moment as she gave a small smile and a nod toward Niamh. Then, extending her hand to Lidia, she greeted her with a firm but warm shake.

Lidia, however, had other ideas. With a mischievous glint in her eye, she brought her knuckles to her lips and planted a soft kiss on them. She straightened up with a playful grin, her cheeks coloring slightly as she giggled. "Pleasure to meet you," she said, her voice light. "Heard you've been wandering the halls. Surprised I haven't seen you around yet."

Njeri raised an eyebrow, but there was a hint of amusement in her gaze. "I try to keep a low profile. I've been busy." She glanced around the room. "Besides, not much for me to do here except train."

Lidia's face softened. "I hope I'm not annoying anyone," she said with a touch of sincerity. "There's just not a ton to do by myself."

"I'm sure you'll find your place here soon enough." Njeri's voice was steady and reassuring, though there was a quiet edge to her tone. "In the meantime, you can always keep me company. But now, Niamh, I believe we've got some magic to work on. We don't want anyone else indirectly related to the magical community getting hurt again."

"Yeah, we heard about Aoife's friend getting hurt. That probably affected everyone," Lidia remarked, her voice quiet but full of understanding.

Njeri's expression darkened slightly, the memory weighing on her. "Yeah, I'm not sure how much they've told you, but I assume it isn't much. The coven didn't believe in protecting humans back then. They almost let her die. Aoife's been great for Nick, though. She's pushed him to become a true leader. Got the coven in line and even formed a pact with other creatures to protect humans connected to our world. It's been a big change. For the better, though. I think you'll both find your place here soon enough."

Lidia exchanged a glance with Niamh, her gaze softening at the mention of Aoife. "Sounds like a good shift. Aoife's really stepped up, huh? I can see why you respect her so much."

"She's earned it," Njeri said, giving Niamh a look of quiet encouragement. "I think you can find your place here, too. I'm excited to see what you bring to the table now."

"Thanks for telling us," Niamh replied. "Cami mentioned some of it, but we could tell she was upset, so we didn't want to push her."

Lidia, ever the playful one, batted her lashes at Njeri. "Yeah, we were trying to be considerate," she teased.

Njeri offered a small grin before turning serious again. "Of course. Now, let's get started. Lidia, is it? How about you take a seat in the first room on the right? The barrier's fire and bulletproof, so you shouldn't be able to hurt yourself." She gave a wink.

Lidia rolled her eyes dramatically. "Har, har. Bulletproof? What exactly are you getting us into here?" she muttered, walking toward the clear-walled room with mock reluctance.

"I'm ready. Overly full, but ready," Niamh said with a half-smile, trying to shake off the unease she felt building in her chest.

"Chef hook you up?" Njeri asked, her tone light but teasing. "I hear he's been busy sending food to the three new guests."

Niamh paused for a second, the mention of Chef instantly pulling her back to the moment. She had noticed Lidia had been eating quite a bit, and it made her wonder about the third guest. She could only assume it was Bain. The thought of him made her stomach twist, not out of hunger, but because he seemed to always linger in her thoughts. Between his blonde, curly hair, those high cheekbones, and piercing blue eyes, he had an uncanny way of occupying her mind.

She mentally cursed herself for drifting back to him. Everyone around her seemed to mention him, as if the universe was determined to make it harder for her to keep him out of her thoughts. She shook her head, trying to clear her mind. *Focus, Niamh. Focus.*

"Chef's the best!" Njeri laughed, breaking her from the spiral. "Had to add an extra hour to my workout just to make up for the calories."

Lidia's voice rang out from across the room. "Well, whatever you're doing, it looks great on you!"

Niamh could hear the warmth in Lidia's words, and despite the heaviness of her thoughts, she smiled. Lidia's carefree nature always had a way of lifting the mood.

Njeri shot Lidia a half-grin and a playful wink before turning her attention back to Niamh. "I'm no pyromancy expert," she said, her voice carrying an undercurrent of seriousness, "so I asked Dr. Aba to join us. She has more insight into this topic." She gestured toward the door, and Niamh's gaze followed to see the tall, iridescent-skinned doctor standing there, her presence imposing yet calm.

"Hello again, my dear," Dr. Aba's voice was warm yet clinical, a soothing contrast to the intensity in the room. "It's good to see you doing well. I'm sorry your stay here hasn't been more relaxing. It rarely is for newcomers, but rest assured, you are not alone." Her eyes held a glimmer of empathy, but her focus quickly shifted back to business. "So, let's get to the matter at hand. I believe you have a general sense of how to summon your magic from within, but I wanted to show you something more advanced. Most with the gift of pyromancy still require an external heat source; you do not. You *are* the source."

Niamh's heart skipped at the weight of that. She wasn't just a vessel for flame. She *was* the flame. Dr. Aba motioned toward the center of the room, her voice steady and calm. "I want to see how far your powers extend. I've been doing some research on pyromancy, and it turns out that some had extremely rare abilities and had multiple colored flames. Each color held unique properties." She paused, her gaze intense as she focused on Niamh. "For instance, green flames could travel long distances, like an arrow aimed at its target. Blue flames? They can be put inside someone, causing their blood to boil... resulting in death." Her words hit Niamh like a cold wave, and she swallowed hard. "The purple flame is extremely rare, but it's said to keep someone's heart beating forever, provided they have pure intentions. If they don't... well, it can wither them."

Niamh's stomach churned. This was so much more than she'd ever anticipated. *Fire* was one thing; she could handle that. But now, it was about *intentions* and consequences she wasn't sure she was prepared for.

"I think we should try some of these variations," Dr. Aba continued, her tone firm yet filled with an unspoken reassurance. "Along with your traditional flame, I believe you'd have a fighting chance against your... Queen Cailleach."

The mention of her mother, the woman who wanted her dead, dropped like a weight in Niamh's chest. She had no illusions about the battle ahead, but hearing it spoken aloud made the reality of it more daunting than ever.

She hesitated for a moment, the fear of failure and causing harm creeping up again. "Is this safe?" she asked softly, her voice barely above a whisper. "I don't want anyone else to get hurt by me."

Dr. Aba's eyes softened, understanding the depth of Niamh's concern. "Oh, it's quite safe. We have all the necessary safety precautions in this room. This is the safest place to experiment with new techniques like this." She met Niamh's gaze, holding it with quiet confidence. "That being said, we're entering uncharted territory. There isn't much documented on these rare flames, so we may need to experiment a bit to figure things out."

Niamh glanced over at Lidia, who was still sitting in the clear room across the way, looking relaxed despite the heavy conversation. Lidia offered her a small, reassuring wave, and Niamh felt the weight of the moment lighten, if only slightly.

Niamh nodded slowly, feeling the gravity of the situation settle in. She wasn't just about to train her magic. She was about to uncover parts of herself she wasn't entirely sure she was ready for. But for Lidia, for the people she loved, and for herself, she would push forward. The flames were hers to command now. And she wasn't about to let fear extinguish them.

"Okay, any direction on how to start?" Niamh's voice was uncertain, betraying the tension she felt inside. She wasn't sure she was ready for this. She had always chosen the safe, practical, and predictable path. Her magic had been a source of fear, a reminder of how out of place she was in her own life. Now, the idea of manipulating fire, changing its colors and effects, felt more like an untamed beast than a tool at her disposal. But she knew she had to try. She'd already gone too far down this road to turn back, and the weight of her decision pressed heavily on her.

"Let's get that dummy set up here, Njeri," Dr. Aba's voice was firm, her tone the epitome of professionalism as she gestured toward a glass cubicle room along the side of the space. "That one has the strongest extinguishers in it… just in case," she added, leaning closer to Niamh with a smile that didn't quite reach her eyes.

Niamh gave her a weak smile in return, trying to keep her composure. She appreciated the effort to reassure her, but the unease in her gut didn't dissipate. She was about to experiment with fire, magical fire. There was no real way to prepare for that, no matter how many safety protocols were in place.

Njeri, ever the efficient one, dragged a heavy, human-sized plastic doll into the room, setting it down carefully in a chair. The doll was disturbingly lifelike, dressed in a plaid flannel shirt, blue jeans, and tennis shoes. Its plastic face was blank, almost unnerving in its stillness. Njeri adjusted its clothing as if it were a person, tossing the limbs into place with an ease that made Niamh wince.

She felt an odd pang of guilt. This wasn't real. This was just a doll, a practice target. But still, the thought of her magic, her *wild* magic, being unleashed on something, anything, felt wrong. The doll seemed so innocent, so unassuming, and yet here it was, about to bear the brunt of something she could barely control.

It was easier to think of this inanimate object than a real person. At least she wasn't about to burn someone alive. But even so, Niamh's heart twisted. That doll represented something more to her, something deeper than a simple target. All her life, she had been the odd one, the one who didn't quite fit in. She had been the one left behind, the one told she was too much or too little. The doll, with its blank face and lifeless form, was a mirror to those feelings she had buried for years. It was the embodiment of the shame, the sense of undesirability that had followed her since childhood.

"I'll make sure the extinguishers are ready," Njeri said with a nod to Dr. Aba, noticing Niamh's lingering hesitation. There was an unspoken understanding between them. Njeri had seen the unease in Niamh's eyes, but she didn't push, instead giving her the space to work through it.

Niamh inhaled deeply, her breath shaky. She couldn't allow herself to hesitate. Not now. Not when she had already come this far. "Okay," she whispered to herself, more as a reminder than a declaration. "Okay."

Njeri stepped back, her expression calm but encouraging, letting the doctor take the lead.

"You're going to become more in touch with yourself than you've ever been before," the doctor began, her tone gentle but firm. "The magic is a part of you, a part you've been hiding for a long time. You need to recognize it, embrace it, and make peace with that hidden part of yourself. Only then will you be able to truly control it."

She paused, clearly choosing her next words carefully. "You also need to understand how you *connect* with your magic. For some, it's a whisper inside their mind, a voice guiding them. For others, it's a tingling sensation deep in their soul. And for some, it's a vision, an image they can see clearly. You need to find what works for you, what lets you understand your magic."

Niamh nodded, taking a steadying breath as she let the words sink in. *Find the magic and embrace it.*

It sounded so simple, but her chest tightened as doubt crept in. When she thought of her magic, acceptance wasn't what came to mind, fear was. Fear of its unpredictability, its overwhelming power. Fear of what it could mean about her.

But then again… her magic had saved her. Time and time again, it had been there, pulling her back from the brink. It seemed to know her better than she knew herself, responding to her deepest wants and needs.

Maybe it wasn't the magic that was scary, she thought. *Maybe not accepting it is what made it so terrifying.*

She closed her eyes and waited. She waited for a feeling, a sound, *something* from her magic. But nothing came.

She felt warm, but that was nothing new, she always felt warm. It was simply part of who she was.

Deciding to try a different approach, Niamh shifted her focus. Instead of listening or waiting, she imagined what her flames might look like. She knew they came in different colors, so she searched for the darkest place inside her, the one she rarely dared to explore.

She pictured a green flame flickering wildly in the wind, lively and unpredictable. Then a blue one, tall and steady, its strength unwavering. Finally, she imagined a purple flame, pulsating as though the wind was teasing and tugging at it, yet it refused to extinguish.

As she visualized these flames, something incredible happened: they leaped higher, as if excited to finally be seen.

Niamh's fear ebbed away, replaced by a growing sense of connection. These flames weren't enemies to be feared; they were her friends. They didn't want to harm her, they wanted to help her.

An overwhelming urge rose within her. She wanted to touch them, to reassure them in return. She imagined a hand reaching out her hand and gently caressing the flames. The moment her fingers brushed against them, they glowed brighter, their colors intensifying with the small act of kindness.

She felt a sense of completeness, as if a missing piece of herself had finally clicked into place.

But then, a tugging sensation in the back of her mind disrupted her peace. A nagging feeling whispered that something wasn't quite right.

A nagging feeling, insistent and sharp, broke through the calm. She couldn't ignore it, no matter how much she tried. Something wasn't right.

She peered past the three flames, through their translucent bodies, and for a fleeting moment, she thought she saw more. Shadows of other colors flickered in the background, faint and hidden. She strained to see them, but they wouldn't come closer, retreating just out of reach.

The uneasy feeling persisted, clawing at her focus, but she pushed it aside. She couldn't afford to be distracted now, not when she was finally learning to connect with the flames she could see.

For now, she would focus on the three she'd discovered. They were enough.

"I got it. I see them," Niamh announced, pride swelling in her chest. She kept her eyes closed, almost afraid to open them.

What if opening her eyes made the flames disappear? She didn't want to lose them. She'd endured so much hurt already, and in the brief time she'd known the flames, they had become a part of her, a part she knew she couldn't bear to lose.

"Great! Good job, Niamh!" The encouragement was firm and excited, cutting through her nervous thoughts. "Now," the instructor continued, motioning to the far corner of the room, "I'd like you to stand over there."

Niamh hesitated, reluctant to let go of this quiet, powerful connection, but she did as instructed.

"Summon a green flame," the instructor said, their voice steady and calm. "Focus on it and then think about where you'd like it to go. When you're ready, release it, willing it toward the target." They pointed to a distant, circular target on the wall, marked with faint scorch marks from previous training sessions.

"Your mind must be free of distractions," they added, their tone serious now. "Or it could be disastrous."

Niamh's hands flexed at her sides, nerves buzzing through her fingers. She took a steadying breath, trying to block out the room, the lingering doubts, and the weight of expectations pressing down on her.

Niamh tried to clear her mind, to banish any distracting thoughts. She pushed away the image of Lidia's frightened face, her distraught parents' tearful expressions, and most stubborn of all, Bain's irritatingly sexy smirk.

She pictured darkness, a blank, black canvas in her mind. But it was easier said than done. Little snippets of her family, fleeting memories, and *his* face kept flashing across her thoughts like unwelcome intruders.

"Niamh," Dr. Aba's calm but firm voice broke through her trance, pulling her back. The doctor must have sensed her struggle. "You're overthinking. I want you to clear your thoughts and then reach deep inside yourself. Feel for the green flame; it's there, waiting to get out."

Niamh nodded, taking a deep breath as the doctor continued.

"Only take a little. A small ember is all you need. Grab that tiny piece and hold it in your mind while you think about where you want it to go. Do not release it until your intended target is clear, *only* that target. Don't let other thoughts creep in. Once the image is steady in your mind, release the ember and visualize it reaching and penetrating the target. Got it?"

"I'm ready," Niamh said, though her voice lacked conviction. She spread her feet apart, planting herself firmly. "As I'll ever be."

Closing her eyes tightly, she focused on the dummy sitting in the chair. She pictured its lifeless, plastic body in her mind.

What will it look like when the flame hits? she wondered. *What damage will it do to that poor, melted-looking face?*

Her concentration wavered as her mind betrayed her, veering sharply into forbidden territory. She thought about Bain's body instead, how it looked so perfectly chiseled, more sculpted than the finest ice sculpture. Her cheeks heated as her thoughts lingered on the feel of his chest beneath her hands, the way she'd rested against him not long ago.

Her heart raced as she remembered his strong legs next to hers, the way his touch. *Focus!*

She panicked, pushing the thoughts out of her head with force. *Focus,* she told herself harshly. *You're not here to think about him. The dummy. Picture the dummy.*

Taking another deep breath, she steadied her trembling hands, forcing her mind back to the task at hand.

Reaching deep within herself, Niamh felt the place where her flames nestled, a restless, shimmering energy waiting to be tapped. As she descended into the depths of her magic, a rainbow of colors unfolded before her. Each flame radiated a unique presence, evoking different emotions that swirled and churned in her chest.

Together, the riot of colors made her anxious, their collective power overwhelming her. Their energy spilled over into her emotions, heightening her unease. She realized with startling clarity that there were too many flames, more than Dr. Aba had described.

For now, she shoved that revelation aside, focusing on her immediate goal. She reached for the green flame, forcing herself to ignore the others.

But they didn't make it easy. The flames jostled and surged, shoving and pushing against each other as if competing for her attention. Each one vied to leap into her grasp first, their flickering forms bouncing off each other in an unruly dance of chaos.

Focus, she told herself, taking a deep breath.

With quick precision, she mentally grabbed hold of the green flame, closing an invisible hand firmly around it. The moment she did, the other flames roared higher inside her, their energy flaring with what felt like anger or jealousy. Their discontent spilled into her, making her stomach churn.

The green flame, now isolated, quivered in her grasp. It felt wild, untamed, but she held on tightly, refusing to let it slip free. She willed it closer to the surface, dragging it upward with every ounce of focus she could muster.

It resisted, bouncing wildly within her like a pinball in an arcade game, ricocheting from one side of her mind to the other. It took everything she had to keep it steady, to hold it in one place long enough to focus.

Beads of sweat began to form on her forehead from the internal struggle. It took much more strength, mentally, than she ever imagined. It wasn't as easy as letting her heat fill up her body like before. She squeezed her eyes shut more, focusing on her target, the dummy with a body not like Bain's. The flame felt her thoughts and began shooting around in her again. She struggled to keep it where she wanted, where she felt like she had control of it. It felt like it had a mind of its own, and it was trying to escape. It shot around her so forcefully that she didn't have time to catch it and hold it still. She worried for her parents, for Lidia, and for Bain if she couldn't get it under control. And with one final jolt, the flame escaped her body. Niamh screamed as the flame exploded out of her chest with what felt like atomic bomb strength.

Her eyes flew open in terror. She knew she didn't have control of where it was going. She saw the fear in the doctor's eyes, and Njeri was already running to push the doctor to the floor in anticipation of it being out of control. The green flame shot around the room, seemingly with no target. It bounced off the steel beams and hovered for a brief second, giving Niamh a small hope it might not hurt anyone. Then, the flame shot through the floor.

Chapter 21

Niamh's heart was beating too fast; she thought she might die. She knew exactly where it was going. She ran to the stairs as fast as she could, knowing the elevator would be a slow and painfully quiet ride for her. She darted down the steps, several at a time, as fast as she could until she reached the infirmary floor. She flung the door open. Fluorescent lights were flickering on and off, sparks releasing from broken wires the lights were hanging onto for dear life. Screams filled the air as she ran through the hallway, avoiding the downed wires and lights.

She knew the way; even in the dark, she could find her way to him. She walked the steps in her mind several times, wanting to go to him but not allowing herself. Her feet slipped out from under her as she ran to his room. She pushed herself up, but a thick, sickly liquid stuck to her hand. Even in the dark, she could tell it was blood, the notorious copper smell filling the air. Her heart sank. She didn't want to look at what she'd done. A grunting sound broke her trance.

She crawled into the room, unable to make herself stand, the thick liquid clinging to her hands and knees. She pulled herself up using the rails of the bed. As her eyes were level with the bed, she saw it. He looked sickly white.

Njeri and Lidia ran in seconds behind her, nearly pushing her over when they bumped into her. Taking in the surroundings, Njeri turned to stand in front of Niamh. She grabbed Niamh's face, forcing her to look into her eyes. "He's okay. You didn't hit him. You hear me? You didn't hit him."

Lidia stood frozen in the hallway, her breath caught in her throat. The sight before her was almost too much to process. She'd never seen so much blood before, never seen anyone die, and she didn't want this to be her first time.

Her instincts screamed at her to run, to get as far away as possible, but her feet stayed planted.

She clenched her fists at her sides, forcing herself to stay. She had to be strong. Not for herself, but for her friend.

Her brain took what felt like hours to register what Njeri had told her. *He's okay.* She hadn't hit him with her flame. He was okay. But she knew she hadn't imagined it. The thick, sticky liquid was still coating her hands and soaking through the knees of her pants. She looked around the room to see who else had gotten hurt. That was far too much blood for anyone to live through. Her hands began to shake as she inspected them, watching the blood drip off her fingers.

She saw the panic in Niamh's eyes, she was close to losing it. Njeri quickly scanned the room to understand the situation fully. Bain was lying on the bed, propped up on his elbows, his eyes wide in shock, his skin too white to look healthy. The doctor and nurses were huddled around him and the machine. The machine was pouring out blood. The nurses were quickly ripping out the tubes jutting out of Bain's arm and hurrying to unplug the machine from the wall. The green flame had left a scalded round outline on the machine next to Bain. It was spewing blood all over the floor. The screams from the machine competed with the doctor and nurses yelling orders at each other.

Njeri shook her again. "It's the machine. No one's hurt."

The beeping of the machine stopped. The doctor was checking Bain, but he ignored the doctor's efforts to get his attention and looked directly at Niamh. His white face and wide eyes made him less attractive, but still handsome by most people's standards. Niamh stood next to his hospital bed in silence, tears threatening to overflow and expose her emotions.

A few minutes went by with them staring at each other, taking in the reality of what had happened. Niamh was about to crumble into a million pieces when Bain did the unimaginable. He held his arms out to her.

She slid on the bloody floor over to him, plowing into his body with a thud. He wrapped his long, strong arms around her as much as he could with the restraints. Letting her break down in safety, he held her tight while she shed tears that carried the weight of what could have happened, the fear of what almost happened. She felt safe in his arms, allowed to show just how truly scared she was at that moment. He didn't pull away in terror, he held her together because he wasn't afraid of her.

Her feet slipped on the gooey floor, sending her legs out from under her. Bain, with a grunt of effort from his blood loss, pulled her higher onto the bed. She found a spot on his shoulder, his body feeling like it was made for her at that moment. His strong arms wrapped around her, holding her in place firmly. His arms were cold, though, not his usual warmth. It snapped her back to reality and the memory of what had just happened. She almost killed him. The machine had taken most of his blood out of his body, and he could still die.

The doctor worked around her to get a new IV hooked up in his other arm. Bags of dark red liquid were hung above them on a metal hook. The nurse wheeled in a new machine, pushing buttons on it as the doctor attached Bain to the device.

Niamh looked at him, his eyes lacking their usual shine but still showing deep feelings for her. His gaze showed nothing but care for her. She didn't know how he could even want to see her, much less hug her. She almost killed him.

Njeri walked slowly up behind her, making sure not to startle her. She put a hand softly on Niamh's shoulder. "We should let the doctor work. He's okay, but he needs attention."

Niamh sniffled and pushed away from Bain, his weak grin pulling at her heart. He wiped away her tears as she reluctantly left his body. The brief, uneven smile he offered her made her feel as if her heart might break. Njeri took her turn holding Niamh as the doctor continued his work, placing stickers and tubes on Bain's pale body.

His muscular chest, exposed from the doctor's work, made Niamh's stomach flutter. Even in his weakened state, he was still undeniably handsome. Her eyes moved up his body, taking in the image of him, his pride still visible in the way his gaze lingered on her, even as sick as he was. He was vain, even in this state, and yet… he made her feel something she wasn't sure how to name.

"The dialysis machine he was hooked to took most of his blood," the doctor said, noticing the alarmed look on Niamh's face. "He's lucky to be conscious right now. We're replacing it with fae blood now."

Niamh's eyes widened, but the doctor continued, "Fae blood has healing properties. Bain's lucky he's magical himself, or he probably wouldn't be here. You've got a tough guy here."

Niamh wanted to correct her, to explain that Bain wasn't *her* guy, but she didn't have the energy. Bain didn't do anything to correct her either. In fact, his grin seemed to widen ever so slightly when Niamh let the comment slide. It gave him a glimmer of hope that maybe, just maybe, she would give him a chance.

Aoife burst into the room a few seconds later, coming to an abrupt halt as the scene unfolded before her. She stood frozen, her breath hitching, unable to process the full weight of what she was seeing. But her instincts quickly kicked in.

Carefully, she moved toward Niamh, her steps cautious on the slick, blood-covered floor. "Come on," Aoife said gently, slipping an arm around her friend's shoulder to guide her out. Niamh leaned heavily against her, her body trembling, silent from the shock.

The group, led by Aoife, made their way to the lobby, which was mercifully empty. Bloody footprints marked their path, a haunting trail that followed them across the tile floor.

Huyen, seated at the front desk, immediately moved quickly, stepping over the streaks of blood with practiced calm as she brought a bottle of water to Niamh.

"Here you go, honey, this will help," Huyen said softly, her concern evident as she pressed the cold bottle into Niamh's hands.

Niamh's fingers wrapped around it reflexively, but she remained silent, her gaze distant. The lobby felt eerily quiet, the only sound the faint hum of the overhead lights and the muffled echo of their steps.

Someone had draped a soft blanket over her shoulders. She didn't need it to stay warm, she never did, but the gesture was comforting. The gentle weight of the fabric pressed down on her, keeping her grounded as her mind reeled with chaotic thoughts.

Aoife let her sit in silence for a few minutes. When tears started to stream down Niamh's face again, she gently cupped her face, wiping away the wetness on her cheeks. "Niamh, listen to me," Aoife said softly, her voice full of quiet strength. "You didn't kill him. You didn't even hurt him. He's alive. And he's not going anywhere. You hear me? He wants to see you. He trusts you, even after everything. You can't punish yourself for this, love. You *can't.*"

Lidia's hand rested on Niamh's back, her touch firm and comforting. She knew this wasn't something that could be fixed with words alone, but she wanted her friend to know she wasn't alone. Not now. Not ever.

Niamh's eyes dropped to her lap, her chest heaving with the weight of the emotions crashing over her. She didn't know how to let go of the terror, how to ease the guilt that clung to her like a second skin. "I don't know if I can do this," she whispered. "I can't keep putting him in danger. I can't keep being the reason he's hurt."

Aoife kneeled in front of Niamh, lifting her chin gently so their eyes met once more. "You didn't do this, Niamh. Your magic it's powerful. And sometimes, it's unpredictable. But this is not your fault. You're learning. You're growing. And so is he." Aoife's eyes softened. "Bain sees you. Not just the magic. Not just the danger. He sees *you*, Niamh."

Niamh's lips trembled, the weight of Aoife's words sinking in, but the storm in her chest didn't calm. "But I... I don't know how to handle this. How do I keep him safe? How do I *fix* this?"

"You don't have to fix it," Lidia said quietly, her voice steady. "You just have to be you. And that's enough. You're not alone in this. We're here. And so is he. You don't have to carry it all on your own."

A long, heavy silence stretched between them. Niamh closed her eyes, inhaling deeply as if to steady herself. For a moment, she allowed herself to feel the weight of her emotions without fighting it. Then, when she spoke again, it was quieter, but the tremor in her voice had lessened. "What if… what if I'm too much for him?"

Aoife smiled gently, brushing a strand of hair from Niamh's face. "You don't get to decide that. He does. And he's chosen you, Niamh. No one said this would be easy, but it's worth it. You're worth it."

Lidia leaned forward, her eyes soft with compassion. "You're not too much for him, Niamh. You're exactly what he needs. But fighting this connection might be causing some of your internal struggles. You've fought against this bond so hard, maybe it's time to stop resisting it. Maybe it's time to start accepting it."

Aoife and Njeri nodded silently, their expressions supportive but firm.

Niamh's chest tightened. She knew Lidia was right, *they were all right.* She had been stubborn about Bain from the start, always keeping him at arm's length. But it wasn't just for his sake—it was to protect her heart, to shield herself from more pain.

Except, instead of keeping her safe, it had only caused her more hurt.

She exhaled shakily, the weight of her emotions pressing down on her. Deep down, she knew it was time to stop fighting. To stop pushing him away.

Aoife rose to her feet, her eyes full of understanding. "How about you take a few minutes, or as long as you need. Bain's going to be okay. And when you're ready, we'll go see him. On your terms."

Niamh nodded slowly, the soft blanket still wrapped around her shoulders, her friends' presence a steady reminder that she wasn't alone in the weight of this moment. She took a deep breath, finally willing herself to look up and meet Aoife and Lidia's eyes.

She sat in the pristine white lobby, its festive decorations of Christmas trees and poinsettias clashing with the streaks of blood on her clothes. The cheerful warmth of the holiday decor only heightened how out of place she felt, but that wasn't new for her.

Her thoughts churned as she recapped everything that had brought them to this moment.

Fighting their connection it's what had caused all of this. Granted, Bain hadn't made it easy with the whole kidnapping ordeal, but even then, she couldn't deny the pull she'd felt from the very beginning.

She had resisted it, stubbornly guarding her heart to protect herself, but it had only made things worse.

It was time to stop fighting. It was time to let go of her pride and face what was already there.

"Okay," she said, her voice small but resolute. "I'm ready."

He was lying on the hospital bed, his head turned away from them, when he heard footsteps coming. His pale face turned to look over his shoulder. His light eyes lit up a bit when he saw Niamh standing in the doorway. "You came back." It wasn't a question, it was a statement of pride. She came back, so she must like him, at least a little, he hoped. "I'll be okay, don't you cry for me, I've been in worse spots than this before. I'm so proud of you, Niamh. For embracing your magic, you're beautiful, all of you."

Niamh's chest tightened with the weight of Bain's words. His warmth, the steady rhythm of his breathing, it all felt too good, too comforting for someone who had been responsible for so much damage. She wanted to believe him, to trust that he truly understood, but the doubt still lingered, the fear that the next time she lost control, she might not be able to stop herself.

"I'm scared," she admitted, the words slipping out before she could stop them. "Scared of what I could do, scared of what I've already done."

Bain's hands held her tighter, pulling her flush against his chest. His breath hitched, but his voice remained calm, steady. "I know. But you don't have to be scared of me, Niamh. I'm not afraid of you."

She pulled back slightly, enough to meet his eyes, searching for any sign of doubt. But all she found was the same quiet determination that had been there since they first met. "You should be," she whispered, the pain of the past still clinging to her.

Bain shook his head, his expression softening. "No. I won't be. I'm not afraid of what's inside of you. I'm only afraid of losing you." His voice cracked slightly.

Her heart twisted at the raw emotion in his words. He had been through so much, far more than she could imagine, and yet, here he was, telling her he wasn't afraid. Telling her he was still here, still fighting. She wanted to believe him.

"Bain," she started, her voice trembling. "I can't lose you."

"You won't," he assured her, his hand cupping the back of her head, pulling her back down to rest against him. "Not as long as we're together. Not as long as we both fight for this."

The room was quiet, save for the steady hum of the machines and the soft sound of their breathing, as Niamh let the moment settle over her. She wanted to believe him, wanted to believe that they could get through this. Together.

She closed her eyes, letting herself melt into his embrace, even as doubt and fear gnawed at her insides. But Bain was right. She didn't have to do this alone. And as long as they were together, there was still hope.

"I'm fine. I just want you to know that. You didn't hurt me." And with that, the fragile resolve she'd been holding onto shattered. She hadn't remembered herself as much of a crier when she was younger. She'd built a thick skin early on, especially when she looked the way she did. But this feeling was something she couldn't make sense of. It was different than anything else. Different than the love for her adoptive parents, different than trying to make friends, even different from her love for Lidia. This feeling was far harder to navigate. She had to break down walls she'd built to protect her heart after years of boys pretending to like her, only to make fun of her when they thought she wasn't looking. The wall was there for a reason. Now, she had to undo years of self-preservation.

"I don't know what I'm doing," she choked out.

"What do you mean?" he asked, wiping the tears off her cheek.

"I only put you in danger. Why would you keep wanting to be around that?"

"First off, I want to be around you. I could live without the danger part, but

I've accepted it as part of being near you. Second, you're worth everything you can throw at me. I'd prefer if you threw it near or next to me, but whatever you can do is fine," he said, trying to lighten the situation. "I don't think your life will be like this forever. You're only in these situations because of me. So don't put the blame on yourself. I introduced you to Queen Cailleach. I regret that more than anything else I've ever done, and trust me, I've done a lot I regret."

She pushed herself up on his chest to look at him. "I don't know how to get a hold of my magic. I'm afraid to try again."

"Well, the stubborn woman I know wouldn't just give up. You're the strongest person I know, and if anyone can do it, it's you. What went wrong the last time?" he asked, gently probing.

Her cheeks flushed. "Well, I was supposed to be aiming for a dummy across the room, but I guess I thought of the wrong one." She tried to joke.

Bain burst into laughter, his deep, rumbling voice filling her with an unexpected warmth. That voice filled voids she didn't even know existed in her heart, mending wounds that others had left. It made her feel safe. It made her feel happy. She had no idea that one single sound could shift everything inside her.

"See what I mean? You are amazing! And if you don't see it yet, just see what I see. I'll be your eyes until you realize that you're worthy of everything good in this world and beyond." He paused, hesitant but driven by his feelings. "Would it be inappropriate to ask for a kiss?"

"You… you want to kiss me?"

"With every fiber of my being."

Blinked slowly, trying to read his face for any sign of insincerity. But she found none. He only looked at her with pure desire. He truly wanted her. She slowly leaned down, and when their lips met, it was as if two waves had collided, intense, inevitable. She felt the warmth of him, the softness of his lips. His tongue gently coaxed her mouth to open, and when they finally came together fully, it felt as if her entire world shifted. She had never been a fan of open-mouth kissing, but this… this was different. It wasn't just a kiss, it was something deeper, something that touched parts of her soul she had kept hidden for years. His kiss seemed to absorb every insecurity, every past rejection, every ounce of self-doubt she carried.

Sinking into that blissful ocean of safety and care. She floated on clouds of reassurance, drifting down rivers of comforting caresses, dancing across fields of encouragement. She felt out of place in her own body, these emotions so unfamiliar but so welcome. She let him break down the walls she had so carefully built, and when he did, he didn't leave rubble. He took it all, and instead, he built something new, something sacred, a place where he could worship her.

She pulled away first, her breath coming faster than before. His lips, however, still reached for hers, unwilling to let go. He blinked as if trying to grasp reality again. His mind was a haze, overwhelmed by the warmth of their connection. It had left him feeling fuller than he could have ever imagined.

"I think I love you, Niamh."

Her breath caught, and for a moment, she couldn't find the words. She was frozen, her chest tight, unsure how to respond to the gravity of his confession.

"You don't have to say anything back. Don't say it until you're sure," Bain continued, his voice soft but sincere. "But I fell for you the second I first saw you. And I just fell more and more each time you talked, looked at me. Even those disapproving glances just made me fall deeper in love with you. You hold me to a higher standard, you expect more from me. I want to be a better man, a better being, because of you. So, no rush. However long it takes, whatever I have to do to make you see that my feelings are true."

She nodded slowly, unable to breathe, unable to think clearly. Her mind raced, emotions in turmoil. "I, um… need to go practice more."

"I hope I didn't make things harder for you," Bain said, his voice quieter, tinged with regret. "I just wanted you to know, in case… well, you know, stuff happens. I just wanted you to know how special you are." He hesitated but didn't add the part he was truly thinking—*in case you kill me*. If that was his fate, then so be it. At least he had that moment. That felt more real than all the hundreds of years he'd spent in the dimensions.

"I appreciate you opening up to me, Bain," Niamh said, her voice barely above a whisper. "I'm just not sure how I feel yet. Too much has happened. I can't think straight."

"I understand," Bain replied, his expression soft and patient. "No rush. But, consider joining me for dinner, please. We can talk more... if you want."

"Is that safe? Are you well enough for that?" she asked doubtingly.

The doctor yelled from behind the curtain, "He's fine, the fae blood is working its magic, literally and figuratively." she laughed at her own joke, "But seriously, he'll be close to normal, using that term loosely for him, in no time."

Niamh tried not to laugh at the doctor giving him a hard time. "I, um, think dinner would be nice," she replied, her voice quieter, trying to regain some composure.

"My place, say... eight?" he joked, rattling his handcuffed wrist.

She chuckled, the tension easing a little. "Sure, eight is fine."

"I'll wear my best hospital gown for you!" he teased with a mischievous glint in his eye.

"Can't wait to see it... the gown, that is," she stumbled over her words, suddenly aware of the thought that had crossed her mind. She quickly forced the image away, but it lingered. *What if he wasn't wearing any underwear under the gown?* Being a virgin didn't mean she'd never seen a naked man, just not one that wasn't running across a yard at warp speed. This one could be for her. The thought of what she may be encountering overwhelmed her as she left the room.

Aoife, Lidia, and Njeri met Niamh outside the room. Aoife, always better with feelings than Njeri, gently suggested, "Honey, why don't you go get changed, take a moment, and when you're ready, meet us back at the training center, okay?"

Niamh just nodded, too overwhelmed by everything that had just happened to speak. Lidia, sensing her friend's need for quiet support, grabbed her hand and led her back to their room. In a silent daze, Lidia helped Niamh strip off her blood-soaked clothes. She turned on the shower and gently guided Niamh into the warm water. To some, it might have seemed odd for Lidia to stay, but for Niamh and Lidia, who had been practically sisters since grade school, it was just what they both needed. They didn't need words to understand each other's hearts.

Lidia stood outside the shower, giving Niamh the space she needed but also silently offering her strength. Niamh cried, releasing the stress and pain of the day, of the past few days. She cried for the uncertainty in her heart, for the love she so desperately longed for but wasn't sure how to trust. She wanted to be loved, but could she trust Bain after everything that had happened between them? She just wanted to be accepted for who she was, and for the first time in her life, K Corp had felt like that, a place where she was beginning to feel like she belonged. Could this be her home? Was she finally finding it?

After the shower, Lidia had a towel ready for her. She wrapped it around Niamh and enveloped her in a hug, offering the comfort and security only a lifelong friend could provide. Together, they sat on the edge of the bed, both silently reflecting on the chaos of the day. Niamh wasn't sure how to move forward, but she knew she needed to; she had to practice again, push through the fear and uncertainty.

Lidia stood behind her, a steady presence. As Niamh gathered the courage to get dressed, Lidia, without a word, began to braid her hair, carefully leaving out the bangs, knowing how important that small detail was to Niamh. It was her security blanket, a piece of her past that had always made her feel more grounded, more in control.

As Lidia worked, Niamh took a deep breath. She knew what she had to do. She couldn't give up now. She'd never given up on anything before, not when her mom had signed her up for soccer, and the other kids had mocked her, not when she had to sing in front of the church, feeling the weight of everyone's eyes on her deformities, not when she was nominated as spring dance queen as a cruel joke. She'd gotten through all that. She wasn't about to give up now, not when she was finally starting to understand who she truly was and what she was capable of.

As the seconds passed, Lidia noticed a shift in Niamh. She sat up straighter, her shoulders pulled back, and a determined look settled on her face, a look of a woman on a mission. Lidia's heart swelled with pride. She could see it now, the strength Niamh had always had deep inside her, finally surfacing. She was growing into the person she was meant to be, and Lidia felt honored to witness this transformation, this glow-up. She stayed in the room, silently watching, not wanting to add any distractions after what Niamh had just been through. She knew this was something Niamh needed to do on her own.

Chapter 22

Niamh took a deep breath, steeling herself before stepping into the training room again. Aoife and Njeri were already there, working to patch up the hole in the floor. Embarrassment crept up her cheeks.

"Don't even worry about this," Njeri said with a grin. "We had a Jinn possess a bowling ball once because he was mad he got the lowest score. He did quite a bit of damage around the building."

Niamh managed a small smile, though she thought it was probably one of those stories that was funnier to witness than to hear about afterward. Still, she felt some relief. She wasn't the only one to have made a mess. She just hoped her mishap wouldn't become one of those stories people shared as a cautionary tale.

Aoife, watching her closely, asked, "Are you sure you're ready?"

Niamh straightened, trying to channel the same determination she had felt just moments ago in her room. "Ready. I have to learn about myself to keep my family safe. I have to do this."

Aoife nodded, a quiet appreciation in her gaze.

Njeri, ever the enthusiastic one, slapped her on the back with a little too much force, sending Niamh forward a step to catch herself. "Let's get started then!" she said with a grin.

Niamh steadied herself, her resolve firm. This was just the beginning.

She was ready.

"We had the witches put a cast on the room for extra protection," Njeri said with a grin. "Your fire seems to be very strong. We weren't prepared for that. Now we know what we're working with. So, do your worst."

She leaned in closer, her tone lighthearted, "Well, maybe not *your* worst. I like working here, so try not to burn it down. Kay?"

Niamh didn't know whether to laugh or groan. It didn't exactly boost her morale, but she knew Njeri meant well… or at least, she thought she did. The women stepped outside the room, securing the door behind them. Aoife gave her a reassuring nod, and Niamh took a deep breath, trying to focus.

She reached deep within herself, to the part of her that she'd been keeping locked away. She found the green spark once again, the others still fighting to break free. She felt the internal battle raging inside her, but she held onto the small green flame. It wanted to be free, dancing excitedly in her mind, eager to be released.

This time, she was ready. She knew it wouldn't be a repeat of last time. She understood now how to control it, how to keep her mind steady and focused. The consequences were too dire to let her thoughts wander. She closed her invisible fist around the flame, holding it tightly, and pictured in her mind exactly where she wanted it to go.

With determination, she opened her hand and released it.

She almost didn't want to open her eyes to see what had happened. But when she did, she was stunned. The dummy, wearing a flannel shirt, now had a large hole burned through its chest. Plastic dripped from the edges of the hole, and small flames flickered around the wound.

Aoife and Njeri burst through the door, rushing to her with wide smiles, their arms around her as they screamed in excitement. She'd done it.

Niamh could hardly believe it. Her heart raced, and her body was flooded with a mix of exhilaration and fear. It was both exciting and terrifying. She had that power. And one day, she might have to use it against someone. She hoped it wouldn't come to that. She didn't want to be a killer, but she knew that the evil coming after her had to be stopped. She couldn't wait for someone else to save her.

Finally, she managed to grit out, "I did it. I actually did it."

Njeri grinned, her voice full of pride. "Yeah, you did, girl! Good job!"

"You did so well, Niamh. We're so proud of you for not giving up," Aoife said, her voice calm and reassuring. "Are you ready to try more?"

Niamh shook her head slightly, trying to appear braver than she felt. "I'm not sure. But I have to tell you something. I think there are more colors than the doctor said."

Aoife raised an eyebrow. "What do you mean?"

"Well," Niamh hesitated, "she said there were three, but I swear I saw a whole rainbow of colors inside me. Maybe I saw them wrong, but I can feel them, too. They all feel different. And they all want to get out. I had to fight to take only one at a time."

Aoife was silent for a moment, processing what she'd just heard. "Well… that's interesting." She nodded thoughtfully. "I'll relay that to the doctor. She had some things to do earlier, so she couldn't come back up, but she may want to for this. She won't believe it, though. She's a woman of science, after all. She'll want proof. Do you want to explore them?"

Niamh felt a spark of excitement mixed with uncertainty. "Um, sure. Let's do it. I'd like to know what's hidden inside me."

Njeri bounced up and down, unable to contain her enthusiasm. "This is so exciting! I thought Aoife's magic was going to be the highlight of my year, but you may give her a run for her money!"

Both Niamh and Aoife turned to Njeri, their voices in sync as they said, "It's not a competition."

They froze for a moment, then looked at each other, laughing. The shared moment of levity helped ease some of the tension in Niamh's chest. She wasn't alone in this anymore.

Njeri backed up a step, holding her arms up in a surrender pose, still laughing. "Alright, alright, back to business. We need to figure out exactly what powers you have."

"We know you've got the green flame and what it does. Did you see blue and purple in there, too?" Njeri asked, her voice now focused.

"Yeah, they were there. There was also red, pink, black, and white. What does that mean?" Niamh replied, her mind racing with the new discoveries.

"Girlfriend, we're about to find out. Hold onto your panties because it's about to get exciting!" Njeri said, way too enthused for Niamh's liking, but she couldn't help but smile at her energy.

Aoife, always the grounded one, stepped in. "We know the blue can boil someone's blood, and the purple can make someone's heart beat forever, or stop depending on the intention. So how do we find out about the other colors?"

Njeri grinned. "Well… we've got a few ballistic dummies stored away for a special occasion. I'd say this qualifies." She hauled a large, person-sized torso from a nearby storage closet and set it in a metal folding chair, pointing her arms at it like it was a grand prize.

Niamh felt a flutter of nerves in her chest. "So… what now?"

Njeri slapped her hands together. "So, I guess pick a color, and we'll try it out. But let us get behind the barricade first, yeah?"

Aoife moved quickly to the side, nodding in agreement. "Safety first. And if anything goes wrong, we want to be ready."

Once they were safely tucked away behind the thick, clear wall, Niamh reached down with her invisible hand and felt for the flames inside her. Each one gave off a different feeling, distinct from the others. She could tell them apart by the way they vibrated, the way they whispered to her.

Her fingers brushed over the red one. It practically jumped into her hand, eager to be released, prickling with pink excitement that danced under her skin. Niamh's anxiety flared, but she tried to steady her breath, reminding herself that she had to be in control. She closed her eyes for a moment, releasing a slow exhale. The flame was restless, but she focused, holding her hand open, aiming at the dummy. The red flame obeyed, and when she let it go, it exploded in a rush.

The impact hit with such force that it sent a shockwave through the walls, shaking the room as if an earthquake had ripped through it. Red flames engulfed the dummy, pieces of ballistic gel flying in all directions. Niamh instinctively bent down, covering her head with her arms, bracing for any debris that might fall.

Gel rained down, splattering across the room, while dust swirled in the air, thick and unsettled. The women stared at each other in disbelief for a beat, taking in the destruction. Then, without warning, cheers erupted from Aoife and Njeri.

Niamh stood frozen, still in shock, her heart pounding in her chest. Aoife and Njeri rushed to her, lifting her up in excitement, their laughter ringing out.

"What in the sugar cane forest happened here?" Nick's voice echoed from the stairwell door. He stepped in, wide-eyed, looking around at the damage. The room looked like a warzone, pieces of the dummy scattered across the floor, a few lights flickering from the force of the explosion. "It shook the whole building. Are you guys okay?"

Aoife, laughing, waved him off. "Yeah, we're fine. We know what the red flame does now."

"Red go boom," Njeri added, her voice bubbling with laughter.

Nick ran a hand through his hair, his nervous habit clearly on display. "Okay, if you're sure. Do you need anything? Or is this all under control?" He surveyed the mess, his eyes narrowing with concern.

"All under control," Aoife said with a wide grin, her voice full of confidence. She knew how to work him. "We have a few more to test out, so don't be alarmed if you hear more sounds."

Nick let out a low chuckle, still shaking his head as he turned to leave. "Alright, just please don't blow the building up. Again."

With an unsure look, Nick left the women to continue their investigation.

"What color next?" Njeri asked Niamh, her voice tinged with curiosity.

Niamh hesitated, the memory of the red explosion still fresh in her mind. The power she held felt so unpredictable, so dangerous. But she knew she couldn't back down now. She needed to learn about her abilities, to understand them before they overwhelmed her. "Let's try the black," she said, though something in her gut told her that black meant bad. There was only one way to find out.

Njeri nodded eagerly, her enthusiasm not dulled by the tension in the air.

She pulled out another ballistic dummy and a fresh chair, one that wasn't bent or broken from the previous tests. Setting it up carefully, she gave it a quick slap on the shoulder before running behind the barricade, giving Niamh a nod to signal that it was safe to proceed.

Niamh closed her eyes for a moment, feeling her breath settle. She reached into herself, seeking the black flame. It pulsed in her hand, almost alive, and she could feel the weight of its potential. She took a deep breath, knowing what she had to do. With a shaky exhale, she released it, willing the flame to fly towards the dummy.

The room reacted instantly, a pulse of air expanding outward as the flame shot forward. But then, as if it had a will of its own, the black flame pulled itself back into the air, creating a deep, dark hole in the center of the room. It seemed to absorb everything around it, the very air, the objects, the light. A hungry void was opening in front of her, its pull becoming undeniable.

Niamh's grip on the flame began to falter. She slid closer to the growing hole, her body drawn in despite her will. In panic, she grabbed onto the nearest metal support pole, her fingers clenching around it for dear life. Her legs began to lift off the ground as the force of the pull grew stronger. The wind sucked the air from her lungs, leaving her with only the deafening sound of its pulse.

She could see Aoife and Njeri shouting at her, but their voices were lost beneath the roar of the force. She couldn't make out the words. Fear was rising in her chest, her grip slipping from the pole as the wind howled louder.

No. She had to stop it. If she didn't, they wouldn't survive.

With every last ounce of strength, she clung to the pole, her fingers slipping one by one. In a desperate scream, she commanded the flame to stop. "Please, stop!" The words echoed in her mind, a final plea to control the chaos.

Slowly, the wind began to die down, its pulse weakening, and the flame receded. The pull faded as if the flame had heard her command, obeying the desperate plea in her voice. The winds settled, leaving nothing but silence. Niamh's legs hit the ground with a hard thud, and the wind's last whisper faded.

She let go of the pole, collapsing onto the floor. For a few moments, she just lay there, breathing heavily, her body still vibrating with the adrenaline. A pair of hands gently rolled her over, urgency in their touch. Aoife and Njeri loomed above her, wide-eyed, their hair standing on end.

Niamh lifted a shaky arm and gave a thumbs-up. She was okay.

Aoife and Njeri let out a collective breath, their faces relaxing in relief. They both collapsed beside her, laughing nervously, their bodies still tense with the aftershock of what had just happened.

After a few moments of silent recovery, the room began to settle. Niamh still felt the weight of what had just happened, her hands shaking, her breath still a little too fast, as if she couldn't quite believe what she had done.

"Girl, you got some tricks up your sleeve, don't you?" Njeri said with a laugh, trying to lighten the mood.

"I… I don't know what that was," Niamh admitted uneasily, her voice shaking slightly. She couldn't wrap her mind around what she had just created, the overwhelming force it carried.

Aoife glanced at her, her eyes thoughtful. "I believe that was a black hole."

Njeri squealed in excitement, clearly thrilled by the spectacle. "Holy shit! That was awesome!"

"Awesome isn't the word I'd use," Niamh said quietly, her voice edged with uncertainty. The power she held was terrifying. She couldn't ignore how close she had come to losing control.

Aoife, ever the calm one, nodded slowly. "I don't know. That was pretty cool. I didn't know things like that could happen. You have some power inside you, Niamh. You're a rare treasure."

"Or a ticking time bomb," Niamh muttered, her face shadowed with concern.

Njeri, however, remained confident. "Nah, we'll have you mastering those powers in no time." Her voice was full of assurance, but Niamh wasn't so sure.

Niamh just nodded, offering a small, closed-lip grin that didn't quite reach her eyes. She wasn't sure if she felt reassured by her friends' confidence or more afraid of the power growing inside her. Would she ever truly be able to control it? Or was she destined to one day lose herself to it? Only time will tell.

Njeri clapped her hands together excitedly, her energy uncontainable. "Ready for the next one?"

Niamh let out a big sigh, her shoulders tense with the weight of what she had just experienced. *How much worse could it get?* she wondered. The idea of what was to come next was enough to make her stomach twist. But she knew there was no avoiding it. She had to learn, had to gain control, or risk everything slipping out of her hands.

As Njeri quickly replaced the dummy and chair, Niamh noticed the scattered remnants of the blow-up obstacles, sucked away by the black hole. They'd be another problem for later. Right now, the focus was on what new power she'd have to face.

She shook her shoulders, trying to loosen the tight knots from the stress of it all. Her heart still raced, but she knew she had to keep going. With a deep, steadying breath, she reached inside herself once more, seeking out the next flame. She felt the sharp zing of the white flame, its energy almost tangible in the air, eager to be released.

Niamh focused, aimed, and with a flick of her wrist, she sent it flying. The room exploded in bright white light, and before she could react, a powerful gust of wind shot out from the flame, sending her crashing to the floor. She coughed, struggling to regain her breath, the force of the wind too much to handle.

Niamh couldn't understand what was happening. The force of the wind whipped her hair around, objects returning to their original spots, the entire room seemingly resetting itself. She turned in confusion to the others, seeing Nick walking backward into the room as if he was pulled along by some unseen force. She couldn't make sense of it.

Through her dazed vision, she saw Aoife and Njeri sprinting backward, retreating behind the barricade. The wind was relentless, howling around her. Then, suddenly, she saw something strange, everything that had been sucked away by the black hole moments before, like the blow-up obstacles, the dust, and the debris, was now being replaced, reversing almost. It was as if time itself had shifted, pulling everything back into place.

Remembering that she had somehow controlled the black hole earlier, she focused, reaching for the same kind of command over this new force. She yelled, "Stop!" And just like that, everything stilled. The rush of air ceased, and the white spot of energy collapsed in on itself, vanishing completely.

Njeri emerged from behind the barricade, clapping slowly, her voice full of awe. "Girl, stop it with these amazing powers!" she exclaimed. "You just fucking reversed time!"

Niamh blinked, her brain struggling to catch up. She looked at Aoife, confused. Aoife nodded, her smile wide with admiration. "Yep, you did it. You literally reversed time in the room. That's… that's incredible."

A quiet moment passed as Niamh absorbed the weight of what she had just done. Reversed time? It didn't seem possible, but she had seen it with her own eyes. Everything that had been displaced, everything that had been sucked into that black hole, was now back where it belonged.

"Now I don't have to replace the obstacles," Njeri said, snapping her fingers with a mock pout. "I was getting excited to try some new styles out, though." She grinned, unable to hide her excitement, though Niamh wasn't sure whether to laugh or take a moment to collect herself.

Still feeling the overwhelming rush of energy coursing through her, Niamh couldn't help but feel both exhilarated and terrified. What was happening to her? And more importantly, what would she do if she couldn't control it anymore? She knew there was more to come, and she wasn't sure she was ready. But she couldn't stop now.

Niamh winced at the slap on her back, but she managed a small, tired smile. Her body felt drained from everything she'd just experienced, and she couldn't deny the exhaustion starting to settle in her bones. She'd never imagined her magic would take so much out of her, but here she was, learning things about herself she hadn't even known existed.

"I think I have one more left. Let's get this done." Niamh said, her energy was clearly crashing.

"If you're sure, girl," Njeri said, unsure if she was truly up to it.

"I have to."

Njeri nodded, appreciating her *don't quit* attitude.

Her friends safely behind the barricade reached in once more and called to the last flame the pink one. It was small, dainty almost. She admired it as she pulled it to the surface. It sat quietly in her hand, not excited like the rest.

With the dummy replaced, she took aim and willed it to its chest.

The flame hit its mark but fizzled quickly and died out. It didn't leave a mark, no burns or any sign it had fire hit it.

"Well, that was… not as exciting. Maybe you're just tired. Let's call it a day and try that one again tomorrow." Njeri called as she walked out of the safety room.

Maybe she was just tired. It got her thinking. *Can magic go impotent?* she wondered.

Aoife, sensing the exhaustion in Niamh, gave her a sympathetic smile. "You did amazing today. You've learned so much already. Don't be too hard on yourself."

Njeri, bouncing with uncontained energy, grinned and gave Niamh another encouraging pat on the back, this time a little gentler. "Yeah, girl. You've got powers no one's seen before. Take a break, get some rest. You'll be even stronger tomorrow. And who knows? Maybe tomorrow, the pink flame will surprise us. It's not all about explosions, right?"

Niamh chuckled weakly, her mind still trying to make sense of everything. The pink flame had been such a mystery, she hadn't expected it to just fizzle out like that. But maybe that was a good sign. Maybe it meant she had control over it, or maybe it wasn't as volatile as the others. Still, there was a nagging feeling in the back of her mind. What if the pink flame wasn't what it seemed? What if it was hiding something more dangerous, waiting to show itself when she was least prepared?

"Alright," Niamh sighed, stretching and feeling her muscles protest. "Maybe a break is exactly what I need. I just… I don't want to mess up again. I don't want to hurt anyone."

"You won't," Aoife said, her voice gentle but firm. "You're learning. You're getting stronger every day, and you'll be ready for whatever comes next. We're here for you, Niamh. You don't have to face this alone."

Njeri added with a smile, "Besides, we're all still figuring out our powers, too. You're not in this by yourself. And hey, tomorrow we can try out the pink flame again. Maybe it's just a little shy today."

Niamh nodded, grateful for the support, but her mind still churned with questions. How much longer would she be able to keep up this act of control before everything got out of hand? The pressure to understand her abilities was immense, but she knew she couldn't stop now. There was too much at stake, and she couldn't afford to let fear stand in her way.

"Thanks, both of you," Niamh said softly, her voice filled with quiet determination. "I'll rest. But tomorrow… tomorrow, I'll figure it out."

Aoife smiled and gave her a reassuring nod. "That's the spirit. We'll be here when you're ready."

As they gathered their things and left the training room, Niamh lingered for a moment, casting one last glance at the spot where the pink flame had vanished. *I'll figure you out,* she thought. *I have to.*

Niamh wanted those answers; she needed them more than anything. But she also knew that pushing herself too hard could be dangerous, not just for her but for everyone around her. She trusted her new friends to help her make the right decision. They'd been nothing but supportive, and she didn't want to push them further than necessary. She nodded in agreement, knowing it was the right call to pause for now.

Chapter 23

It was getting close to eight. Time was ticking down to her meeting with Bain. She hesitated at the word *date*, it felt foreign, uncomfortable on her tongue. A word that didn't fit who she had been. But it was the truth. She had to admit it. She needed to see him. She felt that gravitational pull when they were apart, irresistible and confusing. Her mind told her to hate it, but her body betrayed her. She wanted to see his smug, handsome face again, and the frustration that stirred inside her only made her hate it more.

The shower did little to ease her tension. Her mind kept swirling back to what she had learned about herself today: literal bombs of power, locked away inside her, waiting to go off. And then there was Bain, his presence just as heavy in her thoughts. Between those two overwhelming realities, it felt like the weight of the world rested on her shoulders. She was stepping into uncharted territory, and it was a place she hadn't been prepared for.

But she wasn't the same woman he had taken just a few days ago. No, she had changed. She had found her power, both metaphorically and physically. She had grown into herself in ways she hadn't expected. And she wasn't going to let anyone, least of all Bain, think she was someone to be trifled with.

She walked down the hallway toward the hospital area of K Corp, her steps slower than usual as she passed a large window. She glanced into it and caught her reflection. The woman staring back at her was unfamiliar, yet not. She straightened her shoulders, tugged her shirt down to smooth it over her skin, and lifted her chin. *This* was the new version of herself.

With a rare moment of self-acceptance, she swooped her bangs to the side, the skin that had been hidden there a foreign sight. It didn't feel uncomfortable to her, though, her eyes in full view. She was the image of someone who had found herself, had reclaimed what was hers. For the first time, she didn't mind looking into her own eyes. They didn't feel like a burden to her anymore. They felt like a source of strength, something she could draw power from rather than run from.

All the years of shame and embarrassment had led her here. They had shaped her, forged her into someone who refused to back down. And she wasn't about to give up now, not when she was so close to feeling whole, to understanding who she really was.

One last deep breath, her large yin-yang eyes locking with her reflection. With renewed resolve, she turned and walked into the hospital area. The familiar aroma of food filled the air, guiding her steps as she neared Bain.

He looked better, his natural color was returning, the pallor in his skin fading. The dark circles beneath his eyes were lighter, though they still hinted at nights without sleep. She hoped it was just exhaustion from all the stress and not the lingering effects of what she had done.

A small table covered in white linen sat nestled between the curtain and the hospital bed. Restrained to the chair by the handcuff still strapped to his wrist.

But as she took him in, she couldn't help but think, *God, he still looks good.* The thought irritated her more than it should have. It would be so much easier to hate him if he were ugly. But instead, she found herself fighting that pull, that attraction to him she couldn't seem to shake.

Bain was sitting at a small round table, much like the one in her room, his usual confident smile lighting up his features. But there was something different about it today. Something warmer, more genuine. He was pleased to see her, and for a moment, she wasn't sure whether she should feel relieved or frustrated by that. But either way, she couldn't ignore the electric tension that flared between them the second their eyes met.

"Hey," he greeted, his voice smooth, with a hint of that same smugness she knew so well. "You look… beautiful." The words caught in his throat. The sight of her made him feel whole again.

"Hi." she glanced down at the table, an unlit candle sat in the center. On either side were two plates covered with clothes. She smiled a little at the setup.

He leaned back in his chair, studying her in that way that always made her feel both seen and exposed at the same time.

For a moment, Niamh felt herself retreat, the weight of her powers and the weight of their connection pressing on her. She wasn't sure if she was ready for this, for him. But she was here. She had walked this far, and she wasn't going to turn away now.

"You came.", his voice gentler now, his usual cocky edge replaced with something more genuine. Something that made Niamh feel like maybe, just maybe, there was more to this than she'd allowed herself to believe.

"I considered my many options and chose the short straw," she joked, trying to lighten the mood, but it fell a little flat.

He placed his unrestrained hand over his chest dramatically, as though wounded. "I'm wounded. No, really, I am. So, take pity on a temporarily disabled person."

Niamh couldn't help herself. She fought the smile tugging at her lips but lost the battle. She slid the empty seat next to him around the table and positioned herself to face him. His eyes sparkled with mischief, and before she could settle in, he scooted his chair closer, subtly shifting toward her like gravity pulling him in.

She sighed, unable to suppress her smile. How could she be mad at him when he was so… adorable?

He nervously fiddled with his straw, an absent gesture that somehow felt a little more personal than it should. "I hear through the grapevine that you've been practicing your powers."

Niamh took a slow sip, weighing her words. "I have, but you knew that," she waved at him, displaying his still pale skin.

"How's that going?" he prodded, clearly wanting more, his gaze intent and focused, pulling at her with that subtle charm of his.

She went for something light. "Good. No one's died… yet." She added the last part almost as an afterthought, hoping to see a flicker of unease in his expression.

He leaned back in his chair, that typical confidence radiating off him. "I'm well-acquainted with death. We've crossed paths a few times. That doesn't scare me."

She couldn't suppress the half-smile that curved her lips. But there was an uncomfortable tightness in her chest. *Bad boys.* They were the ones brave enough to break through the walls she'd built to protect herself, only to leave them broken and scattered in their wake. So why was she feeling drawn to him? Why did his roughness call to something inside her that she wasn't sure she even wanted to acknowledge?

Bain saw it, the tension in her shoulders, the guarded look in her eyes. The walls were there, strong and high, and he could feel them pushing him away. But he wasn't ready to give up. Not yet. He wanted to climb those walls, not break them. He wanted to be the one she let in. But he knew he had to be careful. Push too hard, and she would retreat even further. It was a delicate balance, walking that line between curiosity and caution.

"You're really not going to tell me about any of your training?" he asked softly, a teasing edge to his voice but something more sincere lingering beneath.

She sighed, knowing he wouldn't stop until she gave him something, anything. "Training went well. We figured out most of the flame powers… except for one."

His interest was piqued. "What color is the last one?"

She raised an eyebrow, her lips curling slightly in amusement. "You know there are different colors?"

"Of course I know. I pride myself on knowing about powerful magics," he replied confidently, though she caught the hint of something else in his eyes. He knew she thought he only wanted her for her power. And maybe, in the past, that was true. But now, as he sat across from her, he felt a pull toward *her*, not just what she could do. How could he prove that to her? How could he show her that he wanted *her*, the woman beneath all that power, more than anything else?

She looked at him, waiting for the answer, and he sensed her hesitation. "So?" he pressed gently, pushing her ever so slightly.

She relented. "Pink."

"Pink?" he asked, the word rolling off his tongue in disbelief. "Pink?"

"Yeah," she said, her voice firm. "I was there."

Bain leaned forward, clearly intrigued. "I've just never heard of a pink flame."

"So, you don't know everything after all," she teased, giggling as the moment lightened. The ease between them, for just a moment, felt like a breath of fresh air.

He chuckled, his grin widening. "Don't get used to it."

His smile softened as he leaned back, the teasing edge fading into something more thoughtful. "So how are you going to find out what it does?"

"I don't know yet," she admitted, running a hand through her hair in frustration. "We tried it on the dummy, and nothing happened. I'm not sure what Aoife and Njeri have planned now."

He raised an eyebrow, an almost predatory gleam in his eyes. "Well, try it on me."

Her eyes widened in shock. "No. No way. It's too dangerous. You could blow up."

He shrugged, that same smugness flickering back to life. "Maybe it's something that needs a living person to work. I happen to be a living person."

She hesitated, her thoughts tangled in the possibilities. Maybe it did need a living person. But the weight of the idea felt heavy on her chest. Could she risk it? She couldn't test it on a stranger, not after everything she'd learned about her power. But Bain? Could she test it on him?

There was a stillness between them, the tension palpable. She looked at him, studying his face, searching for something, anything, that would tell her she could trust him with something so dangerous.

But maybe the real question was: could she trust herself?

"No. Bain," Niamh's voice was firm, though doubt still lingered in her mind.

"After everything I did to you, this in no way makes up for it, but it's a start. Whatever happens, I don't hold you accountable," he said, his voice low and sincere, as if he was trying to convince both of them.

She shook her head, uncertain. "I can't… I can't risk it."

"I volunteer. Let me do this for you, Niamh," he said, his words earnest as he reached for her hand. His touch sent an unexpected jolt through her, a burst of warmth that made her pulse quicken, the flames inside her stirring to life again.

The feeling was intoxicating, like something inside her was waking up, something powerful, something dangerous.

"Look," he continued, his voice steady but with a hint of passion behind it. "The other flames, I'm assuming, were big and bad. But not all of them are like that. Purple is a love flame. Lovers have used it for centuries to stay together, to make sure they never outlive each other. Not all flames are dangerous."

"But it can also be used to stop someone's heart," she reminded him, her voice cold with caution, the reality of the danger creeping back in.

He grimaced but didn't back down. "True. Just don't think ill thoughts towards me when you do it, and we should be okay."

She met his gaze, still unconvinced. The words she'd heard about her flames echoed in her mind, the destructive potential of each one. But she couldn't ignore the truth: she had to know. When she faced her mother, when the battle truly began, she needed to be prepared for everything. Her powers, her gifts, they weren't just for show. They were weapons. She couldn't afford to be caught off guard.

Reluctantly, Niamh nodded. She knew this was a test. But was she ready to face it? She wasn't sure. She needed answers, and Bain was offering them in a way she wasn't sure she could refuse.

He let go of her hand and clapped them together, rubbing them in anticipation. "Let's get started."

"You don't want to eat first?" She hoped, desperately, for a moment of normalcy, something to ground her before this unknown power consumed her.

"No stalling. Let's get you sorted out," Bain said, his voice carrying that unyielding edge that made her stomach tighten with nerves.

She pouted, but there was nothing she could do to delay the inevitable. "Okay," she muttered, her throat tight.

Bain sat tall in his chair, bracing himself for whatever was about to come. His fingers gripped the armrests with an anticipation that bordered on nervousness. She could see the tension in his posture, the way he was preparing himself for the pain, for whatever might happen. His eyes met hers, and with a single nod, he silently gave her permission to begin.

Niamh took a breath, steadying herself. She reached inward, her thoughts swirling with uncertainty. Her invisible hand reached out, pulling the pink flame from the depths of her power. It was wild in her grasp, sparking with energy like a live wire. It zinged against her palm, sending an electric current through her fingers, urging her to release it. She fought to focus. *Good thoughts. Only good thoughts.* She had to make sure Bain didn't get hurt. She couldn't let this go wrong. At least with the white flame, she could reverse things if need be. But there was no going back with this one.

Bain smiled at her, his expression wide, filled with something genuine, something that made her chest ache. He was calm, even in the face of potential danger. His smile was an invitation, a reminder that, at this moment, she needed him. No hesitation, no regrets, just the quiet assurance that, no matter what happened, he was here because he wanted to be. *Because he wanted her.*

With a deep breath, she let the pink flame fly.

The moment it touched his chest, the flame splashed across him, seeping into his skin, disappearing with a shimmer that made her heart stop. Bain gasped, his head thrown back, face towards the sky, his entire body going rigid for a split second. His eyes widened, distant, as if he were somewhere far away. His gaze unfocused, his breath catching in his throat. She saw something flicker in his eyes, a flash of something darker, or was it pain?

The seconds stretched like hours. She stood frozen, fear gripping her heart as she waited, watching for any sign of what the flame had done to him.

"Are you okay, Bain?" Niamh's voice trembled with fear, but he didn't respond. He couldn't, even if he wanted to.

She shook him gently, her hands desperate but unsure. "Bain, please, say something, anything," she pleaded, her heart pounding as panic began to rise within her.

"Anything," he rasped, his voice rough and strained. But his body remained unmoving, his eyes unblinking, fixed on some distant place that Niamh couldn't reach.

The chill of uncertainty swept over her like a wave. "Bain, look at me," she whispered, her voice breaking, almost too soft to believe in. Slowly, almost agonizingly slow, his head turned, his eyes lifting to meet hers. But what she saw there made her breath catch in her throat, his gaze was vacant, distant, empty. They were nothing like the lively eyes that had always carried a spark of mischief, of life.

"Okay, this isn't funny. You can stop now. You hear me? Stop this." She wished with all her heart that it was some cruel joke, that Bain was pulling a prank. But deep down, she knew it wasn't. He wasn't playing.

His eyes blinked. Once, slowly. Twice, then faster. A normal pace returned to his blinking, and suddenly, *there* it was. The sparkle. The life. The depth. His eyes were Bain's again, but it wasn't enough to dispel the lingering fear inside her.

"Bain?" Her voice quivered as she asked, her hands hovering just above him, unsure whether to touch him again.

"I'm back," he said, and the excitement in his voice startled her. "That was wild!"

She frowned, a knot tightening in her stomach. "What happened?" Her voice was barely a whisper, the weight of the situation settling on her shoulders.

He looked up at her, eyes still gleaming, but his expression seemed almost dazed. "I don't know. I couldn't move, I couldn't talk. It was like I wasn't even in control of my body. It was… it was like you were."

Niamh blinked, struggling to process the meaning of his words. "What?" She barely dared to ask. "What do you mean *I* was in control?"

"You had control over my heart from the first time I saw you," he said, his grin pulling at the corners of his lips, mischievous as ever. "Now, I guess you can control my body, too."

The way he said it, playful, teasing, sent an uncomfortable heat to her face. She could feel her pulse quicken, but she fought to keep her emotions in check. He didn't understand the weight of his words. But he was still Bain, the same arrogant, playful, infuriating man she couldn't seem to shake off.

He paused, looking at her with an almost knowing smirk. "You're planning on making me do things to you, aren't you? I can tell. Your kink list is getting longer by the day."

Her breath caught, and she froze for a moment, horrified. The thought had never crossed her mind. *Never.* But the way he said it, so casually, made her heart race in confusion. Was he joking? Was he serious? Did he *want* her to be in control like that? No. No, it couldn't be that simple. She wasn't like that.

She gasped, feeling her face flush. *No, stop. This isn't you, Niamh.* She scolded herself, trying to banish the thoughts that had no place in her mind. It was too dangerous, too complicated, too… wrong.

Bain's grin deepened, his eyes playful, his tone low and teasing. "I'm into it if you are," he added, a gleam of mischief in his eyes, hoping to pull a reaction from her, anything to get her to respond.

But she remained silent, too caught up in the strange mix of emotions swirling inside her. She didn't know what to say, what to feel. She couldn't bring herself to even look at him for a moment, afraid of what he might see in her eyes. And then, when she did glance back, she noticed the nervousness on his face. His confidence faltered just a little, and she realized that he wasn't just teasing her for fun. There was something deeper there, a vulnerability he didn't often show.

Finally, she broke the tension with a dry laugh. "I'm not going to do that," she said, her voice a little shaky, but trying to mask the chaos within. "Pink is off-limits. But it's tempting. I could always get you to do the dishes or clean the bathroom for me instead," she added with a playful grin, hoping to change the subject, to steer them away from the awkwardness.

"That's not what I had in mind," he said, his grin widening. "But whatever tickles your tongue, baby. Naked cleaning coming up!"

"Oh my god, stop. Please stop," she groaned, burying her face in her hands. The tension broke as they both laughed, but the heaviness still hung in the air between them.

"Really, though," she said more softly, her voice sincere now. "Thank you. Thank you for volunteering for that. It was very brave of you. Or stupid. Not sure which yet." She paused, her tone softening as she met his gaze again. "But I do appreciate it."

"Anything for you." His face was genuine, sincere. No hint of teasing now. There was only raw sincerity, and it made her heart flutter unexpectedly.

She stared at him for a moment, realizing how much he meant it. He had never cared about anyone the way he cared about her. At that moment, she understood that he would do anything to make her happy. The weight of his loyalty pressed against her chest. *He would do anything for her.*

The thought was overwhelming, more than she was ready for. But one thing was clear: Bain wasn't just a playful trickster. He had something deeper, something real. And that, more than anything, scared her.

"Can we eat now?" Niamh asked, her voice tired but with a hint of hope in it. She needed to change the subject, and frankly, her stomach was growling louder than her thoughts. After all the magic she'd used today, it felt like she had run a marathon.

"Of course, princess," Bain replied automatically, immediately regretting the title the moment it left his mouth. He could see the tension in her face. He knew how much she hated anything to do with her mother. And frankly, he didn't blame her. Her mother was a monster, *and that was saying something,* considering the many monsters Bain had met in his long life.

Niamh didn't respond to the word choice. She was too exhausted to engage, too tired to argue. She just wanted food and rest, and she needed them now more than anything.

They ate in relative silence, only broken by the occasional appreciative sound from Niamh as she tasted each bite. She let out a soft moan of approval as she chewed, her eyes fluttering closed, savoring the meal. The sound was so simple, yet it made Bain's breath hitch. Those little sounds went straight to him... well, you know. There was something about hearing her pleasure that made his pulse quicken, even if he wasn't the cause of it.

He tried to focus on his own plate, but his eyes kept drifting back to her. She was so close to him, so effortlessly close, and it made him feel... unsettled, in the best way. She was here, *willingly,* eating beside him. She was sharing this space, and that was more than he'd ever hoped for.

Her eyes would flutter shut with each bite, as though every flavor was a tiny pleasure to savor. It was endearing, the way she immersed herself in the experience. And Bain couldn't help but want to see the world through her eyes, to taste the joy she found in the simple things. It was strange. She wasn't just a woman to him anymore; she was something... more. She was a revelation.

This was the best night Bain had had in hundreds of years. The thought hit him like a wave. He had never, *never* put someone else's needs above his own. But now, with her, it felt natural, instinctual. She was everything he never realized he needed. He thought he could get used to it. Loving someone wasn't so foreign to him, but being *loved* in return was something he'd never truly allowed himself to hope for. He'd get there. He was sure of it. He just needed time.

He wasn't known for giving up, and Niamh, he knew, was worth the wait.

She didn't stick around long after her plate was empty. "I'm gonna head back to my room. I'm really tired," Niamh said, her voice softer than usual. It wasn't a lie. She was exhausted, having spent the day channeling flames, blowing things up, and wrestling with the weight of the knowledge that she could kill an entire building of people with just a thought. It took more out of her than she wanted to admit.

Bain didn't argue. He could see it in her eyes, the weariness, the heavy sighs she tried to mask. She was drained. Instead of pushing her to stay or asking her to linger, he quietly agreed. He didn't want to cause her any more discomfort. He nodded, softening his tone. "I'm tired too," he said, though the truth was far from it. He had spent the day planning the dinner, convincing the doctor to let him use a candle in the hospital area; she'd refused, of course. It wasn't the same, but it was something. He could live with that. Baby steps, he reminded himself. It's a marathon, not a sprint.

"Will you swing by tomorrow?" he asked, his voice hopeful but calm.

"I'll think about it. Good night, Bain." The words were simple, but they felt like a gift; those three words made his entire year. *Good night*, such a small phrase, yet it meant everything to him at that moment. He had never heard anything more beautiful.

"Sweet dreams, Niamh." The words felt tender on his lips. She smiled at him, a smile that seemed to shine with something real, something raw. It was genuine, unguarded, and for the briefest of moments, Bain allowed himself to believe that maybe, just maybe, this was something more than a fleeting connection.

She turned to leave, and as she did, her smile lingered in his mind. But he didn't leave her thoughts. As she made her way back to her room, the quiet of the hallway wrapped around her, and she replayed the evening in her head, his touch on her hand, the way he was willing to sacrifice himself to help her, how he seemed to know just how to push her to be better without overstepping. He understood her, maybe better than anyone ever had. It was a feeling that was both comforting and unsettling.

But trust didn't come easy. Not for someone like her, who had learned the hard way that people who got too close could hurt you the most. The past trauma she carried made it almost impossible to believe in the sincerity of anyone else's intentions. Even Bain's kindness, his willingness to be there for her, was wrapped in layers of doubt. Could it be real? Or was it all just a long con, a well-crafted scheme to gain her trust only to tear it down when she least expected it?

Her heart ached with the question. It would be easier to believe in him if she didn't have to worry about the damage she'd suffered in the past. But for now, she pushed those thoughts aside. She was too tired to untangle the web of doubts spinning in her mind. A knock at the door drew her attention.

She opened her door, and before she could even step inside, Lidia's voice rang out, "So how was it?"

"Hello to you, too," Niamh joked, grinning at the playful intrusion. They had no boundaries in their friendship; Lidia never held back.

"Hello. Now, *how* was it?" Lidia asked again, impatience creeping into her tone. She was practically bouncing in her seat, waiting for all the details.

Niamh flopped down on the bed next to her friend. "It was… good. He was the perfect gentleman."

Lidia's face fell in mock sympathy. "Oh, I'm sorry."

"That's a good thing, Lidia," Niamh chuckled, rolling her eyes.

"So, nothing? He didn't try to get into your pants? Or at least make out?" Lidia prodded, her curiosity impossible to contain.

Niamh let out a startled laugh. "Lidia! No. But he did offer for me to test my magic on him. It was… brave."

Lidia raised an eyebrow, not entirely following. "Brave?"

"Aoife and Njeri had me working on my magic, trying to figure it all out. We got all the flames except one. So, Bain volunteered to be the test subject. He could've literally exploded or died, but he still offered." Niamh's voice softened at the memory of Bain's reckless yet genuine willingness.

Lidia blinked, processing. "Wait… *What* did it do?"

"It controlled him. Like, he couldn't move or speak unless I told him to. It was so strange. I've never felt so powerful or that in control of someone else. It was like having a puppet at my disposal." Niamh shivered a little, the weight of it settling over her.

Lidia's grin spread wide, mischief dancing in her eyes. "You had the opportunity to make him do all the things you've been dreaming about, and you didn't take it? Really?"

Niamh rolled her eyes. "You're just as bad as him."

"I'm just saying," Lidia teased. "If it's consensual, it's not bad, right? You could've made him *do* something he'd never do willingly. Think of the possibilities."

"Lidia!" Niamh laughed, shaking her head. "I won't take advantage of him like that."

Lidia just shrugged. "Fine, fine, you're no fun." She leaned in closer, clearly hoping for some more drama. "So, what did you guys talk about? Give me the tea."

Niamh let out a soft sigh, thinking back to the conversation. "Not much, just magic. We ate, and then I left. He asked me to come back tomorrow, but… I don't know if that's a good idea."

"Why not?" Lidia asked, raising her eyebrows, clearly concerned.

"Because I don't want to get attached," Niamh admitted, her voice quiet. "Because he still could be using me to gain power and standing. Because I'm dangerous until I get better control of my magic. There's a million reasons, Lidia."

Lidia's expression softened, but she pressed on. "But is that really it? You're telling me that's all? Because I think you're scared. And I get it. You're scared of letting someone in, of getting hurt. I've seen it before. But you can't shut yourself off forever."

Niamh bit her lip, not sure how to answer that. She wanted to say that Lidia was right, that the real reason she hesitated wasn't about control or power, but about vulnerability. She was scared of opening herself up to someone again, scared of letting someone see *too* much. But instead, she stayed silent, looking away.

Lidia was relentless, though. "I'm not saying marry the man, Niamh. I'm just saying, give him a chance. From what I saw, he genuinely seemed into you."

"When did you talk to him?" Niamh's tone was sharp, her hands on her hips as the familiar sting of betrayal flickered through her. Had her best friend been talking to him behind her back?

Lidia winced, raising her hands in mock surrender. "You were training, and I was bored. I was just walking around the building, and I stumbled on the hospital area. He was there. I didn't go see him on purpose, Niamh! But even if I did, I didn't give him any secret information about you or your social security number or anything."

Niamh shot her a look but couldn't help a small laugh at the absurdity of the accusation. "You'd better not have."

Lidia winked. "I didn't. I just thought he seemed like a decent guy, and, you know, I was *curious*."

"Curious, huh?" Niamh said dryly, sinking back into the bed. "I don't know about this, Lidia. I want to trust him; I do. But it feels too easy. And with me, nothing's ever easy."

Her friend's expression softened. "I get it. But trust your instincts. And trust that, at least for tonight, I'm not the one you need to worry about." They hugged as Lidia left, a small bit of comfort at the end of a long, stressful day.

Niamh lay down in her bed, the soft sheets a welcome comfort after a day full of emotional and physical exhaustion. Lidia's words echoed in her mind, but the more she thought about them, the more she realized how much she was letting her fears control her. She was so scared of being vulnerable, of letting someone else in, but Bain had already proven he was willing to face danger for her.

Why am I fighting this so hard?

She didn't have an answer, at least not one she could put into words. It felt safer to keep her distance, to protect herself from whatever this *thing* between her and Bain was becoming. She closed her eyes, letting her mind wander freely, hoping it would take her to a place where she could simply breathe and not think so hard.

Her thoughts inevitably drifted back to Bain. Even in the quiet solitude of her room, she couldn't help but picture his smile, the way he'd offered himself so freely, with no hesitation, even when he had no idea what would happen with the magic. His willingness to put himself at risk for her was a rare quality she didn't often see. And it made her question everything she thought she knew about trust.

The room was still, safe, and her mind felt oddly clear for the first time in days. She could feel the subtle pull of sleep coming on, but before she surrendered to it, she whispered into the quiet, "I'm not ready for this."

Her room, her sanctuary, wrapped her in its comforting embrace. She could let go here, in this space where no one could intrude, not even Bain. And yet, the dream realm was a different kind of freedom. A place where she didn't have to hide, didn't have to fight.

She let go of her waking thoughts and surrendered to the dream.

And just like that, she was in his arms, safely, without fear, without judgment.

The night passed slowly, but her dreams were vivid, unfiltered, exploring what was buried deep inside her heart. The desire she felt for Bain, the way he made her feel alive, was no longer a fear to suppress. In her dreams, she could let herself feel it without the weight of reality.

She was back in the cabin, the scent of pine and the earthiness of the mountains filling the air. The overstuffed couch beneath her was a comforting weight, soft but sturdy, wrapping around her like an embrace. The crackle of a low fire flickered in the corner, casting dancing shadows across the rustic wood walls. The warmth of the room contrasted with the chill outside, the snow still falling gently in thick flakes, muffling the world beyond the windows.

As she shifted, she became aware of the arm beneath her, the solid, steady presence of a body behind her. She instinctively reached out, her fingers brushing against warm skin. Her hand traced a gentle path across his chest, lingering on the subtle rise of muscle beneath her fingertips. It felt real, grounding. She was here, with him, in this space where nothing else could intrude.

Her fingers continued their exploration, sliding over the smooth surface of his skin, down to the contours of his abdomen. Each muscle was defined, strong, but there was something tender in the way she touched him, as if she was discovering him for the first time. She stopped, her hand hovering, not wanting to cross into something more, unsure if she was ready, if he was, or if it was just the way the mountain air and the heat of the fire made everything feel so intensely alive.

A groan slipped from his lips, low and drowsy, breaking the silence. She froze, holding her breath, afraid to disturb the peaceful moment. But instead of waking up fully, he shifted closer, his breath warm against her neck. She could feel the steady rhythm of his pulse through the soft pressure of his chest against her back, and the way his body seemed to draw hers in, as though their connection was something deeper than just physical.

A flicker of heat stirred within her as he brushed against her neck, his lips lightly grazing the skin there. She could feel the subtle tension in the air, this intimate space between them where nothing seemed to matter except the quiet rustle of the fire and the sound of their breath, mingling together.

The stillness of the cabin was heavy with unspoken words, but it was the weight of the moment, the shared quiet intimacy of the space, that felt the most telling. Out here, in this place where time felt like it slowed, it was just them. And though she hesitated, part of her wondered how long she could keep pretending that this, this pull between them, wasn't as real as the mountains themselves.

A tired, gritty groan escaped his lips. She froze, afraid she'd wake him up. He moved his head closer to her and nibbled her neck, pinching just hard enough to hurt in a good way. She never found pain pleasurable, but maybe, for him, she would be open to trying it. He made her want to do things she normally wouldn't.

His warm tongue gently danced on her neck. She closed her eyes, fully surrendering to the feeling. A strong, slim hand slid up her hip, finding its way to her stomach, pinning her closer to him. He moved his hips against hers, and they both reacted instantly to the sensation.

Chapter 24

❧

Buzz. Buzz. Buzz.

She was ripped from her dream by the dreaded alarm clock. She wanted to throw the damn thing out the window. With a groan of disappointment, she slammed her hand down to silence it, then pulled a pillow over her head to scream into it, releasing some of her pent-up frustration. Maybe Lidia was right. Maybe she should be open to seeing Bain. She wanted to explore the possibilities; her subconscious wasn't subtle.

Splashing cold water on her face did little to wipe the vivid memory away. She needed a distraction. Food was her first thought. She made her way to Lidia's room on the way to the restaurant, but when she cracked the door open to ask if she wanted to join her, Lidia threw a pillow at her. The subtle hint was impossible to miss. No breakfast with Lidia, then.

With a sigh, she walked down the hall alone.

Walking into the restaurant, it was empty, except for one table where a certain dark-haired man sat. The moment she saw him, she wanted to run, to hide. But he'd already spotted her. Running now would just be awkward. With a reluctant sigh, she walked over to him, forcing herself to be polite, though she didn't trust herself after her last dream.

"You don't have your bracelet anymore?" she joked, trying to mask her nerves.

He rubbed his wrist, a cocky grin tugging at his lips. "Nope. Nick determined I'm not a risk to anyone. So, I'm free to do as I please."

"Well, congrats on your freedom." She turned, intent on sitting at another table, but before she could move, he quickly caught her arm, his gaze locking with hers.

"Would you join me? I'd love the company after being locked up like a prisoner."

"You were a prisoner. You kidnapped me, remember?"

He winced slightly, a touch of guilt flashing across his face. "Oh, that… yes. But I didn't know what she had planned. I thought she just wanted to meet her daughter. I am sorry, once again, for that."

"It's a hard thing to forgive, Bain. You and her actions, both inexcusable. She won't be winning any 'Mother of the Year' awards anytime soon."

"I just hope you can forgive me someday. Or at least give me another chance. I'd do anything to make it up to you."

She stared at him for a moment, her thoughts swirling. "Can we not talk about this all again? I'm pretty over it. I'd like to just focus on surviving the day."

He gave a small nod, a hint of relief in his expression. "Sure. Have a seat."

He darted up, pulling out a chair for her, and for a moment, she hesitated. But what harm could breakfast do? She thought. With a quiet exhale, she sat down, though a small part of her still wondered what exactly she was doing here.

Cami was their waitress. "What can I get you, Niamh?"

Niamh studied her for a moment, empathy stirring in her chest. Being a banshee must be so difficult. Cami was stunning, model material, with cheekbones sharp enough to cut glass and legs that seemed to stretch on forever. Her smile could light up a room. But behind all that beauty, there was so much pain in her eyes. Niamh had always wished for that kind of beauty, but now she understood, sometimes the grass isn't greener. Cami had lived through more death and sorrow than anyone should have to, and no amount of beauty could shield her from that.

In this building, they all shared something. A bond of pain, of understanding. Their struggles may have been different, but they all wanted the same thing: safety. Respect.

"Hi, Cami. I'll have the waffles and a coffee, please."

"No problem. Bain, your omelet will be right out," she said, though her words went unnoticed. Bain didn't take his eyes off of Niamh. Cami saw it, and she gave Niamh a knowing wink of encouragement.

"So, what are you going to do with all your newfound freedom? You leaving K Corp?" she asked, her voice tentative.

"I don't know yet," he replied, his eyes glinting. "I was hoping there'd be a reason for me to stay." His sly smile was both teasing and hopeful.

"Bain, I…" She trailed off, not sure how to continue.

He cut her off with a soft chuckle. "It's fine. I get it; you've got a lot going on. But you can't blame a man for trying." He smiled, but it wasn't his usual playful grin. It was more subdued, a touch disappointed.

The arrival of his omelet and her coffee broke the tension. Niamh sipped her drink slowly, the warm liquid grounding her as she waited for her waffles. She devoured them quickly, not out of hunger, though she was certainly starving, but to keep her mouth full, to avoid any further conversation. Anything to keep him from pushing.

Bain caught on. He didn't try to talk anymore, sensing her discomfort. It stung a little, but he couldn't blame her. His ego would have to get used to rejection if he kept pursuing Niamh. She wasn't someone who gave in easily. And that was part of the fun of the chase.

Breakfast was finished in record time. They both stood up at the same moment, the silence between them thick with awkwardness. Bain waved her forward, trying to be a gentleman, but part of him couldn't help but enjoy the view as she passed him.

"I'll, uh, see you later," Niamh said quickly, hurrying toward the door and making a beeline for the training center. She couldn't bring herself to look back at Bain. The last thing she wanted was to see the disappointment on his face or worse, see him try to push for another conversation she wasn't ready to have.

As she entered the training room, Aoife and Njeri were already there, setting up the last ballistic dummy. The sight of it made Niamh realize she had completely forgotten to tell them she had figured out the last flame.

"So, uh, I know what the last flame, the pink one, does," she said, her voice barely above a whisper, hoping they wouldn't be mad that she tested it on Bain.

Both women turned to her, their faces filled with shock, waiting for her explanation.

"It controls people," she added quickly, bracing herself.

Aoife and Njeri exchanged looks, their confusion evident. "I've never heard of such a thing," Njeri said, her voice full of disbelief.

"How did you come to find this out, Niamh?" Aoife asked, her tone almost cautious, as if she was afraid to know the answer.

Niamh hesitated. She could feel the heat rising in her cheeks. "Bain offered to let me test it on him. He thought maybe the flame needed a real body to control, that the dummy wouldn't be enough to activate it. He was right." She gave a sheepish smile, trying to avoid their eyes.

"You. Tested. New magic. On. Bain?" Aoife asked slowly, her voice tinged with disbelief.

Niamh nodded, hoping they wouldn't press her further. She could already feel the weight of their judgment.

"Well, it didn't work on one dummy, but it worked on another, apparently." Njeri's laugh broke the tension. "He must like you if he offered to be your test subject. That was pretty dumb."

Niamh chuckled nervously, relieved that Njeri wasn't angry. "I know, I shouldn't have done it, but he wouldn't stop pushing."

"No, I mean he was dumb, not you, honey. He may be good-looking, for a man, but not much upstairs, huh?" Njeri laughed again, and this time, Niamh joined her.

She realized she wasn't in trouble, at least not as much as she had feared. She let out a breath she hadn't realized she'd been holding.

"Well, that's a relief," Niamh muttered, a small smile tugging at her lips. "Glad you're not going to yell at me."

Aoife spoke up, her voice steady yet tinged with a hint of concern. "Well, with that sorted, I guess we can move on to the next topic. We got an invitation, well, more like *you* got an invitation. From Queen Cailleach." She paused, watching Niamh's reaction. "She's proposed an accord, a truce, to keep this war from killing any more innocents. It's… it seems out of character for her, but I think we need to consider it. A truce would be the best thing for both realms. As much as I'm leery about it, we should at least think it through."

Niamh's stomach twisted at the mention of Queen Cailleach. She didn't want to be in the same room as that woman again, let alone make any kind of agreement with her. But she knew, deep down, that she probably wouldn't be able to avoid it. Cailleach wasn't the type to take rejection lightly.

"What would I have to do?" Niamh asked, trying to mask the unease that was settling deep within her. She hadn't felt this much pressure since the early days of her magic training, but this was on an entirely different level.

Aoife's gaze softened, sensing Niamh's discomfort. "Well, you'd travel to her dimension with a team of guards and negotiate an agreement with her. We want to save as many lives as possible, so preventing an inter-dimensional war would be the best course of action."

The weight of it settled in Niamh's chest like a lead anchor. A truce… but she had no idea how to form a peace treaty. The most responsibility she'd ever had was running her flower shop back home, and even that felt like a stretch some days. Now, she was being asked to negotiate peace between realms? She felt dizzy, her breath catching in her throat. Her body swayed slightly, and for a brief moment, she thought she might collapse, but Aoife was there, steadying her with a hand on her shoulder.

"You don't have to do it if it's too much. We'll find another way," Aoife said gently, her voice reassuring.

Niamh shook her head, trying to push the rising panic away. "I think you should go," she muttered, almost to herself, as if the words would somehow make the weight of the decision lighter.

Aoife stared at her for a moment, then shook her head in return. "We can't. Nick and I have been refused entry. She'll only allow you as our delegate. But the guards? That's non-negotiable. You'll have a team of them to protect you. Not that I think she'd try anything. It wouldn't be in her best interest." Aoife's lips curled slightly into a half-smile. "Your powers are a force to be reckoned with. Her snow doesn't stand a chance against your... well, flame." She chuckled softly, trying to lighten the mood.

Niamh's heart pounded in her chest, but Aoife's words did bring a small sense of comfort. She *was* powerful. Even if she wasn't sure how to negotiate peace, she knew she had the strength to stand her ground. The thought of facing Cailleach again filled her with dread, but Aoife was right; she had no other choice. The realms were counting on her.

"Okay," Niamh said, her voice quiet but firm, "I'll do it. But I'm going to need a hell of a lot of preparation."

Njeri's voice cut through the tension, her words firm and full of conviction. "I know you're scared. And that's okay. But girl, you are *so* bad ass! Don't let her think she can walk all over you. Go in there, reclaim your power, and show her what she's been missing out on all these years."

Niamh's chest tightened, but something deep inside her stirred. Njeri was right. She wasn't the same person she'd been just a few days ago. The girl who'd once felt lost and small had become someone stronger. She had power now, real power. And it was hers to wield, no one else's. She wasn't going to let Cailleach have any more control over her. Not now, not ever.

She pushed her shoulders back, straightened her spine, and took a deep breath. "I'll do it," she said, the words firm and resolute, though her heart was racing in her chest.

Njeri slapped her back with a grin. "That's my girl!"

A smile tugged at the corners of Niamh's mouth, but her nerves were starting to kick in now that she had agreed. She tried to keep her voice steady as she asked, "So, when do we begin?"

Aoife, always the calm presence, looked at her with a reassuring nod. "I guess now, if you're ready."

The question made Niamh pause. She hadn't thought this far ahead. "Can I tell Lidia first? So, she doesn't worry about me?"

"Of course, honey. Take all the time you need," Aoife reassured her gently.

Niamh nodded, grateful for the understanding. Her feet moved mechanically as she walked toward Lidia's room, her mind racing with thoughts she hadn't had time to process. She wasn't just about to face her mother, she was about to face her destiny, something bigger than herself. The pressure weighed heavily on her, but she knew she had to do this.

She had a responsibility to K Corp, to the people who had supported her and given her a place when the world outside had turned its back. She had a responsibility to herself, to the woman she was becoming, the woman who wouldn't hide in the shadows anymore.

Her father had been a shadow creature, but she was part goddess, too. She didn't need to be ashamed of that, of who she was, or where she came from. The unique blend of powers inside her was a gift, not a curse. And she wasn't going to let Cailleach or anyone else define her.

She reached Lidia's door and knocked lightly, her hand trembling only slightly as she braced herself. No matter what came next, she had made her decision. And now, there was no turning back.

Niamh gently pushed open the door and stepped into the room, her eyes immediately landing on Lidia in front of the mirror, expertly applying her makeup. It felt almost normal, the same routine they'd shared countless times back in Georgia. Niamh, as she often did, perched herself on the counter, her body instinctively finding comfort in the familiar spot.

But the second Lidia turned and saw the look on her face, her hands froze, the makeup brush suspended in mid-air. Lidia didn't need any words to know something was wrong.

"What's wrong?" she asked, setting down her makeup tools, her voice soft and full of concern.

Niamh sighed, bracing herself. "I need to tell you something."

Lidia's expression shifted, and she leaned on the counter, eyes never leaving Niamh. The unspoken understanding passed between them, this wasn't just another one of their typical talks.

"I have to go to a different dimension to make a truce with my birth mother. It's something I have to do. She won't let Aoife or Nick go. I... have to do this." The weight of her words settled heavily in the room, and she let out a long, shaky breath, trying to release some of the tension coiling in her chest.

Lidia stared at her, her gaze wide, processing the words. Then, slowly, she set the makeup bottles down and crossed her arms, her expression a mix of disbelief and concern. "Okay. That's a lot. That's a sentence I never thought I'd hear come out of your mouth. Is it dangerous?"

"Probably," Niamh shrugged, the uncertainty hanging in her voice. "But Aoife's sending guards with me. That's supposed to make me feel better."

Lidia's brow furrowed, but she didn't press further, just nodded and said softly, "When do you go?"

"Now." The word was like a stone, heavy and final.

Lidia's eyes welled up with tears, the emotion quickly threatening to spill over. Niamh felt a pang in her chest as she watched, but she couldn't let herself crumble. Not now.

"Don't do that," Niamh whispered, her voice trembling. "If you make me cry, I won't be able to hold it together. I can't break down right now, Lidia. This is the first step in taking back what they took from me. My birth parents... they stole my sparkle, my confidence. I need to do this. Please... just support me."

Lidia's tears flowed freely then, but she wrapped Niamh in a tight embrace, squeezing her so hard it almost took her breath away. "Of course I support you, honey! I support you in everything you do." Her voice cracked, but she held onto Niamh, as if trying to hold onto the moment, the strength of their friendship. "You go kick some Queenly ass, okay?"

Niamh let out a small, bittersweet laugh, pulling away slightly to look into her best friend's eyes. "That's the goal," she said, trying to sound confident, even as doubt swirled inside her. They both knew how dangerous this was. Neither of them needed to say it out loud. But they couldn't deny the fear that lingered between them.

Lidia swallowed hard, nodding, trying to steady herself. "Just promise me you'll come back. I'll be lost without you."

Niamh's heart ached, but she didn't know how to promise something she couldn't control. So, she simply said, "I'll try."

That was all she could give, and both of them knew it was enough.

"I need to call my parents real quick. I just wanted to let you know," Niamh said softly, sliding off the counter. She forced a smile that didn't reach her eyes, knowing Lidia saw right through it.

"Okay, I'll be here," Lidia replied, her voice thick with unspoken emotion. Niamh knew Lidia didn't want to say goodbye, not like this, but there was nothing more to be said.

The phone call to her parents was a different kind of stress, the kind that twisted in her stomach. After everything they'd been through together, she couldn't help but fear that this might be the last time she'd speak to them. It wasn't an irrational thought, everything felt like it was teetering on the edge of something too dangerous to control. But she had to call. She couldn't leave without at least hearing their voices, knowing they understood.

"Hi, honey! How are you doing? We've been waiting for an update from up there," her mom said, her voice bright, full of that signature warmth Niamh had grown to cherish. It felt like a weight on her chest, her mother didn't deserve to carry this new burden.

"I'm okay, Mom," Niamh replied, her voice wavering. "I've been learning a lot about myself here. I feel more like myself than I ever have. But there's something I need to do. I have to take a trip. I may be gone for a while." Her throat tightened with each word.

Her mother's tone shifted slightly, sensing the gravity in her voice. "What kind of trip, honey?"

Niamh swallowed, knowing her mother would sense the truth before she said it. "It's something to do with my birth mother. I'm sorry. I have to do it, to keep everyone safe."

"You don't have to apologize, honey," her mom said quickly, the softness in her voice almost making Niamh break down right then and there. "I know she wasn't who you were hoping she'd be. You've been dealt a hand of cards that was stacked against you. But you are the strongest person I know. You've succeeded and excelled at everything you do. You just make sure you come back home safely to us, okay?"

The words were like a balm to her raw soul, but they also tore at her heart. Her mom was right, and yet, how could she promise that? There were no guarantees, no way to know how this would end. But hearing the love in her voice, the quiet plea to come back, made Niamh want to fight harder than ever.

"Thanks, Mom," she whispered, her voice barely above a breath. "I needed that. I'll, uh, call you later, okay?"

The lump in her throat threatened to suffocate her, but she had to hold it together. She couldn't afford to break down now. She hung up before the tears could fall, her chest tight with a sorrow she couldn't put into words.

Without thinking, she rushed to the bathroom and splashed cold water on her face, trying to force herself back to some semblance of control. The cool water didn't stop the tremble in her hands, didn't silence the growing knot in her stomach. But she couldn't cry, not yet. Not until the mission was over.

She had to be strong. She *was* strong.

She looked at herself in the mirror, her reflection no longer something to shy away from. Slowly, she was starting to see the woman she had become, not a mutant, not something broken, but a strong, powerful goddess. A force. The woman staring back at her was someone who would no longer stand by while a bully hurt her family or friends. She had the strength to protect those she loved. And, most importantly, she had the power to take control of her life. To define who she was.

Chapter 25

Aoife was waiting for her in the lobby, flanked by Nick, Njeri, and Bain. When Bain saw her, he gave her a sheepish smile, one she didn't quite recognize. It was new. He looked nervous. She couldn't help but notice how much stronger she appeared now, how much more in control of herself. He seemed to see it too. She was no longer the uncertain woman he'd once tried to hold back but someone else, someone formidable.

He wasn't sure how to approach her. He had his reasons for being there, reasons that had nothing to do with causing trouble. He wasn't there to make things more complicated but to protect her. Even if she didn't need him, even if she didn't want him there, he couldn't shake the feeling that he couldn't let her go into that dimension without him. If something went wrong, if she was in danger… he couldn't forgive himself for not being there to try and stop it.

Nick led the way to the large lab-looking room with the machines, their whirring hum so loud that it was nearly impossible to hear anything over the sound. White-coated scientists were scattered about, engrossed in their work, too busy with their tasks to even glance up as they passed. The hum of technology and machinery created an odd kind of coldness in the air, and yet, it felt oddly appropriate given what she was about to do.

Aoife stopped in front of Niamh, gently taking her hands in hers, her eyes full of a quiet strength that Niamh admired. "I'm so sorry I can't go with you," Aoife said, her voice steady but tinged with regret. "But you have a great group of guards, our best. They'll keep you safe. And Bain… well, he wouldn't take no for an answer. He promised to be good and not cause any trouble."

Niamh didn't know how to respond. She didn't want Bain there, didn't want the added complication of his presence. He could cause drama, create doubt. There was always the chance he could double-cross her or distract her when the stakes were high. But there were bigger things at play now. She couldn't let herself be swayed by the small uncertainties. She had to stay focused on the bigger picture: securing peace, finding some measure of control over her chaotic life, and facing her birth mother with the power she had only just started to understand.

She didn't speak, didn't try to argue or voice her thoughts. Instead, she nodded silently, trying to push aside the nervous lump in her throat. Her thoughts were clouded, but she knew one thing for certain: she couldn't back out now.

She looked over at the group of guards, standing tall and unwavering, a picture of readiness. Their black body armor hugged their frames, sleek and functional, designed to protect the most vital areas of their bodies. Their faces were shielded by thin mesh, some kind of high-tech protective gear, but Niamh could still see their focused eyes. Beneath the armor, they wore full-body suits, black as night, a perfect blend of practicality and efficiency. They were ready for anything, and she felt a slight sense of reassurance knowing they were there.

Bain, however, stood apart from the group. He was dressed in a perfectly tailored light grey suit, the fabric smooth and crisp, designed to highlight his slim frame. The top button was undone, revealing just enough skin to make Niamh's breath catch. It was an outfit made for a business meeting, not a battle. And yet, there was something about the way he stood, confident, determined, that made her feel like he was ready to face whatever challenge lay ahead. When his eyes met hers, he gave a small nod, his firm smile saying everything he couldn't voice. He wanted to protect her. More than that, he *would* protect her, no matter what.

Aoife snapped her attention away from Bain and reached into her pocket, pulling out a small bracelet. She handed it to Niamh with a reassuring smile. "Here," she said, her voice steady, "take this. The button on it will let me know when you need a portal. Just push it, and I'll send it back as soon as you're ready. Do you have any questions?"

Niamh didn't know how to respond. Her mind was swirling, her nerves tightening. How was she supposed to form a peaceful alliance with someone like her mother? She felt a wave of doubt creeping in, making her stomach churn. She had never been good at diplomacy. What if she failed? What if she couldn't make the truce? Aoife seemed to sense her hesitation, her voice soft but firm. "You got this, Niamh. I've seen so much growth in you. I know how powerful you are. Do not let her bully you. You're stronger than her."

Niamh swallowed hard. Could she be stronger than the Queen? Her mother was a goddess, a being of immense power, banished for a reason. The weight of that history pressed on her, a reminder of what she was up against. But Aoife's words rang in her ears. She had come so far, learned so much. She couldn't let doubt take hold now. She was part goddess, too, and she wasn't going to let her mother define her future. She had power, her power, and no one, especially not her mother, could take that away from her.

With a deep breath, Niamh pushed the doubt aside. She had a mission. A goal. And she would not let the shadows of her past hold her back.

Bain stepped closer, his presence like a force of nature. His eyes were steady on hers, a little too intense, but his smile was warm, sincere. "You ready? Let's go kick some queen butt," he said, trying to lighten the moment.

Niamh couldn't help but shake her head at him, the weight of the mission pressing down. "No, this is a peace mission. We're going to find common ground and protect people. No butt kicking."

She turned back to Aoife, a question on her lips. "Does he have to come?"

Aoife's lips curled into a sympathetic smile. "I tried talking him out of it, but he wouldn't take no for an answer. And he does know Cailleach, so he might be able to give you insight into her next move."

Niamh shot Bain a sidelong glance. She was still uncertain about him, and a small part of her feared what his presence might complicate. She looked back at Aoife, her voice low. "Do you trust him?"

Aoife gave a light shrug, as though the decision were clear, yet still not easy. "He seems to be genuine when you're involved. He's been nothing but helpful. I like to think the best of people. But some say I'm an optimist." She chuckled softly.

Niamh stared at the floor for a moment, the doubt and hesitation swirling in her chest. She wanted to believe Aoife, to trust Bain's intentions. But the walls she'd built for so long, the ones that kept her safe from hurt, from disappointment, wouldn't come down so easily. It was safer this way. *Better* this way.

Her breath was steady, but her heart was in a tangle of conflicting emotions. She sighed, looking up again to see Bain's eager expression, though it softened when he caught her gaze. He was always stealing glances at her, but there was something different about the way he looked at her now, more earnest, as though he was trying to prove something to her, maybe even to himself.

For a moment, their eyes locked, and a small smile tugged at the corner of her mouth. It wasn't much, just a glimmer, but Bain's heart skipped at the sight. To him, it was everything. She hadn't pushed him away completely. And that was enough for him to hope, to believe, that there was still a chance for him to be someone worthy of her trust, someone who could be better for her.

"I'll be watching your back," Bain said softly, his voice laced with determination. He wasn't just here for the mission. He was here for her, whatever that meant.

Niamh met his gaze again, trying to read him. She knew what this was, he had a history, one he wasn't proud of. But *this* was different, or so he claimed. She couldn't afford to dwell on what he had been; she had to focus on the mission ahead. She could only hope he was telling the truth.

Aoife's hands moved with graceful precision, the air around her rippling as she summoned the gust of gold-tinged wind. She pulled her hands apart, widening the cyclone until it swirled in the air, and with a swift motion, she tipped it to its side. The cyclone flattened, creating a seamless portal that shimmered like liquid gold. Half of the guards stepped in front of Aoife, ready to protect her, while the other half formed a protective line behind Niamh. Bain slid beside her, his presence a comforting weight. His shoulder brushed hers, sending a ripple of warmth through her. She didn't pull away this time. She was starting to realize just how much his proximity made her feel… more.

Aoife's voice broke through her thoughts as the guards moved in formation. "Stay close," she murmured, her voice calm but urgent. The rest of the team nudged Niamh forward, keeping her moving with the pace. Her eyes flicked back to Bain, and he squeezed her hand. The warmth from his touch melted away her doubts, even if only for a moment. He wasn't here for a distraction, not really. He was here because he wanted to be.

The wind washed over them, sending her hair flying in wild circles. Squinting through the stinging hits, she stepped through the golden circle, into the unknown.

When the wind died down, the gusts fading as fast as they had come, Niamh's feet landed softly on the ground. She glanced around to find herself standing on paver stones, not stone, but something far more intricate. The crystals beneath her feet lit up with an ethereal glow, white and intense, casting a radiance that felt otherworldly. Her heart skipped a beat. These crystals, the same ones from her first journey, were impossibly beautiful. They seemed to pulse with energy, like they were alive, and they stretched up into towering mountains that surrounded her on every side.

The guards gently nudged her from behind, a signal to move forward. Her breath caught in her throat as she walked, eyes wide with awe. The mountains rose higher than she could have imagined, their jagged peaks crowned with clusters of shimmering crystals. The landscape was breathtaking, eerily beautiful in a way that made her feel both small and powerful at the same time.

Her mind drifted to the task ahead. Her birth mother was somewhere out there, among the towering mountains and glowing stones. Niamh's stomach fluttered with a mixture of anticipation and anxiety. She wasn't just walking into enemy territory; she was walking into her past, into the place where her power, her bloodline, and her very existence were shaped.

She stole a glance at Bain, his profile strong and steady beside her. His eyes were focused ahead, but the tension in his jaw betrayed his concern. He was here to protect her, yes, but Niamh wondered if he, too, was thinking about the looming confrontation that awaited them.

The distance ahead felt like an eternity, but they continued, step by step, the crystals beneath their feet guiding their path toward the unknown.

The doors loomed before them, towering at least 30 feet high and adorned with intricate crystal designs that sparkled like stained glass. The shapes were organic and flowing, as if nature itself had sculpted them, adding to the ethereal atmosphere of the palace. Niamh marveled at the grandeur of it all, her footsteps echoing in the vast hallway as they approached the entrance. The doors creaked open as they neared, groaning under their weight, signaling the beginning of what could be a very long and tense negotiation.

The guards' footsteps sounded like thunder against the smooth stone floor, their synchronized stomps reverberating through the cavernous space. Niamh kept her eyes ahead, taking in the sight of the grand staircase that spiraled upward. It was made of clear crystal, gleaming in the light like an opal, but she quickly averted her gaze. Heights were not her friend. She didn't need to go up there, and she was glad for it.

As they walked deeper into the space, Niamh's thoughts wandered to the task ahead. This place, this palace, felt ancient, its air heavy with power and history. The walls were adorned with more crystals, glowing with more light than what was natural. She was still in awe of the beauty of it all when the guard in front of her suddenly stopped. She wasn't prepared for the sudden halt, and she bumped into his back, her body jolting forward. Her foot stepped awkwardly to the side, pushing him out of line. The guard quickly recovered, but Niamh flushed with embarrassment. She muttered an apology under her breath as she straightened herself up, trying to shake off the awkward moment.

But then, she saw her. The queen.

Sitting on a raised dais, Cailleach looked like the picture of opulence and disdain, her presence undeniable. She wore an extravagant gown that somehow managed to be even more ostentatious than the last. Huge puffs of fabric cascaded over her shoulders and down her front, ending at her hip. The fabric sparkled with embedded crystals yet still managed to leave delicate skin exposed under a shimmer of mesh that caught the light. It was a sight designed to command attention, but it didn't intimidate Niamh. Instead, it filled her with a quiet fury.

As the guards parted in unison, Niamh felt vulnerable, the space around her feeling suddenly too vast, too open. Yet she stood tall, her confidence bolstered by the fact that she was surrounded by her team. She was safe, even if she was momentarily exposed.

"Niamh," the queen's voice cut through the space like a whip, laced with venom. Her eyes narrowed as she spoke, her lips curling into a smile that was anything but warm. "So happy you were brave enough to come. I wasn't sure you would after last time."

Niamh straightened, her eyes locking with the queen's, unflinching. "You mean when you tried to kill me?" she replied, her voice sharp and unwavering.

Cailleach waved a hand dismissively, as if to brush off the accusation. "What's a little tiff between family?" she quipped, the casualness of her tone laced with a deep, cutting malice. "You weren't injured."

"No, because Bain saved me," Niamh shot back, her gaze never leaving the queen's.

The queen's smile faltered for a split second before she regained her composure. "Ah, I was wondering when I'd see that cockroach again. They just don't die, do they?"

Bain, standing at her side, took a step forward. He was calm, too calm, as he met Cailleach's gaze. "I'm tougher than I look," he said, a devious grin tugging at the corners of his mouth.

Niamh could feel the tension crackling in the air as Bain addressed the queen. It was clear that he was no longer the man who had once sought favor with Cailleach. His words were a declaration, a sign that he had realized his worth, a realization he might not have come to without Niamh's influence. She saw him, really saw him. And she didn't hold his past against him. She understood him in a way no one else had.

Cailleach's gaze flickered over Bain, disdain dripping from her every word. "You've changed, haven't you? I'll admit, I didn't expect it. But you're still a nothing, Bain. Always will be."

Bain straightened, his chest puffing slightly. "Maybe, but not in the ways that matter." His eyes flicked to Niamh for just a moment before he turned his attention back to the queen. "I've learned there's more to life than seeking your approval. You don't control me anymore."

Niamh felt a sense of pride swell in her chest as she watched Bain stand his ground. He was no longer the man who had been so eager to please Cailleach. He was someone else now, someone stronger, someone who would fight for what mattered, even if it meant standing against the very person who had once held power over him.

Cailleach's eyes flashed with anger, her lips twisting into a tight smile that didn't reach her eyes. The tension in the room could've been sliced with a knife as she studied Niamh, clearly not accustomed to being spoken to with such defiance. The queen's silver crown, perched grandly atop her head, glinted in the light, but it did nothing to soften her appearance. If anything, it made her look even more intimidating, like some deity perched above everyone else.

Niamh sat straighter, refusing to let her mother's regal aura unsettle her. The room, with its long crystal table and towering walls, felt like a cage. It was grand and intimidating, meant to make her feel small and insignificant, but Niamh wouldn't let it. She had too much at stake.

The queen leaned back in her seat, her fingers tapping rhythmically against the smooth surface of the table, as though she was pondering her next move. "You *owe* me everything, child," she said slowly, her gaze narrowing. "Without me, you would be nothing. You would have no power, no purpose. I gave you life. Don't forget that."

Niamh's heart tightened at the reminder of her mother's twisted hold over her existence. She wanted to shout, to scream about how she didn't owe her anything, but she bit her tongue. Now wasn't the time for that. "You may have given me life," Niamh said, her voice low but firm, "but I'm not your puppet, and I'm not a tool for you to use to get what you want. I came here to find a way to stop the destruction, to make sure no one else suffers because of your hunger for power."

Cailleach's lips twisted into something that wasn't quite a smile. "You talk of *peace* as though it's something easily achieved. Do you think you can walk into my domain and dictate terms?"

"I have my own legacy now. I've built it with people who care about me, who fight with me. And I'll protect them, no matter what."

The queen laughed maniacally, "Little girl, you have so much to learn. I am queen here; I speak first. You obey me."

Niamh squinted and tilted her head questioningly. "You seem to think I am one of your servants. That you can boss me around. Newsflash, lady, I am not someone you can talk to like that. So, take a breath, pull that stick out a little, and let's talk like people."

Her entourage that stood behind her let small gasps out as some jaws dropped open in surprise at what Niamh said. The queen squinted her eyes at her, glaring directly at her. "You come here and treat me like this?"

"You started it. Now can we please stop the pissing contest and sort out this accord?" Niamh pushed. "We don't want a war, and I'm sure you don't either."

"What I want, I can't have. I want my heir by my side to help me rule. We could rule the 26 dimensions together!"

"You're right, you can't have that. You only want me for my power, so you can enslave even more people. Your subjects you have now look terrified of you. Why would I give you more power to do even more harm to people?"

"I have enough!" She was quick to defend herself.

Niamh crossed her arms over her chest. "Oh, you do huh? Then why haven't you done it yet? I hear you can barely hold onto your subjects here. Your power is wavering." She didn't know if that was the truth, but she knew it would wound the queen and throw her off her game.

"I, I have enough. I'm just waiting for the right time. If you won't join me, maybe I'll have to offer the position to someone else who's stronger. I doubt you'd have enough power to help anyway. My sources say that you can melt my ice. I doubt that would do much to help me." She smirked. She had no idea how powerful Niamh was. Boy, was she in for a surprise if she pushed her too hard.

"Bain, would you like the job? I didn't have an opening to take you onto my team before, but there seems to be an opening now. Care to join your queen again?" She smiled innocently at Bain, he knew it was a tactic to get to Niamh.

"No, thank you, you're highness. I would like to stay by Niamh's side. Thank you for the offer, though." She gasped, offended to be rejected by him. That was the first ever offer of power he had refused in his very long life. It felt good to make the right choice for once.

"Okay. Back to the accord." Niamh blew her off.

"There will be no accord!" she yelled, echoing through the room, slamming her fist onto the table, shattering the large crystal down the center.

Bain reached out, his hand instinctively moving toward Niamh as if to shield her from the flying debris. It wasn't much; it would do little against the queen's wrath, but the gesture spoke volumes. His instinct to protect her was undeniable, even in the face of hopeless odds.

She took note of that, filing it away for later. When the time came to make a decision about him, she'd remember these signals, these moments when his actions spoke louder than his words ever could.

But now wasn't the time to dwell on Bain. Right now, she had to deal with the tantrum-throwing toddler of a queen.

"If there will be no accord, we shall get going," Niamh said firmly, reaching for her bracelet to press the button that would summon Aoife's portal.

Before she could make contact, a thick layer of ice shot out, encasing her hand and wrist in a freezing bind. The bracelet was trapped beneath the ice, its button completely inaccessible.

Her eyes widened, but before she could react further, another ball of ice hurtled through the air, striking one of the guards beside her squarely in the chest. The impact sent him crashing to the ground, the sound of his fall echoing in the frozen silence. His body cracked and broke into pieces, sliding across the smooth floor in different directions. Naimh sat in shock. She just killed someone. Someone who volunteered to protect her. Her adrenaline spiked. Her anger rose, and her body heat flared in response.

The ice melted off her wrist, dripping off into puddles. She could portal home now, but she wanted to make her pay for hurting that innocent guard. She couldn't let that stand. Niamh turned to the broken guard and dug down deep into her inner flames. She called the white one to her, it leapt eagerly into her hand. She willed it to the poor man on the floor, it splattered across him, coating him with white flames that seemed to pull him back together, reversing the actions his body took. Pieces slid back into place, he tipped back upright and was whole once again.

Niamh glanced down at her wrist, encased in ice. Panic threatened to creep in, but she steadied herself as realization struck; her mother's power reversed time. That meant she had a chance to stop it from happening again.

Drawing a green flame from deep within her, she felt its energy sharpen, straightening like an arrow as it readied itself to strike. She pictured her mother's hand in vivid detail, her target clear.

With a mental release, the flame shot through the air, streaking with deadly precision. The sickening sound of impact echoed as it pierced her mother's hand, pinning it to the arm of the ornate chair she sat in.

A shrill scream tore from her mother's throat, sharp and venomous, as blood began to drip from the wound.

Her eyes, glowing an unnatural silver, snapped toward Niamh, filled with fury and seething pain. The air around them seemed to crackle, heavy with her rage, as she glared at her daughter with the full force of her power.

"Guards! Seize her!" the queen screeched, pointing a bony, bloodied finger at Niamh.

Her guards stumbled into each other in their haste, jostling and shoving as they scrambled to obey. Chaos erupted behind the queen as some guards began fighting amongst themselves, their movements disorganized and frantic.

"Niamh, we have to move!" one of her guards urged, attempting to guide her out of her chair.

But Niamh couldn't look away. Her eyes were locked on the queen, watching her every move.

Amid the chaos, a few of the queen's guards broke free from the infighting and rushed straight toward her. Niamh's guards quickly stepped into formation, their shoulders closing ranks to shield her from sight.

The clash was brutal. She heard the unmistakable sound of blows landing, grunts of exertion, and then the sickening *thud* of a body hitting the ground.

Peering through the cracks between her guards' shoulders, she saw one of the queen's soldiers lying motionless, his head resting at her guard's feet on the cold pavement.

Her focus snapped back to the queen, who stood slowly from her throne. The flaming green arrow, now extinguished, was clenched in her hand. With a defiant grimace, the queen yanked the arrow free, blood flowing freely from the wound in her palm.

Her silver eyes burned with fury as she cast a venomous glare at Niamh, her presence radiating menace despite the injury.

Niamh knew her mother would retaliate; she had to stop her before it was too late.

Bain grabbed her hand, his touch grounding her for a moment. "Please," he pleaded, his voice low and urgent. "Be careful."

She didn't reply, just gave him a firm nod before gently pulling her hand free. With determination, hardening her resolve, she pushed her guards aside and stepped forward.

The red flame inside her flared to life, eager and ready at her call. It burned hot and wild, filling her with a fiery confidence. She cast one last glance back to Bain, ensuring he was safely tucked behind the line of guards.

Turning her focus forward, she raised her hand and hurled the flame as hard as she could toward the far end of the table. She had no specific target, she didn't need one. All she needed was chaos.

The flame streaked through the air like a comet, striking its destination with a deafening roar. The explosion rocked the room, rattling the walls as a shockwave sent loose debris tumbling to the ground.

Shards of crystal cracked and chipped from the room's ornate decor, cascading like sparkling snowflakes through the air. The light caught the falling fragments, making them shimmer as they drifted to the floor in a surreal display.

Niamh's chest heaved as she watched the aftermath, her pulse pounding in her ears. The red flame had done its job.

As the dust and smoke began to clear, Niamh scanned the room, her heart pounding in anticipation. She couldn't see the queen standing anymore, and for a brief, fleeting moment, she dared to hope it was over.

But then, a thin, bloodied hand slammed onto the table's edge, followed by another. Using them as leverage, the queen pulled herself upright.

Her crown, once a symbol of her elegance and authority, was now shattered, the broken pieces tangled in her knotted, blood-streaked hair. She no longer carried the image of perfection and poise, she was a vision of wrath, disheveled and seething.

Her bloodied fist shook violently with rage as she raised it, summoning another shard of ice. Its sharp edges gleamed as it formed in her hand, glinting ominously in the fractured light. With a furious cry, she hurled it across the table, straight toward Niamh.

Niamh's instincts flared to life. She didn't hesitate. Willing the red flame inside her forward, she unleashed it with precision. The flame streaked through the air, colliding with the ice chunk before it had a chance to reach its mark.

The ice shattered midair, exploding into harmless fragments that scattered across the table and floor. Niamh stood firm, her jaw set, refusing to back down as the queen's enraged gaze locked on hers.

An explosion to her side drew Niamh's attention. The wall caved in with a deafening crash, sending shards of crystal and stone raining down. The guards nearest her threw themselves over her, their bodies forming a protective shield against the falling debris.

The sound of grunting reached her ears, pained, guttural, and it wasn't coming from the guards. A hand grasped her shoulder, startling her.

It was long and slender, trembling slightly. Bain's hand.

Her heart plummeted.

Scrambling free of the protective circle the guards had created, she slid across the floor to where Bain lay sprawled, clutching his chest. His breaths were shallow, his face pale, and between his fingers, ice crystals spread like vines, quickly coating his hands and creeping up his arms.

"No, no, no!" Niamh whispered, panic swelling in her chest as she tried to brush the ice away, but it reformed faster than she could clear it.

The queen, standing amidst the chaos, saw the moment of weakness and pounced. Her silver eyes gleamed with satisfaction as she raised her uninjured hand, forming another icy projectile.

Bain had no powers to defend himself, no way to fight back. The queen saw an opportunity and took it, aiming where it would hurt them most. The queen didn't need to use her words to gloat; the cruel satisfaction on her face said it all.

Love was his weakness.

And now, it was hers.

Niamh wasn't done yet. She refused to give up. There was more she could do, she *had* to do more.

Summoning the purple flame, she cradled it gently in her mind. It felt warm and calm, as if it already understood her intentions. She leaned in close, whispering to it: *Save him. Protect Bain. He is innocent in this war. Heal him. Keep his heart beating.*

With trembling hands, she pressed the flame into his chest. The purple light pulsed as it sank into him, disappearing beneath his skin.

For a moment, Bain's eyes flew open, glowing a vivid, unnatural purple. Then they shut again, and his body went limp in her arms.

"No!" Niamh gasped, panic clawing at her throat. She gripped his shoulders, shaking him gently. "No, no, no!"

Her thoughts spiraled out of control. *Did I do it wrong? Did my intentions falter? Was my heart not pure enough?* The possibility that she had failed, that she had *killed* him instead, shattered her resolve.

Her tears came fast and heavy as she laid her head on his chest, sobbing uncontrollably. "Please," she whispered through the tears. "Please don't leave me."

Thump.

She froze, holding her breath.

Thump, thump.

His heartbeat grew stronger beneath her ear, steady and sure. Relief washed over her like a tidal wave, her sobs catching in her throat as she sat up quickly.

"Bain?" she whispered, searching his face.

His eyes fluttered open, their familiar shade of blue staring back at her, *that* shade of blue, the one that had quietly become her favorite color.

He smiled weakly, his hand lifting to brush tears off her cheek. "You saved me," he murmured, his voice soft and hoarse. "Again."

"Well, you should probably stop putting yourself in dangerous situations," Niamh said, her voice teasing as she wiped at the lingering tears on her cheeks.

Bain chuckled softly, the sound warm despite his weakened state. "I'll work on that," he replied, a playful glint in his eyes. "Although, I don't mind you saving me. I'll be your damsel anytime."

She laughed, swatting his chest gently. "You're impossible."

Before he could respond, a deafening crash echoed through the room, snapping her attention back to the queen.

Her expression hardened as she turned to the guards surrounding Bain. "Guard him," she ordered, her tone firm. "And don't let him do anything else stupid, like get hurt again."

The guards nodded in unison, their postures stiffening at her command.

Niamh spared Bain one last glance, her heart still racing from the moment they'd just shared. Then she straightened her shoulders, steeling herself for what was to come.

She knew it had to end now. There was no other way.

Niamh had been afraid to use the black flame before, terrified of what it might do, what it might take, but now she understood. Her mother would never stop, not until Niamh and everyone she cared about were dead.

Summoning her courage, she called to the black flame. It responded eagerly, materializing in her hand with a weight that felt alive, pulsing with dark energy. It didn't flicker like the others. It was steady, solid, ready to be unleashed.

Please don't take everyone with you, she whispered in her mind, offering a silent prayer as she clutched the flame tightly. With a sharp exhale, she willed it forward, sending it streaking to the other end of the room. It was a risk, she knew it could take them all away, but she had no other choice, she was out of options.

The queen was yelling at her guards, slapping one across the face for some perceived insubordination, when the black flame hit the ground in front of her with a deafening explosion.

The air shifted immediately. The blackened spot began to expand, a swirling vortex of wind and shadow spreading outward like a living thing. The wind picked up with alarming speed, tearing helmets from the guards' heads and sending them clattering across the room.

The guards began to lose their footing, their boots skidding helplessly on the smooth floor as they were pulled toward the growing black hole. They clawed at the ground, desperate for purchase, but it was useless. They could not fight the force that it possessed.

The queen's silver eyes widened with panic as she shoved her guards in front of her, using them as human shields to block her from the black abyss trying to claim her. Their cries of protest were drowned out by the roar of the wind as she sacrificed them without hesitation.

Niamh's chest tightened as she watched. She felt a pang of sorrow for the guards, wondering if they had known what they were signing up for when they pledged their loyalty to the queen. Did they deserve this?

But it was too late to stop now.

This wouldn't have ended without bloodshed. The queen had been out for war, not peace. Niamh realized how foolish she had been to think otherwise.

Most of her guards had been sucked into oblivion, leaving the queen to fend for herself. She clawed desperately at the table's edge, dragging herself forward with blood-slick hands. The crystal surface offered little grip, her blood making it slippery and unforgiving.

The long train of her shimmering gown was caught in the vortex, whipping wildly as it was pulled toward the black hole. She screamed, yanking at the fabric, but it was futile. The void devoured her dress, inch by inch.

Her screams grew louder as she was dragged closer and closer, her once-perfect hair flying in all directions in the chaos. The remnants of her crown were long gone, lost to the pull of the vortex.

This was how Niamh would remember her mother. Not as the poised, commanding queen she had pretended to be, but as the desperate, barbaric figure fighting a losing battle against the chaos she had wrought. It felt cruel to hold onto this image, but her mother had been far crueler. She had earned every second of this.

Niamh's eyes remained fixed on her mother's hand as it slipped further down the table, her grip failing against the relentless pull. Her gown hung in tatters. Niamh watched as her feet disappeared into the void first, followed by the rest of her.

The queen's final look wasn't one of sorrow, regret, or even fear; it was pure hatred, burning bright in her silver eyes as she vanished completely. That look sealed it for Niamh. This was who her mother truly was. It was a memory she would carry forever, one that reassured her she had made the right choice.

The queen was no more.

Niamh sighed, sinking to the floor, a wave of sadness washing over her. Not for the queen herself, but for what could have been, for the mother she had once hoped to find. Her heart ached with the loss of something that had never truly existed.

"Stop," she whispered to the black flame.

Obediently, the swirling wind slowed, the vortex shrinking smaller and smaller until it finally winked out of existence. The room was left in silence, heavy with the aftermath of destruction and loss.

Niamh's guards were helping each other off the floor, checking for injuries and bracing themselves against the chaos of the room. The heavy silence was broken as a crowd of people began pouring in, their voices rising in cheers and applause.

Niamh froze, unsure of what was happening. The scene was surreal.

Chapter 26

The few people who managed to escape the vortex started to find their balance, standing on unsteady legs. Other workers from around the castle cautiously entered the room, taking in the scene as they walked to their loved ones. Hugs, tears, and cries of sorrow rang out in the debris-filled room. They mourned the loss of people they knew and were thankful for the few that were still there.

They wore stark white linen clothing, their skin pale and almost translucent, as if they were half-frozen. Their movements were hesitant, as though they were still testing their freedom. Relief radiated from them, but their frail appearance made Niamh's stomach churn.

One of them, an older woman with white hair braided down to her feet, stepped forward eagerly, her expression filled with gratitude.

Niamh's guards immediately moved to block her approach, but Niamh touched one of their broad shoulders, gently urging him aside. She could see it in their eyes, these people weren't here to harm her. They were feeling the same thing she had felt not long ago: relief.

The older woman clasped her hands together as she spoke. "Our queen," she said, her voice trembling. "We cannot thank you enough for saving us from her. She was a harsh, cruel ruler. We vow to serve you. You will be a kind queen."

Niamh blinked, stunned. "Oh, no," she said quickly, shaking her head.

"I'm not going to be your queen."

The woman's face fell into confusion. "But… you banished Cailleach. Who will be our queen if you won't?"

Niamh hesitated for only a moment before speaking with calm conviction. "You don't need a queen. I'm no queen. You can go home or stay here if you want. Form a democracy if you so choose. But I'm not a queen."

A heavy silence settled over the room as the crowd processed her words.

Finally, the woman spoke again, her voice barely above a whisper. "We… we can go home?" Tears welled in her eyes, spilling over as her lip quivered.

"Yeah," Niamh said softly, her expression warm. "Go home. It's fine."

The room rippled with quiet gasps, followed by tears and murmurs of disbelief. For the first time in what felt like ages, hope began to bloom in the air.

"We've been slaves here for decades," the older woman said, her voice heavy with both sorrow and longing. "I haven't seen my homeland in so long… I wonder what it looks like now." She paused, her gaze distant. "How do we get home?"

Niamh's heart sank. She didn't have an answer, but she knew who might. Without hesitation, she pressed the button on her bracelet, sending a signal to Aoife.

Moments later, Nick stepped through the portal, his usual confidence faltering as he took in the scene of destruction. His eyes darted around the room, lingering on the shattered walls and the disheveled crowd of pale, sickly people.

He turned to Niamh, concern etched into his features. "Are you okay?" he asked, his voice quiet, almost as if he feared the answer.

"I'm fine," Niamh replied, her voice steady despite the chaos. "The queen, though… not so much."

Nick's brow furrowed as he scanned the room. "Where is she?"

Niamh allowed herself a small, grim smile. "She's taken a trip. A long, dark one."

At that, Nick's lips curved into a faint smile of pride. "Well done," he said with a nod. "I'm sure it was unavoidable. Cailleach wasn't exactly known for her diplomacy." His gaze shifted to the group of people standing behind her. "What's with all of them?"

"That's where I need your help," Niamh admitted, gesturing to the crowd. "They were held here against their will. They wanted me to be their queen, but that's a terrible idea. So, I told them they could go home. The problem is, I don't know how to get them there."

Nick studied her for a moment before his smile widened, full of pride. "We can help them," he said confidently. "I'll get a team together. We'll figure out where they're from and help them get to where they need to go."

He clapped her lightly on the shoulder. "You did good, kid."

"Thanks," Niamh said softly. "I feel good. I hope we changed some of their lives today, for the better." She hesitated, her gaze falling to the floor. "But I feel bad about her guards. I couldn't save them, but I couldn't let her keep hurting people, either." Her voice cracked slightly. "Does that make me a horrible person? For letting them get sucked in with her?"

Nick's expression softened, and he shook his head. "Hard choices have to be made sometimes. We do the best we can, even when the options are awful. Losing people… It's always hard. But that you *feel* bad about it? That shows the kind of person you are. Bad people don't care when others get hurt."

His words offered some solace, but Niamh still felt the weight of her decision pressing down on her. She nodded slowly, knowing he was right. The decision had been made, and now she had to live with it.

As she struggled with her emotions, Bain quietly slipped his hand into hers, his grip firm but comforting. The warmth of his touch reassured her.

He knew how impossible the choice had been, and in his heart, he believed she had made the right one.

But as much as Bain admired her strength, he couldn't help but wonder if *he* could have made the right call. His instincts were hardwired for survival, for gain. If it had been him, his first impulse would have been to offer himself as a ruler, though he knew he'd never be chosen in a matriarchal magical dimension.

And honestly? That was probably for the best.

Deep down, Bain knew he should never lead anyone. He wasn't like Niamh. She had compassion, integrity, qualities he lacked. He'd spent too much of his life chasing more: more power, more money, more of everything. It wasn't how Niamh thought, and that made her special.

She would have made a great queen, he thought, giving her hand a light squeeze.

But, Bain had already made up his mind. He supported Niamh wholeheartedly, she deserved someone who would. But deep down, he knew he wasn't what she needed. He was a profiteer to his core, and centuries of living that way weren't easily undone.

How could he tell her he had to leave? Would she understand?

He doubted it. Changing someone's way of thinking after lifetimes of habit was nearly impossible. And he didn't want to drag her down with him. She deserved so much more, someone better, someone not like him.

No, he couldn't tell her. It was kinder this way. He would leave without giving her a choice, making the hard decision to protect her from himself.

Bain lifted her hand and kissed her knuckles, savoring the warmth of her skin against his lips. The gesture felt final, bittersweet.

She looked at him questioningly, her eyes narrowing slightly as if she could sense something was wrong but couldn't quite place what. He met her gaze but said nothing, forcing a small, soft smile.

She didn't press him. Niamh had bigger issues to deal with right now. A whole queendom of people needed rescuing, and ensuring their safety had become her top priority.

The weight of it all bore down on her, heavier than anything she had ever experienced. How could anyone shoulder the pressure of running a place like this? Perhaps that's why her mother had wanted her to join.

Maybe her mother couldn't handle the responsibility alone. Or, more likely, she had wanted more power, more people to dominate and control.

Niamh shook the thought from her mind. The "why" didn't matter anymore; her mother was gone. What mattered now was protecting the people her mother had oppressed.

Aoife, Nick, Njeri, the entire K Corp team, and even Lidia were stationed on the other side of the portal. They were working tirelessly, collecting information for their system and organizing transport to get everyone where they wanted to go. It was a massive operation, and everyone was pitching in.

Everywhere Niamh went, people surrounded her. They hugged her, kissed her hands, and bowed to her with tear-filled eyes. The gratitude was overwhelming.

"Thank you for setting us free," they said over and over, their voices filled with emotion.

She had never experienced anything like it. It was more affection and admiration than she'd ever received in her entire life. She didn't think she'd done much, just what needed to be done. But as she looked at their faces, saw the hope shining in their eyes, she realized just how much she had changed their lives.

Hours passed, each one blurring into the next, as she moved through the crowd, offering reassurance and guidance.

By the time she finally returned to her room, the weight of the day hit her all at once. She closed the door behind her and exhaled deeply, leaning against the cool wood.

For the first time in hours, she had a moment of silence.

Niamh sat on the edge of her bed, recapping the day in her mind.

She had killed someone. The fact that it was her birth mother broke something in her. No matter how evil she was, she was still her mother. That was a hard reality to deal with.

It was a feeling that refused to sit easy, no matter how many times she repeated it to herself. The woman who had given her life was a monster, a cruel, destructive force who had to be stopped. Niamh *knew* that. She had made the only choice she could.

But knowing didn't make it any easier.

The weight of it clung to her as she stepped into the shower. She let the heat soak into her skin, hoping it would melt some of the tension away. The water poured over her, washing away the grime, the blood, and the tears she couldn't hold back any longer.

Her mother had been an evil creature, yes. But she had also been her mother. The woman whose face, whose voice, Niamh had dreamed about her entire life. The woman she had once hoped to meet, to understand.

And now, she was gone because of her.

The ache in her chest didn't fade, no matter how long she stood under the spray. She pressed her forehead against the shower wall, tears mixing with the water.

The guilt, the loss, the questions- they were too much to handle on her own. She needed to talk to someone who had been there. Someone who could help her process what had happened or maybe offer a perspective she hadn't yet considered.

Because right now, she couldn't silence the voice in her head whispering, *what if there was another way?*

She made her way to Bain's room, her heart heavy and uncertain. The door was slightly ajar, and as she stepped inside, the first thing she noticed was the emptiness.

His bag was gone.

On the desk, where his belongings had been, lay a single piece of paper. She picked it up with trembling hands, her eyes scanning the lone word scrawled in ink:

"Sorry."

Her chest tightened as she stared at the note. *"Sorry?" That was it?*

He was gone.

He hadn't said goodbye. He hadn't even tried to explain. He had just… left, slipping away without a word, hiding from her like a coward.

What was he sorry for?

A million questions swirled in her mind, each one more painful than the last. Had he done something? Was he guilty of some secret she didn't know about? Did he feel bad for leaving? Or had he concluded that he didn't like her after all?

The possibilities were endless, each one cutting deeper than the last.

None of them made the situation easier to swallow.

The truth was simple, even if it hurt: he was gone.

And the only thing he'd left her with was a single word that didn't explain a thing.

He knew she deserved better than a note. He had agonized over it, knowing it was cowardly, but he didn't have the strength to face her.

Those yin-yang eyes of hers, so full of emotion, would tear his heart apart if he had to see them crying for him.

And they *would* cry for him.

He hated the thought of it. He didn't want her to cry, not for him. He hoped, selfishly, that she would hate him instead. That she would believe it was something about him she despised, and not something she had done to drive him away.

Because it *wasn't* her fault. This was a him problem, through and through.

She was perfect, too perfect. She was good and kind and everything he knew he wasn't. And that's why he had to leave.

Walking away from her was the hardest thing he'd ever done. He felt like he was ripping his own heart out, leaving it behind with her. But he told himself it was for the best. She'd be better off.

It had to be.

Niamh didn't have the energy to talk about it. She knew Lidia would listen anytime she needed, but the thought of putting her feelings into words felt impossible.

Instead, she fell into a monotonous routine: go to bed, wake up, and help more people find their way home. Go to bed, wake up, help more people, and on and on it went.

Wash, rinse, repeat.

She became a robot on cruise control, moving through the motions without truly feeling anything. The days blurred together, each one as colorless as the last.

Lidia watched her friend carefully, concern growing with each passing day. Niamh hadn't laughed, not even smiled, in days, and that wasn't like her. Niamh had always been resilient, finding humor even in the darkest of moments. But now, it was as if all the light in her had dimmed.

Lidia couldn't help but worry that her friend was truly broken. Banishment wasn't easy on anyone, let alone having to banish your own mother. That kind of weight would crush anyone.

But this felt like something more.

It wasn't until Lidia caught a glimpse of the note Niamh kept folded in her pocket, the single word written on it, that the pieces started falling into place. She hadn't realized just how far Niamh had fallen for Bain or how deeply his absence had cut her.

Still, Lidia refused to give up. She stayed close, quietly supporting her friend however she could, hoping that one day, Niamh would find the light again.

Niamh fell into a rhythm at K Corp. The work was steady but rewarding, and she began to genuinely enjoy helping the people who came through the doors, or the portal, as it often was.

Little by little, sparks of joy found their way back into her life.

One day, a group of little girls with colorful flowers decorated their hair and antlers giggled together in the lobby. They looked at Niamh in awe and curiosity as she walked up to them. She even let them pull her hair away from her face, no longer trying to hide her mismatched eyes. Their innocent laughter and fascination with her filled her heart with warmth.

The steady flow of unique creatures passing through K Corp made her feel less like an outcast and more like she belonged. Slowly but surely, Niamh began to feel like she was part of a community, a place where her differences were not only accepted but celebrated.

Lidia, seeing the light return to her friend's eyes, finally felt safe enough to leave. She returned to her home in Georgia, where her familiar routines waited for her. She would have spent forever with Niamh, as long as she needed her. But she did not need her anymore. Lidia knew she was with her people, she was finding her place in the world, and she needed to let her have this moment.

Still, the two of them spoke daily. Niamh filled Lidia in on the unique and fascinating creatures she met, and Lidia shared snippets of her more mundane human life and flower shop talk on the regular.

Lidia had grown to love the community at K Corp, too, but she knew she couldn't live there. Humans didn't belong in that world, not permanently. With Cailleach gone and the danger no longer hanging over her head, Lidia's place was back home.

She was happy that Niamh had finally found somewhere she fit, somewhere she could thrive.

Lidia had offered to check in on the flower shop regularly, which made Niamh feel better. The shop was her pride and joy, her heart and soul. Knowing Lidia was looking out for it gave her peace of mind; there was no one she trusted more.

One evening, while Lidia was checking in deliveries, something odd happened. She noticed a strange plant in the shipment, and she couldn't figure out where it had come from. There was no greenhouse name on the receipt or recipient for the order to get shipped to.

She picked up her phone and called Niamh. "Hey, girl, so we just got a shipment in, and there's this weird plant. I don't know what it is, and there's no greenhouse name on the receipt. Do you think it's a gift from one of your new magical friends, maybe?"

"I'm not sure. It's so odd. Can you send me a picture of it?" Niamh asked, her skin crawling with unease. It was extremely weird to receive a plant without a greenhouse name on the order form. Something about it felt *off*.

"Sure, give me a sec," Lidia replied as she began pulling up the camera on her phone she started to describe it. "It's big! It has a green stem and bright red leaves, with little drops of something coming off of it. It's the weirdest thing."

Lidia snapped a picture and sent it over. She couldn't help but be drawn to the shimmering drops, curiosity urging her to touch one. Gently, she pressed her finger against a droplet.

Niamh's heart sank the moment the photo came through. She knew exactly what kind of plant it was, and she would *never* have ordered it.

"That's a sundew," Niamh said sharply. "From the *Drosera* family. Whatever you do, don't touch it."

"Uh, too late!" Lidia's voice shot up an octave, panic setting in. "Niamh, I'm stuck! This thing is huge! And I'm *stuck* to it! I literally can't pull my hand out of the liquid. What should I do?"

Niamh's breath caught in her throat. She could hear the panic in Lidia's voice, and her mind raced. She knew sundews could kill insects in about fifteen minutes once they were stuck to the thick enzyme fluid, but this one was far larger than anything she'd ever seen.

She didn't know how quickly it would work on a human.

"Okay, Lidia, take deep breaths," Niamh said, forcing her voice to remain calm despite the panic rising inside her. "I'm going to make a call and be there right away. Don't do anything; struggling might make you stick to it more. Stay very still."

She knew she had no time to waste. Within minutes, the plant would start dissolving Lidia's skin to absorb the protein.

Hanging up quickly, she dialed Aoife, her fingers trembling. "Emergency. I need to get to Royal Flowers *now*. There's a carnivorous plant eating Lidia."

That was a sentence she never thought she'd say.

"Uh… okay," Aoife replied, her voice tightening with alarm. "I'll alert the network. Meet me in the lobby, and I'll portal us there."

Niamh didn't even bother responding. She bolted toward the lobby, her legs feeling far too slow, like she was moving through molasses. Every second stretched into an eternity, the weight of urgency pressing down on her.

When she finally slid into the lobby, nearly crashing into Aoife, her chest heaved with exertion.

"Ready?" Aoife asked, already bringing up her golden portal.

Niamh could only nod, her burning lungs refusing to let her speak.

As soon as the portal stabilized, Niamh didn't wait for the signal. She ran through without hesitation, her heart pounding like a drum. Aoife followed close behind, ready to support her.

Niamh sprinted through the shop, her heart pounding in her chest as she weaved past rows of vibrant flower bundles. The sweet aroma of roses and lilies seemed surreal, almost mocking, as her focus locked on the back room where deliveries were always sorted.

Bursting through the door, she found Lidia sitting on the floor, her hand still partially coated in the sticky residue of the carnivorous plant's secretions. Beside her knelt a person with dark hair, carefully attempting to wipe the fluid away with a rag, bit by bit.

Lidia looked up and spotted Niamh. "Oh my god, can you believe this?" she exclaimed, her voice tinged with incredulous humor. "This *fucking thing* is trying to eat me!"

Niamh's breath caught as she took in the scene. Leave it to Lidia to crack a joke, even while she was being eaten alive. She admired her friend's upbeat spirit, but her mind struggled to rationalize what was happening.

He looked up from the plant, his blue eyes locking with Niamh's. For a moment, her knees threatened to give out beneath her. Those eyes, *his eyes*, made her almost forget everything he had done to her. *Almost.*

She shook her head, her shock quickly giving way to anger. "How are you here?" she asked sharply, her voice laced with suspicion.

"I, uh, was in the neighborhood," Bain replied, his tone unsure, as if even he didn't believe his own excuse.

"What game are you playing, Bain?" Niamh snapped, her words cutting. "Did you do this?" She motioned toward the plant, her frustration bubbling over.

"No game," he said quickly, shaking his head. "I really was in the area, and I got the call for help."

Niamh's mind reeled. What he was saying made no sense. Before she could fire off another accusation, Aoife leaned in close and said in a low, hesitant tone, "He's been working for a branch of K Corp. One that helps prevent magical issues from going public. He told us not to tell you, but... well..." She gestured toward the room with an awkward shrug. "Obviously, the cat's out of the bag."

Niamh blinked, her anger momentarily giving way to confusion. She said, her voice soft but incredulous.

Niamh's fury flared. Everyone had been keeping this secret from her, and now she was supposed to just accept it? She couldn't help but question Bain's motives. Was he truly turning over a new leaf, or was this just another one of his games?

"So, you… got an emergency call about this and just showed up to help?" she asked, her tone sharp and accusatory.

"Yes, Niamh," Bain said firmly, his patience thinning. "This is what I do now. But can we focus on Lidia *not* being eaten right now? We can be pissed off at me later."

His words jolted her back to reality, she had completely forgotten about Lidia. Bain was terrible for her focus.

"Right," she said quickly, turning to her friend. "How are you doing?"

"I'm… doing… gr…eat," Lidia slurred, her voice sluggish. The enzymes were working fast, and her pale face made Niamh's stomach twist. "This sticky shit really is gross."

"It's mucus, actually," Niamh corrected automatically, the words slipping out before she could stop herself.

"*Ew!*" Lidia shrieked, pulling a disgusted face. "*Why* would you tell me that?"

"I know, honey, I'm sorry," Niamh said, cringing. "We'll get you out of here soon."

She turned back to Bain, eyeing the progress he'd made. It wasn't much. Her frustration bubbled up again. "What are you using on that rag?"

"It's just soap and water," Bain admitted, clearly frustrated himself. "I didn't know what else to use."

"Okay, let me think," Niamh said, her mind racing. She paused, then added, "Hold on. It's a living thing, right? I mean, I know it's a plant, but it's *alive.* What if I tried my pink flame on it? Maybe I could control it enough to make it let her go."

Aoife nodded. "It's worth a try. I have no idea about plants, you're the expert here."

Bain, still crouched beside Lidia, glanced up and nodded in agreement.

They all stepped back, giving Niamh space. Only Lidia and the giant plant remained in the center of the room.

Niamh took a steadying breath and reached down, grasping the pink flame with her invisible hand. The moment it connected to her, it hummed with energy. She willed it toward the plant, pouring her determination into the flame.

In her mind, she screamed: *Obey me, plant. Let her go. You will not eat my friend!*

The flame wrapped around the plant, glowing softly as it made contact. Niamh braced herself for a sizzle or some kind of fiery reaction, but none came.

A slow reaction started.

Its tentacle-like leaves uncurled slowly, trembling as they lifted away from Lidia. It straightened into its natural position, releasing her completely.

Lidia's hand dropped to the ground with a soft thud. The skin was a sickly green, blistered and swollen.

Lidia bent over sluggishly, her movements slow and weak.

Niamh rushed to her side, sliding her friend further away from the man-eating plant. She barely registered the gold tornado swirling in the corner of her eye. *Focus,* she told herself. She trusted Aoife to handle it.

As Niamh reached Lidia, the coven moved gracefully around them. In perfect synchronization, they laid crystals and bundles of plants in a precise pattern. One member of the coven knelt beside Lidia, cradling her swollen hand and carefully applying ointment to the injured skin.

Lidia sighed, her body relaxing into Niamh's arms. She looked up at her friend with a faint smile. "You came for me."

"Of course I did, silly," Niamh replied softly, her voice cracking. "You're my person. I'm so sorry this happened to you."

"Don't do that," Lidia said firmly, her smile fading. "Don't blame yourself. I know what's going on in your head."

And she did. Lidia knew Niamh too well.

But Niamh couldn't stop the guilt from creeping in. This was *her* shop. She should have been there to protect her.

The coven began chanting in a foreign language, their voices weaving together in a rhythmic hum. The energy in the room shifted, calm yet powerful.

Within minutes, Lidia's hand began to return to its natural shade of healthy pink. The blisters and swelling faded before Niamh's eyes.

She couldn't hold back her tears any longer. Relief flooded her as she realized her friend was going to be okay.

As the coven finished their work, they gracefully retrieved their crystals and bundles of plants. Lidia sat up, testing her hand and holding her weight. She smiled at Niamh, her eyes tired but grateful.

Niamh stood, wiping her tears as she approached the witches. She hugged each one in turn, her arms wrapping tightly around them.

The coven witches froze awkwardly, unused to such displays of affection. Most people were frightened of them, avoiding their presence altogether. But Niamh's gratitude was genuine, and though unsure at first, they hesitantly patted her on the back before stepping away.

They returned to Aoife and her portal, their movements graceful and purposeful, leaving Niamh and Lidia alone in the quiet aftermath.

Lidia was standing now and pulled Niamh into a tight hug. "Lucky Bain was close by, huh?" she whispered teasingly in her ear. Ever the matchmaker, Lidia couldn't help herself.

They pulled back, smiling at each other, grateful to be close again after the chaos. Lidia turned Niamh around, gently nudging her to look toward Bain, who was deep in conversation with Aoife.

He glanced up, his eyes locking with hers once more.

Niamh wished he'd stop doing that, making eye contact like that. His gaze had a way of drawing her in, and it was hard to turn away.

What she didn't realize was that Bain thought the same of her. Her yin-yang eyes, full of emotion and intensity, were equally impossible for him to ignore.

Since leaving her, Bain had been working for K Corp. The decision to walk away from her had been the hardest one of his life, but he knew it was necessary. If he was ever going to deserve her, he had to sort himself out.

He wasn't sure he'd ever reach the standard she deserved. She was galaxies beyond him, bright, limitless, and he had nothing to offer her. But she made him *want* to try.

So, he did.

Since joining K Corp, Bain had aided in rescuing several groups of refugees from their burrows, shielding them from attacks. He'd even crossed dimensions to help a family escape slavery under a Manananggal. That mission had been terrifying for him, but he hadn't hesitated.

There were countless wrongs in his past that he needed to make right, and he was determined to try. For her.

Lidia was feeling more like herself. Aoife pulled her aside for a private chat. Niamh raised a brow, already suspecting it was a ploy to leave her alone with Bain.

Bain stood across from her, shuffling his feet nervously, his hands stuffed deep into his pockets. He looked so different from the overly confident, cocky man she had first met. This Bain looked… uncertain. Nervous, even.

The roles had reversed.

Niamh, now feeling more confident in herself than she ever had, stood a little taller. She had grown to embrace her powers, her body, and her sense of belonging. And here Bain was, fidgeting like he was afraid to speak. It was a first for him.

"So, you look good," he finally said, his voice quieter than usual. His hand came up to squeeze the back of his neck in an uncharacteristically awkward gesture.

"Uh, thanks," she replied, her lips curving into a faint smile. "So do you. I see you've ditched the suits for jeans and flannels. It looks good."

His lips twitched into a crooked grin. He didn't know what to say to that, but he was happy she noticed.

Despite everything he'd been through, Bain was still a little vain. He smoothed his hands down his shirt, trying to play it cool, but his mind betrayed him, imagining what it would feel like if it were *her* hands instead.

"Thank you for helping save Lidia," Niamh blurted out, desperate to fill the silence.

"Yeah, it was no problem," Bain replied, his voice low. "You did all the saving. Turns out, I wasn't needed." He glanced down at his feet, his usual confidence nowhere to be found.

"I need you," she said quietly, the words escaping before she could stop herself.

Bain's head shot up, his eyes locking with hers in an instant. He couldn't believe what he had just heard.

She needs me?

Those were the words he had been waiting his entire life to hear. He had always felt disposable, unworthy. But now, hearing them from *her,* they settled into his chest like a balm, soothing cracks he hadn't even realized were there. His eyes swelled with joy, the corners crinkling as a smile tried to break through.

Niamh noticed the way he looked at her, and something inside her shifted. She had never truly considered what Bain's life must have been like. He'd mentioned it in passing, but she had always brushed it off, assuming he deserved whatever hardships he'd faced because of his trickster ways.

But now... she saw him differently.

She had never felt this way before, but now that the word was in her mind, it felt like the right label. Her feelings for Bain weren't simple, but love...

Yes, that felt right.

Niamh stepped closer, her heart pounding in her chest. Reaching for his hands, she laced her fingers through his. Bain's thumb instinctively began rubbing slow, gentle circles over her knuckles, his touch warm and steady despite the nervous tension between them.

"I know we didn't have a great start to our... relationship," she began, her voice soft but certain.

His eyes lit up at the word, his lips parting slightly in surprise.

"But," she continued, her gaze holding his, "I think I'd like to see where this could take us. If you want to, that is. I mean, I know you left, so maybe you don't even want to, and that's okay, but I wanted to let you know I'd be okay with it... If we tried."

For the first time in a long while, Bain was completely out of his element. He was usually the suave one, the lead in any flirtation, always knowing what to say. But now? Now, he felt like his tongue was tied in knots, his thoughts stumbling over themselves as he searched for the right words, words that could capture the enormity of what he felt.

"Niamh," he started, his voice low and careful, "I have never met anyone like you in all my years. You are truly one of a kind."

Her grip on his hands tightened slightly as he spoke.

"You make me want to be a better man. You deserve a good man." He paused, his voice faltering as he looked down, breaking eye contact. "For a long time, I thought you deserved someone better than me."

"Bain, I don't want anyone but you," Niamh said softly, her voice trembling with emotion.

He looked into her eyes, those mesmerizing opposites, the light one giving off a faint, ethereal glow and the dark one swirling with depths of mystery and intrigue. He could swear he could see her inner flames twirling, dancing inside her like a reflection of her strength and passion.

He swallowed hard, his voice thick with sincerity as he replied, "I will be better for you. I'm sorry for everything I've done. And I'm not perfect. I know I'll mess up again, so I apologize for that in advance, too." He let out a shaky breath. "But the important thing is that I will never stop trying to be the man you deserve."

Bain's gaze locked with hers, his eyes shining with hope and vulnerability. "Will you be mine, Niamh?"

Her smile lit up the room, and the glow in her eye brightened, casting a soft, warm light that seemed to fill the space around them. "I was always yours, Bain. You just didn't know how to ask the right way."

A laugh escaped him, low and relieved, before he closed the distance between them. His arms wrapped around her, pulling her into a soul-hugging embrace. In a bold, sweeping motion, he dipped her low to the side, cradling her as though she were the most precious thing in the world.

And then his lips met hers.

The kiss was passionate and unrestrained, filled with years of longing and unsaid truths. At that moment, they both felt whole, as though the missing pieces of their souls had finally fallen into place.

They had spent their entire lives searching for home, wandering through loneliness and self-doubt. But here, in each other's arms, they knew without a doubt, they had finally found acceptance in each other.

About the Author

Teysha W.L. is a fantasy romance author who continues to blend magic, adventure, and unforgettable characters into stories that stir the heart and spark the imagination. Her second novel invites readers even deeper into the realms where the fantastical and the emotional intertwine, this time with a powerful message about embracing our differences and discovering the strength in being uniquely ourselves.

When she's not dreaming up new worlds, Teysha channels her creativity into crafting, sewing, and drawing, infusing each project with the same wonder she brings to her writing. She also lends her voice to a nonprofit organization that she founded and also volunteers with, using storytelling to inspire connection and positive change. Her three children remain her brightest inspiration, reminding her every day that magic lives in authenticity.

Teysha believes that true power lies in our stories, especially the ones that celebrate what makes us stand out. With each book, she hopes to remind readers that even in the darkest moments, there is light to be found in being exactly who you are.

Stay tuned for more books to come in the K Corp series and more fun writing, some with more spice!

You can connect with me on:
- https://teyshawlauthor.my.canva.site
- https://www.goodreads.com/author/show/53110212
- https://www.tiktok.com/@teysha.w.l?is_from_webapp=1&sender_device=pc

Also by Teysha W.L.

⁂

I write fantasy stories rooted in real-life experiences, moments that have shaped me, challenged me, and helped me grow. Writing has always been a way for me to heal, to reflect, and to find my inner strength as my characters discover theirs.

There's something beautiful about adding magic and mystery to the ordinary, because I truly believe life is full of magic, if you're open to seeing it. Through my stories, I explore themes of identity, resilience, and the quiet power that comes from embracing who you truly are.

My stories in the K Corp series are *clean and non-spicy,* perfect for readers who want to step into a magical world filled with heart, hope, and mystery, without X-rated scenes. Whether you're new to fantasy or just looking for a softer adventure, my books are meant to enchant without crossing that line.

Through my stories, I celebrate the beauty of being different, the wonder of finding your voice, and the quiet kind of courage that changes everything.

If my books can make someone feel a little more seen, a little more brave, or a little more magical… then that's the real happily ever after.